My Journey Through the Plant World

ALSO BY D. PATRICK MILLER

Love After Life (fiction)

Instructions of the Spirit (poetry)

A Little Book of Forgiveness (inspiration)

The Book of Practical Faith (inspiration)

Understanding A Course in Miracles
(nonfiction)

my journey through the plant world

a novel of
sexual initiation

by
D. Patrick Miller

FEARLESS BOOKS
Berkeley CA

FIRST EDITION
July 2008

FEARLESS BOOKS
2104 California Street
Berkeley CA 94703
www.fearlessbooks.com

© 2008 by D. Patrick Miller
All rights reserved. No part of this book may be
reproduced, stored in a retrieval system, or transmitted
in any form or by any means (electronic, mechanical,
photocopying, recording, or otherwise) without the
express written permission of Fearless Books.

This is a work of fiction. Names, characters, places, and
incidents are either the product of the author's imagination
or are used fictitiously. Any resemblance to actual events or
persons, living or dead, is entirely coincidental.

ISBN-10: 0615219756
ISBN-13: 9780615219752

DESIGN & TYPOGRAPHY:
D. Patrick Miller

All flesh is grass, and all the goodliness thereof is as the flower of the field.

ISAIAH 40:6

I

1

MY ONLY problem with sex is that it's always so *unexpected*. I don't mean that it occurs unexpectedly (which is sometimes true), or that the particular way in which it happens is not what I expect (which is nearly always true). I mean that the very *nature* of sex is a big surprise.

For example: When a person gets to know someone by talking to her face for hours, does that really prepare him for how her genitals will look? For that matter, does having seen genitals before really prepare anyone for how genitals will look the next time? Not for me—and this is still true at age thirty-five, with eighteen-plus years of experience to season my grasp on the graphic facts of life . . .

Oh, Christ. Now that I've actually started, I'm even more uneasy about this. But June has been hounding me for weeks to start some kind of journal. The other day she said that my everyday malaise—the all-pervading boredom of my life—is "symptomatic of an inner chaos of psychic forces."

"What *psychic forces*?" I asked dumbly, like I didn't get that kind of lingo after listening to her for three years, and she said:

"Grief, guilt, sexual sadness, all those things we've been talking about. We're going round in circles because you're expecting me to sort things out for you. You've led me to believe you have some writing aptitude, Randall. Now I'd like you to use it on your own behalf."

"But, doc," I replied helplessly, knowing that June bristles at any reference to her academic credentials, "where would I start?"

"Start with sex," she said so directly that I flinched. "In fact," she continued with growing certainty, "let's start with your sexual history, going all the way back, as early as you can remember having any sexual feeling or perception. You're carrying a lot of sexual anxiety that you need to sort out. You need to know what's past and what's present, for one thing, and you don't know that right now. It's all happening at once in your head. So . . . Good. Let's try that, all right?"

Instead of answering right away I looked at the top of June's head, where her hair is both caramel and gray, and wondered why I felt like a twelve-year-old told to wash a heaping mountain of dishes from the grownups' dinner party. I wanted to say, "That's not fair!" Instead I whispered quizzically, "*Let's?*"

So here I sit, facing the computer screen with the kind of foreboding I used to feel when facing inventory in my first store—only much worse. How does one inventory the contents of a personal Pandora's box, after all? But I think I'm on to something already, this thing about the nature of sex. Maybe the whole problem of sex is nature itself!

Because the truth is that lowering my attention to the sexual territory of the body is like dropping out of human civilization, and down into the world of plants. Seeds, shoots, blooms, roots, juices—it's all organic down there, raw and unsocialized. All our romantic ideals about sex are like flowers sliced at the stalk, prissily displayed rootless and truthless in cut-glass vases. The damp soil upon which real sex feeds is too, well, *earthy* for most people to contend with. And that's why they're never prepared for what happens next with sex.

IN THE year 1971—when I was in the sixth grade—I was certainly unprepared for what would happen next, but at least I could have pleaded ignorance. After all, what was about to happen was my very first sexual experience. It was subtle compared to adult situations, but oh-so-unsettling—and it set up my lifelong pattern of feeling behind the beat, always playing catch-up to females seemingly more in-the-know about sexual mysteries.

It was the year before, the fifth grade, when I first met girls who were smarter than I. This was a profound shock, but administered early enough in my life to allow me time to recover without developing macho defenses. (At least, I like to think I've recovered.) Intellectually, I was treading water already; I'd mastered the most difficult books in the school library the year

a novel of sexual initiation

before, and spent most of my time since gloating over effortless
spelling bee victories and getting heavily into stamp collecting.
Beyond a nerdy coterie of fellow philatelists, all male of course,
I didn't socialize much with my peers in our semi-rural Georgia
neighborhood. To most of them, being bookish was tantamount
to being Martian.

My professor father, a social climber at Emory, didn't like my
increasingly superior attitude toward education. He tightened
the family budget sufficiently to send me to a private academy
an hour's commute away from home, on the other side of
Atlanta. The change eventually cost my sister Carolyn, who was
fifteen when I was twelve, her riding lessons.

But my father was academically biased. After all, Carolyn
was a mediocre performer at school, and I was possibly an un-
recognized genius moldering away in my room, plastering the
four walls with hundreds of letterless envelopes bearing First
Day of Issue cancellations. The blanketing effect of this decor
frightened my mother, so she readily seconded my father's decision to place me in a more challenging academic environment.

Challenging hardly did the place justice. At Country Day I
was an ordinary middle-class scrabbler trying to solicit dollops
of attention from "professional educators" (not mere teachers,
mind you) more attuned to the well-oiled manners of the
school's Ivy League-bound majority. My first year there I floun-
dered about in the panicky loneliness of feeling inferior, barely squeaking by with a B-minus average. My parents had to
come in for a long conference to discuss "the most pragmatic
course for Randall's academic future," to quote the principal's
condescending letter at year-end—the most pragmatic course
turning out to be summer school that would "equalize my opportunities" with those of my more fortunate peers. That was when
Carolyn had to say so-long to Mariah, her favorite at the stables,
and take a couple of long walks with Mom in order to find a way
to speak to me again.

But summer school didn't bring me up to par; JoEllen Jones
did. JoEllen Jones was a miracle delivered to me at Country Day
in my second year. Like my father and mother, her parents were

overextending themselves on behalf of her brilliance. She was a natural-born writer who had won an *Atlanta Constitution* essay contest for young people during that year I was being cut down to size in private school. (I remember looking forlornly at the essay contest rules in the paper, too deep in shock over a failed geometry test to imagine actually competing.) JoEllen's piece had accidentally been transferred from the 9-12 age group into the high-schoolers' competition, and *she beat them all.*

JoEllen was middle-class and lived on our side of town, but she came to Country Day as a minor celebrity. When our two sets of parents discovered in the first week of school that we lived only a few miles apart, they began taking us to school together in alternating family cars.

Suddenly I had an ally who was a star—and I pretty much hitched my wagon to her. JoEllen became my living, breathing crib sheet, my warm-blooded abacus, my arts and crafts muse. I shamelessly took advantage of her friendship in order to equalize my opportunities at Country Day. At that age, it wasn't a scheme on my part—it just happened out of sheer necessity. But as JoEllen would tell me later in high school, we inadvertently struck a fair deal—because poor little JoEllen had no other friends. She had suffered socially at public school even worse than I, because little Southern girls were neither encouraged nor expected to be quite so frighteningly smart. Hence I was the first kid, male or female, to be her real true pal.

Actually, what JoEllen would tell me in high school was that she had *loved* me—desperately—way back in the sixth grade. Could that have been true? The notion of desperate love was only dawning on me at age sixteen, so it's just as well that I was completely oblivious to it at age twelve. I was likewise oblivious to JoEllen's precocious physical development until the very end of the sixth grade. What I mean is that she had noticeable breasts and very round hips at twelve years of age, and she already walked in a rumba-like fashion that would later make her the butt—so to speak—of crude jokes among our adolescent peers.

Anyway, back on the cusp of adolescence, I was getting along swimmingly at Country Day as my second year there came to an

a novel of sexual initiation   5

end, all thanks to JoEllen. I guess we were pipsqueak valedictorians, because we were chosen to present twin graduation speeches before an assembly of the entire school. JoEllen's mom was a former actress—"a bit of a tart" in my mother's stern appraisal—and she dressed up JoEllen that memorable day in a flaming red, low-cut party dress and patterned sheer stockings. (Perhaps I'm not recalling this with total accuracy, but the past I must deal with is the past I remember.)

SO OUT comes JoEllen, stage left, onto the purple velvet-draped Country Day auditorium stage, amidst a swell of admiring—or scandalized?—parental murmurs and some giggling among our peers. I was already standing on the other side of the stage, nervously running over the beginning of my three-minute oration in my head. I had learned in rehearsals that remembering the whole speech depended upon recalling the beginning. After the first thirty hellish seconds I was always okay.

But this was not another rehearsal. This was IT, a pass-fail test if ever there was one, and I felt weak-kneed, weak in the bladder, and far too weakly prepared for such a public demonstration of my *savoir-faire*. As the auditorium quieted and it became obvious that one of us on stage was supposed to do something, I desperately wished that I was back in my room poring over tiny, engraved squares of adhesive paper. In fact, I was so stage-struck that I wasn't quite sure of where I was. The thought crossed my mind that perhaps if I shut my eyes tight enough, I could be magically transported to some other world, anywhere away from the awful test about to take place in this one.

Instead, by the grace of God, I cast a sidelong glance across the stage and saw JoEllen smiling ever so kindly at me. This reminded me that I was supposed to repeat my part of the oratorical duet JoEllen and I had been practicing in this very hall for weeks. *Okay*, I thought, *I can do that*. I turned away from JoEllen, my life-support system, and toward the soulless mike thrusting toward my face from atop its skinny silver spine, and bellowed the title of my speech:

"The Golden Opportunities of YOUTH!"

MY JOURNEY THROUGH THE PLANT WORLD

On the last, over-emphasized word my voice cracked for the first time ever—what a moment for puberty to announce its onset!—and something about the squeaky-booming timbre of my voice caused the PA system to have a major feedback crisis. A hair-raising mechanical howl went through the room, causing adults to cover their ears and a couple of infants to howl back, like little dogs, and causing Mrs. Smyth-Fifer, our amateur stage manager, to rush out and fumble with the microphone. I stared dumbly at her as she scurried back into the wings and frantically turned knobs on something back there. I kept staring until she turned her face toward me, half-obscured in the darkness of the wings, and theatrically flashed me a big "OK" sign with her right hand.

With fake professional aplomb, I turned back with a big smile to the audience—now edgy and justifiably fearful of what might next be done to them—and promptly forgot my speech.

Never before had I known that time could stop like that! . . . that a glacial eternity could interrupt the normal course of one's life and bring the crushing sense of death—no, not death, but an *endless dying*—so terrifyingly near. Like an antediluvian fly snagged on a glob of tree sap, I felt irretrievably trapped in a gluey ether of stupidity. All I can remember from this public display of dumbness was fixing my eyes upon a thin Chinese gentleman in the front row of the audience and thinking, *Who is that!?* I couldn't recall any Oriental classmates, and this fellow's etched prominence among a sea of bemused Caucasian faces was clear evidence of a rip in the fabric of the universe, admitting an alien anomaly into this mundane Southern school auditorium.

Then I realized that this fellow's face reminded me of Chiang Kai-shek on one of my stamps. I was mentally attempting to confirm this identification when JoEllen's sweet voice broke the silence, filling the hall with light, order, and salvation:

"Never before have young people faced a future so bright with possibilities!"

I turned like a doll on a music box and looked at JoEllen as if she had just handed me a peanut butter and jelly sandwich back at her house. "What?" I mouthed silently across the stage,

a novel of sexual initiation

desperately wanting to be at her side, and not only because I was in trouble. There was something odd, novel, and heated in the feeling, something that had slipped in through the new fracture in my voice. JoEllen grinned warmly but urgently at me and leaned closer into her microphone.

"Never . . . before . . . have . . . young . . ." she intoned patiently, as if she had taken on the task of teaching English to the toddlers in the audience.

It was my first line! In the same instant that I realized JoEllen was prompting me, I realized that she had probably memorized my entire speech along with hers, and would selflessly recite it and let me take the bows if a full-scale intervention proved necessary. I was so grateful for this rescue that tears sprang to my eyes as I picked up the latter half of my deathless opener—"future so bright with possibilities!"—and I have no doubt that I finished my speech in the most impassioned manner that a sixth-grader has ever delivered such a sentimental mash of parentally incited homilies.

JoEllen followed with a faultless delivery of her own address—"How Young Women Are Changing the World"—and the applause was so lengthy and deafening that Mrs. Smyth-Fifer broke into a wild antic of arm-waving in the wings, the message being that JoEllen and I should take a bow together.

I was slow on the uptake, so JoEllen came over, took me by the hand, and led me to center stage where I followed her lead of bending at the waist and bobbing up and down a few times.

It was during the downs of this up-and-down motion that I first noticed JoEllen's shapely calves, sheer and shadowy in those grown-up stockings. Somehow it hit me that these sensual lengths of flesh were magically congruent—not to mention intimately *connected*—to the rest of her precocious form. This abrupt recognition of JoEllen's physicality is what I consider to be my very first sexual initiation. That, and the sensation of a squishy electricity passing between our sweaty, hot little palms.

I wonder to this day what was going through JoEllen's mind at that moment. I never did confess to her that I first lusted for her, inchoately to be sure, at that peak moment. I do know that my hand ached for the rest of the day, she had squeezed it so hard. Perhaps that's because she really was in love with me already—being ahead of the curve on so many other counts—and somehow she also knew what was going to happen next. Because that near-apocalyptic, peculiarly sensual day was the last time I would see JoEllen for four years. Our two families went out to a festive Chinese dinner that night (I suspected the weird, lingering influence of Chiang Kai-shek), and agreed that JoEllen and I should remain the best of friends over the summer. It's even possible that our folks were trying to set us up for the future—what a dream couple, after all!

But the very next day my father received the crushing news that he was not going to get tenure at Emory. In a huff he quit the university entirely, spending the next several weeks initiating his drinking problem. Private school was off, our summer vacation was off, my mother's long-standing art lessons were off. The whole Kendricks family sank into an ugly funk, with the notable exception of yours truly. For all I could think was that I could spend the rest of my life gleefully collecting First Days, with only the minor interruptions of high school and college somewhere off in the vague future. Plus: I would be free of the intense, mixed-up feelings I was having about JoEllen Jones.

Because along with my novel lust, I felt a disturbing resentment of my girl savior, who was so smart and collected that she remembered my speech in front of the whole school when I couldn't. With everything else that was going on, I guess that's why I never called her again. JoEllen would tell me later that she called several times in the week following our speeches, but I neatly avoided picking up the phone. My dad was too drunk to answer, and Carolyn seldom took messages for anyone, especially not her smart-ass little brother. My mother did call me to the phone once. My response was to light out the front door for the woods, the only haven that felt safer than the little world of my room.

2

NEEDLESS to say I was stunned when, on the first day of high school four years later, I nearly ran over JoEllen Jones while hustling to my orientation class.

"What are *you* doing here?" I blurted artlessly, at which JoEllen blushed and demurely lowered her eyes to the floor of the crowded, noisy hallway.

"Hi, Randall," she said softly.

I felt like a total jerk. "Yeah, hi, I mean."

"My dad died this summer," JoEllen revealed with adult seriousness, raising and locking her large, deep green eyes onto mine. "I had a scholarship to a prep school in Massachusetts, but . . ."

"Oh, wow," I interjected, trying to sound suitably mournful but feeling up to my knees in fifteen-year-old shallowness.

". . . my mom needs me at home for a while," JoEllen finished, her eyes tearing slightly. Then, at completely the wrong moment, I noticed that she was drop-dead gorgeous, with the sixth-grade promises of her womanly sensuality already fulfilled. Her face was round and intelligently angelic, lit with a healthy glow, and skillfully highlighted with make-up that I naively took to be her natural colors. Scanning down her body with doubtless obviousness, I noticed that JoEllen's breasts seemed ready to emerge at any moment through the violently stretched fabric of a white cotton turtleneck. Daringly enough for a Georgia high school sophomore, she was wearing very tight jeans with an oversized, shiny black belt around her waist. Her thick brown hair was pulled back into a generous ponytail. In a uniquely JoEllenish touch, she had a pair of mod sunglasses perched atop her head.

She looked, in short, like a precocious Gloria Steinem, which wasn't far off the mark. After all, she had spent three more years in the accelerated liberal social atmosphere of Country Day after I departed. Hence she was well on her way to becoming one of the "young women changing the world" she had once spoken about so eloquently. Or so it seemed at the time.

Do I have to confess that I was in love from that day forward? The old resentment peeled off from my memories like a brown and wasted leaf; all I could recall was that JoEllen was the smartest girl I had ever known. Now she was also clearly the *sexiest*, a word I delighted in conjugating to myself while riding the bus home in the afternoons, whenever I took a break from reading JoEllen's spirited letters. I guess she'd forgiven my grade-school disappearing act because she wrote me the first note, sharing some silly joke that was going around school, the day after we ran into each other.

Soon she was writing to me all day long, as we had hardly any classes together. She always finished off her quizzes and assignments wickedly fast, leaving her with time on her hands. Before her mom picked her up every day, JoEllen ran breathlessly to me and delivered that day's thoughts. I answered her in my own hand almost every night—though never as prolifically—and gave her my letters in the morning. We always met by the school store and stood there, hardly speaking a word, sometimes holding hands if it wasn't too obvious, while she read what I had written. As I remember, it was a very literary affair.

I knew JoEllen was the sexiest of the girls because my pals in the stamp club, often lunching informally in a library conference room, never let me forget it. "JoEllen Jones—oooo-wee!" they would hoot at every opportunity, one or two of them launching into a raunchy rendition of her hip-swinging walk. I was secretly pleased, although I always acted embarrassed and would start punching the guys to get them to stop making fun of my beloved.

"My beloved" was something else I would repeat to myself on the bus. I even used it in my letters a few times, but the words *girlfriend* and *boyfriend* made me nervous. All the other kids had girlfriends or boyfriends. I saw JoEllen and myself, intellectual overachievers as we were, as somehow above all that—the gossip,

a novel of sexual initiation

11

the intrigues, the dating.

In fact we didn't date. JoEllen's mother was traumatized by the recent disaster in her life, leaving her with JoEllen and a younger son to raise alone. She worked nights and weekends, which meant JoEllen was babysitting whenever she wasn't studying. About twice a week we talked by phone at night, for hours, until my mother put a limit on us.

"You're entirely too young to be so wrapped up with a girl this way, even if it's that smart JoEllen Jones," my mother would say after I hung up the phone at her stage-whispered insistence. Thus she skillfully managed to make me feel that my personal immaturity was the only thing standing in the way of a full-blown, passionate romance with my beloved.

But I suspected it wasn't really my immaturity that was the problem; it was Carolyn's. Tired of competing for attention, my crabby sister had done what I could never do: gotten pregnant at the tender age of nineteen and eloped with her seedy, carrot-headed boyfriend Cody. Now the two of them were living in the more-or-less remodeled garage while my father forlornly watched his aging, baby-blue Aston-Martin deteriorate rapidly in the Georgia sun, rain, and hail.

By that time my father was honing his capacity as a functional drunk. He had gotten a department chair position at Stone Mountain Tech, a local community college, while he sent quixotic applications to Harvard, Stanford, Berkeley, and all the rest of the best. My mother tried to keep painting her pale and precise landscapes in the dim light of her tiny sewing room, and also tried to keep the peace between C & C, as I called them, who were usually squabbling after the young father-to-be got home from the motorcycle shop every day. Needless to say, nobody was very happy around this time. One result of Carolyn's life-altering indiscretion was that the clamps on my social life were screwed down tight.

"No dating until your senior year, and until you've had a full year of safe driving," my mother had pronounced one night at dinner, my father nodding gravely as if he'd actually given some thought to the matter. But this was clearly a Kay Kendricks regimen. Then Mom had smiled tinily, even gently, around the corners of her thin pinkish lips, and added, "I guess you and JoEllen will have a volume of great letters to publish by then."

But we did have a date when we were sophomores, on a spring night that I still remember with embarrassment and a lingering thrill. Once a year the school held one of those Sadie Hawkins dances where the girls took the reins of the patriarchy away from their acne-ridden suitors. It was an event that JoEllen looked forward to for an entire quarter. Four weeks in advance, JoEllen told me she'd hired a cousin to babysit her little brother the night of the dance, and did I want to be her partner, please say yes? In a tone both helpless and grave, I told her my mother had said I couldn't date yet. Within two days JoEllen had gotten her mom to talk to the student counselor, who called my mom and made things OK.

Talk about taking charge! In the week before the dance, I was experiencing the same mix of feelings that had visited me years before, after the speech-and-rescue operation. Again JoEllen Jones had saved me, made my life miraculously better, and made me feel like a total incompetent in one fell swoop.

But as the night of the gymnasium ball drew closer, the ghost of past misgivings paled before the spectre of oncoming anxiety—which I knew I would soon meet head-on in the shadowed confines of a flimsy, tackily decorated Kissing Booth.

ON THE way to the dance in Cody's growling, bucking Mustang, I could think of nothing but the Kissing Booth. Cody's vulgar innuendoes weren't helping the situation.

"Hey, I hear tell that leetle JoEllen Jones is a real ice cream sundy," he muttered, leering at me while we roared through a red light three blocks from the house. "You gonna get in a lick or two tonight?"

I squeezed my eyes shut and said nothing, inwardly writhing over the vulgarizing of my beloved's image by my sister's greasy impregnator. At the same time, he had me—and in a male conspiratorial way, he knew it. Now I couldn't help seeing that JoEllen *was* a real ice cream sundae and I *did* want to . . .

a novel of sexual initiation   13

Fortunately these sick, implanted sentiments evaporated upon my entrance to the dimly lit, romantically decorated gym—where I immediately spotted JoEllen, dressed in a fantastically inappropriate knockoff of a 19th-century ball gown, white gauzy frills at her shoulders and waist and, I swear, hoops and layers of petticoats. Maybe it wasn't that bad, but I do remember feeling the strangest mixture of pride—this amazing creature was mine, all mine for the night!—and a paternal embarrassment about JoEllen's tendency toward excess. She swooped toward me, an unabashed *Gone with the Wind* aura about her, and put her face right up to mine like a flashlight. Now she was so luridly made-up that I couldn't miss it.

"Hi!" she said excitedly, then giggled and seemed to shiver all over. "Hi there," she repeated seductively.

"Yeah," I said coolly. "So here we are." As JoEllen's attentive gaze was making me nervous, I attempted to scan the room in a sophisticated manner. It seemed important to demonstrate that we weren't really part of this scene. We were Intellectuals, after all, culturally slumming for the evening.

I could confidently project this air because I was wearing one of my father's soft, elbow-patched jackets and his corduroy pants. The only problem was that maintaining this image seemed to require a certain gravity and detachment, and suddenly JoEllen had taken me by the hand and was leading me decisively toward the punchbowl. My heart sank when I saw her best friend Lainie McEwen over there—her habitually unhappy face looking like pink cotton candy dirtied with zits and a lot of sooty, scary eye shadow. By the darting of Lainie's worried eyes I could see that she had come alone, probably at JoEllen's insistence. That meant we were likely to become a threesome for most of the evening.

Now I had nothing against Lainie personally; I just didn't understand her appeal to JoEllen. Lainie was what my mother would unhesitatingly call "trailer trash." In fact she lived in one of those double-wide mobile homes up on blocks, maintained a slovenly C average and a very smart mouth, and was rumored to be a sexual veteran—even to the extent, darkly hinted by some, of having terminated a pregnancy. I knew Lainie was a down-the-road neighbor of JoEllen's, but otherwise I didn't get the connection. Most of the time I wrote the friendship off to JoEllen's social naïveté. Smart as she was, she hadn't had enough friends in her childhood to know better than to hang out with Lainie's type.

The really damnable thing about Lainie, though, was that she could read me like a clock on the classroom wall. As JoEllen and I came abreast of her at the refreshments table, Lainie took one look at me, smacked her bubble gum loudly, and asked, "So what's the matter with you?"

"What do you mean?" I said stiffly.

"Oh, you know," she said, blowing an obscene red bubble, sucking it in, and grinning with gum-spackled lips. "Looks like you're too good for the rest of us."

"*Lay*-nee!" JoEllen whined, obviously taken aback because her accent came on so strong. "Now be nice," she added, issuing a motherly look.

"I didn't *do* anything," Lainie muttered childishly, casting her eyes to the floor.

Fortunately, at that moment the band of long-haired, scrawny nineteen-year-olds up on stage blasted their way into a pop rock tune we had all heard done better on the radio, and further hostilities between Lainie and myself were narrowly averted. Given that start, the evening would have been a total wash if not for the Kissing Booth—actually a caravan-style tent set up in one corner with Christmas lights strung around the open flap. It opened for business about halfway through the evening.

For fifty cents, a couple could kiss briefly in the privacy of the tent—a privacy compromised by the presence of the student fee-taker, an adult chaperone, and two or three voyeurs at any given time peering through rents in the tent fabric. The money would go to the construction of a new outdoor track, said to be a good cause by some. You could legally commit as many kisses as you wanted as long as you waited in line each time and dropped another fifty cents. I guess JoEllen didn't want to appear too eager for once, so she waited until there was a line of seven couples before formally asking, near the end of a clumsy slow

a novel of sexual initiation   15

dance, "Shall we go?"

"Sure," I said confidently, slipping one hand into my pocket to finger the surprise I had for JoEllen. I was going to break with the reversed tradition and pay for the kiss myself—an event that would surely draw gasps of surprise inside the tent. Then I would bend JoEllen over and show the peeking rubes what passion really meant.

But when we gained entrance to the inner chamber I was struck cold with chagrin. I had known there would be other people in there, yet somehow I'd imagined they would be anonymous functionaries shipped in from parts unknown—but not Mr. Driscoll, the shop teacher, and Holly, the supercilious head cheerleader! Julius Driscoll was a kindly, balding, half-grizzled black man who took particular care to keep me out of harm's way in shop, away from whizzing bandsaw blades and potentially lethal electric drills. More often than not, he just let me draw plans for elaborate gizmos in his office. Once we had even sat back there while the other boys made wall plaques, and talked about his family like we were adult buddies. His family was a fascinating subject for a kid like myself, avowedly liberal like my sociologist father but with little real experience of minorities.

Holly was that bouncy, vapid kind of cheerleading girl— someone I ordinarily didn't pay any attention to — but here she was, about to take the money for my romantic ambush of my beloved. The sight of her, flanked by a paternally grinning Mr. Driscoll, was paralyzing. I was so ready for someone to start laughing out loud that I almost missed my cue. Holly had opened the gray metal change box and was staring at the two of us intently, while JoEllen fished around in her little fake-pearl purse, before I remembered my plan.

"Wait a minute," I barked harshly, when I had meant to be suave, placing one hand over JoEllen's on her purse. "This one's on me." (That was a little rougher than I had rehearsed it: *Please allow me, my love.*)

"Oh," JoEllen cooed dramatically, like I had just unveiled the Taj Mahal to her. Mr. Driscoll chuckled in his deep baritone before murmuring "Attaboy!" I dropped two quarters in Holly's delicate, bony palm and turned to JoEllen. Startled by the reality of her wide, red lips simultaneously parting and approaching me, I tilted my head sideways and planted a near-miss, shearing kiss on JoEllen's cheek, making a short transit from the left corner of her lips almost to her ear. Basically, I slid off her jaw.

Then I drew back and, to my heart-stopping horror, saw a deep frown of disappointment clouding JoEllen's face. She sighed, glanced quickly at Mr. Driscoll and then at the line behind us, and in a blindingly quick movement drew two more quarters from her purse and dropped them in the change box. Holly had no more gotten the word "But" from her mouth before JoEllen had lunged at me, one hand going up behind my neck, then fixed her lips firmly on mine and shockingly pushed her tongue well into my mouth. It fished around, warm, strong, and persuasive, for a few eternal seconds during which my head reeled and my groin tightened. Then JoEllen abruptly backed off, her eyes half-closed and a floating, dreamy smile on her smeared lips.

"Sweet Jesus," muttered Mr. Driscoll, seeming to suppress a laugh in the tent's semi-darkness. "Randall, you better get yore lady outta here before she takes ever'body's turn."

I nodded dumbly and stumbled out of the tent with one arm around JoEllen's waist, no doubt flushing red from head to toe. As we came out of the tent Lainie came rushing up from behind it, arched her eyebrows at us and exclaimed, "Wow!"

THUS began two months of foolish and frustrating seduction—more or less mutual, but always spiked, it seemed to me, with superior knowledge on JoEllen's part. Ever after the kiss that night, I wondered if JoEllen hadn't learned a lot more from Lainie than I had suspected. After all, I'd heard some seamy rumors that Lainie and JoEllen actually *practiced* things together. I always laughed off such scuttlebutt, but then wondered darkly about the possibilities when I was alone in my room at night.

One thing was for sure: Lainie never seemed far away when JoEllen and I were getting heated up. Our trysts usually occurred at lunchtime, when we would skip eating and take a long walk

a novel of sexual initiation   17

down the Ecology Trail, deep into the verdant, viney woods, and find a little shaded glen to lie in the grass and talk, kiss, and fumble. To me sex seemed to belong in the woods, as if the leafy foliage had been designed to camouflage the kind of action that would have seemed too stark in a bedroom or, God forbid, the back of a car.

But we were both brought up so well, as my mother would have put it, that we never got beyond rolling around and kissing. Once I unbuttoned JoEllen's blouse and she, blinking with excited eyes, pulled one of her substantial breasts out of her bra, holding it in front of me like a soft trophy.

I wasn't sure of what to do. I extended my index finger to her soil-brown nipple, half-expecting to get electrocuted, and found it instead to be incredibly tender. I watched with surprise as it contracted and pushed itself out under my circling touch.

Then there was a noise way off in the bushes—a bird, a wolf, the principal?—and JoEllen rapidly stuffed and buttoned herself back into her clothes. We hastened back toward the school hand-in-hand, running as if we had narrowly escaped an emergency. About halfway back we bumped into Lainie coming down another branch of the trail, munching an egg salad sandwich and wiping her brow as if she'd been on a vigorous hike. Only that night did I realize that Lainie was hardly the hiking type. She usually smoked at lunch.

A few days later, the three of us were sitting out on the front steps of the school at noon. It was quite hot—too hot for slipping away down the Ecology Trail—and getting near the end of the school term. I didn't catch on right away, but eventually I realized that JoEllen was upping the ante on our sexual anticipation by wearing some daring short-short culottes that day. The loose fit of her shorts bared one of her thighs all the way up to the crotch, and she openly let that leg rest in the sun that way. Both Lainie and I could see the trim of her panties and an ample fringe of dark, curly hair jutting out from underneath. I was transfixed by the sight, and Lainie kept winking at me. I tried to glare back, but my gaze was always drawn back to JoEllen's commanding thigh.

MY JOURNEY THROUGH THE PLANT WORLD

"Girl, you are pushing the line with those kew-lots," Lainie finally said a few minutes before the homeroom bell would ring.

"Why?" JoEllen said innocently, batting her eyelashes.

"Shit, you know why," Lainie retorted crudely, casting a dirty glance at me. "We can see your frizz and everything. If Mrs. Amberley sees you like this, she'll send you home to change."

JoEllen patted the cuff of her shorts to cover her inner thigh, then raised her other knee and skillfully turned toward me so that I could see up that leg anyway. Leaning back like a magazine model and pulling down her sunglasses over her eyes, she replied defiantly: "Well, I didn't dress for Mrs. Amberley today. I dressed for Randall."

That really got to me. I don't know why exactly, but I was cool toward JoEllen for the following—and last—month of school. We still took our walks and kissed, but my ardor was leveling off. Hers was heating up, probably because she sensed that I was too cowardly to make a big effort to see her over the summer. So I think she wanted to get something going that I wouldn't be able to resist. Without understanding my motives, I was determined to maintain the status quo. I just wasn't ready.

By the end of school, JoEllen was pretty mad at me for my mysterious distance of the concluding few weeks. Still, we had both arranged unnecessary do-gooder tasks for ourselves on the last half-day, when virtually everyone else had lit out for the lake. Being teacher's pets was in our blood since elementary school, and we weren't above using that status to arrange some last-minute trysting time for ourselves. We both knew that while we were supposed to be filing records for Mrs. Chastain in the school office, there would be plenty of time to sneak off together into vacant halls or empty classrooms—or perhaps down the deserted Ecology Trail—one last time.

But the day turned out to be weirder than either one of us could have imagined. The school was so lifeless that it was downright spooky—my footsteps echoed queerly down the halls—and JoEllen came in crying. She wouldn't even speak to me for an hour. That only left two hours, and getting in some kissing had suddenly become a life-and-death matter, because of my news.

a novel of sexual initiation

But if I told her. . . well, she might not even touch me.

Finally, with less than an hour left, I crossed the empty office and gingerly seated myself on the desk facing JoEllen, who had been staring disconsolately through the window at white cottony clouds in a brilliant blue sky. It was a beautiful early summer day, but neither one of us could feel it.

"What's the matter?" I said as softly as I could.

JoEllen's eyes immediately teared up. She violently slammed the desk and said, "Are we going to see each other this summer or not? You haven't said *anything*, and soon we have to go home!"

I tensed up, chagrined that I should have said something by now instead of waiting for a cue. Then I remembered that things were already beyond my control.

"I have some bad news," I said evenly, as if I were announcing that the film projector was broken and we couldn't see a movie in English class that day. "I found out last night that my father got a job in California, and we have to leave now. Next week, I mean."

JoEllen raised her watery eyes to mine as if she were going to ask me to repeat what I'd said, but the shock had clearly registered. "You're going away?" she whispered.

"Yeah," I said, smiling painfully, crossing my arms, gazing out the window.

"Not again," JoEllen sighed, her tone suddenly adult and world-weary. "Not again."

3

WHY IS the vivid link between the two women who sexually initiated me made up entirely of dark, prolific pubic hair? Does the image linger because I'm unbalanced? Or are my suspicions about the vegetative compulsion of sex — that the tendril is mightier than the mind, in this case — well-founded in natural fact?

I worry about this, I really do. It's the kind of thing that I withhold from June, because no matter how objective she may be as a therapist, she's still a woman (and a native Berkeley crone at that) with doubtlessly thin patience for men's obsessive physical neuroses about women. Perhaps I shouldn't be seeing a female therapist at all. Perhaps I should be pounding antelope-skin drums in a circle of men with our shirts off, stomping about in a funky sweat deep in the dark woods, questing for a vision . . . but frankly, the notion strikes me as ludicrous.

I like June's analytic style. She has that down-to-earth yet high-class refinement that Jungian academies magically impart to their graduates, and she helps me frame my problems more profoundly than I could alone. As June once remarked, "People lose their will to act when they regard their predicaments as overwhelming yet insignificant." Translation: You've got to afford your fuck-ups some dignity to make life worth the struggle.

Still, the pubic-hair connection between JoEllen and Anna feels too weird to bring up in our meetings, even those open to the sky on June's sunny back patio. Perhaps that's why she suggested I undertake this journal of my sexual history. I'll bet she knows I'm keeping secrets.

But when you get right down to it, I've been pretty damn open for a Southern expatriate. I even cried when I told her about that last day with JoEllen, about how it took me all these years to feel the grief that JoEllen seemed to suffer then. She was literally rendered speechless by the news of my departure, sobbing with her head on the desk while I helplessly petted her long brown hair, feeling the most awful mixture of guilt and mad desire. There was something almost criminal in the way that I was secretly relieved to be getting away from JoEllen's directorial presence in my life—an uncanny replay of the end of the sixth grade—while at the same time I was wanting to consummate our long-checked passion (like I would have known how) right there on the floor of Mrs. Chastain's office.

"I think it was the closest I ever came to a psychotic split," I dramatically confessed to June about that long-ago, conflicted hour of parting, my eyes stinging as I looked up to her lined, birdlike face for confirmation. June only nodded, silently and inconclusively. I wondered if that was the wrong diagnostic term.

Finally, JoEllen had raised her head from the desk, got up and crossed the room to get some tissue. After blotting around her eyes, she smiled weakly but courageously—what a magnificent young woman she was becoming!—and meekly inquired, "Will you write me a lot?"

"Sure," I said with warm certainty, eager to prove that there was an intact bone of decency somewhere in my body. "Every week. As soon as we get settled maybe you can come visit!"

It was a lame offer and she knew it, but she nodded her head vigorously, grinned sweetly and rushed over to hug me. For about fifteen minutes I'd say we were as close to heaven as we ever got, leaning there against the desk in a fierce embrace, kissing now and then, no longer speaking. Our urgent, final intimacy was broken by a brief squeal of brakes and the insistent blaring of a car horn out in the school's nearly empty parking lot, visible through the office window. Carolyn had arrived to pick me up, surely not an errand she was enjoying, and she wasn't about to walk in and look for me when the horn would suffice. It was just as well. My farewell to JoEllen was not a scene that I wanted Carolyn walking into.

As JoEllen and I untangled I looked at her sheepishly and shrugged my shoulders. "Call me tonight?" she asked softly.

a novel of sexual initiation   23

I nodded, said "Bye," and walked off, leaving her virtually alone in the whole school. *Christ, what a bastard.*

I did call her, but I don't remember what we said. I couldn't talk for long because our house was in an uproar of dislocation. My father was being a totally officious jerk, his head dangerously swelled over the miraculous acceptance of his application to the University of California at Berkeley, "the finest public institution of higher education *in the world*," he kept saying for the family's edification. Later I would learn that his unexpected appointment was the result of a suicide in Cal's sociology department. They desperately needed someone to help complete a federally funded poverty study. Despite his thin, moth-eaten *vitae*, my father was the only candidate with anything near the right research background.

But if my father was happy, Carolyn was on the edge of ecstasy. The way things were working out, she and Cody were inheriting the whole house, while Mom, Dad and I were entrusting our future to the largesse of the university in far-away California. Despite complaining of nausea from the miracle of my nephew-to-be piecing himself together inside her, Carolyn was the most helpful and industrious I had ever seen her. She couldn't wait for us to get out.

Shocked and numb as I was over the pace of change, I was in harmony with her. Georgia already seemed like history to me. California, as I vaguely pictured it, was the land of no limits or frustrations, where every rebellion or indulgence was allowed. I was devilishly curious about it. My mom pursed her lips tensely through the whole ordeal of leaving, methodically saying her good-byes to neighbors, neatly wrapping up the loose ends that the rest of us were too frantic to remember. That California would liberate her more than anyone was a possibility that occurred to none of us at the time.

TO REALLY appreciate California, I think you have to come from the South. You couldn't come here from any other region and experience quite so profound a cultural shift. Nor could you stay for years and retain so much of your root identity for contrast. Your typical Midwestern expatriate is likely to tell you that he came to California from "oh, nowhere really," or from "it doesn't matter." Within a few years he indeed forgets his shallow wheatfield roots and becomes innately, inconspicuously Californian.

Not so for the California Southerner, who will be able to tell you to his dying day every blessed detail of the crooked corner of the county he came from, back there in North Carolina or Georgia or God-forbid Alabama—and who lived just down the street, and where their folks wuz from. The road map of back-home is stamped like an indelible tattoo on the consciousness of Southerners, forever in the view of their inner eye.

To this day, I still experience occasional shocks when the crusty earth of my upbringing is fractured anew by the impudent thrust of California Reality. What I mean is: bearded women in the grocery store; noisy protests by mobs in wheelchairs; winsome mocha-colored children playing in the park, children whose parents over on the bench are not merely black and white, but West African and French-Canadian; those kinds of things.

I'm cooler about these shocks nowadays. At most I might raise an eyebrow or chuckle. But my first two years in California occasioned countless lapses into open-mouthed bewilderment. On the very first day that Mom, Dad, and I pulled into Berkeley on a mid-summer day, we got slowed down behind a classic old Volvo driven by a woman with closely cropped, multi-hued hair, and sporting one eye-catching bumpersticker which mysteriously announced

WILD WOMYN
TAKE BACK THE NIGHT!

A few weeks later when I had gained a sympathetic pal at Berkeley High, I had this message deconstructed for me, and I marveled at how succinctly it revealed the zeitgeist of the town in just a few words. Back where I came from, bumperstickers mostly conveyed the retorts of rednecks to decent society, like:

GAS GRASS OR ASS
NOBODY RIDES FREE

In this fathomless cultural chasm between the Southeast and Far West lay the rocky proving grounds of my encroaching manhood. Would that I had known, on the aforementioned dusky-golden evening of our arrival in the West, just how soon my manhood would be summoned! When I think back to the dating ban that was still ostensibly in effect when our family trundled into town, I still get a big kick out of it. Because I didn't exactly break that ban before my senior year of high school. It's just that my sexual initiation lurched into high gear and plowed right through it without my folks ever knowing. And what's more, they arranged the whole shebang!

Of course, they thought they were only hiring a gardener. In another incredible turn of luck for my father, our family ended up with the suicided professor's house—an enchanting if small-ish stone-facade cottage perched about halfway up in the Berkeley hills, on one of the narrow European-style streets that charmingly wind this way and that. (I loved that house and tried to buy it from the University when I came into my first real money about ten years later. But like People's Park, they would not let it go for hell or a hoedown.)

In the steeply ascending backyard was a stunning profusion of drought-resistant flora that Mrs. Chedderly, the pince-nez'd octogenarian next door, said was the former inhabitant's "pride and joy." Dad's vanity and obsessive desire to fit in led him to hire a gardener to tend to it, just like Mrs. Chedderly said he should. For better or worse, he hired *her* gardener: the guileless, river-haired Anna.

I first saw Anna from the rear in the back yard, bending over to inspect a huge but shriveled cactus. From my vantage point behind the dirty kitchen window I couldn't quite tell what I was seeing. Anna's butt-length, lightly tangled tresses almost covered her deep green sweatshirt, and one of her bare legs was hidden in the profusion of unidentifiable plant life up there on the hill. If I were of a more fanciful bent, I could claim that she simply arose from the vegetable kingdom right then and there, but this is not one of those therapeutic fairy tales. This is supposed to be a truthful accounting of my troubled past.

Within a minute I had discerned that the form out there was female, youthful, and by itself. Being almost seventeen, I was naturally curious to investigate. We had been moved in for about three days; my folks were having lunch with some very important people on campus, and I was enjoying the unprecedented feeling of being absolutely on my own in a new land. I could as easily say a whole new world, the way things felt so utterly different from Georgia. What I was spying on reinforced the delicious alienation. Back in Atlanta, young women in canvas shorts and flowing cascades of hair generally did not materialize in your back yard.

I walked out the open back door, hands jammed in the front pockets of my jeans, and called out coolly, "Hello up there!"

The young woman jerked clumsily, almost losing her balance before righting herself against the trunk of the oversized plant she'd been inspecting. She leaned against it gingerly while peering down at me. Then she spoke plainly, factually: "I'll have to dig this one out completely. It's got some rot at the base."

"Oh," I replied, somewhat confused. "Okay by me." We both stood in our places for a few awkward moments before the woman—I was sizing her up to be in her early twenties—smiled and took the role of an adult in our exchange:

"I'm sorry, I don't mean to be rude. My name is Anna. I was working on Mrs. Chedderly's garden and she said you might be . . . needing me?"

"Oh, I replied uncertainly. "I guess." Then I shrugged my shoulders and added, "I'm Randall. I'm here with my folks. I mean, they're not here right now. We just moved here. From Georgia." I felt my face flushing red; I wasn't sure whether what I had just said made any sense.

"Really?" Anna called out as she turned her back, then twisted her way out of all the foliage above me and started to step down the hillside, holding a spade in one hand. "My folks are from North Carolina, but I was born in Colorado." By this time

a novel of sexual initiation　　　　　　**27**

Anna had made her way down to the stone porch where I was standing, and I was amazed to see that she was barefoot. Things certainly were casual out here!

"So you've been around," I said lamely, raising my eyes to hers. I realized I shouldn't be looking her over so obviously.

"Yeah, I guess so," she replied, laughing uncertainly. Then she stared at me blankly for a moment and blurted out, "I hope your folks will let me take care of things back here. I don't even care if they pay. But it would be nice."

"Well," I said uncertainly, "I'm sure they'll . . ." Actually I had no idea of what to say, because I wasn't sure what they would do. Then I recalled a bit of conversation between my father and Mrs. Chedderly, and everything fell into place.

"Oh, wait a minute! Mrs. Chedderly told Dad he should definitely keep on the gardener. Said you were the hardest-working young lady she'd ever seen."

"That's nice," Anna remarked emotionlessly, bending over to tap dirt off the spade against the low stone wall framing the back side of the porch. When she turned back toward me she looked conspiratorially from side to side, then leaned close and whispered in my ear. "I'm surprised Mrs. Chedderly remembers me from one day to the next. You know what?"

"No," I whispered back. "What?"

"Sometimes she pays me twice for the same week!" Now Anna's face was very close to me. I was struck by the broadness of all her features—eyes wide apart, wide mouth, nobly long nose, all combining in a handsome way, but not a particularly feminine way. My mind rapidly made the connection: *Carolina . . . Cherokee*, although her hair wasn't completely straight or coal-black like the Indian women I remembered from our summer visits to tacky Gatlinburg in Tennessee. I was about to ask about her bloodline when she continued:

"But it's all right. She can afford it, with those two sons of hers practically running the Bank of America. Anyway, I give half of the extra money to the Free Clinic."

"The free what?" I said, abruptly diverted from my concern about her heritage.

Anna sat down on the top of the stone wall and inelegantly crossed one leg on top of the other to peer at the bottom of one foot. "The Free Clinic is where you can go to see a doctor if you don't have any money. I volunteer there sometimes because I've always been *so* grateful they told me I didn't have herpes."

"What?" I exclaimed, more ignorant than surprised. I wasn't familiar with the word and I thought she was talking about some kind of bedbugs, or . . . what?

"Oh, I'm sorry," Anna laughed, covering her mouth with one hand. "I didn't . . . oh boy, sometimes I just don't think!" Then she pounded one side of her head with the palm of her hand. "That's dumb ol' Anna for you! Just blurt out everything in public, why doncha?"

Even through her dark complexion I could see Anna blushing as she began to back away from me toward the side entrance to the backyard. "Look, I gotta go now and check another garden down the street. It was very nice to meet you. Tell your folks I'll be back on Saturday and I hope we can talk then. OK?" By now she was turning and exiting through the gate, not waiting for any reply.

I half-heartedly said, "Sure," in the direction of her disappearance, then turned and looked at the sunny back yard. I stood there awhile, admiring the western light in the backyard, feeling invigorated, a little smarter somehow. Perhaps because now I knew the first thing about this place that my parents didn't also know. Meeting Anna was like arriving on my own.

BUT THAT moment of confidence was short-lived. When I started my second year of high school, I was as green as a kudzu shoot and I took a lot of ribbing for it from the native kids. Jimmy Carter was getting himself elected to the White House that fall; I had no more than introduced myself in an orientation class as a native subject of the Governor than I picked up the nickname "Peanut Man."

A thin, very expressive black boy named Pierce started it. I would have taken offense if he hadn't gone out of his way thereafter to offer his friendship along with the silly derision. I didn't

a novel of sexual initiation

comprehend everything that was going on there. But that was just as well, or I wouldn't have had any friends at all for the first year at Berkeley High. Certainly I wasn't about to make any headway with the ladies.

The girls at school were all a blur, an unfamiliar sea of hip, West Coast femininity. They all seemed to speak a sassy, self-possessed lingo I couldn't grasp. Although I had never liked the coy and coquettish Southern-belle archetype, it was at least familiar to me. The only girl I talked to much was Ariel, a plump, smoke-wreathed pal of Pierce's. During my first six months at Berkeley High we became a habitual threesome at lunch. It would be a little while before I heard, and then understood, the term *fag hag*— that is, as long as it took me to understand why Ariel paid so much attention to Pierce and he was paying so much attention to me.

If I had apprehended all these dynamics right away, would I have behaved any differently? I honestly don't know. Pierce was a great and unusual pal, that's all. He didn't act very black, certainly not Southern black, probably because he lived up in the hills with his professor mother and had spent most of his childhood in Cambridge—England—so he had a sophisticated frame of reference, and a rather tony accent, for a high school junior. He also had an eye for clothes, and was constantly making disdainful comments about the predominant hippie style of dress on campus.

Pierce's own style leaned toward expensive, tweedy jackets with contrasting but subdued vests and what appeared to be some kind of Continental school tie, an almost miniature hand-tied bowtie in deep crimson, teal, or mocha. Neatly folding his jacket and placing it carefully beside him on the low brick wall where the three of us always had lunch, he would sit with his spine perfectly erect and pick out passing victims for his vicious, quietly muttered fashion reviews.

"The lady has rather too much thigh to be showing it quite so shamelessly, don't you think?" he might say about a girl ambling by in ripped jean shorts, causing Ariel to pull roughly on her own too-short skirt. "Bloody slob!" might be all that a typically grungy hippie guy got out of Pierce. Ariel and I would giggle conspiratorially while Pierce graciously nodded his head and smiled toward the very passersby he was sartorially eviscerating under his breath. I guess we were an odd group. Looking back, it's no mystery that I wasn't making much headway with girls. Anyone who might have cast an eye in my direction would have assumed that I was already socially engaged.

4

IT'S FUNNY how circumstances can conspire to create secretive, hothouse situations in one's life. There I was with a narrow, bent social life at school and, by the time of Jimmy Carter's election in November, a new driver's license in my wallet. Something was bound to happen. With the first winter rain, it did.

'76 being a drought year, the rains arriving in the last two months of the year were sporadic. But one of them came on strongly enough on a Thursday afternoon to bring Anna down the back yard hill, away from her gardening and into the kitchen where my mother and I were reading recipes out of a California-style cookbook.

My mother was still fretting over the dinner she had thrown a few evenings before for my dad's departmental peers. She'd done her absolute best—the sticky fried chicken with lumpy mashed potatoes that I dearly loved. But my father had gone pale when he came in the door and smelled the familiar aromas. He had taken Mom aside to whisper to her in urgent, didactic tones while I tried to make small talk with all the frizzy intellectuals jostling into the house. I felt weak in the knees when I saw her rush into the bedroom, her eyes obviously tearing up. My father strode into the living room and gamely announced that everyone would be treated to a "real, authentic Southern dinner!" I knew he was beside himself with anxiety when he uttered such a redundancy.

My mom returned in five minutes, bright-eyed and smiling bravely. I thought everything came off well—the two finicky vegetarians in the group got by on peas and mashed potatoes—but that night I heard Mom and Dad arguing in controlled, not quite decipherable voices until at least two a.m., when I finally drifted off to sleep with a new Harris Professional stamp album on my lap. Today, Mom and I were boning up on a new cuisine.

MY JOURNEY THROUGH THE PLANT WORLD

Or at least she was, since I had been casting frequent glances up the hill where Anna was working. I did that a lot—glancing at her—when she came by weekly to work on our vegetation. I was happy to have Anna around as a sexually stimulating spectator sport: a youthful woman dressed in shorts in every kind of weather, with an assertive, athletic style of movement that fascinated me. I assumed it was the Indian part of her coming out.

We didn't talk much about anything important, as I remember, but she was always friendly. Anna was like a sister except that it was all right to fantasize about her. That was the extent of my interest. After all, she was an adult, and hired help besides.

Anna opened the back door as Mom was reading out loud from *The Vegetarian Epicure*, and immediately apologized: "I'm afraid I'm dripping all over the floor, Mrs. Kendricks. It's really coming down out there."

My mother had been unusually warm with Anna from the start—or perhaps California was warming her up in general. "Anna, how many times have I told you it's 'Kay'? I don't even know what you're doing back there in this weather. Randall, get Anna a towel, will you honey?"

"Sure!" I said, and took off running, slowing myself down when I realized that I probably looked too eager. In the master bathroom linen closet I dug out the biggest, lushest, deep green towel I could find. I thought Anna would like the color. When I returned to the kitchen I heard Mom utter the words that would change my life:

"Nonsense, young lady, I won't hear of it. You are not walking down the hill in this weather to catch the bus. Randall can drive you home. He just got his license and he can use the practice. Can't you, dear?"

I nodded mutely, holding the towel out to Anna with two hands like a dumb eunuch, wondering why everything in the room had gone into slow motion. Anna was smiling at me in the most curious, conspiratorial way, as if something we had previously schemed had fallen into place. But there was no scheme. Because we never talked about anything but the weather and the plants, mindless chatter spiced every now and then with weird,

a novel of sexual initiation   33

titillating little things that slipped out of Anna's mouth, like the herpes bit when we first met.

In this sudden arrest of time I felt something both cold and fiery contracting in my solar plexus, like a birthing star, then expanding and spreading a tingly warmth downward . . . and then Mom was peering at me incredulously while the car keys dangled in front of my eyes. *"Rann-dall?"* she was singing. "Mother ship to Rann-dall? These are the keys that start the car that takes Anna to Anna's house. Get it?"

"Oh . . . oh yeah," I stuttered as time slipped back into gear. "Oh, sure. I can use the practice!"

"The boy would lose track of his head if it wasn't screwed on," my mother replied in her cold tone of voice, then smiled tightly at Anna, who had been toweling her hair for the few eternal seconds that I'd been out of it. Then Mom walked down the hallway to the bedroom and shut the door. That was classic Mom: on and off, here and then gone. I shrugged my shoulders at Anna, who neatly folded the towel and left it on the kitchen counter.

Outside we got into the enormous Chevy station wagon that was increasingly embarrassing for me to drive around town, given Berkeley's small-car ambiance. My father, who had unloaded his old Aston-Martin on an unsuspecting rube back in Atlanta, had somehow financed a new Porsche for himself within our first month in California.

The cropped, fringy remains of jeans Anna was wearing that day were nowhere near new. Her lithe, naturally coppertoned thighs coming out of them were a major distraction as I maneuvered the car down the narrow winding streets of our neighborhood with all the grace of a supertanker barging through the Carquinez Straits. Anna lived a good piece away, in Piedmont, so the drive really was good practice for me. Or at least it would be in the months to come, when I was calmer than on this maiden voyage. Hardly a word was spoken on the way, save Anna's directions mixed in with a little tour-guide information.

When we pulled up in front of a house with a glassed-in porch on the second floor, Anna said, "Hey, you wanna see my place?" and I said, "Sure."

It was as easy as that.

She lived in the high sunroom, which was filled with plants and had only a bathroom and a tiny kitchen behind it. Another apartment took up the back two-thirds of the second floor; a third unit occupied the entire downstairs. Anna's bed was in one corner under the long window that fronted the street. At the other end of the rectangular room was a cheap, scarred wooden table with two chairs. I sat at one of them, excited and uneasy, as Anna disappeared into the kitchen.

"Do you drink anything?" she called out after a few moments.

"Well, I, uh . . ." I didn't want to tell her I didn't; beer gave me a headache. "Anything's okay," I finally lied.

Anna appeared with a bottle of nondescript red wine and two plain drinking glasses. She sat down across from me and started to pour, then stopped herself and asked, "How old are you again?"

"Just turned seventeen," I said.

She smiled, resuming the pouring, and said, "Does that mean I'm contributing to the relinquishing of a minor?"

"Delinquency," I corrected her, and we both laughed a little too hard. "You know, I'm really not sure," I continued in as low and steady a voice as I could muster. "Maybe I'll let you know in a little while."

Oops, I thought, as Anna bolted from the table, brushing past me to stand at the window with her hands jammed in her pockets. Had I said something offensive?

"It's so nice to see the rain come down," she murmured. "It's been really dry ever since I got here. I just came to town a year and a half ago, you know."

"Oh," I replied, remembering that I did know that already, unsure of whether it was significant at this moment. "Oh, yeah . . . and how old are *you* again?"

Now she turned toward me and smiled a smile that made her mannish, dark-browed features soften and her eyes have lights in them. "Twenty-three," she said. "Old enough to be your. . ."

Her voice trailed off as she broke the gaze we were sharing and walked with a bouncing lilt over to the end of her bed. She was taking off her flannel shirt as she did so. By the time she sat

a novel of sexual initiation   35

down she was wearing only an army green t-shirt and her shorts. Her feet were bare, as they often were, but they weren't drawing my attention. The nipples pushing forward behind the thin, worn cotton of her shirt certainly were.

"Come sit over here, Randall," Anna said softly. I had never heard her use my name that way.

I was beginning to feel tight and erect; I hoped it wouldn't show as I obeyed Anna's call, aware that I was blushing from head to toe. I picked up my glass, then realized there would be no place to set it down once I completed the fateful transit to the bed. "I guess I won't bring that," I stage-whispered, put the glass back down on the table and went over to the bed.

As I sat down she immediately lay down on her side and it was obvious I should do that too. For a few moments we lay there, both of us with our elbows crooked, our heads resting against our palms, her glorious dark hair cascading around her arms and over her chest.

"Hi," she finally whispered.

"Hi," I whispered back.

Some moments passed. Then Anna's eyes darkened a bit as she asked, "What would you like to do, Randall?"

The openness of the question caught me unawares. What did she expect me to say? Play Monopoly? Watch TV? I shrugged my free shoulder and dropped my eyes to the bedspread.

"You stare at me all the time in the back yard. I thought you liked me," Anna said in a faintly accusatory tone.

I fought back a peculiar impulse toward tears, instead letting loose with a petulant sigh, like a twelve-year-old. "Well, I do like you, Anna, I just . . ."

Suddenly she rose and, leaning forward on both hands, looked down into my face like a solicitous mother. "Randall, haven't you ever, um, you know. . ."

I rolled onto my back, thoroughly embarrassed. "Not really. I mean, I've made out and stuff." I closed my eyes tight; I didn't want to see her facial reaction.

"Oh my," I heard her mutter. When I opened my eyes and looked over sideways at her, I saw that she had sat back and was clasping her hands in her lap. "Now I feel really weird," she said to no one in particular.

"It's not my fault," I blurted.

Anna chuckled, rocking forward and bringing her face close to mine again, and the still-damp, earthy smell of her hair close too. "Sweetie, I'm sure it isn't. You seem pretty mature, so I thought, you know, we've been building all this sexual tension and everything. . ."

We have? I thought to myself, stunned that I had been missing that kind of build-up. Or had I? Was it rather that Anna was admitting what I wouldn't admit? Momentarily lost in thought, I didn't notice right away that Anna was pulling her t-shirt up over her head, revealing her breasts—just a shade paler than the rest of her, not very full, but pointed, with dark and exceptionally protruded nipples. I thought that her breasts looked like ripe, exotic seed pods.

Then I didn't think anymore because she had moved over to lie on top of me, her breasts softly mushing against my shirt and her long hair making a curtain on either side of my head. It was dark in there, where our faces were.

"Hi there," Anna said again.

"Hi."

We stared into each other's eyes for a long moment and then she gave me just the barest mouth-to-mouth kiss before whispering, "Will you hold me a little while? Then I think you should go."

"OK," I said. I felt a fleeting disappointment but then, to tell the truth, a sense of relief. Anna lowered her head down beside mine, occasionally wetting my neck with her lips. I traced up and down her back with my hands for a couple minutes as she made soft, cooing sounds of gratification.

Then she sat up. "Thanks," she said, picking her shirt off the bedspread and pulling it back on over her head. "That felt great." With a mischievous grin she added, "What if it rains next Thursday and I need another ride home?"

I sat up, tingling all over, very hard in my crotch but otherwise unexpectedly relaxed, and said, "Okay by me. I don't have any big plans."

a novel of sexual initiation

THE ONLY problem was the drought. After a few more half-hearted showers that weekend, the school week opened hot, sunny, and dry. The tired blue sky looked like it was going to stay that way forever. I sat in class day after day staring at the out-doors, alternately praying for rain and dreaming up Plan B's: Anna could pretend to hurt her ankle and need a ride home; Anna could have some car-requiring errands; or hell, I could walk up to my mother and say, "Kay, Anna and I didn't go all the way last week. Is it all right if I take her home again this week so we can finish the job?"

I found the last alternative pretty amusing, and came up with increasingly brazen variations in my mind as the week ticked down. By Wednesday lunch, I had Anna and myself doing it on the kitchen floor while my mother puzzled over her cookbook. Then I added in the highlight of my father coming home and wordlessly stepping over our writhing mass on the way to his study. I kept chuckling to myself about these scenes over my sandwich, garnering knit-browed looks of puzzlement from Pierce. But I kept the source of my secret glee to myself. By the end of classes on the next day—The Day—Pierce was waving me home with the cry, "You just keep on smiling that mystery smile, Peanut Man! It looks good on you!"

When I got off the bus at 3:30, three blocks downhill from the house, I was worried about the time. Anna usually came to our yard at about 3, and worked until 4:30. Last week we had left the house together about 4:45, and I got home by 6 without provoking comment. Dinnertime was still following our daily Georgia conventions, 6:30 on the dot, although Dad was often missing. He said there was an awful lot to learn for "the new man on cam-pus," a phrase that struck me as rather silly and self-important.

Here was the problem: I didn't know how long it would take for Anna and me to do what was on the agenda. What if I got home late, and questions were asked, and I looked different? I suppose I was worrying about the scheduling of the thing because I didn't want to worry about the thing itself.

I had already dispensed with worrying about an excuse to drive Anna home, having settled on "Mom, Anna has some errands," which would be easy enough to fix with Anna—and then it hit me. Of course! The errands could take longer than either of us expected. "You know how the Co-op market is right before dinner," I could say to the folks when I trooped in at, say, 7:30 or 8 that evening after hours of multiple, mutual orgasms.

As I entered the house, I was amazed at how well it was all going to work out. I called out for Mom but there was no answer. In the kitchen I found a big note on the refrigerator door: "Randall—out for a walk down the hill—we'll go out to dinner—Mom." It was a little strange, Mom opting not to cook without consulting anybody, but I decided it was probably good for her to be getting a little more independent, a little less schedule-bound.

But I wasn't really focusing on Mom's changes at that moment; I was pretty interested in the one coming my way. Putting down my books on the counter, I leaned over the sink to look into the garden out back, where I could barely see Anna crouching in the far right corner of the upward slope, spading something. Although it wasn't raining, it had clouded over during the afternoon. This being early November, it was already getting dark.

I went out the back door and called out, "Hey up there!" Anna stood up—she was wearing a red sweater and long pants for a change, army fatigues matching last week's t-shirt—and waved, then skipped lightly down the inlaid stone pathway to within about ten feet of me, and stopped. I noticed that she was wearing little gold circle earrings for the first time ever. She looked great.

"Your mom's not here," she said matter-of-factly.

"I know," I said, smiling expansively and lifting my eyebrows. "Do you think you might need a ride home?"

Anna grinned, looking up. "It isn't raining exactly."

"Well, you might need help running some errands. The kind of errands that require a station wagon and give me some more driving practice."

"Oh," Anna replied with a wink. "I hadn't thought of that."

"Errands we should get started on right away," I added assertively.

Anna turned and looked up behind her at the garden, almost

a novel of sexual initiation

longingly it seemed, then turned back and smiled warmly, her eyes flashing. "OK. I might have a couple of those errands."

It was as easy as that. I left a note for Mom.

In Anna's tiny sunroom twenty minutes later, it seemed that night had already fallen after she lowered and turned all the blinds on the windows. She lit two candles near the bed. She took off her sweater and t-shirt—*does she ever wear a bra?* I wondered—and walked slowly over to me, appearing very conscious of her seductive power. We had hardly said a word on the drive over, and that was just as well with me. I didn't imagine this kind of thing as a talking experience.

When we started kissing, I noticed right away how lightly and briefly Anna brushed lips. JoEllen had been a tongue-plunger from the get-go, something I'd always found both unnerving and extremely stimulating. Anna retreated every time I put any pressure on her mouth. Then she'd hang her head around my neck and slowly, subtly, rotate her hips. She was almost my height, and strong, muscular all over. *A lot of yard work*, I thought as I brought my hands down her back to the top of her rump.

"Uhm," she hummed softly, pushing her groin against mine. "Uh-humm."

After two or three cycles of semi-kisses, sensual hugging, and pushing groins together, Anna suddenly backed away, dropped her arms to her sides and whispered, "Let's take off our clothes, okay?" I had begun to wonder how that transition would take place. I was glad she was directing.

Taking a deep breath, I rapidly unbuttoned my shirt, took it off, unbuckled and zipped down my pants, took them off. Feeling embarrassed to be standing in front of a woman in my underwear with a hard-on pushing against my shorts, I rapidly removed those without further ado. So there was my grown penis, standing straight out in front of a grown female for the first time ever. It felt hot in a cool room. I watched Anna unsnap and drop the loose fatigues from her waist; she was wearing plain, ordinary pink panties. As she slipped her fingers under either side of them, she looked coyly at me, then slipped them down to her ankles, and stepped out.

I marveled that her pubic hair, which started almost halfway up to her belly button and swirled a little against her thighs, looked less curly than riverlike, just like the hair on her head. Besides pictures, I had only seen fringes of a female triangle—JoEllen's—before now. Anna was hairier than I had expected, although I had noticed the dark hair on her arms a few times when we chatted in the garden. I was beginning to feel frozen and awkward, standing there in the dim light, nakedly facing Anna, when she lifted one hand toward my erection.

"Look at you," she said wonderingly, clasping me as she might a garden trowel, gently pushing me backward to the bed. When we got there she lay beside me, on her side, with one breast against my chest. We kissed more intimately than before while she played around my crotch area, tickling my balls, lightly caressing my electrified penis. I was a little dizzy with inarticulate fright and desire, one part of me ready to charge ahead and another part of me not knowing where to charge. Anna's tongue was flicking into my mouth every few seconds like an evasive lizard. When I would go after it or try to push my tongue into her mouth she would turn her head again. I was getting so distracted by these maneuvers that I wasn't fully cognizant of the building mountain of tension within my pelvis. My whole body was so much more alive and goose-bumpy than when I masturbated that things were getting out of hand.

Suddenly, from out of nowhere, Anna finally did plunge her tongue—into my ear!—and I yelped, my torso bucking upward, which induced her to grab my cock firmly and start pulling up and down on it. She had done this no more than five or six times before I came, shooting fizzily this way and that, then I went, "Aaahh . . ." and jerked around a little. Then I just lay there. Both of us were wet, me all over my midsection and Anna on the exposed side of her rump. Anna chuckled softly in my ear. Then she said kindly, "You're pretty excited, baby."

"Yeah, I guess so," I confessed in an exceptionally tiny voice.

She started to get up. "It's all right," she replied, now very motherly, "I'm sure there's more where that came from." She

a novel of sexual initiation　　41

disappeared into the bathroom for a moment, then came out with a worn hand towel and started mopping up both of us. When she was done she nonchalantly dropped the towel on the floor and lay back flat on the bed, our arms barely touching sides as we both looked up toward the ceiling. I saw the room shade a mote darker as we lay there silently for about a minute, a soft dreaminess starting to fog up my head. I didn't know what came next, but I was starting not to care.

A moment before I would have actually fallen asleep I was surprised to hear Anna take a sharp, short breath and whimper slightly. I blinked and lifted my head, looked down over her body and saw her right hand massaging the dark hair of her crotch. She noticed my movement, turned her head toward me and said in a husky undertone, "Do you want to help me out a little?"

"Uh, okay," I said, getting up on one elbow and placing my other hand on her upper thigh. I wanted to look as studious as possible. I stared intently at what her hand was doing as it softly rotated between her slightly parted legs, pushing her hair around and occasionally exposing mysterious dark pink rivulets of genital tissue. Suddenly I thought of JoEllen again—how I had missed all this with her. I felt sad and elated, a paradox of emotions that was, like the rest of sex, novel and unexpected.

And as I watched Anna building her own excitement, her torso starting to lift toward me, I felt a gravity I'd never known before, as if her pelvis were part of the earth itself, a wild territory rising and opening before me, calling me to set forth into its grasslands, forests, and subterranean caves. Everything felt both close up and far away: here I was in bed with the gardener, a Cherokee maiden, and here I was in California, spinning dizzily away from the past like a spaceman cut loose from his ship.

5

I DON'T know what possessed me. An archetypal instinct, as my therapist might put it, or a past-life compulsion, or the faint genetic memory of making a beeline to an aromatic flower? Whatever drove me, I found myself wanting to take my mouth to Anna's sex as I watched her rub herself. It was also partly the feeling that I had no confidence in using my hand on her. At any rate, I lowered my head and kissed her a couple inches beneath her belly button. She immediately withdrew her hand, exclaiming, "Oh, yes, Randall!"

As I gradually moved lower, kissing to this side and that, starting to lick a little, it became clear that I wouldn't have the right kind of access leaning over her. I sat up, confused. Anna looked at me with alarm, saying, "Please don't stop!"

"I'm not," I protested, "I just don't know. . ."

Immediately Anna raised her knees and spread her legs wide, and whispered urgently, "Come this way. . ."

Getting between her legs, wrapping my arms around her lean thighs, I went right for the thick of it, my face nosing into an unfamiliar bramble of hair, soft tissues, wetness, and unexpected odors—something urinelike, and something very perfumed. Was she wearing some kind of sex perfume? I would never know; as I would learn in the months to come, Anna could be both sexually overt and secretive at the same time. What she revealed and what she didn't followed a logic never revealed to me. I tried a variety of actions: kissing, sucking, licking, JoEllen-style tongue-driving; and I must have done all right, because with a modicum of direction from Anna—"Oh, lower, honey . . . No, don't bite, that hurts . . . Slower . . . Faster!" we got rocking and rolling pretty soon. I was amazed at how loud she could be, making a variety of little religious screams between the stage directions—"Jesus! Oh, oh, yes God"—and how violent and powerful her movements could be, considering that she had my heavy head on her middle and her legs held down.

Soon I felt like I was bronco-busting, trying to keep my mouth in the general vicinity of her opening and what I believed to be her clitoris (I'd read enough *Penthouse* letters to know vaguely what to look for). Then Anna really bucked hard a couple times, mashing my lips against my teeth painfully. She invoked the deity one more time with a vulgar laugh, then pushed my head away and started giggling, rolling from side to side, wrapping up her breasts with both her arms. I could see goosebumps all over her. I sat up on my haunches, pleased with myself, a little surprised to see my penis standing up again.

When Anna stopped rolling, her knees up and her legs together, she brushed some moisture from her eyes and said happily, "Good golly, Miss Molly! You've done *that* before, haven't you?"

"Nope," I said nonchalantly.

"Well, what do you know," she replied. "I found a natural."

I shrugged, happy to be a volunteer. Anna gazed at me warmly and silently for perhaps fifteen seconds. Then she broke her smile and said with an almost depressed neutrality, "Do you want to fuck now?"

That word and her unexpected change of tone really disturbed me. Something alien and unhappy had entered the room's atmosphere, and I was too inexperienced to intuit its source. "Well, sure, I guess," I ventured, placing a hand on her knee. She nodded mutely, pushed herself up toward the head of the bed a little more, opened her legs again, took hold of me and guided me into her.

Needless to say, I had never felt anything like it—a warm, enveloping wetness which, as I moved around slowly and tentatively, let its limits of tendon, muscle and skeleton be known. *I'm really doing it!* I kept repeating to myself silently, perhaps because Anna seemed half-withdrawn, accentuating my feeling of "doing it" instead of any feeling of togetherness. Before, when I had my head between her legs, it was like we were both doing our best to keep up with something happening to both of us, like rafting a wild river with our bodies roped together. Now, in

a novel of sexual initiation

between delicious moments of almost overwhelming sensation, I had the bad feeling that I was merely poking around inside Anna's body. I almost stopped moving a couple times, searching her face for a clue. She looked masked in a friendly way, like a store clerk trying to be a little too helpful.

Now I know—like it does me a lot of good—that I should have stopped everything and asked her what was wrong. At the time I couldn't be sure anything was wrong—maybe women just didn't like this part as much?—and I certainly wasn't going to miss the sensation of coming inside her. As I started to build up toward that, I became oblivious to her blankness. She started reacting a little more, although she was only grunting—"Unnh, unnh . . ." in a low tone.

Finally I came, not too fast this time. I felt every iota of the peaking. This time the surprise was that as I released, I didn't feel big, powerful, and victorious, like soft-porn stories suggested men always felt. Frankly, I felt scared. There was a much bigger loss of control then when I masturbated. I didn't know where I was for an instant, and the closeness, no, the *thereness* of Anna, all around part of me . . . all this was disorienting. Without realizing it, I had pushed myself up into a straight-arm position. With the sudden feelings of release, weakness, and mild fright, I lowered myself slowly back to her body, my face to her face, and we kissed chastely.

In a few moments, Anna whispered in my ear, "Pretty good, baby. You're a good learner." Then she started squirming to disengage us. I was still half-hard and a little disappointed, but I said nothing. In a flash she was up and going into the bathroom, drawing shut the sliding door. I eased onto my back and shut my eyes.

When I opened them Anna was rocking me gently, saying "Hey, loverboy, wake up." I blinked a couple times, feeling incredibly soft and heavy all over, then noticed that Anna was already dressed. I turned my head to look at the clock by her bed and saw that it was ten to six.

"Oh, OK," I replied groggily, sitting up. "I'd better go home."

Anna was sitting on the corner of the bed, hands in her lap, a slight smile playing at the corners of her mouth. "How do you feel?" she said, a little bit too much like a nurse.

"I'm all right," I said defensively. I rolled over to the right side of the bed looking for my clothes. Anna handed them to me. It felt weird being watched while I dressed; suddenly I wanted out of there. The way Anna had changed moods right in the middle of making love had discombobulated me; the feeling that I had possibly done something wrong was taking root. We said nothing while I buttoned my shirt, checked for my keys in my pockets, and put on my shoes. Anna's smile had faded and now she seemed a little anxious, like she wanted to say something but wouldn't.

As I headed out the door toward the wooden stairway, Anna touched my arm and said weakly, "Hey, give us a kiss, okay?" I obliged, not feeling as affectionate as I thought I should, so I held her extra long. In my embrace she still felt strong and shapely and I was getting a little stirred-up again.

I was surprised to see that Anna's eyes were moist, so I said, "Are you OK?"

She nodded her head vigorously, wiping her right eye with the back of her hand, and then grinned gamely. "I think you're a sweet guy," she said. "I hope . . ."

"What?" I asked, running one hand through the hair falling over her chest.

"Oh, nothing," she concluded with a sigh.

"OK." I started quickly down the steps, relieved that I might have escaped some kind of last-minute complication. As I gained speed I half-turned my head and called out, "See you next week!"

"Sure," Anna said simply, and closed the door.

WHEN I got home at 6:15 Mom was sitting at the kitchen table with the newspaper open, a cup of coffee before her. She didn't seem to be reading, but staring out the window toward the side of the house. While I wondered whether I should be the first one to say anything—would that give it all away?—she spoke in her chill monotone. "Your father won't be having dinner with us."

a novel of sexual initiation 47

"Oh," I said calmly. "Another faculty meeting?"

"I don't know," she said without breaking her gaze at Mrs. Chedderly's house next door. "His secretary said he was hung up."

"Well," I answered coolly, "don't worry about dinner for me, Mom. I've got a big paper due Monday that I haven't even started. I have to call Pierce and pick his brain."

"How about Chinese?" Mom asked abruptly, rising from her chair and going to the sink, automaton-like, to wash her cup. It was as if she hadn't heard me at all. The offer sounded good, though, and I quickly forgot my fear of being found out.

Thirty minutes later in a quiet little place called Shin Shin on Solano Avenue, Mom seemed bent on sampling the entire menu: we ended up with soup and potstickers and four main dishes. Only when we were obviously overburdened with plates, their rims hanging precariously over the edges of the table, did Mom seem embarrassed enough to say, "We can always take some home for your Dad. He's probably missing dinner." Though we had been small-talking up to this point, miraculously avoiding the subject of Anna, I was getting a little edgy. Because everyone in our extended family knew that when the slender and fastidious Kay Kendricks pigged out, something portentous was brewing.

Finally Mom pushed herself away slightly from the table, held her stomach at both sides like an attenuated Santa Claus, and said firmly, "Okay, that's enough!" Still going myself—this was only my third bout with chopsticks—I nodded at my mother with my mouth full and waited for whatever was surely coming.

"Randall, we need to sort out our schedule for the next little bit of time," Mom said pleasantly, clearing away enough space on the table to put her elbow down, rest her chin on her hand, and smile at me like a true friend.

"Mmph," I replied.

"You know that your sister is about to deliver any day now." I nodded. Actually the news was a bit of a shock. I hadn't been thinking about anything going on in Georgia, including my

MY JOURNEY THROUGH THE PLANT WORLD

pregnant sister—and including JoEllen Jones. I had a stack of her increasingly plaintive letters on the far corner of my desk; I'd been replying with scenic Bay Area postcards and promising her more thoughtful expositions when I got around to it. Now the mention of back-home brought up all kinds of nostalgia and guilt. Maybe I would really, seriously try to write JoEllen tonight . . . then suddenly I saw Anna heaving beneath me, grunting, her mouth open and her head turning rapidly from side to side, wreathed in her own long hair. I put down my chopsticks and swallowed hard.

Mom seemed oblivious. "At first it didn't look like I could get back until Christmas," she continued. "But I've decided to visit your Aunt Grace in Augusta over Thanksgiving, then stay home til the first of the year to help Carolyn and Cody get settled with the baby."

"Wow," I said with interest, immediately realizing how much easier it would be to arrange trysts with Anna during such a prolonged maternal absence. To divert attention from my real thinking—*Great timing, Mom!*—I said sardonically, "I bet Cody'll be a great dad. He'll have that kid on a Harley in no time."

"Now, Randall," Mom replied mischievously, looking down and folding her napkin over uselessly on the table, "don't get me started on Cody. There's always hope. For divorce, I mean."

"Mom!" I exclaimed, astonished by her joke. She would never have said such a thing back home. When she looked back up she was grinning widely, her pale blue eyes crinkling at their corners. I could clearly see the desirable beauty of her light, crisply defined features, like a fragile portrait sketched in white sand. (Sometimes, at moments like that, I've been in love with my Mom, and I don't care who knows it.)

Neither of us spoke for a few moments, a new line of openness having been crossed between us. Then Mom said magnanimously, "Oh, Cody's a good boy, I guess. I just wish he wasn't a boy still. He's got a lot of responsibility on his shoulders now. He's going to have to be a man sooner than he thinks."

"Yeah," I said thoughtfully, nodding my head like I understood all it took to be a man. The experience I'd gained within

a novel of sexual initiation

the last few hours made me feel like I could handle manhood all right. My inner eye was watching Anna in bed again.

"When I get back after Christmas, Randall," Mom was saying, "we should talk about your future."

"Oh?" I said, genuinely curious, having no idea where she was going.

"Yes," she answered crisply. "Next year you'll be a senior, and that's when you get ready for college."

I had picked up my chopsticks again, but held them in mid-air and looked at her, confused. "What about it? I'm going to Cal, aren't I?"

"Well, probably, honey—if that's what you really want." Now Mom was looking at me with a strange intensity. "We know it's what your father is planning, and of course it's much easier and cheaper with him on the faculty, but . . ." She was fiddling with her napkin again. "Be sure that you do what *you* want to do, all right?"

This was strange. A few weeks ago Dad had walked both of us all over campus, showing us all the academic buildings and the Student Union; my future there seemed as certain if it were already printed in the catalog. At the time my mother hadn't even peeped. What was she getting at? I said, "Uh, okay, Mom. I guess I'll talk to a counselor this spring, and see what my options are."

"Good," she said, nodding her head with finality. "Good. I want you to live *your own life*, you know." Tears were welling in her eyes.

"Mom?!" I exclaimed, urgently leaning forward. "Is there something wrong?" Of course there was something wrong; she had eaten two and a half of her normal meals in one sitting.

She seemed to choke back a big sob, pursing her lips very tightly before looking at me with large, alarmed eyes. "Randall, I think you're grown-up enough to know something important about our family, something that could affect your life in a big way pretty soon."

I tensed up. This wasn't going to be good. "What is it, Mom?"

She looked at me sadly, dropping both hands beneath the

table. "Your father had an affair last year at Tech." Then she turned her head to look at the blank wall beside her, as if some kind of invisible message had appeared there.

A chill ran through me, and the remaining food looked entirely unappetizing. I put down my chopsticks for good. "An affair?" I said dumbly, like I didn't know what that meant. But I saw Anna touch my arm and ask for that kiss as I had left, the soft light from a single bulb inside a round Japanese lantern glowing behind her.

"Yes. With another teacher at Tech, a young woman teaching glassblowing."

"Glassblowing?" I repeated incredulously. My mind played with a few potentially vulgar meanings for such a bizarre detail before I refocused my attention on my mother's face, which was visibly gravitating from a set of defeat to defiance.

"Don't get me wrong," she said assertively. "Phil's an attractive man and I'll bet he's turned away a lot of temptations in his time. I know he was having a rough time of it before we came here. We all were. What upsets me is that he hasn't apologized. He acts like it was his right to—to *be* with that girl—and now he wants me to just forget about it. 'My little indiscretion,' he says. I'm afraid this new appointment has gone to his head."

I leaned back in my chair and sighed disgustedly. "Yeah. A little bit." Then I felt incredibly angry, thinking I was putting two and two together. "Mom, is that why Dad's not home for dinner a lot? Is he doing—do you think he's having another affair?"

"N-no," she stuttered quietly, as if she hadn't considered the possibility. I felt like a jerk. "No, I doubt it," she continued tentatively. "I think he really is busy. He's probably gotten himself in over his head. But he doesn't seem to have very much time for us. And I don't think I want to put up with it any longer."

"What do you mean, Mom?" I asked fervently, feeling cold and afraid.

She put both hands on top of the table and regarded me seriously, but kindly. "I'm going away until the new year to give your father some time to think. If I come back and he hasn't . . . well, if he doesn't show some change in priorities, I'm afraid I'll be

a novel of sexual initiation 51

moving out. I thought you should know. By springtime I might not be in the house anymore. I'll stay close by, at least until you enter the University."

"Wow," I said, amazed. The young Chinese waiter who came to the table with the take-out boxes could have knocked me over if he'd had a feather with him. I glanced up at him and smiled insensibly, then looked around the room, not knowing what to say. Knowing the situation rapidly reduced my fear; I even felt mildly excited for Mom and her new boldness. She calmly took the check, laid some money on top of it while the waiter dished our leftovers into the boxes, and then looked back toward me with a silent lift of her eyebrows. When the waiter departed I found my tongue:

"Well, Mom, I can't say I blame you. Don't worry about me; I'll be okay. But if you leave I'd rather live with you until college. I could get a job next year if we needed money."

Mom smiled condescendingly, going cold on me as she put her billfold back in her pocketbook. "Let's not get ahead of ourselves, Randall. Phil and I both have some thinking to do on our own before all these big decisions are made. Will you be all right for Thanksgiving? You don't mind just being with your father?"

I grimaced. "Maybe I can get myself invited to Pierce's house. I haven't met his mother. She's a real Nigerian."

"Well, whatever," Mom said remotely, standing as I got up to help her on with her coat. "I'm sure you'll find a way to have a good time."

In the car on the way home, nothing was said between us for most of the ten-minute trip. As we started climbing steep, straight-up Marin Avenue, the station wagon groaning with the stress, Mom said, "By the way, it was very nice of you to help out Anna this afternoon."

I flashed on exactly what Anna had asked me to help her with, and my brain screamed, *How does she know that?!* But I kept my mouth shut, thankful that it was night and Mom couldn't see my face inside the dark car. Then I remembered my diversionary note about the errands. *Thank God!*

"She's certainly had a hard time the last few years," Mom

continued nonchalantly. "You know she was recently divorced?"

"No," I said as neutrally as possible. "Really?" I thought the same: *Really?*

"Yes, she told me the other week that she was married a few years ago. They lost a baby only six months old, and then her marriage fell apart. I think she was in college for a little while, but she said she couldn't concentrate on anything. Poor girl. I guess she finds some solace working in people's gardens."

"Yeah, I guess so," I said sympathetically, mystified. How could I not know the basic biography of a woman I had just gone to bed with? Why was Anna withholding from me? What had we been talking about almost every week for months? Just the stupid plants? How could I not know *anything?*

"Anyway," my mom continued, "I think Anna's trying to collect herself and decide how to get her life started over. I don't know how long she'll stay out here. It seems like all her friends are back in Colorado. But it would be nice if you can help her out sometimes like you did today. You know, give her a ride when you can. You don't mind, do you, son?"

I turned my face to the passenger window, grinning hysterically. "Uh, no, Mom," I said, leaning my forehead against the cool glass. "Of course not." To cover my hilarity I straightened my face, turned and asked matter-of-factly, "Mom, do you think Anna is part Indian?"

"Indian?"

"Yeah, doesn't she look a little Cherokee to you? I haven't really talked to her much personally, but she told me that her parents were from North Carolina. I didn't want to ask her right out, but I was curious that she might be Indian."

Mom pulled the car abreast of the house and killed the lights and ignition. "Native American, Randall."

"Say what?" I queried, confused.

"Only Columbus thought they were Indians. Your father is becoming a prominent liberal sociologist, and I know he doesn't want his son going around asking people if they're Indians. *Native Americans.* Try to keep up, son." With that Mom opened her door, got out of the car, shut the door and was striding up the

a novel of sexual initiation   53

walk before I'd even grasped my door handle. At moments like that, I really couldn't stand my mother. She hadn't even answered my question.

6

ONE THING quickens another at a certain age. Later that night as I sat at my desk, staring blankly at the notes for a history paper on the Teapot Dome scandal—could anything have been more irrelevant to my situation at the time?—I was growing certain that I needed to find a job. If my parents actually did split, I didn't want to live with Dad; he was a traitor. Either I would live with Mom or strike out on my own.

The thought made me laugh out loud. A year before I was grousing about the dating ban; now I wanted my own apartment. Working didn't scare me, though my teen employment record was not impressive. I'd mowed a few lawns in my time, but my first real job at an Eckerd's drug store in suburban Atlanta had not gone well. When I started smart-mouthing the manager— some junior-college business major shipped down from Charlotte whom I secretly called "Spam-for-Brains"—I was doomed. Even though family money was tight at the time, my father was relieved by my failure in retail. I'm sure he thought it beneath his male progeny. But I chafed under our allowance arrangement, in which Dad cut me a check for a couple hundred dollars every time I stooped to poormouthing. It made me feel like a son on salary, except that payday was never reliable.

Suddenly I could smell Anna's hair, as if she were standing close to me again inside her tiny, candlelit room. These intimate moments from a world of the very recent past had intruded in a largely pleasant way all evening. Dating ban, indeed! Why did Mom want me to be so friendly to Anna, I wondered briefly—did she know what was going on and was tacitly granting her permission? No, I decided, she wasn't that liberal yet.

Then a scary thought that had been flitting around the edges of my awareness like a disease-carrying mosquito finally bit me. Anna could be pregnant. *She could be pregnant already!* We had made love without taking any kind of precaution—unless she had, but I couldn't tell and we hadn't said anything about it. I certainly hadn't said anything about it, and I had known since sex education in the seventh grade that you were supposed to say something. But Anna was the experienced one. Shouldn't she have said something? How responsible did I have to be? What would a jury say?

This paranoid self-interrogation eventually drove me from my desk to the bed, where I tossed and turned for a while. Perhaps I could call Anna tomorrow, apologize profusely for being so dense, and find out if she was pregnant yet. Would she know already? Probably not, I decided, so I wouldn't call. In fact, any thought of contacting Anna before next Thursday made me nervous. I wasn't sure why, but it seemed important that this relationship be kept within its original bounds.

The next morning at school I begged Pierce for an emergency Saturday session at the downtown library to help me finish my paper before Monday. He exacted a price: "You must come Christmas shopping with me in the morning. We'll do your paper in the afternoon." That was pure Pierce: Christmas shopping two weeks before Thanksgiving! I was lucky he didn't want to trek over to Union Square in San Francisco. In truth, by noon it had turned out to be a dry run for Pierce—he'd bought nothing but an anklet for Ariel from a hippie vendor up on Telegraph Avenue—but he was in good spirits, as always, by the time we sauntered downtown to Shattuck, looking for lunch.

I always say that I owe my success in business to a fallen letter. Pierce and I were walking by a nondescript storefront with a dirty window when I noticed an antique, chipped and scarred wooden "S" about six inches tall lying on the sidewalk. I picked it up and showed it to Pierce, who immediately began soft-shoeing and singing, "Ss-wonderful, sss-mahvelous . . ." Laughing, I backed away to look up at the rectangular sign that spanned the entire top of the storefront. In the same wooden lettering it said

DIVER IONS OF BERKELEY

a novel of sexual initiation   57

"Ah, dear Watson," I said to Pierce in a flimsy Brit accent, "the solution to the case of the fallen letter," and we trooped in.

Inside we found a mystery of nearly Holmesian dimensions. It took a few minutes of adjusting my eyes to the dim light to figure out what kind of store Diversions of Berkeley was supposed to be. An antique cash register sat atop a dusty glass case holding five or six chess sets, in ivory, wood, and fake silver, all of them covered with the same fine layer of grit that seemed to be a theme in the place. There was a deathly silence all about; the front door had been slightly ajar but there was apparently no one around. Pierce was visibly recoiling from the dirt everywhere as I took note of sloppy stacks of board games on two tables—Clue, Risk, D-Day and what have you—and a vertical rack of vacuum-packed Frisbees. It was some kind of game store. But why did it look like a tornado had recently visited the premises? And why did everything stink in a musty, fruity kind of way?

The answer soon came out of a door in the back, as a pudgy little fellow with thick glasses, a monkish fringe of hair around his bald head and a smoking cigar appeared. He looked to be about thirty-five and aging fast.

"Hullo there," he called out, trudging nonchalantly to the front of the store. Pierce took a half-step back as he came within breathing distance of us. "What's up?"

"You lost a letter out front," I said, helpfully holding the letter out toward the troll.

"Ah, dammit," he scowled, biting down on the smelly cigar as he took the letter and laid it on a counter. "Now I'll have to get the goddamn ladder out." The way he said it suggested that this little chore might well be forgotten for the next year or two. Simultaneously chewing his stogie and grinning, he tried to be a salesman again: "So what can I do you guys for?" he growled cheerily.

"Oh, nothing really," Pierce said immediately. "Just out taking some air." He touched my elbow and tilted his head at me as if to say *Let's get out of here.* But something in the air besides the smoke was piquing my interest.

"Do you sell any stamps?" I asked.

"Nah," the storekeeper said, finally taking the cigar from his mouth and flicking some ash on the floor, "no money in 'em. I tried to carry coins for a while but I had a break-in and that was the end of that. How about a vintage game o'Life?" He crinkled his eyes, smiling rattily, like this was an old, favorite joke.

I winced; this guy was hopeless. Why would he think that a serious stamp collector would be interested in a silly board game? Suddenly I felt another pull on my elbow; Pierce, looking anxious, said, "I'll meet you down at Edy's, okay? I'm famished." Without waiting for my reply, he slipped gracefully out the door. It was as if he didn't want to see what happened next.

What happened next was that I fell into an extended conversation with Chuck Berquist, the "owner and originator," as he put it, of Diversions of Berkeley. I can't quite remember how it happened. I think Chuck's next words after Pierce left were "Stamp collector, eh?" I gave him quite a pitch about why he should stock all the various paraphernalia of interest to philatelists, citing evidence of massive consumer interest—evidence, of course, that mostly had to do with my interest. He kept saying "Uh-huh," nodding noncommittally. Finally he interrupted my spiel with a wave of the cigar and said:

"You got any experience in retail, son?"

"Uh, sure," I said matter-of-factly.

"Wanna make some extra Christmas dough? I'm gonna need some help for the rush this season."

Not if you don't clean up this joint, I thought to myself—and then, startlingly, he added:

"If you don't mind clean-up detail, I could give you all the hours you want." Chuck's eyes brightened considerably behind his distorting spectacles.

"Well," I hesitated, "maybe . . . I have been looking around for something steady I could do after school. You know, if it pays enough."

"Start you out at minimum," Chuck said, leaning in toward me as if passing on some kind of trade secret, "and raise you a buck if you want to stay on after the season. Sound good?"

"Okay." I didn't know if it sounded good; it just seemed to be happening.

a novel of sexual initiation   59

"How many afternoons can you spare?" Chuck was moving right along, looking happier every moment.

"Most all of them, I guess"—then I panicked—"except Thursdays."

"Great. How about five, six hours on Saturday too?"

I nodded, starting to feel a little fearful about what I was rushing into. *What about school? . . .* Who cared?

"Do you have an application I should fill out, Mr. Berquist?"

"Chuck! Call me Chuck! Don't worry about it," he said, turning abruptly and starting to retreat to the back room from whence he had first come. He waved backward and yelled, "See you Monday, Randall!"

I SLIPPED into the booth at Edy's across from Pierce, who shrugged apologetically as he chewed a half-eaten burger. Sometimes it was reassuring to see Pierce do *something* that normal teenagers did.

"I was genuinely famished," he explained. "It wasn't just that I had to get out of that dustbin. Although I *did* have to get out of there."

"I got a job," I replied smoothly.

Pierce stopped dead in the middle of a chew, swallowed something too big and sputtered, "You must be out of your mind! In that underworld den? With that weird little chap?"

"Chuck Berquist," I responded. "The owner and originator of Diversions of Berkeley."

Pierce shook his head slowly and then leaned it against one hand, gradually dropping his forehead almost to the table. He always overreacted that way. When he raised his head he said, "Do you have time for this? What about school?"

"School is not big on my list of worries right now, Pierce. I have to get a job because—and this is a secret between us for now, okay?—because I have to help my mother. She's leaving my dad because he's . . . They're not getting along anymore."

Pierce's eyes widened as his mouth opened slightly. I knew he would love such an intrigue. "Really?" he whispered. "Has she moved out?"

"No, but she's going back home for Thanksgiving and staying until New Year's. My sister's about to have a baby. Mom's going back to help out but also to let my father think things over. That's what she says, but I know him. He won't change. It's all over. When she comes back I'm going to move out with her." I leaned back in the plush seat and crossed my arms, feeling victorious.

"Well then," Pierce said with certainty, his composure returning, "you and your father must come to our house for Thanksgiving. Ariel's coming, and a few of my mother's colleagues. You'll be quite welcome."

I had been angling for this invitation, but Pierce's inclusion of my dad was unexpected. "Do I have to bring my father?" I whined.

"Really, Randall," Pierce admonished me, simultaneously miming to one of Edy's middle-aged waitresses that I needed a menu, "be a sport." That was Pierce for you: fair-minded to a fault in every realm but fashion.

That same evening, after Pierce had helped me salvage my history paper at the library, I accosted first my mother and then my father to tell them about my new employ. At home they were increasingly relating like two ships passing in the night, and that was all right with me. I knocked first on the door of the tiny spare bedroom where my mother had set up her painting studio. She didn't answer, which generally meant it was all right to come in. I called it the Kay Code, Mom's indistinct method of telegraphing her feelings.

Standing behind her easel, facing her half-obscured face behind the large watercolor board she was staring at in the inadequate light from the ceiling fixture, I said, "Hey Mom, guess what? I got a job today at a game store downtown."

She glanced at me briefly and then back at her work. "That's nice, son. What kind of game store?"

"A really dirty and disorganized game store. The owner needs a lot of help. I can work all I want to, straightening the place out."

"Hmm," my mother murmured, barely audible.

"So," I ventured, "I'll be making some money of my own when you get back from Georgia . . ."

a novel of sexual initiation   61

"All right," she replied noncommittally, obviously not getting it. "Come around here, Randall. Tell me what you think."

Mom didn't often show her works in progress, especially since we had moved out West, so I was curious to see what she was up to. At first glance, the watercolor looked like one of her conventional, hard-to-tell-apart landscapes, although the scenery was now Californian instead of Southern. The subject was the East Bay hills we were living upon. Then I did a double-take, because I saw something that didn't seem to have been there on first glance. In the upper right quarter of the scene, inexplicably floating in the air above the crest of the hills, was a deep purple, bug-eyed, crimson-streaked fish, partly blocking a full, vibrantly orange moon. The effect of this overcolored, preternatural scene was drug-like; I just stood there staring for several endless moments.

"Wow, Mom," I said finally, "that's wild. Wild in a good way, I mean."

"Hmm," she said faintly. "I don't know. I just don't know."

Crossing and going down the hallway to my father's more spacious den a few moments later, I found him leaning back on his recliner as usual, a book on his lap and a stack of papers, abstracts, and other academic what-not on the floor beside him. Sometimes I could see what my mother meant about his opportunities for temptation; he was at once approachably handsome, professorial, and peculiarly vulnerable in his appearance. Perhaps the vulnerability came from his size. At five-foot-eight, he was barely taller than my mom and his physique was slight though lean and well-proportioned. He still had all his dark brown, wavy, collar-length hair, and an undeniably cool and well-kept mustache over an easy smile that could sell anything—including, apparently, illicit propositions to young glassblowers.

I could hardly look at Dad now without thinking about his betrayal of my mother. This restive hostility combined with an uneasiness about my announcement made me unusually awkward in his presence.

"Dad, can I talk to you about something?" I ventured.

"Anytime, son," he said gently, putting his book aside and

MY JOURNEY THROUGH THE PLANT WORLD 62

regarding me benevolently, playing the role of the attentive father to the hilt.

"So I was downtown this afternoon and met this guy in a game store—I mean, he owns the game store—and anyway, he said I could have a job. I mean, I didn't ask for a job, but he had one. For after school, I mean. You know, for Christmas rush." Boy, what a disaster! Why did I feel like I was nine years old?

My father's smile vanished. "You've gotten a part-time job?"

"Yeah."

"Well son, if I had known . . . I'm sure I could have arranged something for you on campus. Do you need money?"

"No!" I said sharply, fearful and a little offended. "I mean, I will, now that I'm getting older and everything." I heaved a big sigh, giving up the ghost. "It just happened, Dad, and it seemed like a good idea. I'll be helping this guy out a few afternoons per week. Just till Christmas." I was fudging, of course, but I had to sell this thing.

"Well, it's all right with me if Kay doesn't need you around the house and this doesn't get in the way of your schoolwork. You have to keep up those grades to get into Cal, Randall. I can't do everything for you."

"Right, Dad," I said manfully. "I'll stay on top of it." And then I got out of there.

By Monday afternoon I had started working at Diversions. Chuck walked me around the store's layout, showed me the cash register and his method of recording sales and tracking inventory—such as it was—and then asked me to sort through an antediluvian pile of junk in a back corner of the store. He had been tossing stuff he couldn't sell back there. I had just got started when he retreated to his back office, leaving the door half-open so he could see anyone coming in the front door.

From three to six p.m., that came to a grand total of two kids about nine and eleven years old, each of them coming in alone—the independent kids of Berkeley!—looking for some miniature lead soldiers that Chuck kept in a locked display case back near where I was working. I helped them out, ringing up sales of $6.75 for the afternoon. On coffee break—the timing and duration of

a novel of sexual initiation 63

which Chuck left entirely up to me—I sat at a nearby cafe and tried to figure out how Chuck made a living, and what he did in the back office that was so captivating to him. I reached no brilliant conclusions.

That was the week that was, as they used to say. I lost my virginity, found out about my parents' upcoming split, and started a career all in the space of a few days. By the next Thursday, the appointed time for my next coupling with Anna, life had turned unexpectedly hectic. With my afternoons devoted to the store, I was maxed out on schoolwork at night. My mother, who had not quite paid attention to the announcement of my employment, was kind of exasperated with me. There were a few errands she was used to having me run in the afternoons; now I wasn't around until dinner.

With a growing sense of panic I saw her adding daily to a refrigerator list entitled "Randall—Things to Do Thursday for Mom." She handed me a revised list Thursday morning before I went to school. The top few things, to be done on the way home from school, kept me away from the house until 4:30. Then she was on my case for at least twenty minutes, so that I didn't even get a chance to say hello to Anna, although I caught glimpses of her in the back. Of course I couldn't make a big deal of going out there to greet her, like we were lovers or something. So I bided my time until Mom had retreated to the laundry room in the basement, and snuck outside.

It was nearly dark. Anna was packing garden tools away in the little mini-shed against the back wall of the house. I came up silently behind her, figuring that the open door of the shed obscured us from any view from the house, and put my arms around her waist.

"Hi there," I whispered, burying my face in her hair.

Anna twisted around brusquely, leaned forward and gave me a peck on the cheek. "Hi," she responded, "I haven't seen you around much."

"Yeah, I know," I said, sighing loudly for effect, "Mom's got me on the run. And I started an afternoon job on every day but Thursdays. Because, you know, of us and all . . ."

"Really? That's sweet," Anna replied, not sweetly at all. She had turned out of my embrace and was shutting the door of the shed, looking like she was getting ready to go. Everything was racing forward, getting beyond my control. Was Anna angry with me? What could she possibly. . . ? and then I remembered, with a sick feeling in the pit of my stomach. I glanced briefly over my shoulder toward the kitchen window and said in a low voice:

"Anna, look—I've been kind of worrying all week about whether you could've gotten pregnant because we, we didn't . . ."

That got her attention. She looked me straight in the eye, a faint smile playing at the corner of her lips, and said, "Well, Randall, I'm glad that you asked about it, at least. Makes you classier than the average guy. Maybe you could've asked about it a little earlier?"

I was thunderstruck. All week I had been expecting judgment, yet when it came, I was unprepared to defend myself. "Well, I-I. . ." I stuttered.

Anna lifted a hand to my cheek and smiled, warmly this time. "It's all right. I'm not trying to give you a hard time. And don't be afraid, because I have an IUD." Then, shaking her index finger at my nose, she teased, "But, *next girl*, Randall darling . . ."

I must have been as red as a beet by that time; I was thankful that the enclosing darkness was obscuring our features from each other. However embarrassed I was, I was also heartsick because the day's sexual opportunity was obviously gone. And next Thursday was Thanksgiving! As I was trying to figure out what our romantic agenda could possibly be, Anna spoke.

"Did I tell you I'm going back to Colorado for a little while?" She sounded bright and chipper about it.

"No," I replied wanly.

"Yes, for a whole month!" Obviously she was really happy about it.

"I'm flying home Tuesday and staying through Christmas. I'm gonna do some cross-country skiing for a week, and see my folks, and . . ."

Since Anna could hardly see my face, it must have been the

a novel of sexual initiation   65

stock-stillness of my stunned reaction that got through to her. Her voice trailed off and she took my hand. "I'm sorry, Randall. Now you feel bad. I should have told you sooner."

I sighed through my nose, deliberately petulant. "It seems like everybody's taking off. Mom's leaving too, but she won't be back until after New Year's."

"Yes, I know," Anna replied. *Great*, I thought, *I'm glad you two are keeping in touch.* I was so mixed-up by this point that I was ready to stalk back into the house. But then Anna pulled on my hand and led me to the back corner of the house, away from any potential views but Mrs. Chedderly's (who couldn't see beyond her nose anyway). She put both arms around my neck and brought her face close to mine.

"You know what I already figured out?" she said soothingly, conspiratorially. "If it's just you and your Dad around here on New Year's Eve, maybe you could find a way to come spend the night with me."

So what if I was a complete pushover—I was young. "Uh-huh," I choked, trying to keep my cool but getting aroused right there on the back porch. "That could possibly be arranged."

"Great," Anna cooed, kissing me firmly but tonguelessly for a few seconds. "Do you think you can wait that long, sweetie?"

"Sure," I said quietly, tears unexpectedly stinging my eyes. "I guess so." Anna turned abruptly, waved in the darkness, and left by the side of the house.

7

I CAN'T say it was the greatest holiday season of my life. I think it was during that span of time—from the Thursday before Thanksgiving until I saw Anna on New Year's Eve—when I first learned to bury my feelings in work. (June would appreciate that insight; I should tell her about it.) I concentrated on doing everything that was expected of me at school and at home, and doing much more than lazy little Chuck could have dreamed of. By the beginning of the next year, the store would be spic'n' span and there would be a new, neatly drawn floor plan, compliments of yours truly, for a complete reorganization of the stock . . . but I'm getting ahead of myself. I have to deal with the unpleasant stuff first.

Like my father and me in his Porsche, on the way to Pierce's house for Thanksgiving. I suspected that he had already been drinking somewhere, somehow, that morning. I couldn't smell it on him but he had an unmistakably boozy arrogance about him. He'd been a little shook up since Mom left a few days earlier, calling a cab to take her to the airport while he was in class, leaving us only a terse "Merry Christmas, guys!" note and a to-do list for me.

We had mostly avoided each other until now. My father kept nervously glancing over at me, obviously hesitating to say something. But finally he did. He was peering in the rearview mirror when he managed to spit it out.

"Son, I guess your mother has told you why she's taking a long holiday back home. Besides helping out your sister, I mean."

"Yeah," I said curtly.

"That kid's over a month late now," he added, laughing inappropriately. "Isn't that something? You know how fidgety Carolyn gets just if supper's late!"

MY JOURNEY THROUGH THE PLANT WORLD   68

"Uh-huh." I was staring disconsolately out the window. I could try silently counting the days to Anna's return, but I'd totaled them twice already this morning.

"Anyway," Dad continued tentatively, "I guess we're all having a pretty tough time."

I wasn't responding. He could twist in the wind for hours for all I cared. The light changed and he popped the car aggressively into first.

"Moving out here has been a really big transition for all of us, especially your mother. She left a lot of friends behind, and I think she misses them pretty badly."

I turned and looked at Dad with genuine curiosity. What was he getting at?

"So my guess is that when Kay's had some time back home she'll feel a lot better, and we'll get everything back on track for the new year." Grasping the top of the steering wheel with both hands, Dad was staring straight out the window, an utterly false grin playing about his mouth. I couldn't speak. *You asshole* was all I could think.

This little scene ruined my whole afternoon, despite Pierce's best attempts to lift my spirits. I did enjoy meeting his mother, a short, powerfully built woman wearing a traditional African wrap and headdress, who spoke with a British accent even more pronounced than her son's. And that's all I remember of Thanksgiving that year.

I don't want to think about Christmas at all. Dad disappeared for the day; I don't know where he went. Thankfully, we had done nothing about presents. I had the key to the store, and I continued the seemingly endless clean-up there for a few hours, then walked disconsolately down University Avenue in the afternoon and had some pancakes at the IHOP that was open back then. Mom called in the evening. Since Dad was still out we talked freely for an hour, she filling me in on Carolyn's birth story. For a week and a half I'd had a nephew named, unbelievably, Frank, not even Franklin, just Frank. I filled Mom in on . . . what? I don't remember. How could I have had much to say?

Even Pierce was gone by Christmas Eve for a few days. I was

a novel of sexual initiation

pretty much alone. That week was peculiarly hot and dry, and I took a few long walks up in Tilden Park. Feeling a little up after a good hike, I tried to call JoEllen Jones. Her mother said she was in Florida but of course she'd love to hear from me, could I call back after New Year's? "Sure," I said. *Not very likely*, I thought as I hung up, deadly depressed.

Perhaps that explains why everything was so weird when Anna got back. I felt lower than I'd ever been in my life, and I couldn't climb out very easily. I wasn't even very excited when she called on the thirtieth to set up our New Year's rendezvous. Although it hardly seemed necessary, I made up and wrote out a story for Dad about a stay-over party at Pierce's, boldly leaving his number on the fridge for Dad and not even asking Pierce to cover for me. Actually I had kept this whole affair a secret from Pierce.

When I got to Anna's house near dinnertime on the thirty-first, after a gray and misting day, I was vaguely angry. It seemed unfair that Anna had been gone all this time. To make matters worse, she was bubbling over with ski stories and snow stories and Colorado this and Colorado that. While she was fixing spaghetti, she asked me to open a cheap, grocery-store bottle of champagne.

Now I've never been a snob like my father, but he had taught me a few things about civilization. I looked at the sweet champagne, then at the thrift-store conceits of Anna's interior decorating, and suddenly everything felt tawdry. I'm not proud of what followed. I drank a lot of that shit and was growing a headache by the end of dinner, when we started making love, at first being silly about it and then aggressive.

Like the first time, Anna seemed to enjoy everything but actual intercourse; maybe that's why I got a little mean and pushy about it. She kept saying, "Take it easy, honey," with her legs splayed wide in the air, me pumping away in her like a machine. Once I turned her over and roughly pulled her rump up to me, trying to figure out how to take her from behind, at which point she twisted away from me like a wrestler and said firmly, "I don't like that. Okay?" We stared at each other in the candlelight for a moment. Then she said, much more softly, "What's the matter with you?"

I collapsed dizzily backward onto the bed. "I don't know," I whimpered. "I have a headache now."

Anna came to the head of the bed and sat beside me, stroking my hair. "I think we're overdoing it, babe. Let's slow down. We've got plenty of time." Her hands felt so good on my scalp that I finally began to take deep breaths and slid off to sleep. It must have been about nine o'clock. Later I dimly remember Anna sitting up in her bathrobe, watching her old black-and-white TV, but I missed the drop of the ball in Times Square ushering in 1977. I slept straight through until morning.

I woke up feeling like a creep, and a hungover creep besides. It was early but Anna was already up making eggs with some fresh, good-smelling herbs. A warm light was spilling in from one end of her apartment, and everything seemed transformed. I didn't know how guilty to feel about the night before. Maybe not too much, because Anna was humming quietly in the kitchen, and I liked the outline of her ass underneath her translucent robe.

At the table I finally ventured a peacemaking effort after some friendly small talk. "Anna," I said with a grave charitability, "Mom told me about you being married and everything. She said you had a child that, uh . . . that died. That must have been pretty hard for you."

Anna was chewing a piece of toast. She finished and swallowed hard before looking at me like I was a salesman at the door. "I don't need to talk about that," she said curtly.

Oops. So much for that approach. "Okay," I said quietly, feeling for the first time since I'd met Anna that she really regarded me as a youngster.

I GUESS we never recovered from that night. Sure, I kept seeing Anna about once a week until the middle of spring, but we both guarded our boundaries carefully. It was convenient to play along as if I needed to keep our liaison a big secret from my folks, but in fact they were too distracted to have cared much. My

a novel of sexual initiation   71

mom didn't move out when she got back. Instead, by February
she had dragged Dad into couples therapy, the net result of
which seemed to be that they started having big, theatrical,
shout-it-out fights instead of all the evasive maneuvers that were
the Kendricks family's stock-in-trade.

I kept up with school, although I was dropping steadily into
the unfamiliar B range—a territory I had not visited much since
my first year, so long ago, at Country Day. I worked at Diversions
like a man possessed, squeezing in 25 or 30 hours a week by
springtime. With the store cleaned up, reorganized, and
restocked, Chuck was having to stay out front by the cash register. He didn't like this much, so he hired some day help to cover
for him until I got in after school. Diversions was practically
going big-time.

I say that Anna and I guarded our boundaries, but in fact she
tried to break through them once. In April she called me on a
Saturday morning—Mom handed me the phone with a quizzical
look in her eyes, saying "It's Anna, honey, for you?" and I gulped
as I took it from her, standing there in the kitchen. I had a phone
in my room but I couldn't very well act like this needed to be a
private conversation, could I?

So I said, "Hi, Anna, what's up?" as cheerily and neutrally as
possible, keeping an eye on my mother who, thank God, smiled
at me and walked out the back door into the garden.

"Isn't it a gorgeous day?" Anna squealed on the other end of
the line.

"Sure," I said cautiously, a little confused. "It's really pretty
out."

"Is it okay to talk?" Anna stage-whispered, giggling.

"I guess. Mom went out in the garden."

"It's so nice out, Randall, and I was thinking about you this
morning. . . I thought maybe you could come meet me for lunch.
There's this great little place I found on College Avenue called
the Edible Complex, and . . ."

Alarms were going off in my head. "Anna," I interrupted
severely, "we can't *date*."

Several heartbeats went by on the silent phone line. Then

Anna said, "What?" in a tiny, tremulous voice.

"You know we can't start going out like that. It can't be that way. I mean, I'm still in high school." I knew this sounded brainless as soon as I said it, but by then it was too late.

Anna was sniffling: "All right," she murmured. "I'm sorry. It's such a beautiful day, and I felt like seeing you."

Now I felt like a criminal. I wanted to apologize but at the same time I didn't want to take anything back. For some reason I was deathly afraid of any change in our situation. Tongue-tied and distracted, I was completely unprepared for what came next.

"You know what, Randall?" Anna challenged, breaking the silence.

"No, what?"

"I just might *love you!*" Her voice rose to an angry near-shout on the last two words, then she hung up. With a shock I realized that neither one of us had ever said words like that to each other. Hot in my head and weak in the knees, I quickly went into my room, shut the door, and sat against it, hanging my head down for a long time. I didn't know who I was anymore.

I COULD never tell how much my mother knew about things. She never asked me what Anna had called about on the weekend, but on the following Wednesday she took it upon herself to call Anna, presumably about something she wanted done in the garden the next day. When I got home from work, Mom stopped me in the kitchen and said, "Randall, do you happen to know why Anna's phone has been disconnected?"

"What?!" I said, genuinely alarmed. I'd really meant to call her, I had just been. . . *chicken.*

"Yes," my mother said. "I tried to call her this afternoon about the garden, before she comes tomorrow, but her number says it's disconnected."

"Wow," I said, now trying to feign neutrality, "I really don't know."

"Maybe you should take a drive over there if you're not too tired," Mom suggested, "just to make sure she's all right. Did she say anything unusual to you on Saturday?"

a novel of sexual initiation

Oh, Mom, I thought, *you don't know the half of it.* All I said was, "Uh, no, she just wanted me to look for something she'd left here."

"Well, I worry about her sometimes, you know. Can you go check on her for me?"

I drove the big wagon to Anna's like a bat out of hell. As I came up her street I could see that the windows of her porch apartment were empty of plants. I bounded up the side stairs and confirmed, with a sickening wrench in my stomach, that the door was locked. Anna was obviously gone, and our little world of secret intimacy gone with her. I knocked on her downstairs neighbor's door and a young guy opened it, looked at me and said simply, "Randall?" After I nodded wordlessly he retreated to a table in his living room and came back with an envelope. I took it and went to sit on the stairs to Anna's apartment. Her letter read:

Dear Randall,

I have to go back to Colorado. I'm very lonely here and I don't think the way we are being is good for me. I don't want you to feel bad about anything, it's just me, I have a lot of things I haven't worked out and I need to go home. I think you are really sweet and I will always be glad that I helped you become a man, if you know what I mean (and I know you do!) I'm sorry I got mad on the phone, but things got really clear for me after that.

Thank you for being honest. I will write when I'm settled again.

I love you.

Anna

II

8

IS THIS doing me any good? This autobiography is supposed to be my way out of melancholy. Look where it's gotten me so far: slogging through an ancient history of youthful misfires, leavings, and indiscretions, until I am mired in regret. At this stage of my sexual memoirs, what's ahead looks even more dreadful. June says it's a necessary stage of the "alchemical process":

"You're entering the *nigredo*," she informed me (I had to ask her to spell it out), "the dark, shitty phase of transformation. Don't expect to find any light down there; you'll only be disappointed. Your companions will be worms, rats, corpses, anything that stinks of decay. The old ruler of your consciousness is dying, and his whole kingdom is rotting away with him."

Great, I thought. *And I'm paying you one-fifty a pop for this charming travelogue.* What really got to me is that June was sitting there with a bright, beatific grin on her face, her eyes sparkling through rose-tinted, rimless octagonal lenses. Without wanting to reveal too much—I haven't showed her any of this, and I've shared only the broad outlines of the story—I made a ploy for sympathy.

"The thing is, June," I began heavily, staring at my fingernails, "the more I look back on myself as a young adult, the more I despise what I see."

"Good!" she exclaimed, lightly tapping her desk several times with her fingertips.

I was outraged. "I'm supposed to hate myself?! What kind of therapy is this?" I sat up straight, abandoning my usual slouch, grasping both arms of the chair for effect.

"Oh, hush," June said sardonically. "Randall, we both know that you have enough ego strength to weather a little self-criticism. You're not a suicide or a namby-pamby."

"Gosh, thanks, doc."

MY JOURNEY THROUGH THE PLANT WORLD

June continued without missing a beat. "What's important right now is that you pick up all these dark, sad pieces of your life and look them over one by one, reviewing exactly what has caused you to feel shame and regret. The truth is that you've been hating yourself for some time, but it's been too vague and unformed to be an instructive emotion. This journal—and I'm so proud of you for sticking with it, Randall—you can think of this journal as a glove in a hot box. It gives you a way to pick up the hurtful, radioactive elements in your life and examine them without doing yourself any further harm. The self-hatred is a temporary phase of recognizing your errors, and wrong turns, and things that just couldn't be helped. What I'm trying to say is that your self-hatred is becoming more analytic and specific, and that's a good thing, a way to clarify the muddy waters. So don't worry about it. You'll probably find more reasons to hate yourself before this phase is over. But you'll be fine."

WELL, IT'S my journal—I can remember what I want to, right? I can spend some time on the fun things before I deal with the stuff that brings a hotness to my face even now. I guess June knows what she's talking about when she calls pieces of the past "radioactive."

After I got over Anna's disappearance that spring I realized the importance of taking the course of my life into my own hands. Girlfriends and jobs weren't going to keep falling into my lap, and I certainly couldn't depend on my folks to usher me into adulthood with a trust fund and a loving pat on the back. By the end of my junior year of high school, Phil and Kay Kendricks were really on the rocks. I kept waiting for the other shoe to drop.

Later I would learn from Mom that their last couple of months together constituted a showdown over who would move out. Therapy had emboldened Mom to speak out for herself and stake a claim to what she wanted. What she really wanted, she eventually confided to me, was Dad's den, which occupied the sunny southwest corner of the house. Mom told me that the day after Dad left in July, she threw open the curtains in the den, moved in her easel and art supplies, sat down on her stool "and

a novel of sexual initiation   79

cried and cried". . .

Oh, but the fun things. Let's see: I remember a Saturday in
June right after school let out. Against my father's objections I
had immediately gone to work full-time for Chuck Berquist. Dad
wanted me to do a special summer school session on the Cal
campus for local kids who were UC-bound, especially since I had
let my grades slip that year. With my mother assuming neutrality on the issue, I was emboldened enough to stare him down. I
told him I didn't want to take his money anymore, for summer
school or for life itself. Didn't he believe in the work ethic? I had
asked pointedly.

That was early on a Friday evening. Dad was so steamed he
went wordless—a rare event—and then went out the door, probably ending up in the toniest bar he could find in the East Bay.
Feeling supremely triumphant, I went to the phone in the
kitchen and returned a call from Pierce, who had invited me out
to breakfast before I went to work at Diversions Saturday morning. Footloose for the summer, Pierce had accelerated the cultural education program that he had been administering almost
since the day he dubbed me Peanut Man.

It was surprising how much Pierce already knew, how much
he had gotten around town with just a year more of local resi-
dence than myself. He was, after all, a cosmopolitan character.
His dress and poise made many people mistake him for someone in his late twenties. Me, I thought I still looked like a kid,
although Anna had once said something about how mature I
seemed to her. That was nice, but still puzzling.

Promptly at 8:30 on Saturday morning, Pierce honked the
horn of the baby-blue mini-pickup he drove back then and I
bounded in the passenger door.

"So where's this great breakfast taking place?"

"The Brick Hut," Pierce replied, shifting into first and pulling
away from the curb. "Have you heard of it? It's simply a wonderful little spot."

A little spot it was indeed, occupying a tiny corner building
at the busy intersection of Adeline and Ashby in the far southern part of Berkeley. As we entered, jostling around patrons

already in line to get our name on a waiting list, I simultaneously picked up a seductive vanilla-cinnamon scent in the air and an unusual nervousness in Pierce's demeanor. He kept nodding and smiling in a false, ingratiating way to one or another of the all-woman staff, who seemed neither to know nor to notice him.

Since we decided to take a seat at the counter, facing the hot grill, we didn't have to wait long for a seat. As a solidly built, tough-looking woman with bushy red hair wiped a space in front of us and nodded for us to sit down, Pierce leaned down to my ear and whispered, "You see, it's a *collective*," as if that explained something.

"Oh," I said noncommittally as I eased onto the stool, my eye falling upon a refrigerator whose top half was covered with solo and group pictures of women only, plus a few news clippings. One of them bore the logo of the *San Francisco Bay Guardian* atop a restaurant review headlined **BEST FEMINIST GREASY SPOON**, referring to the very establishment we were visiting. Laughing out loud, I pointed Pierce's attention toward the headline and said, "Sounds yummy, doesn't it?"

"Shhhh," Pierce hissed forcefully, "don't make fun."

The whole breakfast went like that. I had a great time, downing one of the best waffles I had ever been introduced to, and soaking up the kind of bohemian atmosphere that you simply couldn't imagine finding in in the South. I kept twisting half-around on my stool to survey the scene: one booth was taken up by two male hippie architects looking at plans held precariously above their food; another booth was taken up by two gay (I assumed) moms and their babies. It seemed that at every crowded table there was a conversation of great cultural or political import going on.

This view is romantically nostalgic, I suppose, for this was one of the first times that I felt like a real citizen in Berkeley, The Town That Goes Out to Breakfast. And I had a suitably exotic guide: Pierce was wearing a fashionable African Pride t-shirt and a striped bandanna to match. It was one of many times when Pierce's colorful flair helped me feel like I fit in on the West Coast. Otherwise there was too much Dixie white bread in me.

a novel of sexual initiation   81

In contrast to my upbeat curiosity, Pierce seemed beside himself with anxiety, not doing much more with his scrambled eggs and potatoes than pushing them around on the plate. This earned a stern grimace from the redhead when she picked up my clean plate and motioned impatiently toward Pierce's, saying, "Do you always fill 'er up *before* you come to breakfast?"

I was sure she was joking in her gruff way, but Pierce looked genuinely crestfallen and raised both hands mutely, palms toward the ceiling. I felt it behooved me to rescue the poor chap.

"Candy bars," I muttered gravely to the redhead, "candy bars under the bed. Soon as he wakes up, it's Hershey time." I had this image at the ready because I had once found such a stash under my sister's bed back in Georgia.

Our waitress—I probably shouldn't call her that, but the word was still active in my vocabulary at the time—just snorted and took away Pierce's plate. Shortly she returned with a check, which, due to the rush she was in, totaled our two orders and indicated the proper tax, but didn't give the full amount due. This would prove to be Pierce's undoing. Through set teeth he insisted on paying everything, so I offered to pay the tip. He laid his large but delicate hand over one of mine and whispered, "No, don't!"

"Why not?" I replied, confused.

"It's unnecessary to leave gratuities on the counter. Besides, they'd rather that men wouldn't leave them extra money."

I peered incredulously at Pierce, who refused to meet my eyes. He was really going weird on me now. "You mean, like our money's no good here?" I joked.

"Shhhh," Pierce buzzed urgently as the redhead flashed by in front of us, burdened with five or six plates of food. "Let's go." He put the check and his money down on the counter, and we went.

We were fifteen feet away from the front door, starting to get in the truck, when we heard a voice bellowing behind us.

"Hey, you guys!" It was the redhead, leaning out from inside The Brick Hut, propping open the door with one foot.

Pierce pointed to his chest and opened his mouth quizzically, but no sound came out.

"Yeah, you!" She held up a small rectangle of paper—our

check, flapping in the morning breeze. "You didn't pay the tax!"

"Oh, my goodness," Pierce responded, slamming the truck door, fumbling in his pockets, and rushing back to the cafe. I saw him count out change into the redhead's hand, his head bobbing up and down apologetically, before practically running back to the truck, his eyebrows arching upward in alarm as I caught his eye. As Pierce opened his door again, another bellow came from down the street:

"And no tip either!" Shaking her head in disgust, the redhead disappeared inside the door. Pierce held a hand to his chest, sighed hugely, and started up the truck with the urgency of a getaway driver.

I didn't have a clue to what was going on with Pierce until a few minutes later, when we were sitting in the truck with the motor running in front of Diversions. I was forty-five minutes early, my standard arrival time when opening for Chuck. It gave me time to open the back door, get the fan going and air out the stale cigar fumes left over from the day before. I was already dramatizing the events that had just transpired at the Brick Hut, replaying the final bellow of the redhead with special gusto, but I couldn't get Pierce to appreciate the humor of the situation. He kept staring straight ahead and drumming his fingers on the top of the steering wheel. Just before I was about to get out of the truck, he asked, "Are you working tomorrow?"

"Nope," I said innocently, "we're not doing seven days a week yet, although I think it would be a great idea . . ."

"Have you ever been to Half Moon Bay?" Pierce interrupted, his voice low and distracted.

"Uh, no," I replied, feeling a strange tingle of apprehension.

"My mother and I took a drive down there one Sunday. It's really very quaint. You should see it sometime."

"Okay," I said dumbly.

Pierce turned to face me, his eyes dancing. "Would you like to drive down tomorrow afternoon? We could take a walk on the beach and then find a nice dinner somewhere. I can promise you a sublime expedition."

The import of Pierce's invitation hit me like a tidal wave.

a novel of sexual initiation

I couldn't have been less ready to handle it—should I say this?—like a man.

"Well, I-I don't know," I stammered clumsily. "I think my mom asked me to work in the garden tomorrow." *I think my mom asked,* I cringed inwardly. Could I have come up with a more transparent dodge? "You know, our gardener left us."

Pierce held my eyes with his for a moment before turning back, looking straight out the windshield again, rapidly conceding defeat. "Oh, quite right," he said softly. "I understand."

I felt a mortifying relief, and a peculiar sense of taking the first step down a path diverging from my first true friendship in California. "But let's do breakfast again soon," I blurted awkwardly. "That really was a great place."

Pierce nodded gamely, shifting into first as I slipped out the door. He drove off without another word. I stood silently for a moment in front of the shop, eager to get in and start the work that usually kept me too occupied to deal with raw and confusing feelings like those I was having at the moment.

I felt sorry for Pierce, but I felt right in having shielded myself from . . . from something I should have seen coming.

I mean, I'd heard enough cruel jokes about Pierce at school not to be in the dark about his tendencies, but still, he'd never said anything overtly sexual about anyone, except for sniggering little jokes that he shared chiefly with Ariel. I was pretty sure he hadn't had any intimate relationships yet. Now he was stumbling toward his adult sexual identity, looking for a sense of belonging, apparently searching for someone to belong to—but he'd made a little mistake. It didn't have to be a big thing between us, I decided. I went to work and forgot about it.

Only now do I realize that, at about the same time Pierce was stepping clumsily from the closet, striving to bring his secret desires into the light, I stood poised before a shadowy stairway leading down to my own sexual cellar, a place where I would stash desires that could thrive only in a sullen obscurity. As my family came apart and I became prematurely absorbed with business, the door to my erotic netherworld was surely swinging open.

MY JOURNEY THROUGH THE PLANT WORLD

ONE WEEK after the scene with Pierce, Chuck invited me to breakfast on a Monday morning at ten, our opening hour. He said that he had something important to tell me, so the store could wait until we were done talking. I almost told him that was bad business, opening up whenever we felt like it. But the invitation was unprecedented in our half-year relationship and my curiosity overcame my fondness for doing things right. Chuck said it would be his treat, and we could go wherever I liked. I said I always went to The Brick Hut.

Business was booming that day; by the time we got an old wooden booth to ourselves it was nearly eleven. The big strong redhead—Brenda, I heard someone call her—was taking our orders, and I asked her how she was doing to show Chuck that I was a regular.

"Can't complain," she said matter-of-factly, squinted at me momentarily, then blinked in recognition. "Hey, you gonna tip today?"

Chuck grinned at me over the top of his menu. I felt my neck turning hot but kept my wits about me: "That's up to the boss," I said with a laugh.

Brenda peered soberly at Chuck now; she really wanted to know. "Hey," he said, "this guy's making me so much money, I should pay all his tips."

"Cool," replied Brenda, cracking a smile as she turned to me again. "I hope you keep coming in with him instead of that weird skinny friend of yours."

I was about to offer a word in Pierce's defense, but a bell rang in the kitchen and Brenda was gone. Chuck leaned back against the booth, his hands clasped behind his head and his elbows stretched back, heaving a big sigh. That was probably his exercise for the day. Still in that posture, he said "Sooo, Randall. I guess you've noticed I don't like to work much."

I laughed out loud so that I didn't have to say yes or no. In fact, Chuck's nonwork habits were my favorite story to tell about daily life at Diversions. When I'd recovered my composure, I tried to be diplomatic: "Well, I assume you're into something really interesting back there in the office."

a novel of sexual initiation

Chuck relaxed forward and rested both elbows on the table, scratching his recent but already bushy moustache. "You know, to tell the truth I am. I know I haven't told you a lot about myself, so here's the straight poop. I'm not really a businessman. I'm actually an anthropologist, and I'm working on my doctoral dissertation right now. Right now and for the last ten years, that is." He sighed hugely, then added, "The business just keeps some chow on the plate."

I must have thrown Chuck a skeptical look; he couldn't possibly have made any money before I made Diversions presentable to the public. Before I could say anything he continued:

"But it doesn't work the way you think. Ever heard of the Berquist Foundation?" I shook my head, curious. "Etty Berquist, my grandmother, she's kinda rich. Well, not kind of—filthy rich." Chuck cast a sidelong glance to a table of nearby patrons, as if suspicious of eavesdroppers. "My grandfather died of a heart attack when he was fifty, but he left her a pile of dough, a great stock portfolio, and a work ethic that's absolutely out of control."

"What do you mean?" I said, smiling attentively, finding myself attracted to the notion of filthy riches.

"I mean she thinks higher education is a complete waste of time." Chuck pitched his voice high and squeaky, shaking a finger at me: "Your grandpa didn't need any fancy dee-greez to make a name for himself, so why should you, little Chuckie?"

"Little Chuckie?" I chuckled.

"Yeah. Here I am almost thirty-six, and I'm still little Chuckie. Anyway, the upshot is that I inherited a trust fund when I was eighteen. But I could only draw from it as long as I owned and ran my own business. That is, for twenty years or until Grandma Etty passes away."

"That's really strange."

"Tell me about it. Her idea was to keep me away from higher education until I was old enough to realize that I didn't need any. But I fooled her. I used some of the money to open up the store and I went to school as best I could. Etty's pretty cagey, though. I know she sends these seedy private eyes by to check that I'm really in the store sometimes. That's why I do most of

MY JOURNEY THROUGH THE PLANT WORLD

my work there. Anyway, I got my master's in anthropology and now I'm working on my doctoral thesis, about this tribe in New Guinea that uses plant-derived psychoactives in their religious rites."

Oh, I thought, *that explains it*. I had sneaked into Chuck's office a couple times when it was unoccupied and puzzled over a few books poking out of the clutter on his desk: a fat paperback entitled *Altered States of Consciousness*, edited by one Charles T. Tart; *The Doors of Perception* by Aldous Huxley; and one in worn manuscript with a controversial name on the cover—Timothy Leary — *The psychedelic experiences: a manual based on the Tibetan Book of the Dead*. So I had figured Chuck for an aging hippie. Several times thereafter I had stared closely at his eyes when he came in the store to see if he was all there, or off tripping in some other world.

"Here's the thing," Chuck continued. "Grandma Etty's never gonna die, but I'll be out from under this trust clause in a couple years. Then I can travel for my research and do whatever I damn well please. My plan was to let the business go at that point, but then you came along."

"What do you mean?"

"You're making it a real enterprise, Randall. Six months in the store, and you've got things looking so good I'm about to start making money. It's scary, man. You've got a knack for this." Taking a sip of black coffee that Brenda had just delivered, Chuck held his cup in front of his mouth with both hands and pointed at me with an index finger. "You should be Etty Berquist's grandson."

I shrugged, not knowing what to say. A considerable silence ensued because Chuck had turned his head to the side, watching and waiting on the grill. For a few moments I entertained a vision of pot-bellied Chuck in warpaint and a loincloth, dancing wildly around a tribal bonfire in the dark, wearing a pair of gag spectacles with spinning eyes painted on them. In the flickering light of the fire, headhunting natives pawed through a pile of Chuck's books, ripping out the pages and eating them, laughing uproariously.

a novel of sexual initiation

I was sinking rather deeply into this vision when Brenda arrived with the food, snapping me out of it. I was entertained for a few minutes by Chuck plowing wordlessly through his omelet, grunting and mumbling his appreciation. When he was about two-thirds of the way through he slowed down enough to speak again.

"So look, Randall," Chuck said, wiping sloppily at his mustache with a well-stained napkin, "what I'm trying to get at is, I don't know what your college plans are, but I hate to see a good kid like you work so hard for nothing. When I leave, the business is yours if you want it."

"What do you mean, it's mine?" I said quizzically.

"I'll sell it to ya. For a symbolic buck or something. My lawyer can handle the whole deal. The only thing is"—Chuck paused to lean forward and whisper conspiratorially—"I'm gonna need you to manage the joint until then. You know, learn the inventory and the ordering and handle the hiring and firing, all that stuff."

I wanted to blurt out, *I'm just a kid!* but something made me hold my tongue. Chuck explained further. "This business is a burr up my ass, Randall. I'm tired of it. I just want to work on my research in the office, and you can do whatever you like out front. If the private dick comes by you can call me out and I'll tell him what a great manager you are. Maybe Etty will even cut you in on the will!"

I stared at Chuck for a while. I can't remember what I said next, except for vaguely going along with the idea and saying college was no big deal, maybe I could put it off for a few years. That is, I tried to sound casual about a change of life direction that I knew my father, for one, would consider catastrophic. On the way back to the store in Chuck's battered Datsun, I stared out the window at downtown Berkeley going by and realized I didn't know what I thought was important anymore. Only one thing I was sure of: Chuck was nuts. What did that make me for going along with him?

I called my folks into the living room one evening of that same week. The household was pretty broken up by that time.

Mom had stopped cooking dinner for us all, using her evening art classes at UC Extension as an excuse. Feeling sorry for my father sometimes, I would cook for the two of us, making my own forays into California cuisine. But I didn't do it often enough to get Dad into the habit of expecting that kind of service.

Anyway, I had managed to get both parental units into the same room that evening, though I was conscious that they took seats almost at opposing corners. I sat on the same couch with my mom. I could reasonably expect her to be an ally, or at least a buffer to help absorb some of my father's inevitable explosion. When I sat down I noticed that Mom's hair was different, sort of shagged in the back. I was about to comment when I noticed my father drumming on the arm of his chair.

"What's this about, son?" he inquired testily, looking at me in a way that avoided looking at his wife. "I've got a meeting on campus at nine."

That was good, I thought; this scene wouldn't drag on for hours. "Dad," I ventured, glancing over at Mom to include her, "I need to talk to you about college."

"There may not be anything to talk about, Randall," my father replied with unusual harshness, "if you don't pull up your grades next year. You could have made up some lost ground if you'd spent the summer on campus instead of working."

"That's just what I need to talk about," I said brightly. "Chuck wants to train me as a manager for the store. He says if I stick with it, he might sell me the business in a couple of years when he . . ." (I didn't want to get into the particulars here) ". . . when he goes back to finish his Ph.D."

My father crinkled his brow, apparently uncertain of what I had meant. "How can you train to be a store manager, Randall, when you've got to get ready for Cal?"

All right, I thought, *time to detonate*. "I don't think I want to get ready for Cal just yet, Dad. I think I could use a couple years working after high school. You know, to grow up a little first." (I thought it would be good to sound humble.)

My father's eyes started flashing like a TILT alarm on a pinball machine. "Are you trying to tell me you're not going to

a novel of sexual initiation
89

college so you can work in a *toy store?*"

That riled me. I sat back on the couch, folding my arms and looking over at Mom—who was staring distractedly at a corner of the ceiling—and replied evenly, "Diversions of Berkeley is not a toy store, Dad. We have games for adults, and chess, and . . ."

"Oh, fuck it," my father sighed. "I'm too tired for this crap." Removing his glasses and pinching the bridge of his nose, Dad sat there for a few moments shaking his head. I was shocked by the vulgarity of his language. Is he learning to talk this way in therapy? I wondered.

Then he shocked me again, turning his attention to my mother and saying, with clear resentment: "Kay, have you been encouraging this crazy idea?"

My mother let down her eyes from her ceiling reverie, like the big guns on a warship majestically lowering to take a bead on a closer target. An incredibly long time went by—half a minute?—before she locked eyes with my father and spoke in a cool, calculated tone.

"Phil, I think it's time for you to go. I'd like you out of the house by this weekend. Randall will stay here with me until we sort things out. We'll talk about school and his job a little later."

Kaboom! Talk about your one fell swoops! Just when I had expected the air to go thick as butter, it was as if a firestorm exploding from Mom's direct hit was sucking the atmosphere out of the house entirely, leaving our three flimsy souls to carom crazily off the walls and ceiling. That's how I felt, anyway. Mom was so steady and strangely detached that I couldn't tell if she felt anything; Dad was white as a sheet. He had no comeback. The war of the last few months was over, won decisively with a winner-take-all gambit. Rising unsteadily from his chair, Dad spoke in a small but steely voice.

"All right, Kay. I'll take that apartment over by Lake Merritt. But I don't know how long you'll be able to stay here if we're going to be separated. This is faculty housing, you know."

If the threat registered with Mom, she didn't show it. She still had her eyes locked on Dad as if to drive him out of the house with some kind of force beam emanating from her retinas. Her hostility was awesome; I was beginning to cower just by dint of being Dad's gender. He turned and started to leave the room, then wheeled about and shook a finger at me like a stern father in a bad television drama.

"This discussion about your future is not over, young man," he declaimed, then left the room. His script was worse than I had imagined. Sinking back into the couch with my eyes closed, I wondered ruefully what Dad would be like if he ever stopped portraying himself. When I opened my eyes after fifteen seconds or so, Mom had vanished. Did she briefly place her hand on my knee before she left? I can't remember for sure.

9

THAT'S how the Kendricks clan, California retinue, atomized into three independent elements, each of us moving ahead without feeling constrained to answer to one another. My Dad moved to Oakland and I began experiencing life with my first roommate: Mom. She pretty much stopped mothering, treating me like an equal partner she had chosen for shared housing. She liked the fact that I could bring some money into our situation. By the start of the school year she was working at an art supply store, but things looked dicey since she and Dad were arguing over money.

I guess that's why she let me slough off most of my homework in my last year of high school. I remember precious little of that time. I stopped lunching with Pierce and Ariel, instead dropping into the store to check out how things were going. I was there most afternoons too, and Saturdays. Chuck hired a new full-time day clerk, but the guy had all the virtues of a sleazy, till-tempted temp. I knew he needed to be checked on frequently.

Thus I became a solid C student in my senior year, mightily confusing a school counselor who pulled me into her office to confront me with my academic paper trail of tests, provided by teachers from a variety of classes, that were either marked "A" or "Absent." When I gravely told the poor woman that I was a hapless Southern emigré, a child of impending divorce living with an increasingly, how to say it, *artistic* mother, she smiled kindly at me and, I'm pretty sure, sent the word around that I was not to be flunked outright.

Early in the school year, when Dad first got wind of the downward drift of my grades, he dropped by the house to yell at both Mom and me, additionally charging us with a conspiracy to boot him out of the house. He was clearly drunk; Mom never let him get closer than the front step.

After that Dad was out of the loop. Mom and I often cooked dinner together, sometimes entertaining her art-class friends, and the two of us became better chums than ever. A lot of the tightness drained from Kay Kendricks once Phil Kendricks had been out of the picture for a month or two.

I guess I was lonesome in my waning teen years. I don't remember some things I should, like high school graduation, because I had become such a lone ranger. Pierce managed to finish school early so that he could start taking business courses over at Merritt College in Oakland, and Ariel and I had nothing in common without Pierce. By the end of the school year I was deadly bored, angling to get out of school whenever possible to get to work. In the summer of '78, after finishing high school, I began killing non-working hours by driving the old station wagon around the East Bay, exploring without a goal. One Sunday evening I was driving home from downtown Oakland, where I had hung out at DeLauer's newsstand for a while, when I came upon a street-corner movie theater whose marquee proclaimed

HOT AND WET!!
DEEP INSIDE LILA *and* LILA COMES AGAIN
Always XXX—Continuous!

and whose posters, on either side of the ticket booth, showed busty, barely clad women sprawling and cavorting in various poses, leering at the viewer, almost as if they were proffering dirty favors to anyone who might free them from the poster cases.

I drove by the theater, shaking my head with a smile, then abruptly turned right at the next block as if a homing device had taken over the vehicle. I circled the block, then came slowly up behind the big brick theater like a surreptitious cop, slowing to a stop in the middle of the street, suddenly aware of my breathing. For some reason, the dreariness of a dull, solitary afternoon had lifted; I was prickly with curiosity and suspense.

I had never been inside one of those places before. I had never seen a porno film, my only experience with explicit sexual media being soft-focus magazines like *Playboy*. For the first time, a question that would haunt me for years to come entered my mind: *Can I do this without being seen by anyone I know?*

I backed up into a spot along the street and parked, killing the engine and sitting there for a moment, a novel restiveness growing within me. I suddenly appreciated my aloneness in a new light; it was a thrilling independence, really, a kind of permission to cross mysterious and perhaps even dangerous barriers. *Why not?* I thought. *Just once, to see what it's like.*

I got out of the car, feeling unsteady as a drunk, and walked around to the front of the building. I hesitated momentarily before entering a small realm of glare cast against the growing darkness by the lurid marquee.

To my horror, the young black guy at the ticket booth carded me. "ID?" he said dully and I flinched, suddenly afraid that I would have to be twenty-one, and that they might call the cops if I wasn't. But the guy just glanced at my driver's license and murmured, "Uh-huh," took six dollars from me and tore a ticket off a loose roll on the counter. I entered the building, taking note of a run-down popcorn stand manned by a bulbous-nosed guy, wearing a red threadbare sweater and looking like somebody's alcoholic uncle. I avoided his eyes as I turned toward the curtain-covered entrance from behind which I could already hear a woman's sharp cries.

On the other side of the curtain, I cast my eyes over the audience first, which consisted of fifteen to twenty men sitting solo all over the theater, at significant distances from each other, like a few random fish caught in a huge net. Grasping that this was the seating custom without understanding why, I triangulated myself between two men several rows apart in the middle of the theater, took a seat, and looked up at the screen, at first not believing what I saw there.

A man and a woman were fucking, far bigger than life, right there on the screen. Nothing was hidden. I could see his penis going in and out of her, up and down, as her legs sawed in the air, the two of them looking like some extraordinary grasshopper singing in a cheap bedroom. My eyes went with the camera to the woman's face, which was lavishly made up but rather pretty, even with her mouth opening widely in a contorted laugh, as she yelled—not quite in sync with her lips—*"Oh, fuck me, baby! Fuck me with that big, big cock!"*

I grinned. I had never heard anything like that from Anna and I couldn't imagine that JoEllen would have ever said it. This was some kind of comedy, I assumed, but before I could think about it further the camera perspective suddenly changed to a rear and shockingly intimate view of the big, big cock—it was pretty big, actually—plunging into the woman's hairy, rich, wet opening. There was a smacking sound, incredibly broadcast throughout the theater. She moaned, he grunted, and I thrust myself back against my chair in shock, amazed that something like this could be seen for six dollars, that it had been going on inside this building even before I entered, that I had only been carded and not exhaustively interrogated before being allowed to enter and see it—this uncut, triple-X commotion. The camera stayed on the couple's genitals so long, the man's tightening scrotum in unsightly close-up, that I shut my eyes until the soundtrack changed.

"I'm gonna come. Oh, I'm gonna come," the robust but pot-bellied man on screen exclaimed, as I opened my eyes to see him squinting his eyes tight, his forehead soaked with sweat, before the camera switched back to the woman's face.

"Come on, baby, I want you to come on my face. Please, please come on my face!" she whimpered, grasping his waist.

"Uh-uh-unnnh," he growled in response, pulling himself up and out of her. Then the film went into slow motion as his huge, erect, red penis traveled over her body until she reached up and grabbed it, pulling it close to her mouth. In several slow, languorous spurts, the man's semen came out of him and arced onto the woman's lips, nose, and one eye, until he was done and the slow-mo ended. Then the woman was laughing insidiously, almost cruelly it seemed, wiping the liquid from her eye and licking it off her fingers like it was some kind of ice cream.

"Umm, baby," she said unconvincingly, "you're the best."

a novel of sexual initiation   95

I slumped in my seat and stared into the darkness toward the floor. This was unreal! Why would she want him to do that? I thought frantically. I remembered tasting my own semen back during my earliest masturbatory frenzies. I had learned how to jerk off from a Philip Roth novel I sneaked out of my dad's library when I was twelve—a fittingly intellectual initiation, he might have thought, had I ever confessed it to him.

Anyway, the stuff was disgusting, like some kind of slimy thick ocean water. I had worried afterward if I might have poisoned myself. So why would this woman want that guy's stuff all over her face? It didn't make sense, but I had to admit that it was exciting in a peculiar way. It was something one didn't often see. It was something I had never seen.

Abruptly, the film ended, a shaky THE END appearing on a field of black for a few moments before the house lights went up slightly. I felt cheated—two minutes for six dollars?—but then I noticed that with the exception of one or two men making their way toward the front door, everyone was staying in place, no one talking, because no one was sitting close to anyone else.

Then I realized what "continuous" meant—they were going to keep showing the movies over and over, or one after the other. I had thought "continuous" meant that the sex kept going, that it didn't stop or drop beneath the screen like in the regular movies. So I was learning something already.

In a few minutes a series of trailers for porn movies came on—all brief cuts of wild fucking, oral intercourse, and men coming—and then **LILA COMES AGAIN** started. I watched all of it, about ninety minutes of a nearly plotless pastiche of fucking scenes, usually with a man and a woman, sometimes with two women who didn't look like lesbians to me, once with a man and two women, and finally, in a preposterous culminating scene, about six women and six men in an orgy scene of everybody doing everything with everybody. (Except: men with men.)

By the end of this film I was amazed at the unabashed stupidity and unrealness of it all—who had ever heard of a world where everybody wanted to fuck and no one refused an offer? At the same time I was drinking it all in like someone starved for this particular make-believe. It was as if I had stumbled upon a bizarre treasure trove of sickeningly rich desserts, something that I had never known existed but that might have always been denied to me until this moment. I had a demanding erection the entire time. I kept shifting in my seat, wanting to be able to come but not wanting to leave the theatre to masturbate, so that by the time I did leave, exiting hurriedly through the front, I was in kind of a dreamy, hormonally charged state of shock. I got back to the car in the dark, shut the door and leaned my head against the steering wheel, massaging my crotch, closing my eyes and reliving some of the orgy scene in my mind, panting slightly.

But I couldn't come in the car either; it seemed too low. Finally I took a deep breath, laughed ruefully, and thought *Well, there. That's what porn is.* I suddenly realized that Mom might have my dinner waiting—it was probably after nine o'clock. Flushing with shame as I thought of her, I flicked on the wagon's lights and accelerated aggressively away from the curb. At that moment, I thought I would never go back to the porn theater.

BUT I was back there the next Sunday evening, when Mom was out of town for the weekend, then again the next Saturday. When I look back on this incipient stage of my addiction, I see myself as a relative innocent, like a kid who's discovered a whole new section of the public library and has set about reading every book in there from A to Z. In my case, however, it was a pubic library that had opened before my wondering eyes. A bad pun, but it's the truth.

The late summer of '78, going on my nineteenth year, was nothing but work and porn. At least that's how I remember it. Actually, that's somewhat unfair to myself, for lots of other things were going on. I was getting to be good friends with my mom; I was getting to know the other downtown Berkeley merchants, who more or less treated me like a peer, which was a genuine confidence-builder; I was occasionally going to movies—regular movies, I mean—with Pierce, although we weren't as close as we had been in school; and I was trying to start a new relationship.

Oh, Christ. This may be more embarrassing to remember

a novel of sexual initiation

han the pornography because of the letter. Perhaps I thought it would work because I'd had pretty good experiences with letters in my life, from the early romance with JoEllen to the recent rehabilitation of my long-distance relationship with Anna. A few weeks after her abrupt departure, she had written a very diplomatic letter—addressed to "The Kendricks Family"—apologizing for leaving us without notice and saying that she missed working in our garden, but that she had decided Colorado was the best place for her to put her life back together.

"P.S. Write and tell me how's life in Berkeley when you get the chance, Randall," she had skillfully concluded. I was impressed with this parent-fooling maneuver so I begrudgingly answered her after a couple weeks. We got a friendly correspondence going after I decided not to be mad at her anymore. My mother seemed happy that we were communicating, since she'd always liked Anna.

So I thought that letters were safe. Or maybe I was too clumsy to approach a woman straightforwardly; so far in my life, they had seemed to come toward me first. The woman I wanted to approach that summer worked at a downtown salad bar where I had lunch two or three times a week. Her name tag said she was Margaret, a name I didn't much like, but after I developed a crush on her I decided that I could make up a pet name for her later.

I don't know why I liked her. She was a little overweight and full in the face; she seemed very plain and simple but had nice long, dark hair. . . All right: she looked like a plush, big-boned Anna. She was always very helpful to me in the lunch line; the more I saw her the more sure I was that she was flirting. Once she gave me back five dollars too much from a twenty. I didn't think it was an accident.

What an idiot I must have been, coming into that cafe and mooning over a salad-bar girl almost daily! It was a sign of my unbalanced life that I became sick at heart over my phantasmic love for Margaret. I almost thought of asking Mom about how to ask Margaret for a date—although I was emotionally worked-up enough by that time to ask for her hand—but I sensed that Mom just wasn't the right resource. Dad, perhaps? Fat chance. I didn't want to become skilled at his kind of propositions, and I was rarely seeing him anyway.

No, I decided, I'd handle this in my own inimitable way. One Tuesday evening I came straight home from work and typed Margaret a no-holds-barred love confessional, starting with how nice she looked behind the big bowl of greens and the salad dressing vats, then asking her about her background, then veering just for fun into a three-page comparison of lifestyles South and West—then giving her, quite without meaning to, the whole lowdown on Anna. I quake to recall my literary chattering. I hadn't written this way since my youthful romance with JoEllen, and I wasn't self-aware enough to recognize that I was mainly writing to myself. (That's when I really needed a journal!)

At any rate, by midnight I had about ten single-spaced pages. As I sealed it into an envelope I felt confident that Margaret had never been asked out this way—then remembered with a chill that the letter didn't actually get around to an invitation. But I decided that was okay because I should handle that in person, after we began to talk over my extraordinary communication.

Along with my money for lunch the next day, I nervously slipped Margaret the envelope and said, in an almost-choked whisper, "Hey, this is for you." She tilted her head quizzically, then said, "All right, thanks," and turned around to insert it into the pocket of her coat, hanging over a chair behind her. *Thank God she can't read it now*, I thought, *I can eat lunch and get the hell out of here.*

I couldn't eat there the next day. It would be too obvious that I was awaiting her response. Besides, I'd included my business card in case she wanted to call me to order a game of Monopoly or something. The next day, Thursday, I tremblingly went to the salad bar for lunch, and didn't see her anywhere. I was about to leave, worrying about my romantic methodology, when Margaret appeared from out of nowhere and sat down at my table, looking less than glamorous in her oil-stained apron.

"Hi," she said noncommittally, pulling a strand of hair away from her round, moonlike face. I liked the way she did that. We

a novel of sexual initiation

could make a life together, I was sure.

"Hi," I replied.

"That was a really amazing letter you wrote," she said, playing with the end of her strand of hair, like a little girl.

"Thanks," I said.

Now she looked straight into my eyes. "Look, I hope you don't take this wrong or anything, and that was a nice letter, but . . . I think you should find a real relationship."

I stared at her, my face tingling. My head was going light, like a helium balloon let loose and heading for Jupiter.

"I'm twenty-seven," Margaret added abruptly, leaning forward as if to tell a secret. "I have a boyfriend, and we're practically married."

"Okay," I managed to whisper. "I'm sorry."

"No, don't be," she said in an irritating, sing-songy whine, reaching across the table to touch my hand. "It was a really nice letter and I'm sure you're a sweet boy. You work at that toy store a couple blocks over?"

Never mind how I got out of there. That evening, tossing around in my head three or four bitter rejoinders I could have used to salvage my dignity at that awful lunchtime scene, I told Mom I was off to see a movie—the truth—and drove like a robot to the porn theater. I was sure the scenery there would occupy all my attention, and it did. I got an erection like never before. Once while Lila or somebody like her was yelping her head off during a rear entry by some inarticulate stud, I looked a couple rows over and could see, in the semi-darkness, a guy leaning way back in his seat with his face up toward the ceiling, his mouth open, his whole frame jerking back and forth.

Looking away from him and then to either side of me, I quietly reached down and unzipped my pants, then dug around inside my underwear to get my hard penis out of the cotton flap and into the air.

I looked around again; no one was on the same row, no one behind or ahead of me close enough to see. Having my erection out was a great relief. As the woman on screen kept yelping and the man fucking her started announcing his imminent orgasm,

I started working hard on mine. Fortunately, the film did a slo-mo (this was getting predictable) of the man ejaculating onto the woman's bare rump, allowing enough time for me to ejaculate violently as well, pushing down hard on my dick so that the stuff shot out against the back of the chair in front of me, making a wet noise, which scared me, causing me to look around again. I squirted again and again, the last time dribbling onto my own seat between my legs so that I had to wipe the semen off with my bare hand. In a slight panic I wiped that hand on one sock, then I grasped my still-stiff organ again and rubbed it some more along the underside, pushing the last gratifying drops of liquid out of the thing.

My face felt hot and huge and my feet were cold and clammy. I felt like I had really gotten away with something, like a prisoner coming to the end of a long escape tunnel and poking his head out into the air of freedom—but not knowing whether police dogs might jump him at any moment. Hiding myself back in my pants, not zipping up, I sat there in a heart-thumping daze for a few minutes, oblivious to the film seguing into a fake-lesbian scene. After that, when a threesome with two men on a single woman got going, I started paying attention again.

I came twice more in the theater that night over two and a half hours, leaving halfway through the second showing of the first film I had walked in on. When I left, by the back exit into a weedy, vacant lot, I felt nothing at all, except thirsty, drained of my foolish, undiscriminating seed and emptied of caring about anything. I drove home and fell asleep like a stone.

So that's it. That's how I started becoming a weirdo, or a dirty young man as it were. There's a couple years back there that are all the same in my mind, as if they passed entirely within a week of routine activity of going to work, helping Mom around the house, having pointless crushes on women I saw around town, and having my sex life in that seamy theater once, sometimes twice a week. Sometimes I saw Pierce. There was an emotional detente between us but he still did his best to educate me in contemporary West Coast customs.

In fact, my fondest memory of that period was election night

a novel of sexual initiation   101

of 1980, when Carter was given the bum's rush and Ronald Reagan was horrifyingly swept into office just a few days before my twenty-first birthday. I can't say I was much of an activist back then, or had ever been, though I was identifiably liberal like my parents—something which had marked our family as virtual radicals back in Georgia but certainly made us nothing special in Berkeley.

Around this time, however, Pierce seemed to be getting radicalized; he'd started wearing black leather jackets with an ever-changing assortment of political buttons. You could always tell where Pierce's consciousness was going by major shifts in his wardrobe. Late on the afternoon of the election Pierce called me at work, excitedly announcing that there was to be an impromptu protest march through the downtown streets that evening. The exit polls were already handing Reagan the presidency. I'd learned enough Berkeley history to know that the town had a special relationship with the former governor. Back during the People's Park riots, he had said that if the rock-throwing protestors wanted a war, he'd be happy to oblige them, and he sent in the National Guard. Everybody said that's what Ronnie called a fair fight.

So it was little wonder that the march was a pretty good show, some of the best fun I've ever had, running and jumping through the streets of Berkeley singing crazy things like, "Hey, ho—whaddya know—Ronald Reagan's got to go!" This sounded crazy to me because the man had just been elected and wasn't likely to be shamed out of taking the prize by the likes of us, but hey, I was enjoying myself. Things like this never happened in the burbs of Atlanta when I was growing up.

By the time the whole march crowd massed in front of the old city hall about nine p.m., there was a couple thousand of us. Everybody seemed revolutionary in a party-down kind of way. At one point Pierce put his long, bony arm around me, held a fist in front of my face, and said, typically overdramatic, "This is history, my good man!"

I shouted, "Right on!" and immediately felt stupid, but I went to bed thinking, *Who knows? Maybe it was history.* The next evening, I watched the TV news to see if there was any coverage of the protest march, but there was none, not even locally. Overnight it seemed that, outside of Berkeley, the rest of a drowsy nation had merely stretched in bed, clapped off the lights, and turned in for a prolonged and dangerous snooze.

10

HOW CAN you tell when you've gotten off the track of the right kind of life? I suspect that things were a little off for me since birth. Since I started this sexual history project a couple months ago, it's as if the misdirected pace of my life has been slowing—like a train losing steam, like an exhausted horse, like a car running out of gas.

I fear the stillness of an absolute stop. Is that what's going to happen when I've redigested all of my life on these pages? I don't know. Sometimes my hands won't cooperate when I start up at the computer again. Sometimes I have to quit mid-sentence and drive up into the hills, then run for an hour on the Tilden Park trails until I plunge into a deathlike exhaustion.

I haven't run in the woods like this since I was a kid in Georgia. In a funny way, I ran then for the same reasons I do now: the tension inside the house was too much to put up with. As a child, I was escaping the Kendricks family tension; now the tension is all mine.

I've never figured out why a run in the woods clears my head. I don't think it's just that I get more oxygen and get high on endorphins. I hate to sound mystical, but it's like my personal boundaries (I never talked this way before June) partially dissolve, and clean, natural air pours into a breach of my brain fog. Then I have a little more peace, even if it doesn't last.

I was just thinking of walks in the woods because I remember so clearly that fateful one in the month of May, when I was twenty-one. I had just disconsolately moved into my own apartment on Virginia Street, after helping Mom move in with her artist pal Gayle in Albany. On a sunny, preternaturally hot Sunday afternoon I had walked up into the hills to figure out what to do with Chuck Berquist.

Chuck seemed permanently lodged in my store—that's how I thought of Diversions by that time—and he was about as useful as a wart. I was working six days a week to the tune of sixty or seventy hours. Three or four days a week Chuck sauntered in at ten or eleven, mumbled hello and locked himself into his office. There was no longer any pretense of him running things. By my calendar, Etty's bizarre rider on his trust fund should have expired a year earlier, freeing Chuck to pursue his research and also freeing him to sell me the store for a pittance, like he'd originally promised.

But every time I asked about the turnover he would merely say "Iceberg's got the papers. He's working on it." Iceberg was Stan Eisenberg, Chuck's lawyer and financial advisor, and he was becoming as mythical a figure as Etty Berquist herself; I had never seen or spoken to either of them. I was beginning to doubt the veracity of Chuck's whole story.

Most of all, I needed the damn office space. I was doing my paperwork behind a little partition in a back corner of the store, and the situation was getting ridiculous. I'll admit that I was a little afraid to confront Chuck openly, for fear that he would overreact to my disturbance of his routine and possibly fire me. Now I know that this fear was irrational, but there was more than the usual job-loss anxiety involved. I was really attached to work back then. June has helped me understand that I was using work to avoid dealing with my past, avoid contemplating the future, and avoid a close examination of the present.

But I was also attached to the job because I was *succeeding*. Chuck had been right about my instinct for retail, whether it was a matter of predicting consumer preferences in games and distractions six months down the line, or doing in-store positioning of the most profitable products. I had seen Dungeons and Dragons coming, for instance, and laid in the best stock of related paraphernalia in the East Bay well ahead of the competition. I knew to put the fancy jigsaw puzzles close to the front of the store, where their adult purchasers wouldn't have to wade through toy soldiers, fantasy games and other kidstuff. Kids, on the other hand, don't care about where they're seen. They just

a novel of sexual initiation   **105**

make a beeline for what they want; you could literally stock things in a dungeon without dissuading them.

On the other hand, product placement can't be static. You have to keep an eye on things daily, watching what gets bought and in what quantities, and from what part of the store, and be ready to move stock, reorder, and change inventory on the whiff of a strong intuition. I don't know why, but I've always had the knack.

But I didn't have the greatest communication skills; that's why I went up into the hills to clear my head about Chuck. Should I precipitate a show-down, should I slip an eviction notice under his door, or should I wait a little longer and see what happened? I gave these questions a pretty good run on the trails, the first I'd done in several weeks. I was breathless and weak-kneed when I collapsed by the side of Grizzly Peak Boulevard—spread-eagling onto somebody's front yard to rest—hoping wildly that the single, correct answer would pop into my head at any moment. It didn't. After fifteen minutes I got up to trudge tiredly down Euclid Avenue and get some lunch at the Northside strip of cafes.

I was thirsty by the time I got as far as the Rose Garden. I've always loved that place; it made me appreciate the value of the WPA (which I'd always heard my conservative uncle from Mobile call "We Piddle Around"). In fact the Rose Garden is one of the prettiest little civic parks I've ever seen, with its long, quarter-circle trellis overlooking an amphitheatre of terraced rosebeds facing the Golden Gate Bridge. I found the water fountain down by the tennis courts. Then I ambled down the trellis walk, my mood lifting somewhat as I breathed in the rose scent available everywhere. I happened to look down two or three rows of flowers and noticed a small woman with dark, short hair partially hidden underneath one fully blooming shrub of yellow blooms.

She was digging furiously around the woody stem of the plant, and I smiled as fond images of Anna came to mind. My gaze lingered on her a few moments as she straightened up briefly and wiped her forehead with her arm. In the brief moment before she leaned back down again—folded over with her bare knees pressing against the dirt—I saw one side of her face in the bright sunlight. A soft click sounded in my head, then a subtle chill of recognition, not so strong as to bring a name to mind, but still . . . there was something familiar in the woman's unguarded gesture. Slowly, with the forced casualness of an amateur spy, I walked to the next opening in the trellis walk and came down the steps to the row of roses where the woman was working. I was only ten feet or so away from her now, but could hardly see her at all; I'd have to walk right by to check her out. I was nervous. Was this another fantasy-provoking female I was likely to fixate on?

I decided I could breeze by the mystery woman briskly, take one look and figure out what seemed familiar about her, then head for lunch, get on with my life.

It didn't work out that way. As I came abreast of the woman on the ground, she abruptly stood up and wiped her brow again, this time with the tail of her red shirt, exposing a pale white midriff and the bottom edge of her bra on the side.

"Shit it's hot," she mumbled in a distinctly Southern twang before noticing me and taking a startled half-step backward, dropping a spade from her other hand. Now we were face to face with about a foot of height difference between us. There was something so familiar about that precise angle that I caught my breath even before the startling familiarity of her features sent my brain into a spin. She managed to get words out before I did:

"Randall?" she asked incredulously, her eyes widening and her mouth breaking into an astonished grin. "Is that *yew*, Randall?!"

I let my breath go in a chopped expiration that came dangerously close to spitting. "*Lainie?*" I cried. "Lainie McEwen?"

"Jesus!" the little woman suddenly yelped. "Well, I'll be go to hell, Randall! Now look at you right here!" Then she leaped at me and hugged me ferociously. This was the first time I had ever pressed up against my high school sweetheart's best friend.

How quickly one can make a string of unexpected decisions! In the blink of an eye and the brief compression of our embrace, I decided that I was no longer angry at Lainie for the way she'd acted toward me in high school; that I'd been wrong to think of

a novel of sexual initiation
107

Lainie as trailer trash back then; and that I owed it to JoEllen Jones to be nice to Lainie now, to be an ambassador of goodwill in honor of that passionate but truncated love.

Of course, I wasn't aware of those decisions at the time. Maybe I'm just trying to make sense of subsequent developments. But something had sure happened, some fantastic acceleration of a mere accessory relationship from the past. When Lainie and I pulled back from our hug, arms remaining around each other's waist, I looked at her sweaty face with its big, shiny forehead, small dark brown eyes and almost perfect bow-shaped mouth, and thought: *Wow, she's a lot cuter than she used to be!*

Then Lainie broke from our embrace completely, wiping childishly at the remaining moisture on her face with the back of one hand and casting her eyes wildly about as if desperate to find a powder room.

"Gawd, I'm a mess," she said apologetically. "Hope I didn't get you all sweaty. I was so goddamn surprised, Randall! I mean, can you believe it?"

"Nope," I said truthfully. "No, I really can't believe it. What are you doing out here, Lainie?"

Her eyes darkened and she looked uneasy. "Um, I'm visiting my cousin Jeanna for a little while. You know I had a cousin out here?"

I shook my head, now feeling awkward that we were still standing close but no longer touching. Backing off a step I said, "You know, we didn't talk very much back in high school."

Lainie grinned again. Her eyes sparkled, something I didn't remember noticing from the years before. "Yeah, that's right," she said impishly, "cuz you were all crazy in love with JoEllen."

This remark stung unexpectedly—this was the same Lainie, for sure—but the discomfort was rapidly overcome by curiosity. "So whatever happened to JoEllen?" I asked abruptly, impolitely.

"You don't know?" Lainie said, obviously surprised.

"Not everything," I said awkwardly, trying to cover my ignorance—trying to cover up that I hadn't even read the last few letters from JoEllen that arrived during my relationship with Anna.

"You know she moved to Florida?" Lainie said quizzically.

"Uh, yeah," I lied.

"Then you know she quit high school when she got pregnant. Because she met that guy down there."

"Oh," I said tonelessly, the bottom dropping out of my heart without warning. "Pregnant."

Lainie stooped down to pick up her spade again and brushed some dirt off her white socks. "Yup. Now they have a little girl and they live on an Army base down there. Last I heard, anyways, which was about two years ago."

I snorted without meaning to, feeling a genuine sense of tragedy. *How young women are changing the world,* I thought ruefully, and then vocalized the rest: "What a waste."

Lainie raised her eyebrows. "Well, I don't know. . ." she said uncomfortably, twisting around to look at the bay sky behind her. Realizing I was being a little inconsiderate, I put on a cheerful tone and asked, "So you work here now?"

"Huh?" Lainie said, turning back around and regarding me with confusion. "No, not really. My uncle, that's Jeanna's dad, works for the city and said I could fool around here if I wanted. I get nervous just sitting around. I really like to be in a garden."

I was about to say that was like someone else I knew, but realized that bringing up Anna was not the cleverest thing to do at the moment. Lainie looked terribly vulnerable and I couldn't quite make sense of what she had said. Why would she be sitting around? What was she really doing here? Not wanting to make an inquiry that might embarrass her, I frantically searched my mind for the proper thing to say. Then it came to me, suave and sure:

"Hey, Lainie, you want to come have lunch with me? My treat. We can catch up on old times in Georgia and everything."

Lainie beamed like a four-year-old on Christmas morning. "Well now, I might if you asked me two more times, honey!" she said merrily, winking at me, sending us both into gales of laughter over a silly joke that had always convulsed us back in high school.

WHEN WE got down to Northside I picked the place to eat without asking Lainie. Once we were inside looking at a big wall

a novel of sexual initiation

menu, it seemed like I might have made a mistake. Tugging on my sleeve, Lainie stretched up to whisper in my ear and said, "Hey, Randall, what's *fall-awful?*"

"Falafel," I corrected her. "It's ground-up chickpeas that are balled-up and fried. You eat them with some lettuce and tahini in a pita bread."

Lainie was looking at me like I had delivered a lengthy soliloquy in Greek. Already it was clear that she hadn't been out of the South for long, so I translated: "It's like a spicy hush puppy in a sandwich."

"Oh. Sounds weird." Squinting at the wall board with great skepticism, Lainie asked, "Don't they have a hamburger?"

Fortunately they did. Ten minutes later, as Lainie chewed through her burger and I negotiated a sloppy falafel, I had the first of what would add up to, over the years, countless perceptions of Lainie as a child: wide-eyed, funny, and skittish, bouncing in her seat with excess energy. She watched in wonderment as I ate my lunch, refusing several offers to try a little of it, launching into several lengthy, semi-profane riffs of gossip in response to my questions about the old stomping grounds.

I had been so out of touch with the past that I was surprised to find how hungry I was for news, even second-hand. Lainie was pretty second-hand, given that she had an almost entirely different social frame of reference than I. She had grown up in a trailer not far from a drag-racing track and I had grown up in a quiescent suburb. In the South, that kind of class difference can be greater than a racial one. The more Lainie talked, the more it became evident that our only common link was JoEllen Jones, and the more I marveled that they had ever been best friends.

Also, the more Lainie talked, the more she seemed to be avoiding the subject of what had brought her out West. I was increasingly curious about it. Finally interrupting one of her spiels about a high school scandal I had missed, I challenged her:

"So come on, Lainie, tell me exactly how you ended up here in Berkeley. I mean, this is the last place I would have ever expected to run into you." Worried that I might have insulted her, I grinned big and foolishly, as if I might be kidding around.

But Lainie's face had clouded over; she was staring silently out the window. She turned back to face me with a half-defiant wince and replied in a low voice, "They made me leave."

"They? Who made you leave? Why?"

"The Skinners."

Momentarily confused over what Lainie meant—were the skinners some kind of hunters who menaced her trailer park?—I shrugged my shoulders and asked again, "Who?"

Lainie shifted twice in her seat, obviously uncomfortable with the subject at hand. She peered directly into my eyes, as if trying to gauge my readiness for the whole truth, then launched into a rapid-fire, breathless digest:

"Well, you see for about the last year I was living with this guy, Bobby Skinner. We had some fights and his momma Lorene never liked me anyway. About three months ago Bobby came home real drunk one night and started yelling and hitting me. I hit him back and we were both screaming a lot, I guess, so the neighbors called the sheriff and when the deputy came he knocked Bobby down and. . . well, then I hit him pretty good."

"You hit Bobby again?" I asked, a bit breathless myself by this point.

"Hit the goddamn deputy," Lainie confessed, her eyes dropping to the surface of the table, one of her fingers scraping nervously at a dried-up mustard dropping.

I couldn't suppress a laugh, but immediately reached over to touch Lainie's white forearm, lightly sprinkled with fine dark hairs, to reassure her. "I'm sorry," I said, still chuckling. "I don't mean to laugh, but . . . what did you hit him with?"

Lainie raised her eyes back to me and smiled brightly, as if she were proud of herself. "Bobby had this old wooden post out back, like a six-by-six, but split in half. I picked it up and took it 'cross his back. Knocked him out!" "Oh, shit," I murmured, lowering my head and scratching my hairline with one hand. "Lainie."

"Anyways," she continued, "when we got to court there was this judge that Bobby's momma knows. He said he couldn't abide by domestic violence, and he told Bobby he better never show up

a novel of sexual initiation

in that court again. And then he told me to leave the *en-tire* state of Georgia."

"What?" I blurted, shocked.

"Yeah!" Lainie exclaimed, her head bobbing forward like a bird's, "he told me he should put me away for assaulting an officer but instead he just wanted me to get as far away from him as I could. He called it 'our little deal.' If I left the state, he wouldn't put me in jail."

"Is that legal?" I asked wonderingly, as if Lainie had a fine mind for the law.

"I think it's legal to Low-reen Skinner," Lainie seethed. "Anyway, my mom called my uncle Guy who works for the city here, to see if I could come stay for a little while. Then my cousin Jeanna said she had an extra room in her apartment, and I could stay there. So here I am."

"When can you go back to Georgia?" I asked, feeling both curious and vaguely troubled.

"Oh, I don't know," Lainie replied, leaning back in her seat and sighing. "Maybe never. It's really pretty out here, and I hope I never see another goddamn Skinner in my life."

"No more Bobby, eh?"

"Nope," Lainie said decisively. "He beat up on me too much." Glancing conspiratorially to the left and right, Lainie pulled her chair around to be next to me, whispered "Look at this," and nodded toward the underside of the table. Once I looked down, she roughly pulled one leg of her shorts up enough to reveal the side of her right hip. I caught my breath at the sight. Whether it was because of the milky white ampleness of her thigh or the faded-yellow but obviously severe bruise near the very top if it, I'm not sure. Probably both. I nodded gravely, avoiding Lainie's eyes as she continued speaking with the full length of her leg exposed:

"Bobby calls me all the time now, even said he might come out here, but I told him no way. I'm looking for a job. When I get some money I'll move out from Jeanna's and get my own apartment. I like California."

"Me too," I added, ready to move on to less daunting subject matter.

MY JOURNEY THROUGH THE PLANT WORLD

I leaned back and took my eyes from Lainie's body, and she took the cue, pulling down her shorts again. "I just got my own place," I continued, "close enough to the store to walk to work. Gotta buy a car though, since Mom took hers to where she's living in Albany."

Lainie smiled noncommittally, though she was clearly relieved at the change of subject. Then she changed it again:

"You know what?" she said, bouncing in her seat and leaning very close to me. "Jeanna's roommate is a witch."

"A witch?" I replied, uncomprehending.

"Yeah! A real one! You should see the place we live in. August—that's the witch—she has all these bones and feathers and rocks everywhere. Jeanna says August has a convent . . . no, that's not right . . . a coven, once a month at midnight up in Tilden Park. I've never been but Jeanna says she has, and that it's really fun. I might go next time."

"Jesus Christ," I said, shaking my head. "This town. Witches." Then a funny thought came to me. "You go to that coven, Lainie, and they'll never let you back into Georgia."

I expected her to laugh, but instead she looked at me earnestly and said, "You wanna see it? Our place, I mean?"

My brain did a quick assay of the situation and decided to take a step backward. "Uh, sure," I replied clammily. "Sometime." Lainie's face fell and I was abruptly visited by a terrible vision of her trudging home alone, a bruised Dixie refugee wandering innocently into the clutches of a West Coast black-magic sorority. So I reversed myself: "I guess I can walk you home if you want me to."

"Okay!" Lainie assented happily, bouncing again. "Can we go across campus? It's so pretty, I been goin' there all the time."

So we walked across campus, on one of those afternoons that had turned into a dazzling advertisement for the San Francisco Bay area: sunny, bright, and breezy, with thin wisps of a cooling afternoon fog flitting by overhead. Depending on whether you were in or out of the wind, it was either hot or surprisingly chilly—unpredictably changeable, like life itself all of a sudden. I remembered being worried about something earlier in the day;

a novel of sexual initiation   **113**

since Lainie's appearance I felt as if the whole subject of my life had changed. And I guess it had.

A funny thing happened when we got down to the sharply scented, mystically still eucalyptus grove that's close to the western border of campus near downtown. I jumped over the little creek there with ease, but Lainie, wearing flat, dirty canvas shoes with no treads, slipped on the bank after she had jumped over, almost falling to her knees. When she straightened up it seemed as if she was going to cry over nothing. Instead she held her hand out toward me—was she trying to balance herself?—and after a few awkward moments with the two of us standing there looking at each other, she barked, "Hey, you!"

"Oh, sorry," I said sheepishly, descending the bank by a yard or so to take her hand in mine. After I pulled her up the slope, and we walked through a hedge of bushes onto a brilliant green lawn that overlooked the streets of downtown Berkeley, we were still holding hands. It was against my better judgment, but it was mostly all right. Lainie's hand was small and delicate, though her grip was strong. Hers was the first woman's hand I had held in a while. Neither of us spoke about the holding.

I knew what was coming, and I suspected it was crazy, all out of balance and too fast. But I was tingling deep and low, just above my groin. There was something in me desperate to grab this excitement, this unforeseen opportunity. I can't remember what Lainie was talking about as we made our way through downtown. She was chattering a lot, but I suspect she was just making conversation while her head spun with anticipations not too different from mine. Could the route we were taking ever be justified? I don't know. Even now, I can't say much in our defense, except perhaps: *We were lonely, God, and we were both so far from home.*

THE APARTMENT Lainie shared with her cousin and the witch in an old brick complex a few blocks west of downtown was everything she had promised, and then some. As I came in the door my eyes were drawn to a framed picture over the fireplace—a huge, ungodly yellow, red, and chocolate brown portrait of an African woman wearing mannish raiments and jewelry of royalty and magic. Stones, feathers, shells, animal skulls and random vertebrae were piled on the mantle, littered on a coffee table, even scattered over the kitchen counters, competing for space with a few antique appliances and one brightly new Champion juicer. It was the first time I'd ever been in a place that was both so decidedly feminine—a literal no man's land—yet staunchly unfrilly. Remembering Carolyn's pink, girlish bedroom back home, I chuckled out loud as Lainie led me down a shadowy hallway, giving me a tour of the realm.

"What's so funny?" she asked.

"Nothing," I replied, shaking my head. "This is kind of a weird place, isn't it?"

"It's all right," Lainie said neutrally, pushing open the last door on the hallway without going into the room. "My room ain't weird, is it?"

I entered, taking note of an Atlanta Rhythm Section poster on the far wall over a cheap, four-drawer dresser, and replied, "Nope. Looks normal. No skeletons in here." Suddenly I felt trapped; I was inside a small area with no chair, the only comfort being a thin mattress on the floor with a yellow bedspread tangled up with two pillows. Except for the poster, I might have been in an anonymous, underfurnished motel room.

Lainie was still standing out in the hall, saying nothing. I looked all around one more time, shrugged my shoulders and said, "I mean, it's nice."

I was beginning to feel so awkward that I was thinking up excuses to leave when Lainie asked, "Do you want anything to drink, Randall?"

"Sure," I said happily, relieved at the opportunity to get out of the bedroom.

"Help yourself to anything in the fridge," she replied, backing away from me as I came out and turning to another door. "There's all kinds of fresh juices in there 'cuz Jeanna hardly drinks anything else. Or eats anything, for that matter."

Now Lainie was speaking from behind a closed door: "I'm gonna take a shower, okay? You can take care of yourself for a

a novel of sexual initiation 115

minute or two. Jeanna and August won't be back til later."

That last bit of information seemed unwarranted, but the tingle returned to my lower region. I opened the refrigerator door as I heard the water start in the bathroom across the way, and I couldn't say to this day whether I saw a jar of carrot juice or an elephant's head inside that appliance. All my awareness was focused on the muffled sound of water spraying behind a closed door. I was wondering if I had the nerve to go in there, announce myself, and draw back the shower curtain.

11

O F COURSE I didn't do anything of the sort. It would have been the most brazen thing I had ever done, completely out of character and stupid besides. I suspect it was an idea I got from porn, which was full of people approaching each other sexually without so much as a how-ya-doin', then going all the way without a moment of hesitation or awkwardness. I guess that can happen only when you have a director.

When the sound of Lainie's shower stopped, I remember staring at the bathroom door until it opened. Lainie came out wearing a deep blue bathtowel big enough to cover her from armpits to just below her knees. She smiled at me brightly and said "I'll be back in a minute!" as she scurried down the hall.

Instead, in a minute or two I heard Lainie plaintively call "Randall?" from her room. I bolted from the kitchen, then deliberately slowed my walk for the fifteen feet or so down the hall to her open door. When I came in the room we were immediately standing face to face. She was wearing some silky black gym shorts of which I could see only the bottom trim underneath the tail of a coarse white cotton shirt she had on, with the top three buttons undone. On the right side of her chest, the shirt said SHELL in red-trimmed yellow letters, and over her heart appeared the word Robert in a blue stitched script. It was probably a good thing that I didn't make a connection with the name at that moment. Looking back from the present, the symbolism of it is at once piercing and ludicrous.

There was a rubbery medicinal smell in the room that I couldn't figure out, but it didn't seem to be the right time for asking questions. Lainie was looking up at me silently with big, excited eyes, and she was breathing heavily.

"Let's close the door," I suggested, turning and stepping back to do the job myself. I returned to my former position in front of Lainie, a bit closer this time. Momentarily uncertain, I raised both of my hands to her shoulders and lightly fluffed the wet black curls of hair behind her ears. She was smiling warmly and looking right into my eyes, first one and then the other, so that her own eyes were shifting, left, then right, left and right. My own smile felt tremulous, like it would break out into something wild like a yell if something didn't give, so I nervily slipped my hands under her shirt to the tops of her shoulders, and massaged her there. When she closed her eyes, taking a deep breath, I took that as a cue and lowered my hands to start unbuttoning the lower three buttons of her shirt. When I was done I reached inside on either side and, without moving the shirt aside to look, placed my open hands completely over the small mounds of her breasts and squeezed gently.

"Huhhhh," Lainie sighed out loud, like I had opened a valve that let out air under pressure. I squeezed her again. She lowered her head and leaned into me, unsteadily, so I let my hands go around her back, still inside the open shirt, and pulled her to me. Unbelievably, her hands were soon busy at my belt, doing a pretty good job of unbuckling, seeing as how she couldn't be looking at what she was doing. Then she unsnapped my pants just as skillfully, almost rudely pulling them and my jockey shorts down at the same time, to about mid-thigh. This felt silly but was as far as she could reach in the clinch we were in. Then I felt her handling my balls and rapidly levitating penis. When I took a couple of big, sharp breaths she raised her head to look at me, wildness in her eyes, and brought her mouth up to mine.

We kissed, not too deeply but with some pressure, then I pushed her off slightly to take her breasts in my hands again, while she held my solid erection off to the side. We looked at each other for the longest time, Lainie's brown eyes merry with anticipation, as if we two had pulled off the biggest bank job of all time and were only beginning to scheme about all the ways to spend our ill-gotten gains. In all my sexual history, I can't remember a more erotic moment.

a novel of sexual initiation

While I clasped Lainie's secondary sexual characteristics, she kept a firm and playful hold on my primary one, which was starting to twitch a little. In retrospect, I wish we could have stood there that way forever, conjoined without penetration, cooperating in the endless heightening of our sensations. But it's impossible to stop time and almost as hard to stop sex in the middle. For better or worse, we were going all the way.

"Let me get my pants off," I finally said in a strangled, breaking voice, half-falling to the bed as we broke from our embrace. Much more gracefully Lainie removed her shirt, placing it atop the dresser, but left on her shorts, which were cut high enough up the sides of her thighs to let me see that there was nothing else underneath them. Lainie's body was oddly disproportionate but nonetheless exciting to see. Her chest seemed small and underdeveloped, with small button nipples on her modest breasts, but her hips flared wide, making for a very round and generous bottom, as I would later see. Her full thighs reduced at the knees to almost spindly calves; looking at her almost-naked that first time, the word *childbearer* printed itself in my mind and I felt slightly fearful. I had learned my lesson with Anna; now I knew I had to say something about birth control, but I still had absolutely no idea of how to bring it up.

Worried and naked, I lay back on the bed, my penis pointing straight up at the ceiling. I was about to say something, what I don't know exactly, when Lainie abruptly announced, "I already put in my diaphragm," and shockingly pulled down her shorts. Her pubic hair was a brief thatch above her crotch; I could see the folds of her labia as she came and stood over me on the bed, then squatted down to sit on my pubic bone, my cock angling forward to go behind her rump.

Everything was happening so fast now that I was almost overwhelmed with excitement. Lainie's warmth was making my head spin as my hands softly traversed the dramatic flare from her waist to her globe-like hips and then the cool, tender territory of her buttocks. I pushed down on her there, increasing the pressure against my groin, and Lainie started nibbling around my neck and right ear, whispering softly, "Ain't we having fun?"

"Yeah," I wheezed, although *fun* wasn't the word I might have chosen for it, seeing as how I felt both terror and delight at that moment and couldn't tell them apart. After more nibbling, kisses, and mutual squirming, Lainie sat up on me, ran her hands through her hair, and then raised herself up on her knees, angling herself over my erection. I couldn't believe she wanted to do it already! Anna had always wanted to do everything but intercourse first, and when I sometimes came before getting inside her she seemed relieved.

Lainie was already putting a couple fingers inside herself, and moving her hips with her eyes closed dreamily. Before I could make any suggestions she had taken her fingers out of herself, grasped me and put my tip right at her opening. I caught and held my breath, staring at her until she opened her eyes and grinned. Then she slowly, incrementally, lowered herself onto me, our eyes locked, and I was fully in, wetly and warmly enveloped, welcomed and captured.

What are the boundaries we cross when we put bodies together this way? Years later, during my Disastrous Dating Period, I remember arguing with a young New Age-type girl I was trying to get into bed about what sex did to your soul. "I believe my soul mixes with the soul of any man I sleep with," she said earnestly. "Even if we never sleep together again, my soul is a little bit different forever."

The implication, of course, was that she wasn't sure about mixing with *my* soul, as if it would merely contaminate hers. It was an original put-off line, I have to give her that. Though I stomped off at the time, telling her she was living in deep space, I wonder sometimes . . . To this day I feel like I have some of Lainie's soul in me—a soul of lemon zest, black pepper, and cayenne. Ordinary kitchen spices, but always sharp, memorable, and uncompromising. Hard on the stomach sometimes.

If souls do mix in sex, Lainie and I blended ours pretty well that afternoon. After a little while I got over my initial trepidation and realized that we really were having a lot of fun, perhaps because Lainie seemed to be enjoying herself so much. While not doing anything out of the ordinary, so far as I knew, she

a novel of sexual initiation   121

seemed quite uninhibited. While still on top of me, she once rose up and leaned as far back as she could while staying joined to me. There was something she really liked about that, moving slowly up and down over me with her back arched away from me, her eyes squeezed tight and her lips stretched tight across her teeth, muttering "God-damn-it, god-damn-it" so many times over that I started to find it funny. Lainie tended to curse during sex, and I never did find an explanation for it. After making love she was always so embarrassed that she wouldn't answer my questions.

One thing that made the afternoon fun was that I lasted so long, perhaps because Lainie spent so much time on top of me, something I never experienced much with Anna. It seemed to keep me in a hyperexcited state without progressing toward orgasm. After a while I heaved up and rolled Lainie over—always a tricky, awkward maneuver, although I've seen it done in porn flicks with a cold technical flair—and she put her legs way up high, on top of my shoulders, so that her vagina was a little compressed, squeezing me. That was very exciting, so I plunged into her again and again, sometimes so hard I was afraid for her. She yelped and cursed until little streamlets of water came out the corners of her eyes. If I slowed down she would grit her teeth and say "Don't stop" so I kept going and going until things were out of my control. I felt my buttocks tighten like a rock and my plumbing on the underside started its tiny but momentous convulsions. I spurted so many times inside Lainie that I thought a diaphragm couldn't hold it.

Then I slowly lowered myself onto her, our sweat mixing—like souls?—to make a slimy layer between us. Lainie was giving out this little string of laughs: "uh-ha, uh-ha, uh-ha, ha-ha-ha-ha . . ." and shuddering, and I realized she was probably coming. Should I start moving again? Could she get stopped in the middle? Even though I was a little soft, I pushed against her again and she roughly grabbed my shoulders, screamed "Wuhh-wha, no! No, no, no!"

I stopped, chagrined, and said, "Okay, okay!" and then Lainie threw her arms out wide across the bed, laughing and laughing, drawing deep, violent breaths, turning her head far to the left. Then she breathed again, turned her head back and looked at me, smiling and teary-eyed. And then she blushed.

It was over. I lowered my head to kiss Lainie on the lips, slid over a little and kissed one of her nipples. Then I pulled out—a devilishly ticklish, dying sensation—and laid down on the bed beside her. "Wow," I said to the ceiling.

"Yeah," Lainie answered weakly. "We do it all right, don't we?"

"Yes," I confirmed, but my spirit was sinking into a funk. In my psychology readings in recent years I've been reassured to learn that little depressions after sex are not uncommon—les petits morts and all that. But just as vividly as the sex, I remember staring disconsolately at the ceiling that late afternoon, feeling drained, gratified, yet strangely lonesome as Lainie drifted off into the soft breathing of a nap beside me.

Why lonesome? That's something I have to deal with in this journal—the fact that I went to bed with Lainie without having fallen in love with her. I would go to bed with her hundreds of times over the next few years without ever falling in love with her. Is this a sin of some kind? I shouldn't get too dramatic because I did learn to love Lainie by and by. But we never had much of a romance. I'm sorry about that to this day. Sorry for her, sorry I've never apologized. But was it all my fault?

WHOA THERE—back up. I'm into one of my self-flagellating riffs, like the monologues in June's office when she stops me and tells me not to be so hard on myself. I'm beginning to understand what she means about having the past and present all mixed up in my head. Here I was writing about my first sex with Lainie, a sweet and long-gone part of the past, and yet I can't separate it from the global guilt of the present. I guess that's why I have to remember the way things actually happened, in the right order, with all my who's-whos and what's-whats in order.

All right then. I drifted off into a nap that summer afternoon along with Lainie. When I heard a noise in the apartment I jerked awake, my eyes falling on a little clock beside the bed that said ten til six. I turned my head to the other side and realized

a novel of sexual initiation 123

that Lainie was soundly asleep on me, one warm thigh partly crossed over my legs, her hands gathered together like a child's between us. Whatever noise had awakened me was followed by voices and the closing of the apartment door, then a laugh, and the two voices talking. Two women: one voice was soft and musical, the other lower, clipped.

I gave Lainie a full-body nudge without effect, so I trailed two fingers over her forehead, squeezed her nose and said, "Hey, you."

"Hunh?!" she grunted, lifting her head and looking at me utterly confused, her eyes all out of focus, her cheeks puffy with sleep. For a moment she was absolutely adorable. Recognizing me, Lainie smiled sweetly and shockingly moved a hand over my groin. "You wanna do it s'more?" she slurred, bringing her lips to my ear.

"No!" I exclaimed in a stage whisper, causing her to jerk back from me in surprise. "I think your cousin is home. I heard them come in the door."

Lainie raised herself up on elbow and listened intently to the murmur in the kitchen, and said, "Oh yeah. We're supposed to have dinner together tonight."

I sat up and leaned against the cool plaster of the wall. "I should go then."

"Oh, hush," Lainie replied. "Of course you're not gonna go." She sat up, crossed a leg over me and sat on my lap, leaning close into my face. "Let's see if we can fuck without them hearing."

I was about to protest when a light knock came at the door and the soft-voiced woman said, "Lainie? You in there, cuz?"

Lainie clapped a hand over her mouth like a mischievous kid, lifting her eyebrows and rolling her eyes around once. When she took her hand away from her mouth she said, "Uh, yeah, Jeanna. Give us a minute, willya?"

There was a momentary silence at the door before the unseen Jeanna said in a wondrous tone, "Give *us* a minute?" We heard her footsteps receding down the hall and a burble of conversation in the kitchen. Then the Jeanna-voice bellowed out, "Ooo-wee, Lainie! Never mind your roomies! We'll just be in here cookin' dinner, minding our own business!"

There was a lot of laughter from the kitchen. Lainie was beaming with satisfaction, lifting up on her knees to clear away the sheet that had gotten between us, then coming down, flesh to flesh, on my midsection and rotating her rump on top of me. I started to stiffen up but said, "No, wait, really, Lainie. Really, I mean it. OK?"

Lainie pursed her lips in mock agitation, then stood up wonderfully naked and whispered, "Okay, we'll wait until after dinner." She turned and slid back her closet door, and I saw her full, splendid ass for the first time. The room was full of lust, lust full of itself and lust looking to make more of itself. Which pieces of it belonged to each of us was hard to tell. Lust would always serve Lainie and me well.

We dressed quickly and silently, my head spinning with anxiety about how I could introduce myself with a shred of dignity to the two women outside. I couldn't come up with anything plausible before it was time to exit the room and make our entrance. I was sure we stank of sex, but that particular cat was already out of the bag. Would the witch take notice? I wondered. Would she burn some incense to dispel our rank magic?

By the time we entered the kitchen, Lainie having pulled me down the hallway from the bedroom by the wrist, whatever smells we carried were fortunately displaced by the powerful aroma of garlic and onions sautéing in a pan. I could see the backside of a short, bulky woman with curly, dark-blonde and silver-frosted hair at the stove. A few feet from her was a taller, extremely slender woman with black hair hanging lankly almost to her shoulders, wearing shorts, a green t-shirt hanging out beneath a denim jacket, and an Oakland A's baseball cap. Jeanna, I thought, before I first looked her in the eyes and received a warm but suggestive smile.

"Hey Auggie," the long-haired woman said, tapping the cook on the shoulder. August turned around as Jeanna slid next to her, put a long arm around her shoulder, and said, "Looks like Lainie found a *man*."

It was the worst moment I could have imagined; I felt exposed for all the casual happenstance and opportunism that had

a novel of sexual initiation

transpired in the afternoon. I also felt like I was facing some kind of feminine tribunal. The fleshy, impassive face of "Auggie" wasn't making me feel any more at ease.

"Hmmph," she replied noncommittally, turning back to her cooking. Jeanna folded her arms, leaned against the sink behind her, and questioned Lainie directly:

"So where did you dig him up, cuz?"

Lainie crossed the kitchen, breaking contact with me, and going to stand next to her cousin so that they were both looking at me like some kind of animal in a zoo. "Guess what, Jeanna," Lainie exclaimed, "this is my old friend from high school, Randall!"

Old friend? I thought curiously, stepping forward to offer a hand to Jeanna. "Kendricks," I added formally. "Randall Kendricks."

Jeanna extended her slim, cool hand to me but kept her face turned to Lainie. "From Atlanta, you mean? You didn't tell me you knew anybody out here."

"I didn't know I did!" Lainie squealed. "That's the amazing thing! We ran into each other up in the Rose Garden this afternoon, and we had lunch, and then we . . . walked down here a little while ago." Lainie winked and showed her teeth to me during the pregnant pause in her report.

"Well now," Jeanna said, folding her arms again and smiling at me very directly. "It's a small world after all."

That's when it started to happen. I really noticed Jeanna's face at that moment, and an unknown door deep in my heart opened. From that previously hidden room came a wise, irrefutable voice saying *Yes. Here she is.* I don't know how else to describe the sensation.

It wasn't that Jeanna was pretty in any conventional way. She had long, dense eyebrows almost joined in the middle, big gray eyes and a wide mouth, a faint brush of dark hair above her thin upper lip. I could tell that she and Lainie were blood-related. They had the same broad forehead and a subtle resonance to their features, although Jeanna was exotic where Lainie was plain. They were both as white as could be, but Jeanna was infused with an ethereal paleness, as if the blue sky ran in her blood. She was so thin it seemed one might see through her if she turned aside. Something in me moved toward her but couldn't go all the way *to* her, so it stopped in the middle of the room, lost. That feeling of displacement would be something I felt every time I was around Jeanna: a kind of entrancement. I must have been entranced by Jeanna's appearance momentarily because I missed some words she said to August, who turned and offered a chunky hand to me. "Hi," she said guardedly.

"Oh, hi," I answered, trying to figure out what I had missed. "I'm Randall."

"Yeah," said August, nodding her head with just the slightest grin, "I got that." The room froze with silence.

"August," I said factually, trying to sound interested in her existence. Then it slipped out: "Is that a made-up name?"

August glared at me, her small eyes blue and cold. "All names are made-up," she replied testily. Lainie giggled.

"You know what I mean," I said, my hackles rising a little. "Is that the name your parents gave you?"

"Nope." Another frigid silence. I noticed Jeanna giving August a little elbow nudge, as if to say, *Be nice.* It wasn't working, and I felt myself involved in an unexpected test of wills. Perhaps because I was the lone man in the room, I wasn't about to capitulate.

"So, what was your name before?" I challenged. Then it came to me, a really clever thing to say: "Did they name you after some other month?"

"Yes, as a matter of fact," August snapped back. *"April."* Brusquely grabbing a green pepper and placing it on a cutting board next to the stove, she turned away from me again. I shrugged my shoulders and looked helplessly at Lainie, who was in turn looking to Jeanna as if she were obviously the person in charge. I guess she was, because she smiled maternally toward August's back, then winked at me and shook her head as if to say Never mind, it's all right. Then she told me that I was staying for dinner. I was hardly in a position to protest.

As it turned out, August was a pretty good cook. She manhandled some whole-wheat spaghetti and a very chunky, vegetable-

a novel of sexual initiation

filled sauce into a huge wooden bowl, mixing it all up for us in a rather expert way. I couldn't really criticize her style, although she was clearly of the whole-foods-at-any-cost school, not something I had grown up with. As I would learn during a very chatty dinner—just me and the girls—August's day job was at a natural foods grocery up on College Avenue. What she did at night, with the bones and the feathers and a gaggle of unfriendly women just like her (I presumed), I really didn't want to know, and she wasn't telling that evening.

Jeanna worked at Cody's Books and wrote a lot of poetry, she said. I found myself wanting to ask what her poems might be about, but it seemed a little too forward to ask about them. In fact, I had to keep disciplining myself not to ask Jeanna one question after another about herself, because of that odd, enchanting effect she had on me, and because Lainie was sitting right beside me squeezing my leg under the table every few minutes.

For her part, Jeanna asked the two of us lots of questions about school back in Atlanta, which made me uneasy because I didn't want to go into the whole JoEllen history. Lainie did it for me, of course, in her garrulous and unguarded way, sometimes sending Jeanna into gales of laughter and even getting a snicker from August now and then.

After a couple hours of this, August said she had to do her meditation, excusing herself with the curtest of nods to me and good-nights to Jeanna and Lainie. Jeanna and I cleaned the kitchen while Lainie watched the TV in the front room with the sound down low. Jeanna was whispering to me and handling the dishes as noiselessly as possible, so I assumed we were under the aegis of a household meditation rule. That was all right: I could have stood there, leaning close to hear Jeanna speak, and drying off plates and silverware, all night if that had been possible. I felt comfortable with her from the start.

In a warm and rather intimate way, Jeanna told me all about her family—her parents had left Georgia soon after marrying, and she had grown up in Oakland and Berkeley—and she also told me about all the times her folks had helped out Lainie's mother in one way or another. Jeanna said she'd always had a soft spot for Lainie, given that she had it so rough back home. She thought coming to California was the best thing that could have possibly happened to Lainie. Didn't I think so? she wanted to know. Sure, I said. After all, it had been the best thing ever to happen to me, although I said this with more certainty than I felt.

By about ten that night the three of us were sitting in front of the television but not paying much attention to it, still gossiping, this time in almost inaudible whispers about August and the terrible time she had growing up in Texas, according to Jeanna. Her father and uncle had raped her, she'd left home at fifteen and got into some bad (Jeanna didn't say what kind of bad) situations living in Arizona after that, and then . . .

Suddenly I realized that I had been gone from my apartment all day, and perhaps I should get back there, although Lainie and I had been subtly signaling more sex to each other all through the evening. The problem was that I felt embarrassed about going into her room with her, publicly this time, or more precisely, right in front of Jeanna. For some reason I didn't feel very proud of myself, leaving my own place in the morning and ending up sleeping at somebody else's place by night. It felt—what was the old Southern word?—*shiftless* somehow. I was trying to think up an irresistible excuse to leave but I realized I had no pets to feed, no plants to water, no roommate to check on. Finally, I hit on something.

"Uh, look everybody, I have to open the store in the morning, so I guess I've gotta get on home."

Lainie looked at me with open-mouthed surprise, sat up on her knees on the floor, and said plainly, "No you don't."

I was speechless. Of course she was right; Lainie always had the knack of disintegrating my pretenses. Jeanna laughed softly, covering her mouth and looking at me from her plush, ancient chair in an older-sister way. Lainie stood up, came over and took my hand, and said, "Come on."

We returned to her room, closed the door and took off each other's clothes, then made noiseless love, curling up close, pushing and giving, kissing and breathing into each other's mouth. After we had settled down and were both not far from sleep,

a novel of sexual initiation

Lainie pulled back from me and rested her head on one hand. I could just see her eyes in the semi-darkness, a faint yellowness coming in the window from street lights outside.

"So you like my cousin," Lainie said quietly.

"Well," I choked, "yeah, I guess. She seems like a really nice person."

Even in the dim light I could see Lainie's knowing smile. She reached over and pinched my nipple, causing me to gasp. "Well, don't get yourself all worked up, baby. She likes girls, you know."

Stunned, I rolled onto my back and stared at the ceiling, gray and vague in the dim light. "You mean, she and August . . .?" It was not an image I wanted in my head.

"Yes, you dumb-ass," Lainie giggled, climbing on top of me and bringing her face really close to mine. "I used to think you were so smart back in high school. Now you can't see the most obvious things."

"Well, something happened when I came to California," I said. "I'm not so smart out here." Then I was, unbelievably, erect again. When we finished this time I could hardly feel my body anymore, I was so tired. For a few minutes, Lainie kept stroking my chest, keeping me on the threshold between consciousness and a tantalizing sleep. Without warning she said timidly, "I always really liked you, Randall."

I nodded my head slightly but only said "Hmm," partly because I was so sleepy and partly because, even though I wanted to say something nice, I couldn't honestly return the sentiment. Lainie had really bugged me back in high school.

So that's how I fell in love, and fell into the most sexual relationship of my life, all on the same amazing day. Too bad I fell into these things with two different women.

12

WORK equals about 44,000 hours of my life over the last fifteen years; sex, by which I mean actual sexual activity, equals by my most liberal estimate, 524 hours over the same period. So why do I have to write a journal about my sex life instead of my work life? Couldn't it be argued that it's the work life that really counts, since it's taken the lion's share of my time, energy, and brainpower, while my sex life has been a weird but ultimately insignificant distraction?

Oh, well . . . nice try. In my mind's eye, I see June grinning in wise condescension and saying *"Re-ziss-tance!"* like she does whenever I come up with such diversions from the "established therapeutic momentum," as she puts it, of our face-to-face encounters. At least I might be able to start saving some money soon; I've internalized my goddamn therapist.

Besides, I know it's cheating to reduce my sex life to the time spent actually "doing it." What about all the time at work spent thinking about sex?

Hey-o, there-you-go, as Iceberg always says when he's uncovered the secret truth of something buried deep within a legal brief or a ream of financial statements. I can clearly remember the first time I ever heard him say that. It was at our second meeting—the one after Chuck split—which was right after Lainie and I had our startling reunion.

Now there's an irony. I had gone up into the hills that Sunday morning to figure out what to do about Chuck, and instead ran into Lainie, which completely changed the subject. By the next Wednesday, the Chuck problem was resolving itself. Chuck didn't show up at work the first two days of the week; I called his apartment a few times, listened to his curt, never-changed message—"Yeah. S'Chuck. Leave it after the beep"—and hung up, stumped. I would have walked over to his place Tuesday night, but I was at Lainie's for the third night in a row. . . only the two of us there that night, methodically stripping each other in the sitting room lit only by the flickering TV. . .

Anyway, on Wednesday morning Chuck finally showed up with a big grin on his face, hopped into his office leaving the door open, and started feverishly putting everything into boxes and grocery bags.

This was too much. Something was happening and I was clearly out of the loop. That morning I was breaking in a new part-time kid on the cash register, but as soon as I got a free moment I strode over to Chuck's open door, leaned against the frame and said, with a mixture of exasperation and curiosity, "Hey, Chuck! What's up, man?"

Chuck wheeled around, his brow wet with little dots of sweat and a maniacal grin on his face. "This is it, Randall!" he exclaimed, his voice unusually high and tinny. "I'm outta here!"

"What?!" I said, as a cold shiver ran over my arms. "You're not leaving?"

"Sure as shit," Chuck replied. "Everything's a go. I got my grant money, I got my tickets to New Guinea."

"B-but Chuck," I stammered, stunned to have my Chuck dilemma so instantly eliminated, "what do I do with . . .?" I took a dramatic half-step backward into the store, gesturing in a wide sweep toward all the stock I had meticulously organized, and ended up pointing indirectly at the goofy, mop-haired boy who was banging away at the register, obviously having forgotten how to get the money drawer to pop open.

"Do what you always do," Chuck said matter-of-factly, dropping a packed banker's box on his desk with a thump. "Run the store like a fuckin' genius. I haven't had anything to do with it for the last year anyway, right?"

"But Chuck!" I protested, almost making a peeping sound. "It's your store! How am I supposed to . . ."

"Not anymore," Chuck interrupted. "Tomorrow Iceberg's coming over, and I'm signing this turkey over to ya. Just like I promised." He leered at me—wildly, generously, foolishly.

a novel of sexual initiation 133

"Chuck," I said firmly, trying to sound as mature as possible. "This is crazy. This can't possibly be the way this kind of thing is done. Don't we have to go to City Hall or see a judge or something . . .?" I stopped at this point, my hands waving up above my head, because I was sure that I didn't know what I was talking about.

But it wasn't like Chuck would know, or care. He waved his hands in front of his face—our emotionalism was making us look like some nutty vaudevillian team—and cut me off by saying curtly, "Don't worry about it. Tomorrow, four p.m. Iceberg, you and me. Now get outta here and let me pack." Then he started whistling, and I knew that was all I would get out of him.

Next day, Thursday, quarter to four, I was standing behind the cash register chatting with Giselle. Ah, Giselle: talk about thinking about sex at work! I can't remember if I hired Giselle; I think she showed up one day when I was short of help, claiming to have worked for Chuck before and saying she came by at his request. But when did Chuck ever notice that I needed help? At any rate she stayed on. By that day when I was standing there as anxious as a bridegroom, waiting for Chuck and Iceberg to show up with the papers, she had become my assistant manager, more or less. She claimed a vaguely French heritage, sans accent, and had that dyed, ultra-black hair falling close to her eyes in thick bangs to prove it.

And those hip-hugging short skirts. Good God! The weird thing is, Giselle is the only woman I've ever actually known with a *Playboy* figure and a sex-kitten aura, yet in all these years of working at close quarters I've never laid a hand on her, or asked her out, or even seriously flirted. My only attraction to her has always been merely physical; we never had enough neurotic affinity to get involved. So, over the years Giselle and I have become good work buddies. I hardly knew her back then, when Diversions of Berkeley was about to be delivered into my naïve sole ownership (or so I thought).

The odd thing is how quickly it was all over. Precisely at four, Chuck bustled in with the heretofore mythic Iceberg at his side. At first I thought there'd been some kind of mistake; to this day

I'm still not used to the fact that Iceberg looks nothing like what he is. He's as stocky and bluntly developed as an NFL linebacker, but he's a tax attorney and business consultant, and nothing short of brilliant at that. He's always had this weird, tufted blonde hair that goes in all directions; it was a little longer back then, and he looked more counter-culture because he was fresh from passing the bar and not really into his groove as a lawyer. When he came in the door with Chuck, wearing a stretched-tight orange t-shirt and frayed khakis, carrying a well-scuffed brief-case that looked like a toy in his thick grip, I thought Chuck was playing some kind of a joke on me.

Standing beside Giselle behind the counter, I surreptitiously elbowed her and made a face in Iceberg's direction, but she was already mesmerized by his appearance. Was it his sea-blue eyes, his unsubtle masculinity, his buffed-out arms? Whatever the lure, Giselle was regarding Iceberg with an ever-widening smile as he and Chuck approached, shook hands with both of us, and made small talk before Chuck suggested that we three guys retire to his office and get the business done. I took one look back on that fateful short trip, only to see Giselle beaming broadly at me, one index finger idly tracing her cheek, her eyebrows arched to the heavens. *Good God.*

Once inside the office, Chuck brusquely slammed the door behind us, pulled out the drawer of his now vacant desk, and brought forth a single sheet of paper. "Here we go," he said excitedly, proffering a pen and the sheet to me, at which point I turned helplessly to Iceberg and said, "Are we doing this right?"

Iceberg rubbed his head roughly with one hand—*that's why his hair is all over the place*, I realized—and said, "Look, Chuck, I haven't looked over any of your stuff recently. We need to go over your taxes for last year, and check that you've renewed your business license, and . . ."

"Nope," Chuck barked, "you and Randall have to sort out all that stuff out later. Me, I'm flying out of Oakland tonight. I wrote up this statement here, says the business is all Randall's free and clear and so forth. You're the witness, Iceberg. If there's any problems later on, you can leave me a message after I get settled and send you a number from the island. OK?"

Iceberg rested his cheap briefcase on the table and seemed to lean on it, looking tired and frazzled. He picked up Chuck's fuzzily typed statement, entitled by him

TrANSFeR of BUSINESs OWneRSHIP:
DiverSions of Berkeley

and said, "I don't know, Chuck. This looks crazy. Why didn't you tell me what your schedule was?"

My sentiments exactly, I thought, feeling some hope for rescue.

"Look, guys," Chuck said, bridling with obvious irritation. "Either we all sign this thing and I'm outta here, or we don't sign it and I'm still outta here. I really don't give a fuck at this moment. I've been waiting twenty years to get my leg out of this goddamn trap, and I'm goin' tonight. Got that?"

Iceberg defensively held up two big hands in front of him, and replied, "All right, whatever you say, Chuck. Let's sign the thing and Randall and I will work everything out next week." He glanced at me sympathetically, adding hurriedly, "Chuck's already covered me for this, Randall. If you need me around when you're on your own, we'll make an arrangement later."

"Oh," I said in confusion, not quite getting it, then added "Sure. Of course." I cringed inwardly, realizing that I could have been going into hock for the rest of my life and not known it at that moment. Thank God Iceberg seemed trustworthy.

Chuck and I signed what might have proven to be a meaningless scrap of paper. We had no more done that than my ex-boss shook both our hands and rushed out of the office toward the store entrance, backtracking long enough to lean over the counter, buss Giselle lightly on the cheek and say, "Seeya 'round, honey!" Then he was gone.

Iceberg and I wandered up to Giselle, both of us shrugging our shoulders and sharing inarticulate expressions of amazement. The three of us stood there for ten minutes or so, laughing and telling Chuck tales while Iceberg assured me that everything would be just fine, we'd meet next week and sort it all out and that at any rate, I'd gotten a hell of a deal. Giselle was fawning over Iceberg with embarrassing obviousness; I couldn't figure it out. Although he wasn't that much older—maybe 28 to Giselle's 21?—he was clearly cut from less trendy stock. I couldn't imagine them ever becoming a lasting item. When Iceberg exited the front door, Giselle revealed that she had concluded the same, albeit with a twist:

"I think," she said matter-of-factly as she chewed the corner of a business card embossed with the name STANLEY EISENBERG, ATTORNEY-AT-LAW, "that I could sleep with him about, oh . . . three times."

THE MORAL of this story is that I've never known what's going on with my life, what's hidden beneath the obvious, and where things are headed—except that they're never going in quite the same direction I'm looking. If there was ever a time that proved this point conclusively, it was that second meeting with Iceberg, exactly a week after Chuck had left. He showed up again precisely at four, while Giselle and I were standing in almost the same spot as the last time. Except this time he came in with a big smile for Giselle before greeting me. I figured that she must already be one for three.

In the office—my office, finally—Iceberg opened up his briefcase and took out the papers that should have been reviewed the week before. Rapidly flipping and sorting them, apparently for the first time in a while, he kept reassuring me that everything was on the up and up, that Chuck's cheesy document giving me the business was more or less sound, and that he would make sure my new status as owner was nailed down with all the proper authorities. Then he stopped and stared intently at one sheet that appeared to be a private letter.

"Hey-o," Iceberg crooned in a peculiar, sing-songy tone, "there you go."

"What?" I said, leaning in close for a better look. "What is it? Where am I going?"

Iceberg leaned back in my creaky chair and held out the paper at arm's length, as if he were checking for a watermark.

a novel of sexual initiation

Then he turned his head up toward me, smiled oddly and said, "Looks like you have a silent partner."

"What do you mean?" I felt a sudden weakness in my knees.

"This letter from Bettina Berquist, Chuck's aunt, says that she retains a thirty percent interest in Diversions of Berkeley and all future subsidiaries until she's bought out. Chuck certainly never bought her out. So she's your partner now."

"What does that mean?" I whined. "I have to give her thirty percent of everything I make?"

"Not exactly," Iceberg said, pursing his lips. "You see, Chuck never made any money. In fact he kept borrowing from Etty to keep this place alive." Iceberg paused for a beat, then exclaimed, "Oh, shit."

"What?!" Now my heart was hammering in my chest. I didn't want to be where I was.

"It's just that I don't know how much dough Chuck is into Etty for, or if he's paid her back anything since you turned this place around. That little bugger. If he left you in arrears to his aunt. . ."

"Hold it!" I interrupted. "I'm really confused. First of all, who's Bettina? I only know about his grandmother Etty."

Iceberg looked me square in the eyes and blinked like a horse. "His grandmother?" he said quizzically. "Chuck doesn't have a grandmother living, so far as I know. His aunt's name is Bettina. Chuck calls her Etty. She raised him and all that, you know. Pretty rich lady, has quite a spread in Santa Fe."

My head was swimming. I was trying to figure out how I had stumbled into this job and ended up owing an indefinite amount of money, and a third of my business, to some woman of indistinct relationship to Chuck Berquist—a guy who was proving even more unreliable in his absence than he had in the flesh. Iceberg saw that I was about to panic, so he reverted to his reassuring mode and told me that he would thoroughly review the Chuck files over the next few days. He warned me that we'd have to communicate something pretty soon to Etty Berquist, Chuck's something-or-other, because it was a safe bet that Chuck hadn't bothered to tell her what was going down before splitting town.

I nodded my head a lot and thanked Iceberg profusely. Snapping shut his briefcase, he squeezed my right shoulder with one bearish hand and said, "Not to worry. Do what you do best, and I'll take care of the rest." It sounded like a line he was trying out for his fledgling career, but I liked the sound of it. Feeling a little better, I leaned against the door frame as Iceberg headed for the storefront, stopping to lean over the counter and kiss Giselle on the cheek. When Iceberg had exited a moment later, Giselle turned toward me, smiling triumphantly, and held up two fingers.

BECAUSE Pierce had been with me the day I first wandered into Diversions, it seemed appropriate to call him soon after I inherited the place. I couldn't wait to see his alarmed expression. By this time—summertime of '81—we'd been largely out of touch for six months, during which time Pierce had moved to the City and gotten a bank teller job. From brief phone encounters in which he had brushed me off with excuses about busyness and the crushing demands of decorating his new place, I inferred that he was undergoing yet another of his dramatic lifestyle changes. I wondered how his look would be altered this time.

It turned out that more than his look had changed. On a Saturday afternoon Pierce breezed in the door with a shorter, slighter white guy, both of them wearing almost identical black leather jackets. It's strange how quickly you can feel something; almost instantly I felt a pang of abandonment as I realized that Pierce had finally assumed his authentic gay identity and found a companion to explore it with. As always, Pierce had swung into his new identity 110%; he was wearing black leather motorcycle pants too, and had lots of little chains, latches, and oversized safety pins scattered all over him.

Pierce swept up to me at the counter where I was stocking a fresh shipment of the latest revision of Life, gave me a big hug (it was like being embraced by the upholstery of a hearse), and said, "My dear Mr. Chamber of Commerce! Meet my lover, Frankie."

Pierce's brown-eyed, curly-haired *lover* gave him a wry, sideways glance as he shook hands with me, and I said, "Frank. Just like my nephew."

"Yes," he said with a winning smile. "I hope so."

I laughed; he seemed quite clever. Within a few minutes of chatter we had established that Pierce and Frank had a very nice place in the Castro and that Frank, six years older than Pierce, managed a computer store in the financial district. He asked me if I had the store's inventory "on disk" yet, and I confessed that no, currently it was filed only in my head and frequently rearranged in my anxious dreams. Frank gave me his card and said, "Let me know when you're ready to modernize. I can give you a deal on a good system. No pressure, though." The softness with which he said that seemed to certify his sincerity. Pierce gave me a look that said, *What a find, eh?* I couldn't disagree; I felt good for Pierce.

In fact, by the time we three had a late lunch (at Edy's, for old times' sake) I felt almost envious of my high school chum. I had a brand-new lover too, but I was slow to admit it. I felt embarrassed somehow that Lainie was an old acquaintance from the South, as if I hadn't succeeded in finding an authentic California girlfriend.

But it was a good visit, and by the time we shared a round of hugs, promising to catch a movie together soon in their neighborhood, I felt remarkably buoyant and optimistic. It was good to feel good. Despite the fact that Iceberg had been in frequent touch by phone and seemed to be working things out for me, I hadn't been able to escape a sense of entrapment about the business. Everyone seemed impressed that I had a going concern under my own name at the tender age of twenty-one, but I was all too aware that it owed chiefly to my compulsion to stay busy, and to Chuck's compulsion to be weird.

Add to this professional foreboding my growing sense of rootlessness. I hardly lived in my own apartment anymore, sleeping with Lainie every night and hanging out at her place when I wasn't at work. I wasn't sure if I was in love, or just hormonally possessed.

Frank and Pierce lifted my spirits so much that day that when I sauntered back to the store at 4:30, suddenly cognizant of the balminess of an early summer day, I told Giselle and the part-timer to skip out and I shut the place down an hour and a half early. Never before (and not many times since) was I so impetuous.

I walked directly to Lainie and Jeanna's, about six or seven blocks from downtown. It so happened that as I came close to their apartment building I spotted the two of them sitting side-by-side on lawn chairs out front, on a concrete apron descending to the sidewalk. From the angle I was approaching, they couldn't see me, and they didn't expect me at this hour. That's how I surprised them, both sitting there smoking. I had actually cried out, "Hey there, ladies!" before I realized that I had not seen Lainie smoking since high school. When she turned and saw me she literally jumped in her chair, flung the cigarette to the concrete and ground it out with her sandal. Jeanna looked on bemusedly, drawing long and casually on her own smoke.

It's odd, but I can't remember Jeanna ever smoking again. She was probably doing it to be companionable; she often went out of her way to help Lainie feel comfortable. Looking back, I wish I'd followed Jeanna's example more often.

Mussing Lainie's hair with one hand as I came up, I wondered why she was looking at me so wide-eyed. I sat on a low brick wall around a dried-out garden space and said casually, "No smoking in the house, eh?"

Jeanna exhaled like a movie star and smiled at me. "Nope. August says it drives out peaceful spirits. But she burns sage for purification."

I nodded gamely like this might mean something to me, noticing again that Lainie looked spooked. "Are you all right?" I asked her.

"Are you gonna be mad at me?" she said meekly.

"Mad at you?" I glanced worriedly at Jeanna; I didn't want her to think there was some kind of problem in my relationship so soon.

"Yeah," Lainie said defensively. "Because I smoke. I wasn't doing it around you, was I?"

"What?" I said, uncomfortable being treated as an inquisitor.

a novel of sexual initiation **141**

"I mean, no. What does it matter? You can smoke. I don't care."

Lainie relaxed in her chair but still regarded me nervously. "Well, you *useta* care."

"I did?" I said innocently.

"Yeah!" Lainie exclaimed. "Don't you remember? SMOKING IS STOO-PID," she boomed suddenly, miming the stretch of a banner against the open blue sky.

Now I remembered. In a fit of sophomoric priggishness back in my only year of Georgia high school, I had gotten involved with an anti-smoking campaign sponsored by the Young Civitans or the Junior Rotary. I'm sure this was because JoEllen was a Civitette or a Rotarette; she was the joiner type, not me. But it was definitely she and I who helped unfurl that ridiculous banner in the main school building's interior courtyard, in front of the whole student body. How ridiculous! Lainie's memory was phenomenal.

"Oh, that," I said dismissively. "Jesus. I don't care, Lainie. Really. As long as you don't smoke in bed."

Jeanna giggled, apparently reading something into what I'd said. "Oh, yeah?" she intoned seductively.

I blushed. "I mean, because she could start a fire."

Now Jeanna reached over and touched Lainie's arm. "Didja hear that, cuz? Don't go starting any *fires* in bed." Lainie laughed, obviously relieved to be off the hook, as Jeanna cackled on: "Do your smoking afterward, like everybody else."

Only later did I realize how thoroughly Lainie had been covering her tracks. I hadn't ever noticed smoke on her, not since high school. Later that day the taste of it got into my mouth from her mouth, and I found its musty tang oddly erotic.

13

IS IT terrible to admit that, out of almost seven years of being with Lainie, many of my most pleasant memories come from the year before we lived together? It's not just that we were new to each other. It also had to do with seeing a lot of Jeanna.

Jeanna and I were curiously parallel. Her relationship to August seemed to be purely about their emotional dependence on each other. Lainie and I would develop a similar magnetic bind, an oppositional stickiness, rather than any real compatibility. Lainie, for instance, had little of a political view about the world. In the numerous group discussions that went on in that apartment—often in which I was the only man among five or six women in informal dinner parties—Jeanna and I always turned out to be the two people who had actually read the newspaper or *Mother Jones* recently, and had something informed to say about the world. Admittedly Jeanna was to my left, seeing as how a few of my Southern roots still tickled conservative bedrock.

August generally kept her silence until something related to sexual politics piqued her interest. Then she would rumble forth like a volcano about the sins and iniquities of the "ruling patriarchal consciousness," evoking righteous affirmations from any witching pals who might be visiting. This was my cue to hold my tongue for a while, since I was, by dint of physiology, the only representative of the patriarchy present.

And yet, over the first nine or ten months of my hanging out with "the girls," as I mentally referred to them, August and I managed to achieve an almost amiable detente. We chatted guardedly sometimes, like two opposing generals from some 18th-century war who might meet over a chessboard during a lull in combat, trying to psych each other out.

I remember going over to the apartment on a Sunday and encountering August at home alone, sitting in the living room, listening to Holly Near on the record player. After killing a few minutes in Lainie's empty room, deciding against napping while I waited on Lainie and Jeanna to return from a shopping trip, I came back into the common room and sat down in Jeanna's raggedy chair, smiling gamely without making eye contact with August. I let my eyes roam over the room until I focused on the huge amateurish painting of an African princess over the mantel. It was one of the main things I'd noticed in the apartment on my first day there, but its origin and subject remained a mystery to me. I tried to make a little parlor conversation:

"Hey, August, who did that painting?"

"I did," she said aggressively, as if accepting a dare.

"Really?" I replied, genuinely surprised. "It's, uh, really nice. Who is it?"

"In zinger," August replied, or so I heard.

"A zinger?" I responded, confused.

August rolled her eyes and spelled out "N-z-i-n-g-a. The warrior queen of Angola. She fought off the Portuguese colonizers in the seventeenth century."

"Wow," I said, genuinely impressed. "I didn't know there were warrior queens in Africa."

"Well, there *weren't*," August said forcefully, obviously warming to her subject but still eyeing me warily. "That's what made her so great. Sometimes to fool the other tribes she dressed like a male warrior. And she kept a group of male sex slaves that she forced to dress like women."

"Oh, come on," I said. "You're pulling my leg."

"No!" August insisted. "I read about her in a book on all the great queens of history. Nzinga had lots of slaves, male and female. It was the way you did things back then if you were the head of a tribe. Once, when she went to negotiate with a Portuguese official, she took a slave with her to use as a chair. The white man didn't let the Africans sit in their houses, so Nzinga sat on one of her slaves who was on all fours. At the end of the meeting she left the slave there to prove she had plenty of

a novel of sexual initiation   **145**

chairs." August was beaming, as if she had personally counseled the warrior queen to make that ancient display of arrogance.

"How charming," I said sardonically, unable to suppress a smile. "Was it a male or female slave?"

"Who?" August asked guardedly.

"Was it a male or female slave that Nzinga left in the Portuguese chump's living room?"

August shifted in her chair, like a general unexpectedly checked on the chessboard. "Well, I'm not sure," she admitted. "Probably a male slave."

Or maybe not. I just went to the UC library today—twelve or thirteen years after that little chat—and found out for sure. (This is the kind of thing that engages my attention now, when I should be working.) Anyway, it's recorded that it was a maidservant—who could have been in drag, I suppose—that Nzinga left behind. Some versions of the story say she had the chair-slave killed to prove there were always more human furnishings where that one came from. Some feminist icon! I almost feel like calling up August and letting her know, but I guess that would be bizarre. June says that the purpose of a personal history like this is to make my own peace with the past, not to settle scores. I'm not always sure what the difference is.

I guess I have to make peace with the fact that I would have been happier moving in with the girls than having Lainie move in with me. There, I said it. When I look back on it, relating to the three of them was more balanced and fulfilling than any one-on-one relationship I've had since. Lainie and I were griddle-hot sexual partners; Jeanna and I were intellectual peers and almost-soulmates, I wistfully believed; and August and I were loyal antagonists on the battleground of sexual politics. I could have lived with the girls forever.

But August would have none of that. After a while she began making it plain that she didn't like me around the apartment. To be truthful, Lainie had been bugging me for months to sleep over at my apartment more often, although she always said it was a depressing place when we did. (I didn't have any plants, I didn't cook much, I never cleaned up.) Once Jeanna took me

MY JOURNEY THROUGH THE PLANT WORLD

aside, graciously trying not to hurt my feelings, and told me that I really shouldn't regard their apartment as a place I could drop in without warning. I'd had a copy of Lainie's key made, and Jeanna said August was especially unhappy about that.

More than anything else, what got the message through my head was a strange encounter I had with Jeanna and August. Somehow the three of us were in the apartment one afternoon, while Lainie was out. Coming out of the bathroom, I almost bumped into the two women in the hallway. For all her bulk, August was flattened against the wall, and Jeanna was leaning over her. Their faces were very close. Jeanna had one forearm against the wall above August's head, with the fingers of her other hand playing behind August's ear. It was a posture of seductive power, one I would have only associated with a man before that moment. When both Jeanna and August peered coldly and wordlessly at me, I finally understood that I was an interloper in their intimate territory.

I not only hustled myself out of the apartment at that moment; I began mentally laying plans for living with Lainie. It's not that I was really excited by the prospect; it was just that I knew Lainie should get out of the apartment too. The obvious thing to do was to move in with me. Why was it so obvious? I wish I could look back and say that we had so much to look forward to together. Wouldn't that be nice?

But if I'd been asked for the truth and nothing but the truth, I would have said, "Lainie couldn't make it without me." And that's what I really believed, so help me God.

OH — I ALMOST forgot: the love of my life! Livvy! The aging Swedish movie star, Liv Ullman: that was the *nom de fume* of my first and classic automobile, the red lady who would prove to be such a reliable sinkhole for my discretionary funds all throughout the '80s. When I first saw her, I was taking an angry walk through town, going nowhere in particular, trying to shake off the chagrin of realizing that Jeanna and August thought of me as a squatter in their apartment.

I hadn't really talked seriously to Lainie about the situation.

The subject of living together had come up but I hadn't yet devised a firm schedule for it. Back then I never had a serious discussion with Lainie until my decisions were essentially made. Now I know from counseling that that's unfair and imperialistic, but hey, I was in my early twenties back then. I can cut myself some slack in hindsight, can't I?

So there I was, walking along Shattuck Avenue out toward the Berkeley Bowl produce market, and I came upon a corner lot, full of used cars, that bore the sign BUGGY BUFFET. I puzzled over this name for a second or two, trying to figure out the auto-culinary connection. Then I saw her: a faded crimson, crumply-bumpered Volvo with racy, fender-mounted rearview mirrors—a rounded-off sedan of the dated style that seemed so popular in Berkeley at the time. I'd noticed the old Volvos around town before and wondered why that particular vintage was so wide-spread, but *this*—this was love at first sight.

A sign in the rear window clinched it for me:

RARE MODEL
1967 123GT, Domestic Swedish
Performance Model
LOW MILES
Second Owner Must Sell

When I asked at the tiny office shack set against one side of the car lot, it turned out that the "buffet" referred to the fact that you could sample any of the cars right then and there, as long as you left some kind of security deposit. The owners were selling the cars; Buggy Buffet was a broker. I didn't have a credit card yet, but I left my wallet except for my driver's license, and probably promised the guy my first-born, in order to borrow the keys and take the machine out for a spin.

She didn't start well, the clutch was shot, and she needed a tune-up, but on my first ten- or twelve-block foray at the wheel of Liv Ullmann I was happy as a clam. Suddenly my whole life felt resolved: if I had a car of my own, Lainie could move in with me. And of course I was ready to own my own business! In the same way that learning to drive had catalyzed my sexual initiation, buying my own car would inaugurate my adult lifestyle.

Up to this point, if the truth be told, I had been behaving like a petulant baby bird pushed out of the nest before I felt like going. I was peeved with my mom for wanting to live without me. I think that had a lot to do with the shabby shape of my apartment and the way I had glommed onto the girls as a collective surrogate. I remember thinking: *If I put the three of them together in my mind, do they equal my mother?* But this line of thinking evoked disturbing sexual images, so I dropped it.

Two days later I met Livvy's owner at the car lot. Drexel was a mild-mannered, bald, self-deprecating chap in his late thirties who told me that he had shipped the car over from Sweden, meaning to restore it to its full glory in his garage. "But my wife had twins instead." He grimaced when he said it. "I love this car," he sighed. "But, you know, first things first. Priorities." The tone of his voice suggested that it would take a while before his little twins proved to be of greater value than the sacrifice at hand.

Drexel wanted $3500 for Liv, a princely sum to me at the time, and I can proudly say that I wasn't a total mark. It did occur to me that a car that rare hardly belonged in a used-car lot on the funky end of Shattuck Avenue. But my pulse kept racing through the day. In the evening I called Iceberg and described the whole situation to him, leaning hard on the car's classy vintage. After taking in the whole story, Iceberg said simply, "Sounds like money down a rathole to me. Also sounds like you're gonna buy it anyway." He gave me the name of a freelance mechanic, Greg Sykes, who specialized in Volvos and could give me the straight poop on the car's real condition.

I didn't waste any time. I convinced Drexel that I needed the car for a thorough tryout over the next weekend, and took it to Sykes on a Saturday morning. Lainie was with me; we'd slept over at my place for a change. Sykes, who lived near Lake Merritt in Oakland, turned out to be a Richard Gere-like guy with a dark brooding look and wavy black hair. His prognosis on Liv's condition: "If she weren't a 123, I'd say leave her where you found her. If you want a project, we could have some fun restoring her.

a novel of sexual initiation 149

Someday you might get back a piece of what you'll put into her."

Thinking back on it, I hear nothing but trouble in that evaluation. But who pays attention to a realistic assessment of an infatuation? Thanking Sykes and making an appointment with him a couple weeks later for Liv's first physical therapy, I slipped back into the car. Lainie was playing with the control knobs on the dash.

"Greg says go for it," I said cheerily.

Lainie looked out the windshield at Sykes and said simply, "Cute." I thought she was talking about the car.

We bucked and backfired over to Albany to see my mom. Lainie and my mother got along famously; I think it was a relief for Mom to see me bonding to someone, even someone who was distinctly lower-class back in our native state. Perhaps I wanted to show Mom the car to let her know that all was forgiven, that it was all right she had booted me out of her life because now I had a great car. It's humiliating to recall it that way, but there it is.

I hadn't seen much of my mother for a few months, not just because I was petulant but also because I hadn't had use of the station wagon for a while and Albany was a long bus ride away. I thought she'd be more excited about my new vehicle than she was. When I booped the horn in the driveway, she came out, looked at it, and endured about five minutes of my car talk before inviting us in for coffee cake with her housemate Gayle.

That's when it dawned on me, long after it should have. Perhaps it took all those hours of hanging out at the girls' apartment, absorbing the gestalt of a lesbian atmosphere, before I could perceive that my mother's arrangement with Gayle was more than one of convenience. To this day I don't know if they were involved before Gayle moved in. Now I think of my mother as an adult-onset lesbian; she certainly wasn't born that way. I think my father was just too much to take over the years.

At any rate, the recognition hadn't fully coalesced for me until that morning with the coffee cake and the four of us at the table—once again, just me and the girls chatting. This was getting to be a pattern in my life. There was some way in which Mom and Gayle were smiling at each other that wasn't merely the companionship of two women at fifty, both separated from their husbands. Wait, I know what it was: they were deliberately not touching each other, but they *almost* were. Here was a new entry in the Kay Code.

Once I got it, I was sure that Lainie had understood for a while. Lainie was quick. She must have known—because when we got back in the car after the kaffee klatsch, I thumped the steering wheel and said, with mock outrage, "Is the whole world turning gay?" and Lainie said impishly:

"I'm not."

"I'm glad," I growled, pinching her thigh before starting the car. Then a wave of impulse washed over me. "Lainie," I said while gunning the engine, not looking at her, "you remember what we were talking about the other night? About staying over at my place more often?"

"Yeah?" she answered, faintly.

"Well, I've been thinking about—that maybe it would be easier, I mean better for everyone if, you know, you were just staying at my place." Perhaps because I didn't know I was going to say it, I wasn't sure of what I had said exactly. I wished I could withdraw, review, and revise my words.

Lainie was silent. I stared at the vibrating gearshift knob for a moment before I got up the nerve to look over at her. She was rapidly looking at me and then out the windshield, back and forth. She was also biting her lower lip. I guess she didn't know what to say either, because what she came out with after a little while was even more awkward than my clumsy proposition.

"Well," she said weakly, "I guess it's easier to move my stuff now, since you'll have this car and everything."

I smiled wanly, feeling sorry for both of us, sorry for the way in which we had to leave out huge chunks of communication in order to get anywhere at all with each other. It was partly a Southern thing, this indirection around our real feelings, and it was partly just us, but it would always be that way.

"OK," I said simply, backing the car out of the driveway. Nothing else was said inside Liv Ullmann until we were back in Berkeley proper. Then, while we were idling at a stoplight,

a novel of sexual initiation

Lainie leaned over and stuck her tongue in my ear, giggling happily. I knew that we were back on even keel again. Nothing delicate would have to be said for a while, no emotional discomfort acknowledged or surmounted.

Sure, we buried a lot of truth that way — truth that would have to surface later disfigured, starved for air, and furious with both of us. But by no means was the inarticulate bargain we struck that day the worst ever made by two young folks on God's wobbly earth.

14

MY LIFE happens in clumps, it really does. Nothing at all happens for long boring stretches, then something happens that knocks into something else, like dominoes, and things clatter along lickety-split for a while. That's the way it was the fall and winter of 1981. I bought the car by dipping my hand into the Diversions till, although I was later chastised by Iceberg for it. Lainie moved in to my dumpy one-bedroom apartment, bringing in plants and flowers, and hanging curtains and doing other housewifely things. Not long after that, we both met Etty Berquist.

Must have been in January of '82; I remember heavy rain as Lainie and I scurried across the parking lot of the Claremont Hotel late on a Friday afternoon. I was jumpy as a flea. Acting as my legal representative, Iceberg had informed Etty of Chuck's departure (she'd heard nothing, as it turned out) and put several questions to her in correspondence. Her attorney had answered by deferring all inquiries until Etty could meet with me in person. Furthermore, she required that Iceberg not be present at our first meeting, a condition that riled him considerably.

"Don't sign anything!" he urgently drilled into my ear over the phone. "Don't make any verbal agreements either. Tell her you're open to any of her requests, but you can't make any commitments until you've talked them over with me. If she won't deal with me directly, then I'll deal with her lawyer. And look for openings to get her out of the business completely, Randall. She's got the resources to pull a fast one on you and leave you with nothing to show for all your work. She seems more like Chuck every time I have to deal with her. You know: nutty and unreliable. The more distance you can put between you and her, the better. Be careful."

From the moment we met Etty sitting in the bar overlooking the East Bay, it seemed like I was taking every wrong step there could be. Knowing she was red-haired, I recognized her at a window-lit corner table right away.

I strode over to her confidently and said, "Etty?" immediately regretting my use of her familiar.

As she stood and unfolded all of her bone-thin, six-foot-plus frame, she seemed to be bristling. "Bettina Berquist," she corrected me, proffering a slim, age-spotted hand bearing a substantial turquoise ring. "You must be Mr. Randall Kendricks. And . . . ?" she said condescendingly in Lainie's direction, as if she really meant to say: *And what is this?*

"Lainie," I choked, trying to remember what Lainie was short for. The only word that came to mind was *lanolin*, and I knew that couldn't be right. I got so flustered that I inadvertently allowed Lainie a moment to respond on her own.

"McEwen," Lainie offered, her accent especially noticeable as she said *kew-inn*. To my great embarrassment she added, "Nice to meetcha."

Bettina Berquist smiled painfully at the corners of her lips before inquiring coldly, "And your relationship to Diversions of Berkeley is exactly what, Lana?"

Lainie flashed me a panicked look. The older woman's revision of her name didn't seem to be an accident, and Lainie was by no means equipped to play a convincing hand in a game of social intimidation. Nor was I for that matter, but I didn't have any choice. The least I could do was run interference on behalf of Lainie's innocence and shaky self-esteem.

"Lainie," I pronounced emphatically, "is my . . ." (*now what?!* I thought frantically) "my *personal companion.*"

Oh, Christ. If I hadn't known that the game was lost already, Bettina Berquist's half-suppressed grin let me know that she was in control of the field and any further tactical moves on my part would be ruthlessly quashed. I was outclassed in every respect, including the physical. This sixty-ish representative of the ruling class not only had seniority, she also had a few inches on me

a novel of sexual initiation 155

in height. She made Lainie look like a munchkin.

To make matters worse, my personal companion and I were horrendously underdressed. Lainie had put on a dark skirt, stockings, and a nice purple blouse for the occasion; heretofore I had thought she looked civilized. Here in the Claremont lounge, she looked like a bargain basement shopper. And me: a real disaster area! I was wearing black jeans and my only sports-coat, the elbow-patched corduroy job of my father's that Lainie had first seen when she spied on JoEllen and me in the Kissing Booth, lo those many years ago in high school. I was critically in need of a fashion update.

On the other hand, Berquist herself wasn't exactly a model of conservative tailoring. Indeed, her style of dress was not far shy of bizarre, but it clearly breathed money. She was wearing a matching vest and pants of off-white leather, finely tooled with Southwestern sand-painting figures stitched on all the pockets, and a filmy, see-through pink blouse that revealed her bony breastplate and bra wherever it was not covered by the vest. And cowboy boots! In passing I thought that only Pierce could compete with this woman for sheer fashion bravado. If only he had her budget!

"How sweet," Bettina said, snapping me out of my sartorial review, apparently responding to my lame identification of Lainie. "Lana, Randall, please have a seat. Would you like margaritas?"

Ouch. The condescension in her voice was such that Bettina might as well have said, *Would you kids like some Kool-Aid?* I resolved to speak only when spoken to, and whatever came down, to let Iceberg recover my losses on the legal front. Lainie, on the other hand, looked quite happy to have a drink ordered for her. No doubt it was another first in her catalog of West Coast experiences. I nodded that we'd go along. When Bettina signaled the cocktail waitress to come over, the young woman snapped to like her future depended on it. *Bettina Berquist must be known around here*, I thought. *Boy, am I in over my head.* It came to mind that I might as well drop to all fours and let Bettina make the best possible use of me, like a chair of Nzinga's.

"Randall, I'm aware thatyou may not be clear on the precise

relationship between myself and the business founded by my nephew Charles. I wanted to meet you in person to assure you that, whatever Charles may have told you before he decided to surprise us all and leave the country, I will not interfere in your day-to-day operations. You'll have a free hand to run the store as you see fit. While I was not pleased that Charles transferred the business without consulting me, I understand you've achieved quite a turnaround of the store for someone so inexperienced."

"Thank you, Ms. Berquist," I said politely, artfully accepting her continuing deprecations, determined not to fumble again.

"Please, you may call me Etty."

Fine, I thought edgily. *How about you calling my girlfriend by her real name?* But I said nothing, glancing over at Lainie to see her staring wide-eyed at the rim of salt on her just-delivered margarita. Obviously she didn't know what to do about it. When she finally started flicking it off onto the table a few moments later, I had to look away. A pertinent question had come to mind:

"Etty, do you mind if I ask you a personal question about you and Chuck, er, Charles?"

"Not at all."

"Well, he had a curious habit of referring to you as his grandmother. In fact, that's who I thought you were until my attorney clarified the situation after Chuck left. Was there any particular reason he would do that?"

Etty swallowed hard and blushed. "His grandmother?" she said, her voice faltering for the first time. "Why on earth would he say that?"

I raised my hands from the table in exasperation and shrugged dramatically, like Etty and I had always been on the same team, then replied, "I really don't know. He also said that he never meant to be a businessman, but you didn't want him to go to school until after he'd run a successful shop. I couldn't figure out why you required him to keep at it so long."

"What do you mean?" Etty responded, her eyes narrowing in consternation. "What else did Charles tell you?"

"Well," I said, warming to my sudden power in the conversation, "he said he was prevented from pursuing his field studies in

a novel of sexual initiation

anthropology by your requirement that he run Diversions. He left after the time was up because he said he got his grant and he was out from under his obligation to you. He said you sent over private eyes to make sure he kept running the business. He said you . . ."

I stopped because Etty's martini glass was shaking in her hand, and when she set it down it rattled slightly on the table. Lainie looked at me conspiratorially, the bottom half of her face hidden behind the nearly drained glass tilted to her lips.

There was a distinctly uncomfortable pause. When Etty spoke again her voice was low and strained: "That little trickster. That ungrateful son of a bitch." She noticed Lainie's shocked look and, composing herself, said, "Pardon my French, dear. Would you like another?"

Lainie nodded her head up and down in childish enthusiasm. I was hardly drinking; I was too fascinated by the turn of the conversation. Etty returned her attention to me, a tone of dignified sadness now coloring her voice.

"I'm sorry, Randall, I'm just a little shocked by Charles' lies. I don't know why I should be surprised. When my sister and her husband were killed in an air crash and Charles ended up with me, he already had some problems. He was twelve at the time. All his teachers said he made up the most awful stories about the other kids, about me, even about his poor parents. Once he told his class that his parents were hijackers who crashed the plane they died on. I figured he was in such terrible grief at a tender age that I didn't want to put any more pressures on him, and of course, I had businesses to run . . ."

She paused and looked almost tenderly at Lainie, happily accepting her second margarita from the waitress. "I never intended to be a single mother, or a mother at all! I guess I didn't pay enough attention to Charles. He was in a lot of trouble in high school, mostly with these outrageous lies. Once he reported the principal to the authorities as a grave robber." Etty stopped as if she were about to laugh, but instead looked mournfully into my eyes, her thin, lined face showing some vulnerability for the first time. Her eyes were a pale watery gray, and her skin showed the experience of long exposure to the sun.

"If you don't mind my asking," I interjected, "what exactly was the situation with the store? Was it true that you wouldn't allow him to go to the University?"

Etty shook her head vigorously and grimaced. "Of course not. Charles couldn't have gotten into Berkeley if his life depended on it. His academic record was hopeless. He begged me to let him leave Santa Fe and live in California, and do his independent studies, as he called them. I asked him what he would do for money, and he said he'd like to run a store if I would set him up. That was easy enough. Why he just sat there like a mole for so long is beyond me. Every time he'd ask me for help, I felt so guilty I couldn't refuse him."

"So there was no stipulation that he had to. . ." I inquired, still puzzling over the complexity of Chuck's fiction.

"Heavens no," Etty interrupted with a sigh. "Where he got that is beyond me." Pushing away her empty glass and smiling almost fondly at Lainie, who grinned back, her eyes sparkling, Etty straightened her posture and seemed to regain some of her former reserve.

"At any rate," she continued briskly, "the good news is that you're a bright young businessman with a going concern. I'm glad that we'll be associated in the future, and you should feel free to contact me for assistance at any time. If you ever want to expand, I could be quite helpful."

"Well," I said hesitantly, amazed at Etty's celerity, "as a matter of fact, my attorney and I are not quite sure of exactly how things stand, you know, legally speaking . . . with your interest in the store and everything." *That sounded dumb*, I chided myself.

"Oh, don't worry about all that right now," Etty said, picking up a white leather handbag off the floor. "Our lawyers can work that out. I just wanted to see you in person and determine that the situation is in reliable hands. I'm certain now that it is, Randall."

"Thank you, Etty, but I . . ."

"There's just one thing," she interrupted, standing and hoisting the handbag strap over her right shoulder. "I will need you to come to Santa Fe soon to discuss in detail how Diversions fits

a novel of sexual initiation   **159**

into my investment portfolio overall." Etty turned to face Lainie
and said, "It'll be a boring business trip, Lana, so you needn't feel
compelled to come." Then, back at me, with her officiousness in
full voice: "Will there be any problem with that, Randall?"

"No, m'am," I said, the latter anachronism popping out
before I could stop myself. In fact, I was alarmed and confused.
But Bettina Berquist looked pleased. "Wonderful. I'll write and
give you a date and send the airfare. Lana, it was so nice to meet
you. You seem like a very sweet personal companion."

Lainie beamed glassily at her but didn't rise; it was clear that
she was six sheets to the wind on those two margaritas. Lainie
was a little person, after all. I stood and shook Etty's hand, and
then she walked swiftly into the main hallway of the Claremont.

When Lainie and I got back into the car, I leaned my head
against the steering wheel. "Who *are* these people?" I moaned. "I
thought Chuck was nuts, but now. . . What do you think she
means about Diversions 'fitting into her investment portfolio'?
It sounds like she owns me lock, stock, and barrel." I turned to
Lainie as if she would be ready with a detailed answer, but she
was slumped and squirming sideways in her seat, pulling her
skirt up obscenely high, flashing her panties.

"Lainie!" I barked, reaching over to pull her skirt down, nervously glancing out the side window to see if anyone was nearby.
Thank God it was dark and rainy. "I think you had too much to
drink."

"I *luv* mah-ga-*ree*-tas," she cooed.

"Yes," I said, laughing in spite of myself, "I can see that."

Lainie put on a mock-serious face, sat up in her seat, and
asked, "Is a personal companion, like, somebody you're just
doing it with?" Then she reached down and cunningly pulled
her skirt back up an inch.

I laid a hand on her leg just above the knee, unexpectedly
thrilled by the feel of her nylons. "Please, Lana, let's wait until
we get home."

Lainie chortled, thrust her pelvis into the air and came back
down hard on the seat, shaking the car all over. "I *love* being
Lana!" she cried.

15

THIS JOURNAL disturbs me sometimes for what it causes me to remember, but at this point it's disturbing because it asks me to remember what I cannot. That is the everyday reality, the texture, the tone of living with Lainie for six years—especially the first few years when everything was basically all right with us. Or perhaps it never really was all right, and that's why I can recall so little. It's just that the first few years were less troubled than the last few.

It seems important to get this right because I don't want to fall prey to negative revisionism. I don't want to vilify the past in order to shore up some belief in the Better Way of the present. In truth, I don't have a better way presently. I am hardly living any way at all now, obsessed as I am with review and regret. Yet somehow I feel compelled to defend the virtues of the past. . .

Oh, Christ—I know what's bugging me. It's that goddamn letter from Anna that came a couple months after Lainie and I met Etty. Just the sight of the envelope made me feel guilty. To my surprise Anna had proved to be a faithful correspondent since she left, sending me two- or three-page missives every few months, a serial digest of her continuing adventures that I came to think of as the Colorado News & Review. Over time, I'd lost interest in responding and resorted to the same treatment I'd given JoEllen's correspondence: postcard rejoinders. Or sometimes, like when I moved to my apartment, a half-sheet note giving her my new address and bragging on my life advancements.

Not that Anna's letters had been particularly revealing. Sometimes it was all she could do to keep me up with her wanderings, which were frequent but limited to the Rocky Mountain State after her California adventure. She lived in Denver and then in Aspen, and waitressed at a cowboy diner in Rifle for six months (where some "wild goings-on" went on, as she obliquely put it), before finally returning to her home base of Colorado Springs. I'd gotten a couple of letters from there by the time Lainie and I moved in together. Now that I think about it, they'd already been getting weird. She kept talking about going to church for the first time in her life, and all the wonderful new friends she had there. But nothing could have prepared me for The Sin Letter. I'm going to dig it out and paste it in for the record:

Dear Randall,

Hello again. How are you doing? I am writing with some good news and some bad news, although in a way it is all Good News. First, guess what: I am engaged to be married! I don't know what to say about it except THANK THE LORD. Truly I feel like I have been wandering in the wilderness for a long time and now God has shown me the way Home. And He has given me this wonderful man, Kenneth, an associate pastor at the church with such a bright future of service that he wants to share with me. I am so happy, Randall, and I hope you are happy for me too.

It was nice to hear about your new/old friend Lainie in your life, and I hope you will tell me more about her soon!

All right, now I have to say the hard part. . . because Kenny says it is important if I am to go on with my life. Randall, I don't know how to say this, but I realize now that when we met I led you into sin. You know, the sleeping together, which was not just my idea but I should have known better. Kenny says I must apologize to you even if you are not yet saved. He says that if I do my part it will help you confess to Our Savior and find your own way to a new life washed in the Blood of the Lamb.

I am not going into the details of our sinning together because I have done that already with our minister and he says they are forgiven. But from the bottom of my heart I apologize for having led you astray. I hope you will forgive me.

Randall, just between us there is always a little part of my heart which belongs to you. I'm pretty sure that is not a sin.

Pure love,

Anna

a novel of sexual initiation   163

Pure love, my ass! It is a measure of the severe apoplexy that this letter caused me on its arrival that it still evokes an irate vibration in me today. I shook all over then, and I shake a little now. At the very time I was establishing a new life with Lainie on uncertain emotional terms, Anna deeply contaminated the memory of my first romance, a cornerstone of my sexual history. What I liked to recall as a secretive hothouse affair was now a *sin*, in her eyes—a sin that she had apparently confessed in detail to her fiancé and some busybody preacher.

Boy, I bet those repressed fundamentalists hung on every word! Exactly what did she emphasize, I wondered: the first time? Or the second time, on New Year's? How about that time in the spring, not long before Anna left me, when we were kissing behind the tool shed at home while my parents were in the house, and she unzipped me, fished me out and made me come, while we kept kissing, right there, standing up? Did she tell them how I fertilized the fuchsia and we had to immediately hose the stuff off the flowers lest my mother discover it? Did she tell them *that*, for Christ's sake? The sheer betrayal of it all!

I was shaken. I really needed to tell someone about Anna's letter, but there was no one to turn to. It wasn't the kind of thing I would bring up with Lainie. We hadn't discussed my sexual history because I think she was avoiding having to tell me hers, the sordidness of which I could well imagine, considering all the high school rumors. To tell the truth, I would have most wanted to talk with Jeanna, and get her sharp insights. In my mind's eye I could see her sympathetic expression—although I could see her laughing a little too—and then I could imagine us talking for hours about sex, love, and intimacy. It seemed so possible . . .

But Jeanna was virtually quarantined from Lainie and me at the time, August having reclaimed her attention full-time since I had been successfully exiled with Lainie in tow. Jeanna had dropped by our place a couple times to check it out and talk with Lainie, but always left quickly, as if her absence from home might be missed.

Pierce! Yes, now I realize that Pierce would have loved The Sin Letter. But he wasn't around much either, considering his

MY JOURNEY THROUGH THE PLANT WORLD

full-time gay-liberation life in the City. During 1982 I actually saw more of Frank, as he made good on his promise to computerize Diversions at a very fair price. In February he came over and assessed the situation, then got right back to me with an estimate and a very impressive graphic presentation of a computer system that would magically accelerate my ordering and inventory processes, and, "keeping an eye on the future," as he said in his soft but compelling way, allow me to organize and track the progress of additional branches of the store.

Frank had no sooner brought up that notion than Iceberg called to set up an appointment to discuss the same possibility. His correspondence with Etty's lawyers indicated that her investment firm, Southwestern Ventures, was prepared to stake me to branch expansion as soon as we could present a convincing plan of action and a couple of site suggestions. Iceberg was developing some commercial real estate connections and seemed excited by the potential of the situation. By then he seemed less worried about Etty's potential to manipulate me, having been convinced of her good intentions by the investment dollars they were dangling in front of both of us. I guess he saw his retainer growing.

Frankly, I was amazed and sometimes disquieted that all this business development seemed to be speeding along without my instigation or control. On the other hand there seemed to be no reason to put a stop to it. Running the store and scheming with Iceberg kept me busier than ever, and that meant that I could effectively quash any personal anxieties that might demand attention.

The Sin Letter had me going for a couple days, but I guess I just stuffed it. What did it really matter, after all, what Anna called a sin? (It matters now, of course, now that I am excavating every feeling I ever buried; it's all that burying that has made this journal necessary. Now I'm a grave robber.)

By early 1983, Diversions' computer system was up and running, if not exactly humming. Frank's software support did leave something to be desired, largely because he had to turn it over to a less experienced assistant. Frank was ill by then, first with

a novel of sexual initiation   **165**

what he called the flu and then with what Pierce said was some kind of hepatitis. That sounded serious. It would be a while before I understood what was going on—that Frank had fallen prey to the "gay plague" sweeping San Francisco—and what that was going to mean.

Wait a minute—I started this entry trying to recapture the reality of everyday life with Lainie. What did we do? Normal stuff, I guess. I worked all the time, and Lainie worked at odd jobs, never proving reliable until she found her niche assembling sandwiches at the Edible Complex. But that was a little later. So, what else? We went to movies and we ate out a lot because I worked all day and Lainie was no cook.

Sometimes on weekends, though, I would fix a nice dinner for Lainie and me, or we would even have my mother and Gayle over, occasionally Jeanna. August usually declined the invitation. Once, after much cajoling on both our parts, Lainie and I convinced Jeanna to bring some of her poetry and give us a private reading. I remember clearly when this happened because it was the week of the Democratic Convention in 1984, when Geraldine Ferraro was nominated for Vice President. That was worthy of a little party.

August didn't come, and Pierce showed up alone, leaving Frank to rest in bed at home. Pierce looked a little less energetic himself than usual. Still, he came into the apartment pumping his fist and shouting "Jerrr-ol-deen! Jerr-ol-deen!" inducing Jeanna to join him in a brief, wild, ballroom-style dance around the living room. I think the music on the stereo was from Michael Jackson's "Thriller" album, but somehow they made it work. Busy in the kitchen, I peered over the counter at the gaily circling couple and felt a little jealous.

The political talk ranged far and wide over dinner, although Lainie mostly nodded her head and agreed with what the rest of us said, as usual.

At one point Jeanna enthusiastically declared that she thought Ferraro's nomination was just the thing to take the Democrats over the top. I said, "I wish I could agree with you."

Jeanna eyed me over the wine glass she was sipping from

and said, almost accusingly, "What do you mean? You don't think it's important?"

I hastened to defend myself. "Well, of course it's important to *us*," I clarified. "But the rest of the country's not like Berkeley. I think sometimes we actually forget around here that most Americans like Ronald Reagan. He's like everybody's daddy."

"Not my bloody paterfamilias," Pierce interjected, causing Lainie to wrinkle her nose at the big word.

"Obviously," I agreed sardonically. "What I'm getting at is that Ferraro's nomination may scare away as many people as it gets excited. Like most Southerners, for instance."

"Oh, yeah?" Jeanna countered, then turned to Lainie. "Are you scared, cuz?"

Lainie grinned, happy to be playing along. "Nope. I ain't afeered none."

Laughing, Jeanna turned back to me. "Are you scared, Randall? Secretly, I mean?"

I flushed with embarrassment, not because I had any hidden reactionary politics, but because Jeanna was directing her intensity at me in a way that made me nervous. It seemed that she often played little games like this with me, trying to get me to say something revealing, trying to call out something within me—but what? Sometimes I thought she was flirting, but then she always pulled back at just the precise moment that would leave her unimpeachable.

Now I was so flustered I was afraid anything that came out of my mouth would reveal everything I felt—about Jeanna, about Lainie, about Pierce even. I didn't even know what all those feelings were. How could Jeanna do this to me with so few words, and just a flicker in her eyes? This was one of those moments when I heard that inner voice that seemed to speak in Jeanna's presence. This time it said: *Don't be afraid. Speak the truth.*

But I wouldn't have known where to start with the truth, and thus fear won the day. Right before I might have said something regrettable, I came up with the perfect dodge. Shaking my head slowly and peering directly into Jeanna's eyes as if to say *You won't get me this time*, I said instead, "The only thing I'm afraid

a novel of sexual initiation

of is that we'll never get this reading started. How about it?"

Clearly taken aback, Jeanna blinked and looked away, then resumed our mutual gaze with a surrendering smile. My heart leaped. Sometimes it felt as if Jeanna and I communicated more to each other in such brief, subtle moments than Lainie and I did in weeks of idle chatter. My brief reflection on this peculiar fact was broken by Lainie saying, "Yeah! C'mon, Jeanna!"

In fact the poetry escaped Lainie entirely. But she loved her cousin with unfailing devotion, so she could cover her lack of comprehension with expressive cries of pure affection. Truthfully, I could never remember the beginnings of Jeanna's poems by the time she got to the end of them. They were never about anything except the stream of her feelings during the time it took to write a poem. Sometimes a couple of her lines would stick in my mind for days, like an incantation. I can still remember these lines, for instance:

You said our great mother is the ocean
But I am born in your salt and our motion

I assumed this was about sex with August but that didn't bother me. I liked the fact that Jeanna had the nerve to rhyme . . .

There. I've done it again. Betrayed Lainie, I mean. Every time I try to recall our everyday relationship, our hard-earned and gradual love, I end up changing the subject. I really don't think it's because there was nothing there; I'm beginning to see that so much of me was not there.

16

LIFE IS just so complicated. Surely I'm not the only person who's failed to be "all there" in a relationship. Everybody lives their lives in parts, and each part is pulled upon by different people and situations. To keep all the parts going you have to make compromises, perhaps acting a certain way in one part that contradicts the way you live, or who you think you are, in another part. It's not unfaithfulness, really, so much as an unavoidable fragmentation . . .

Perhaps it will be easier if I just stick to the facts. My philosophizing sounds like I'm just making excuses; I know what I'm avoiding now. Here's how it got started:

Etty Berquist sent for me not long after our meeting in February. I flew to Albuquerque for the first time in late April, feeling that I really had something to report, namely the computerization of the store. Iceberg kept saying he couldn't figure out what Etty needed me for. Everything had been going swimmingly between Iceberg and Etty's people. He made me promise to call from Santa Fe as soon as I had a clue.

One thing I have to say for Etty: she was as generous as she was imperious. My flight accommodations were first-class. I was picked up in a limousine at the airport and accompanied by the chauffeur to lunch at a tony airport hotel cafe before we hit the road to Santa Fe. All of this wasn't my style, of course, but it was fun in an aberrant way, and I came better prepared sartorially this time.

Pierce had taken me shopping in San Francisco at Macy's and Wilkes Bashford, even though I was nervous as a cat in the latter establishment. By then I was so Berkeleyized that anything smacking of a lavish lifestyle induced a strong political guilt. On the other hand, Pierce had the time of his life. He obviously needed a break from worrying about Frank, and he'd never had the luxury of spending so much money on clothes, even at one remove. Once I persuaded him that I would not, under any circumstances, wear an ascot, everything went fine.

It was from Etty's friendly driver that I first got a hint of why I'd been brought to New Mexico, but he was too much of a pro, and too long her loyal employee to be indiscreet. Over lunch we mostly talked geography. It turned out that the fortyish, sandy-haired driver, who went by the sole sobriquet of Davis, was a Charlottean. There's nothing like a shared Southern heritage to put two heretofore-strangers at ease. It wasn't until later that I realized how skillfully Davis had plumbed my biography through the device of good-ol'-boy joshing interspersed with casual inquiries like, "Now what did you say your dad taught at Emory?" and so on. I'm sure I was well debriefed by the time we pulled into the outskirts of Santa Fe, where Davis yawned, stretched his arms one at a time while the Lincoln sped along on cruise control, and said, apropos of nothing:

"Well, if there's one thing Etty values, it's her privacy."

"Oh?" I said blankly.

"Yes indeed," Davis replied, regarding me intently by way of the rearview mirror through the glass partition slid partly open between us. His voice was amplified through an intercom, creating a surreal stereo effect. "After five years as her full-time assistant, there are still some things I don't know about her personal life. Whatever I did happen to find out, I certainly wouldn't pass on to anyone who didn't have a clear need to know."

"Of course," I said coolly, aware that we were in mutual good-ol'-boy territory no longer. Was I supposed to say something else?

Davis filled in, speaking with utmost nonchalance as he gazed momentarily at the desert scenario speeding by to his left. "And who would ever need to know certain things of a strictly personal nature?"

The question hung in my little upholstered chamber like an axe on a rope. I felt like I was in the midst of a bad spy novel. I said, "No one, of course," like it was in my script. Davis nodded

a novel of sexual initiation							**171**

silently in the mirror, proffering eye contact to let me know that we had an understanding.

Soon in town, we circled the main plaza, Davis back on casual terms as a chatty tour guide, and then we headed up one street and stopped in front of a remodeled house with a sign out front denoting it as a bookstore and cafe. Davis popped the lock on my door and said simply, "She's in there."

"Oh, okay," I said uncertainly. "You'll wait here?"

"No, I'll be taking your stuff out to the ranch. Etty will need you to drive her jeep. You can handle a stick?"

"Sure," I said, confused by what Davis had said. Things were getting curiouser.

"Great," said Davis. "Welcome to Santa Fe. I hope your stay is comfortable, Randall." His tone of voice had reverted to the conspiratorial. After opening and closing the door for me Davis rapidly inserted himself back into the driver's seat and sped off.

The speed at which things unfolded from that point was remarkable. Inside the bookstore, I was surprised to find that the cafe included a full bar. That was where I found Etty, reclining on an old couch set against one wall, with a half-empty gin and tonic in her hand and, as I would soon discover, at least several more inside her. She tried to maintain her imperial style in greeting me, but her speech was slurred. She asked me about my flight and the drive with Davis, but seemed to pay little attention to what I said, laughing in a short, abrupt manner at inappropriate moments and frequently touching my coat sleeve or leaning against me in a familiar way. There was a Carlos Casteneda book open on the table in front of her, but she couldn't have been doing much reading in her condition.

After about fifteen minutes of extreme discomfort on my part, when I had just begun calculating how to make an exit, gracious or not, Etty asked me to get her another drink. I glanced helplessly at the pony-tailed fellow behind the bar, who interpreted me wordlessly and, tilting his head at Etty in a knowing way, made a slashing movement across his neck. Etty saw the bartender's gesture. Picking up her book, she whispered to me, "Never mind Scott. He's such a fuddy-duddy sometimes."

Then she handed me a thick ring of keys and an index card with a neatly drawn map on it; I figured it was something Davis had prepared. We went to her four-wheel drive vehicle in the back parking lot. I drove us to her ranch, the spectacular late-afternoon light making me feel as if I were on a tour of another world, not just New Mexico.

Etty's ranch, about a half-hour outside of town, was more modest than my expectations, consisting of one large modern adobe structure with a cottage off to one side and some nonde-script outbuildings behind the main structure. It seemed to be in the middle of nowhere, at least ten minutes beyond the last estate, and I guessed that Etty's acreage was substantial. Whatever she was ranching—cows, sheep, horses?—was not immediately obvious in the sunset hour that we arrived. I was struck by the absence of any other beings at all. The limousine was parked out front but Davis was nowhere to be seen.

Inside the cool, dimly lit house, the silence was complete, almost forbidding. Etty showed me the guest room next to the kitchen, and told me to make myself at home and eat anything I liked. She also told me to come to her room as soon as I was unpacked, giving me directions before heading off unsteadily down a dark earthen hallway reminiscent of a catacomb.

I did as I was told. I hung up my suit and changed into jeans and began to feel a little less displaced. I was carefully taking note of all the surroundings, because I knew Lainie would enjoy a detailed rendering of an exotic place. I was supposed to call her later at Jeanna's, where she had elected to spend the weekend rather than staying alone in our place. Every detail of Etty's abode was registering in my mind until I came to the partly-open door of her room. I knocked softly, entering at Etty's mumbled rejoinder only to discover her sitting in a large, exquisitely crafted wildwood rocking chair, wearing a diaphanous, see-through nightgown.

My eyes immediately zeroed in on her barely-veiled breasts as if her pale nipples were homing devices. Surprisingly large for her bony, ascetic frame, her breasts were sagging with age and wrinkled with the weight of hanging. I probably gasped.

a novel of sexual initiation 173

"Will you keep an old lady company?" Etty asked as if she were delivering a well-prepared line, although her voice cracked slightly nonetheless. Then she stood and turned, showing me her backside as she walked to one corner of the room and began climbing, slowly and meticulously, a split-log ladder that led to a loft above.

I don't know if I have ever faced a moment of decision that felt quite so precarious. Part of me immediately wanted to gush forth with lame excuses, but none would come to mind. Part of me wanted to say something outraged, about this being one hell of a way of doing business. Part of me wanted to run without saying anything. But the part of me that won out was someone unfamiliar, someone who was peculiarly reverential of this bizarre situation. When I told June years later about this moment, her ears perked up:

"As if this part of you was *revering* someone?" June had repeated after me. "You mean Etty herself?"

"Not exactly," I recalled. "It was more as if I had stumbled into some kind of sacred place, like one of those kivas or prayer circles Etty used to talk about. There was a part of me telling the rest of me to go along and pay careful attention, because the meaning of what was really happening was different from what was apparently going on. I guess that doesn't make any sense."

June had leaned back in her chair, putting her hands together in a tent just like a therapist in the movies, and said, "It might."

Anyway, I don't know how else to explain why I got into bed with Etty. I climbed up into the loft still wearing my t-shirt and pants, but Etty looked at me in the near-darkness up there and said, "No fair, young man."

I knew what she meant, and stripped, and then lay down awkwardly beside her with no covers on us, parallel but not touching. I was embarrassed to have an erection gaining on me.

The thing has no discretion whatsoever, I thought to myself, but then Etty was sliding one cool leg over my leg. I could feel one large and soft breast against my side; she was actually trying to embrace me. *Oh God.* Again, I was about to bolt, but to my amazement, Etty kissed me ever so lightly near the mouth, her breath an overpowering mixture of alcohol and peppermint, and whispered, "It's nice to be kind to an old lady."

I didn't know what to think. Then Etty touched me down there, where I was now as obvious as a flagpole, and her fingers on my balls were like a bird's claw, feathery but scratching. She had some nails on her! She played with me pointlessly for perhaps a minute, then abruptly rolled away, reached for something on the night table on her other side. The bland perfume of baby oil was soon in the air. Then Etty said, "All right," and flattened herself on her back, spreading her legs slightly.

By now I felt I really should say—or have already said—something, but I heard my Aunt Grace speak in my mind instead: "Don't use words to cover up an empty head!" So I didn't. I got myself up over Etty and leaned over her, at which point she grasped me and, grunting inelegantly, gradually put me inside her. Then the last surprise: Nothing happened.

I mean, I started moving back and forth inside her, reaching to seize one soft, doughy breast in my hand, but Etty did nothing except whimper softly and lock her legs together rigidly. That was it. I moved a little more; she did nothing. Her head was turned to one side. As far as I could see in the dark, her eyes were closed. After a few more moments it came clear to me that she was enduring the situation. *She's frigid*, I realized. Then, surprisingly, she spoke:

"Feel good?" she whispered, the words barely audible in the room's austere silence.

That's when a little part of my heart broke. I realized with utter certainty that this was all Etty Berquist had ever known of sex. And she was at least sixty-five! At that moment, all my building suspicion and judgment of her dispersed, like bad seeds dispersed in the wind, and I could think only one thing: *It's nice to be kind to an old lady.*

I was going to have to carry this off; I was going to have to fake it. So I started moving more rhythmically, knowing I was about ten miles from an orgasm, and made a couple of sharp plunges, causing Etty to breathe in sharply as well. Then I went

a novel of sexual initiation **175**

"Aaahhh," and slumped over to the side, swiftly extricating myself from our union. I lay there nervously for a moment, wondering if Etty was going to notice that my coming was dry. But she only patted my hip softly with one hand and said, "Nice."

Then she started to talk. Lord, how that woman could talk, as I would learn over the next hour and a half, and at every subsequent rendezvous (eight or ten in toto) that we had over the next several years. In Etty's defense, I have to admit that her talk was fascinating. She was a virtual encyclopaedia of knowledge about Navajo and Hopi culture, and the fact that I can now deliver learned if second-hand discourses on vision quests and ceremonial dances and the legends of various kachinas owes entirely to Etty's bedtime lectures. At the time, a lot of what she was talking about went right over my head, although I understood where Chuck's predilection for transcendent explorations was rooted.

ETTY'S unique pillow talk finally trailed off into sleep—during which she muttered absurdities for a little while—but when I ascertained that she was good and gone, I eased myself out of bed, got dressed and promptly stormed the kitchen. Ravenous, I was delighted to find a plastic quart container in the fridge full of an excellent chicken salad made with fresh corn, black beans, and cilantro. I really wanted to ask for the recipe, and amused myself with wondering whether I should put the inquiry to Davis or Etty. Three-to-one it was Davis, I decided. I remember really pigging out, probably because I was a little shook up. Piling on the food calmed me down considerably.

Sitting alone at a gigantic rough-hewn wooden table in the dining room, digesting that excessive repast, I then rehearsed, out loud but softly, how I would describe the evening's encounter to Lainie and Iceberg in the calls that were due each of them. It was easy, really:

"She's a lonely old lady who needs someone to talk to. We just sat in her living room and I listened. No harm done. There are worse ways to spend a weekend, and it's beautiful here. You ought to see it, Iceberg . . . Lainie, we'll make our own trip here someday soon . . ." This sounded good, so I went over it until I believed it. The calls went without a hitch.

Then I climbed into bed about eleven and dreamed, for the first time since I was a child, of flying. First I had to get out of the house. In the dream the natural thing seemed to be to pass right through the walls—a tougher job than I expected, since the walls were earthen and a couple of feet thick. Pulling my body through was like slogging through setting concrete, but I made it. When I was outside, I launched myself like a jet, zooming for the moon. I laughed and sang some kind of a chant, then found myself flying over a broad river in bright daylight. The scene was peaceful and peculiarly familiar, so I brought myself to earth by the water, noticing a beautiful dark horse grazing behind a fence a few hundred yards away.

Right in front of me was an old beat-up card table, of the sort that Chuck used to heap dinged merchandise upon. The table was bare and I had a curious feeling that I was waiting here for someone. But who? I looked toward the horse, who stopped grazing long enough to raise his head and return my gaze. His love seemed sincere, but he was clearly not ready to jump the fence and be my companion. Growing impatient, I felt my happiness with the scenario slipping away, and I started scratching at the cheap surface of the card table with my fingernails, and then Etty was scraping her nails over my scrotum again!

I awoke with a start, thankfully alone in my bed. Outside in the desert scrub, something wild was whistling an ancient and somehow familiar call.

III

17

ETTY Berquist initiated me into an uncomfortable realm of sex with neither love nor desire—the realm of intimacy as commodity, if I still believe that our strange intimacy was the price of keeping Diversions' investment capital flowing. But I'm not so sure anymore.

The more I reflect on it, the more strongly I feel there was something more subtle, perhaps even mystical going on between Etty and myself, something beyond the ken even of her omniscient chauffeur. Or perhaps I'm still trying to find a way to get myself off the hook. Back then the relationship seemed like such a sequestered secret—something happening in a different world —that I didn't think of it as affecting the rest of my life. I certainly didn't think of it as an affair. I would have blithely asserted that it had no impact on my relationship with Lainie, beyond her aggravation with the fact that I was flying to Santa Fe two or three times yearly, always on short notice, never taking her along.

But if Lainie couldn't detect the exact nature of my secrets, she could always see through me nonetheless. It's one thing that glued us together, the fact that one of us understood me—until what there was to understand became too problematic.

For example: our turn for the worse that began at Chez Panisse. By mid-1986 I'd had three or four Santa Fe tête-à-têtes with Etty. My education in Native American spirituality and 20th-century transcendentalism was proceeding apace, while Etty's sexuality remained pathetically static. I didn't even know why we bothered with sex, but it seemed to be a ritual of some importance to her. I just grinned and bore it.

On the home front, Diversions had expanded its reach to branches in Walnut Creek and San Rafael. This growth, and even more grandiose plans for the future, were really Iceberg's doing;

I didn't have the vision. It had become clear that my genius lay only in anticipating what kinds of games, toys, and distractions would appeal most to people, weeks or months ahead of time. I don't know to this day exactly how I did it.

An avid consumer of newspapers and magazines during my early-morning cafe haunts (I usually left the house before Lainie awakened), somehow I could gauge from the news the depth and intensity of current cultural anxieties, and thence conclude what diversions people would find most distracting in their leisure time. Add to that a personal taste for juvenilia (I was still collecting stamps until a few years ago), and you've got a small-time marketing wizard.

Things were going so well on the business front, in fact, that I assumed they were going well on all other fronts as well. Lainie and I seemed, if not happy, at least stable. Lainie's general skittishness was thankfully reduced, largely because she had landed the job at the Edible where she rapidly became something of a mascot, the pet employee of staff and management alike. Maybe it was her accent; I'd tried to lose mine over the years.

So I thought the two of us were getting along swimmingly. The sex was good, if not as charged as it used to be, and we hardly fought, perhaps because we didn't talk a whole lot. I worked all day until seven or later. When Lainie got the Edible job she was there from three to ten. So we just didn't see each other much. Our only whole day together was usually Sunday. We were both pretty good at playing, so we would roam the Bay Area in Liv Ullmann—when she wasn't in the shop getting an expensive nip or tuck in bodywork, or a valve job—and hike, or shop, or ride the ferries, or see movies, sometimes with Jeanna along, which especially lifted my spirits. So I thought everything was pretty fine. Until Chez Panisse.

Of course it's not the fault of that world-class eatery, although I've hardly darkened its door since that long-ago repast. I could very well blame my braggadocio instead. Late one night I mentioned to Lainie that the combined annual gross of Diversions' three branches was approaching a million dollars. Lainie, whose accounting skills were far short of mine, decided that meant I

a novel of sexual initiation   **181**

was personally a millionaire.

This became a news bulletin that she began broadcasting by telephone tree the very next day, causing me no little embarrassment as I tried later to explain to Jeanna, my mom, and half a dozen casual acquaintances the reality of the situation. Sure, Iceberg was allowing me a good salary, I joked to everyone, but a millionaire? Why, that was at least five years off.

Nonetheless, Lainie's excitement was so irrepressible, and her birthday so close by, that I decided a no-holds-barred celebration dinner was in order. When I told Lainie where I was taking her, she looked at me wide-eyed and said, "There's a restaurant named Shay *Penis*?!" and much hilarity ensued as I tried to convince her that not all French words were just English words with different pronunciations. "But what about cherry and *cherie*?!" she chortled lunatically. "Or poo-poo and Pepe *LaPew*?" I confess: I always found Lainie's manic silliness endearing.

Then we set about deciding who to invite. I set the limit at two others, partly because I wasn't used to spending money on this kind of thing no matter how much I had at my disposal, and partly because I knew Jeanna wouldn't come along without August. August must have nixed the invitation, because Jeanna's demurral was flimsy. I knew she must have secretly wanted to come.

My mom said she was in school that night. I had partly underwritten her pursuit of an art therapy degree, so I could hardly be upset about that. Even Mr. Goodtimes himself, Pierce, declined, saying that he was doing an extra night shift at the bank to help make up for Frank's lost work. And so, by the process of elimination, we ended up inviting my father to dinner with us at Chez Panisse. He accepted the invitation immediately, perhaps because it came from Lainie, perhaps because he was so shocked to receive any friendly entreaty from me, even indirectly. I was afraid he would bring along some comely coed, in which case I might not have spoken to him at all. But he came alone. And as he was wont to do, he charmed the lady in closest proximity, my live-in girlfriend, with his fake gentility and polished story-telling capacity.

I wouldn't have been so upset about my father being himself

if it hadn't been for the near-argument that erupted between us. Dad was telling us about some study he was working on, examining the growing sense of doom and purposelessness among unemployed young black men in urban centers like Oakland.

"It's not just the actual lack of job opportunities," he said to a busily munching Lainie, "it's the psycho-social conviction these young men share, that they are out of the loop in our society. And that conviction is fed by subtle cultural signals from all over, including, of course, from our genial father figure in the White House, who psychically menaces the underclass in a manner completely invisible to his well-heeled constituency."

Oh please, Dad, I thought, *this is really not Lainie's field.* Then it just popped out of me, like an alternate personality:

"Well, Dad, there's no cure for a psycho-social conviction like getting a job. I'd have a lot more time to think about how I'd been shafted in life if I didn't have to put in ten or twelve hours a day keeping people employed. I mean, there's that side of things to consider, too."

My father recoiled slightly, and so did I. He didn't expect the reactionary sentiment, and I was ashamed to be mouthing such illogical blather. I was driven by some mixture of feelings I couldn't apprehend. Of course Dad could have moved in for the kill intellectually, because he had facts, figures, and authentic analysis on his side. Instead he got me with a simple, slashing riposte, delivered after an elegant sip of wine.

"My son, the newly minted Reaganite," he said coolly, wiping his moustache with his napkin, "*wizened* beyond his years." Then he leaned over toward Lainie, grabbed her hand playfully and said, "See what happens when you become a millionaire?"

Lainie, damn her, laughed.

I was so frazzled by the end of the dinner that I got confused about the check total, inadvertently leaving an extra twenty on top of an already generous tip. When I realized this as Lainie and I were driving away in Livvy, I felt a cold shock of fear— as if a lost twenty were going to bankrupt me—and the Reaganite remark repeated itself in my head. It still smarted. Lainie,

a novel of sexual initiation **183**

garrulous all through dinner, was strangely silent, but I could hear a familiar rustling in her handbag.

"Please don't smoke in the car," I said testily. "I'm going to have everything in here re-upholstered soon. I don't want it smelling like cigarettes."

Lainie continued with her ritual, rolling down her window halfway. "You don't have new upholstery yet."

"I mean," I said insistently, "that you should get out of the habit *now*."

The rustling stopped as Lainie apparently considered her options. Now I felt bad; I hadn't planned on being a jerk but this evil side kept popping out. Trying to ease the atmosphere I said, in a lighthearted way, "So did you like your birthday torte?"

Lainie was glum. "Oh, it was okay, I guess. What was that gooey purple ice cream that came with it?"

I winced. "It wasn't ice cream. It was plum gelato," I said didactically, realizing even as I said it that I was sounding like a snob. We'd all had too much of an exquisite Pouilly-Fuissé.

"Well, excuse my ignor-*anus*," Lainie sang sardonically. Now I knew she was angry, not just intoxicated. A reversion to adolescent vulgarity was always a sign of Lainie's pique—the flip side of her childlike charm.

I tried to change the subject and enlist her sympathies. "Well, I guess you saw my father in classic form tonight," I began. "He was flirting with you right there at the table."

"Yeah," Lainie replied flatly.

"I don't know if it's his way with women that bothers me as much as him acting so cool and in control. He's such a phony."

Although she'd apparently given up on smoking for the moment, Lainie reached over and impulsively pushed in the cigarette lighter, then settled back in her seat and said, "But you're just *like* him."

It's a testament to my self-control that I didn't veer off Shattuck Avenue and plow Liv Ullman into the laps of the hamburger eaters inside brightly lit Oscar's. I braked harshly at the yellow light and barked, *"What did you say?"* as if Lainie's remark wasn't already burning itself into my brain like a branding iron.

MY JOURNEY THROUGH THE PLANT WORLD

Apparently Lainie missed my shock or she wouldn't have gone on like she did: "I said, you're just like him. You're always acting like you know more stuff than you do. I mean, you're always talking about politics but you don't *do* anything political. Like when August wanted us to come to that gay rights march but you said you had to work. *Work, work, work*," Lainie sang snidely, reaching over to pull out the cigarette lighter as it popped, then holding it close to her nose. Inwardly I was racing to come up with a defense, but Lainie wasn't done: "And *you* flirt with Jeanna all the time."

I heaved a huge, disgusted sigh and retorted, "Jeanna is gay, in case you hadn't noticed."

"I know," Lainie shot back. "That's what makes it so weird. Are you waiting for her to switch so you can sleep with her? Why don't I ask her to do you a favor once, so you can get it over with?"

That was it. *I don't have to take this*, I thought malevolently. So I resorted to the retaliatory measure against which I knew Lainie would be defenseless: silence. When the light changed, I popped Liv aggressively into second, causing just the dramatic buck-and-lurch I wanted, and drove ahead without a word, my jaw set like a stone. When I realized I had missed our turn I circled the next block without saying anything about it. By then Lainie was getting the message.

"I'm sorry," she whined. "I didn't mean it. Sometimes I just think you like Jeanna better than me."

Great apology, I thought sarcastically, but held my tongue. A minute later, as we neared the apartment, Lainie tried again.

"Okay, I'm really sorry, Randall. I didn't mean it, okay? I take it back." She sounded utterly childish.

I parked the car and got out wordlessly, slamming the door, striding through the gate. Lainie got out and came running up behind me, whimpering: "Will you talk to me, *please*?"

BUT I didn't, not for an hour and a half, and I could have held out the whole night if Lainie hadn't marshaled her own formidable weaponry to the front. When we entered the apartment I went straight to the bedroom and watched some cop show and

a novel of sexual initiation 185

the news on TV, hardly any of it registering since I was playing out vengeful dialogues in my head. Lainie disappeared to the tiny closet room off the kitchen, dragging the phone in with her, and shut the door.

Once I got up and stood by the door to try to hear what she was saying, because if I heard her say something to Jeanna—well, I didn't know what I would do. But she was giggling and I couldn't make out any words at all.

After the news I drew a bath. That was always relaxing, and I wanted to put the evening behind me. In about five minutes Lainie timidly knocked on the door and asked if she could brush her teeth; I grunted an assent, not quite breaking my private vow of silence. Then she came in wearing only pink panties. I almost smiled at the obviousness of it. I wanted to say, *So you think everything will be all right if you show me your titties?*, but I held my ground as I slowly wrinkled in the water.

But when I stood up and reached for the towel, Lainie was bending over rinsing her mouth out. Her round ass was right there in front of me, and her tits, reflected in the mirror, *were* kind of stirring. She also used the mirror to flash me a conciliatory smile. What happened next I can neither fully explain nor excuse; I went a little nuts. My cock came up like one of those springy doorstops, and I pulled Lainie's panties down to the floor roughly, pushing myself against her so that I was erect against the top of her buttocks, settling into the top of the split there. I rubbed her that way for a little while, leaning forward to grab both of her breasts. She moaned and braced herself against the sink, then I reached under her with one hand and played with her long enough to get her wet, not long at all. She spread her legs slightly and kept using the mirror to look at me—hopefully, longingly, fearfully.

I remembered seeing a scene just like this in a porn flick, and I remembered how exciting it was to see the woman's buttocks ripple with the repeated impact of the man fucking her from behind. I wanted to see those ripples now, I wanted to see if it would look the same, just like in the world of porn. So I got into Lainie abruptly, causing her to gasp, and started pounding away at her with abandon, watching her ass, which wasn't doing what I expected, so I really slammed into her and . . .

"Owww!" Lainie screeched. "Hey, watch it! Not so hard, honey. And don't come inside because . . ."

Her warning was too late. All the rapid violent action had ratcheted up my excitement, and though I might have been able to pull out in time, I didn't. I wiggled sideways a little and and then came inside Lainie, my knees going weak as I partly collapsed on her back, almost bringing both of us down to the floor. When I looked in the mirror again, Lainie's eyes were wet and I felt a black fire of guilt rise from my groin to my heart.

"I didn't mean to hurt you," I said contritely. "I'm sorry."

Lainie straightened up as we disengaged and said softly, "I'm all right. You just poked me there. I wanted you to stop because we should have used a condom. Are you still mad at me?"

"No," I said truthfully. "I'm sorry I got so upset."

"About what I said about your dad or about Jeanna?" Lainie had moved to the tub and turned on the water, and started vigorously splashing herself between her legs.

I sat down, ass on cold sink, feeling utterly exhausted. "I don't know exactly," I replied. "It doesn't matter."

Turning off the water, Lainie reached for her own towel and crowed, "You couldn't screw Jeanna like that anyway."

"What?!" I choked.

"Cuz August would knock your block off!" Lainie proclaimed, and pranced out of the bathroom, giggling.

That was the perilous way we righted ourselves that night, and we would have to do it again and again as the months went on, although I believe we lost ground in every subsequent crisis. It was partly because I got irrevocably disturbed that night by the incursion of a pornographic imprint into my actual sexual relationship with Lainie. Although I didn't go to the porn theater often in those days, I did sneak off there sometimes, regarding it as my personal masturbatory right, not something that had anything to do with regular sex.

But there it was, a lurid cinematic vision that had possessed me for a minute. I couldn't shake the guilt, especially after

Lainie brought up August. It was from August that I first heard the quote, "Pornography is the theory, rape is the practice," parroted from some of her radical feminist readings during one of the dinners in the girls' apartment. At the time I had just gone silent, not about to speak up from my firsthand personal experience, although I thought what she had said was a crock.

After that evening with Lainie, however, I was shaken. What had happened was hardly rape. It was just an angry fuck, and judging from Lainie's nonchalance, not the angriest she must have experienced in her long history. But I'm pretty sure that it was after that night that I decided porn was, on balance, unhealthy, and I should quit my fascination with it. That sounded easy enough on the face of it: a simple exercise of will over a minor self-indulgence. Even today, years later, as I write this, it seems equally easy. At least I haven't been addicted to something like cocaine for this long. That would have killed me outright. This compulsion has only mortified me a thousand times, reminding me that my sex life goes on in two different worlds— one real, and one all the more compelling for its unreality.

Anyway, after that night, Lainie and I were especially gentle with each other for a little while. It was as if the ground had begun to shift under us and we both sensed that a rough move by either of us could trigger a mudslide. (I know I've become a real Californian by the way I picture my internal emotional landscape: always at the mercy of floods, quakes, and fires.)

But the seed of our next crisis was literally gestating at that moment. The guilty part of me says I impregnated Lainie from behind on the night of Chez Panisse, but it could as well have been during one of our intimacies in the few weeks previous. We had gotten awfully sloppy with birth control, partly because Lainie was often saying, "I don't think I'm fertile anymore," and had stopped using her diaphragm. And I always hated condoms. Even the thinnest of them made me feel deeply weird, walled-off from the most intimate sensations of sex, like trying to take a walk in a wet and verdant wilderness while wearing a telephone booth. I just couldn't stand phoning it in, as it were.

With increasing carelessness, we had ended up frequently

MY JOURNEY THROUGH THE PLANT WORLD

making love with no protection whatsoever, save my pulling out of Lainie just before ejaculation. It amuses me now to realize that this is what they do in porn, for different reasons. There they call it the "money shot," because it's what the dirty old men, and the dirty young men like myself, really pay to see: the proof that sex was really happening, that at least one of the people fucking for public consumption didn't fake orgasm.

About a month after Chez Panisse, Lainie started becoming more edgy than usual, or sometimes excessively sweet as if to placate me for some petty household crime that had so far escaped my notice. Rather than ask her outright what the problem was, I spent a few days wondering what might be afoot. Going over the household bills, I had noticed a gradual increase in the frequency and length of Lainie's long-distance calls to Georgia, about which she had said nothing. I figured she missed her mother or some old friend, and resolved to send her home for a week as her next Christmas present.

I knew I ought to go with her, because I had seen my nephew Frank only once when Carolyn and Cody briefly came to San Francisco a couple years before. Amazingly, I had never been back to Georgia since the family left when I was a teen. Truth to tell, I still didn't want to go. In my mind's eye I could see nothing there I wanted to revisit.

So was it the phone bill? Nah, I couldn't imagine Lainie being anxious about it, especially since our household accounting was about as loose as our birth control habits. Lainie had her own money in her bank account and took care of her personal needs with it, while I covered all the major expenses. The situation seemed to suit us just fine. Sometimes she had to ask me for money but it was no big deal. Then what was she so jumpy about?

Finally, late one night after I had picked her up at work and we were lying in bed half-watching David Letterman, far too late for me to be up, I decided I couldn't stand watching Lainie chew her fingernails raw for another five seconds.

"Lainie, are you all right?" I asked gently, muting the TV with my trusty remote. "You've seemed really tense the last week or so. Is there something you need to talk about?"

a novel of sexual initiation   **189**

Lainie turned her head toward me, the short waves of her black hair contrasting intensely with the white pillowcase. She couldn't maintain steady eye contact. She looked at me briefly and then back at Letterman.

As he was soundlessly heaving a watermelon out the window of a skyscraper, she said, "I might be pregnant."

"Pregnant," I replied tonelessly, my composure dropping with the melon and smashing to kingdom come on a sidewalk in New York.

"Yeah," she confirmed. "I might be. I mean, probably I am. I think I am. I'm really late and I don't feel right. I've had this feeling before, when I've been . . . pregnant."

And what did I say then, at that precarious moment, when my lover might most have needed my reassurance, my care, or in the best of all possible worlds, my enthusiasm? What was the feeling that rose within me instead, and what did I say? I'll write down exactly what I said. I'll put it down right now so that I can deal with it, hopefully in a more responsible way than when I actually said it. This is what this journal is for, after all: to face the facts of my sexual past unstintingly, without compromise, or self-serving partiality, or hesitation . . .

"Oh shit," is what I said.

18

"OH YES," June had nodded knowingly when I told her about the cold fear I had experienced years before at Lainie's announcement. "The pooh-air hates to be brought to earth."

"The *pooh-air*?" I replied ignorantly, knowing I was in for a lecture.

"P-u-e-r," June spelled patiently, "the *puer aeternus*, or eternal youth." The archetype of the Little Prince. You know *The Little Prince,* by Antoine de Saint-Exupery?"

"Of course," I said sardonically, "personally."

"I'm sure you do," June replied." There's a fair amount of the puer in you. The Eternal Youth is a type of man who has difficulty committing to a practical life at the everyday earth level. He never keeps more than one foot planted there. The other foot is always off on adventures, either in his imagination, or externally, climbing mountains, flying stunt planes, that kind of thing. It's as if he's reaching for another world that's far more exciting than the one he's forced to live in every day."

"That doesn't sound like me," I protested. "I've run a business for all my adult life. I've hardly been off seeking adventure."

"That's true," June said, removing and folding her glasses in a sign of partial retreat, "but you have had a tendency to pursue impossible dreams at the price of a more realistic life. Particularly in the realm of relationships."

I stared glassily at June; was she referring to Jeanna?

"That's why Lainie's pregnancy frightened you so much," June continued. "The puer is always shocked to learn first-hand that sex is related to reproduction—it ties him to the earth. He'd rather pursue sex only as pure sensuality, that is, a way to experience spiritual ecstasy in the flesh, without material consequences. But having a baby? Oh, no. Far too earthbound. The puer is hardly willing to put up with his own incarnation, much less be responsible for another one."

Would that I had known that at the time! I could have simply turned to Lainie and said, "Don't worry about all the blood draining from my face and my utter lack of concern for your anxiety. My archetypal possession is just a little put out, that's all. It'll pass."

The amazing thing is how much grief the pregnancy caused us when we had no disagreement about what to do. Lainie had fewer moral qualms about the decision than I did. She had been through all this before in high school; that guy had never even known about it. But I did, and over the next few weeks I went through some of the most painful gymnastics of guilt, shame, and indecision that I have ever experienced — suggesting we should get married, deciding that would be a disaster, contemplating leaving town in the middle of the night, considering suicide (there was a bad day at work on top of everything else) and, most of all, struggling with the awful feeling of having my leg in a trap. Just like a puer, I suppose.

I remember Lainie watching me with frequent looks of amazement, as if to say, *What's his problem? I'm the one who's pregnant.* And she was right. My problem—which I couldn't express openly to Lainie—was the feeling that my life up to that point had gone down the wrong fork in the road and I was deathly afraid there was no turning back. I had seen people who lived their whole lives in the wrong direction, like most of my poor relatives in the South. People like . . . Lainie.

Once she firmly chose it, the abortion was efficiently resolved, at least as far as I knew. Lainie simply moved back to Jeanna's for a month. She disappeared into that den of feminine conspiracy, and the three of them (or the whole coven?) took care of it somehow. I don't know if they used herbs, or spells, or took her to a clinic. All I know is that Lainie refused my repeated offers of monetary assistance and said that I was too difficult to be around at the time of such a "powerful transit." Of course that was Jeanna's language, or August's. Clearly they had taken control of the situation. I was secretly relieved, although

a novel of sexual initiation 193

I grumbled about it.

When Lainie came back, healthy and quiet, I really thought I was off the hook. Our fighting stopped and it was as if nothing bad had ever happened. But a few nights after Lainie's return, Jeanna called me while I was alone at home, and bluntly told me that Lainie and I should see a couples therapist.

"You two don't communicate much," Jeanna admonished me, "and you're obviously careless, in more ways than one. I'm Lainie's cousin, and I feel a lot of responsibility for helping her get her life together. If you're not going to work harder to be good to her, you should get out of the relationship. If you want to work on it, I know someone you can both talk to."

That was that. I wasn't about to leave the relationship; pulling that large a thread out of the fabric of my life could very well unravel it entirely. I shake my head now, realizing that back then I wasn't even taking a serious look at my feelings for Lainie. We were just attached, sexually and emotionally, and I couldn't imagine living without her. Plus: she was my main connection to Jeanna.

Enter Shanti Valentine. Vicki was her real first name, but she'd been given a new one by Bhagwan Shree Rajneesh. I knew I was going to have a hard time taking her seriously when she first greeted us wearing an orange sweatshirt, red pants, and that ridiculous pendant with the old guy's grinning mug on it. For all her suspicion of West Coast cuisine and other regional variations from Dixie norms, Lainie took Shanti in stride and even started bragging about our exotic counselor to friends.

Only now, after several years with June, do I realize what a lousy therapist Shanti was. On my first foray into counseling, I had no way of telling. In the first four sessions, therapy seemed to consist of Lainie and me talking at each other, complaining about this and that—her smoking, my long work hours, her jitteriness, my working on weekends—interspersed with Shanti's penetrating questions like, "And how do you feel about that?"

By the sixth meeting, it dawned on me that Shanti's questions were losing their dumb neutrality, veering consistently in the direction of "How do you *feel* about living with an asshole,

Lainie?" and "How do you *feel* about being a jerk, Randall?" Okay, she wasn't that obvious, but almost. Little wonder that I became increasingly uncooperative.

In session eight or nine, when I was just about fed up with the whole thing, Lainie revealed that most of her expensive long-distance calls to Georgia were to Bobby Skinner, the Southern gentleman who had relied on physical therapy to settle problems in their relationship. I went ballistic. I was jealous that she was finding emotional relief from our relationship by phone-flirting with a proven Neanderthal, and I was embarrassed not to have known it had been going on for six months. Lainie and I got into a real spitting match that session.

Brilliantly sensing the need for an intervention, Shanti gently asked us to settle our energies deep in our bellies and join her in a peaceful visualization.

"Lainie, Randall, let's both close your eyes and imagine being in the most beautiful, relaxing place you've ever seen. Perhaps it's somewhere in nature, or an old favorite room of yours, even your crib as a little baby. . ." She paused. In my mind's eye I was behind the cash register at the Walnut Creek store, the quietest and sunniest of Diversions' three branches. Giselle was nearby, wearing something skimpy.

"There . . . that's nice," Shanti cooed. "Now you both feel safe and at home in your favorite place. I want each of you to take all the arguing and resentment you've had lately, and imagine rolling all that negative energy up in a ball between your two hands. Okay? . . . And now you've got all that negative energy rolled up in a ball, and I want you to throw it up in the air, *up, up*, way up high, and watch it start floating away and turning pink. All your troubles with each other are now as light and pretty as a pink bubble, and it's floating . . . floating . . . floating up into the sky. Let's rest with that image of the pink bubble for a moment."

Barely suppressing a snort of disdain, I took the opportunity of the restful moment to peek out of one eye at Lainie—who was smiling happily and slouching on the couch—and then out of the other eye at Shanti, who was sitting in semi-lotus position

a novel of sexual initiation **195**

with her head bowed and the Rajneesh pendant rolling around in her hands like a small lump of dough. *Jesus, this is dumb*, I thought.

"Now Lainie," Shanti suddenly asked in a motherly tone, "where is your pink bubble? Can you still see it?"

"Uh-huh," Lainie replied dutifully. "It's way up above Stone Mountain—that's near Atlanta—and it looks just like the moon. It's kinda pretty."

"But it's not going any further away?" Shanti inquired.

"No."

"Well, that's fine. Randall, where is your pink bubble?"

I'd had quite enough. "Well, Shanti," I said with grave affect, "my pink bubble has gotten larger and larger, and it's turned into an enormous flaming red fireball that's hanging right over Chicago. It's dripping fire, like napalm, or like when you burn a plastic laundry bag, making that *drooop-drooop* sound, burning the citizens alive and causing havoc in the streets. And—let's see . . . the mayor of Chicago has called out the army! The general of the army is either Peter Graves or Kevin McCarthy, one of those B-movie guys from the '50s, and, uh, he's looking at the fireball through his binoculars, and he's saying, 'We'll have to use A-bombs to destroy the fire bubble! We may lose Chicago, but we can save the nation!'"

I opened my eyes. Lainie was giggling and Shanti, that poor orange woman, was crying.

YEAH, I was a funny guy back then. I was a barrel of laughs; I was full of it. Always dipping and weaving, dancing like a butterfly, stinging like a bee. Now I can look back and clearly see my dodges, sweet moves to the sidelines, and general loutishness in my relationship with Lainie—not to mention the steady deterioration of my moral fiber during the '80s.

"Hell, I was just going along with the decade," as I once remarked to June, and she replied:

"Have you ever noticed that your self-deprecating humor often signals an abdication of the inner throne of conscious self-accountability?" She used too many high-falutin' words, as usual, but I got the point.

But even at my sharpest, I was not the funniest guy on the planet. That award had to go to Chuck Berquist. Aping my style of correspondence with old girlfriends, Chuck had kept in touch since his departure through cryptic postcards, generally arriving from New Guinea months after they were posted. More often than not he baldly begged for loans to keep his "research" going, research which Iceberg and I assumed was being carried out in a sleazy tropical port bar in the company of degraded native women wearing little but the wreaths of Chuck's cigar smoke.

Maybe we were projecting, as June would say, but nonetheless those are the visions Iceberg and I entertained ourselves with as we carefully tacked each card to the wall of Chuck's former office. Every once in a while we killed some time by writing Chuck letters, apologizing for our inability to seed his research due to the continuing personal interdiction of Bettina Berquist. We imagined him going purple-faced and apoplectic over this fiction. We never actually sent the letters, only postcards saying, "Wish we were there!" and so forth.

The real corker was the day we got an official letter from some government functionary of the Independent State of Papua New Guinea, noting the request of one Charles Berquist, "citizen of the Berkley of the United States," to conduct a research expedition into a region of the country normally off-limits to foreigners. The letter had arrived at Iceberg's office in Martinez, but he didn't open it until a meeting we had at the flagship store in Berkeley. About halfway down the page he smiled and said, "Hey-o . . ." but the "there-you-go" got lost in a torrent of chuckles before he handed the letter to me.

I read the letter quickly, and couldn't stop laughing once I got started. "Chuck needs our *character references?*" I howled. Iceberg doubled over with laughter. All the commotion got Giselle's attention, and she came into the office asking us what was so funny. When we told her that Chuck, that pudgy Indiana Jones of the '80s, needed our glowing personal recommendations before he would be allowed to desecrate the native culture of some untouched jungle paradise, she pressed one hand hard

a novel of sexual initiation **197**

against her closed lips before joining in with our hilarity.

Shortly we were all in tears, throwing out possible lines for the character references we would write. Then I suggested that we should take the matter a little more seriously—"for the sake of the well-being of New Guinea"—and I pulled out a one-volume encyclopaedia from the bookshelf to read out loud about the culture and geography of "the world's second largest island." When I got to the line, "Headhunting and cannibalism are still practiced in some inaccessible regions," Giselle exclaimed, "Wow, really?!" and Iceberg tipped over, slipping out of his chair, guffawing and pounding the floor with both fists.

"Lemme at it! I'll write the letter right now!" he bellowed. "Berquist bouillabaise, anyone?" I thought that was really funny and feared I was going to pee in my pants for the first time since age eight. Giselle backed out the office door, shaking her head and murmuring, "You guys . . ."

Giselle—what a princess! I really should have made a move on her back then. It's not just that she's a knockout; she's a decent, caring human too. A case in point: how deftly she handled my embarrassment the morning that I came in the store wearing sunglasses. This wasn't long after Iceberg and I had sent off our glowing recommendation letter for Chuck.

The night before, Lainie and I had gotten into one of our pitched battles in what I called the Menstrual Wars, the once-monthly eruption of our simmering post-therapy tensions into roiling strife. Every time her PMS set in, Lainie's style of arguing would become maddeningly circular.

That particular night the argument was about taking a week-long trip to Georgia. I had rescinded my offer to send Lainie there on her own since finding out about Bobby Skinner, so she had been harping on me to take a vacation there with her. I patiently explained that the situation at work was especially hairy, what with delicate negotiations with Etty's people over new investment funds, and maybe when things were settled, I could see my way clear to . . .

"Why can't we do it now?" she whined.

"Lainie, I just told you. Everything is too weird and crazy

MY JOURNEY THROUGH THE PLANT WORLD

with these expansion plans, and I don't halfway understand it, even though Iceberg keeps explaining and explaining it . . ."

"But why won't you let me go? We never go anywhere! Why can't I have some fun?"

"Lainie, dammit, *shut up!*" I exploded, pounding the kitchen table, suddenly aware of the cramped quarters of our funky apartment. We needed to get the hell out of there, that was for sure. Iceberg had been advising me that I could use the tax shelter of owning my own house. It seemed like such a big step, though—so adult. This distraction was running through my mind at the same time I was staring Lainie down, optically daring her to make another peep, which she soon did:

"I just don't understand why we can't *go* somewhere," she sniveled.

I lost it. I stood up so violently I knocked my chair down, swiftly circled the small table and grabbed Lainie by the arms, standing her up against the wall like a large doll. "Will you shut the fuck UP?!" I screamed, and slammed her against the wall, pretty hard, probably more than once. Three or four times. I heard her head thunking against the plaster. Quick as a mouse, she wriggled away from my grasp and backed off toward a corner of the room, balling her fists and crouching down like a boxer, starting to feint.

Shocked at myself but amused at Lainie's reaction, I raised my hands helplessly in the air and laughed awkwardly, trying to de-escalate the confrontation. "What's this?" I teased. "The championship bout at Madison Square Garden?"

I shouldn't have let down my guard to make a joke; that's why I never saw the right hook coming. Lainie landed a solid wallop for such a small person, right on my left eye socket. As I went down on the cheap kitchen linoleum I realized I shouldn't have taken on an experienced scrapper unless I was prepared to defend myself.

That's how I ended up with the movie-star look at work the next day, but it didn't fool Giselle. As soon as she saw me she came over, gingerly lifted the shades, and said, "Oooh, what a shiner. Did Lainie do that?"

a novel of sexual initiation

I nodded, deeply chagrined. My home situation was getting around no matter how discreet I believed myself to be.

"Poor baby." Surprisingly, she softly kissed me on the cheek below the bruise, and said contrarily, "Tell Lainie she can come over if she needs a place to stay tonight. We'll have pizza."

"Lainie!?" I protested petulantly. "What about *me*? What if I need a place to stay?"

Giselle grabbed my chin with two fingers and shook it seductively. "Ooh, baby, that's no good. We wouldn't want to give her a reason to kill you!" Then she winked and gave me a dazzling grin, and went to her usual post behind the cash register. I stared at her in wonderment. It was the only time she would ever openly flirt with me, and I cherish that moment to this day. It's a surprisingly efficient salve for ancient wounds.

My embarrassment was doubled when Iceberg walked in a little later, having returned unexpectedly early from Santa Fe. He had gone there for the first time to negotiate head-on with Etty. After issuing restrained and diplomatic sympathies for my injury, he launched into some legalese that I had a hard time keeping up with. Perhaps noticing my poor absorption of the material, he interrupted himself to scan the room and lean closer to me.

"You know, Randall, something really weird happened while I was in Santa Fe." Iceberg's voice had grown low and conspiratorial. I had a cold feeling in my gut about what was coming.

"Oh yeah? What?"

"Well," Iceberg said, casting his eyes about to check that neither Giselle nor any customers were within earshot, "Etty tried to put the *moves* on me."

"Really?" I gasped, recoiling, playing for the maximum dramatic effect.

"Yeah!" Iceberg exclaimed, and then raised his shoulders almost to his ears, doing a shiver. "I mean, *ewww*! Can you imagine doing it with that old hag? Gross! She's nuttier than I thought. Right up there with Chuck, as usual."

"Wow," I said softly, shaking my head.

Iceberg eyed me cagily for a moment, then moved closer to

my ear, his voice closing to a whisper: "In all those times you've been there, Randall, has she ever tried to, you know. . .?"

I straightened up and vigorously shook my head. "Nope," I lied matter-of-factly, "she just uses me as a sounding-board. We talk and talk, and she's actually kind of interesting sometimes. But no, she's never done anything funny with me. You must be her type, Ice."

"Yeah, right," he replied sardonically, visibly relaxing. "Yuck." Hoisting his new, expensively tooled briefcase—he was much more professional now than in the old days—Iceberg cast a longing look in Giselle's direction, and half-heartedly waved good-bye to her. They had been history for a long time, but apparently Iceberg hadn't yet quenched the flame on his torch.

"Well, gotta go," he said decisively, and bustled out the door. At that moment, watching Iceberg depart, I decided that Etty Berquist would have her way with me no longer; the whole thing was just too weird. *Yucky*, in Iceberg's terminology. I had silently confirmed this decision, nailing it down in my mind, when the phone rang.

"Diversions of the Bay, Berkeley speaking," I said cheerily, feeling better already.

"Randall?" said a quavering voice.

"Yeah . . . Pierce, is that you? Hey, I'm sorry I haven't been over in a while. Business as usual, you know. Are you okay?"

"No, I don't *think* I am." Pierce's voice was cracking, the last two words almost lost in a sob. "Randall, please come over here now. Frank is very sick."

19

FRANK looked terrible. That's all I could think, witnessing him in the hospital room: *He looks terrible.* I desperately wished I could get that simplistic, panicky thought out of my mind, and replace it with something profound and soothing I could pass on to Frank. Perhaps with a single magnificent thought, something unprecedented in my mental history, I could devise an instantaneously healing incantation that would reverse the vicious war going on in Frank's bloodstream and tissues—the war that was obviously lost . . .

Instead, all I could think was how terrible he looked, his face gaunt and pale except for several angry red splotches scattered from his neck to his hairline, his eyes peculiarly bugged-out, his lips chapped to the point of cracking open. He was conscious when I came in the room, almost two hours after Pierce's call. He waved one hand weakly as I entered. Pierce was draped over a chair in the corner sound asleep, his limbs all askew as if he had been thrown there by some savage force. And I suppose he had been. I went to Frank's side and helplessly touched the arm immobilized by tubes and straps, then shrugged, as if I had somehow failed him.

"Hey there Randall," Frank rasped. "Is it bright in here? Am I losing my eyesight too?"

"Oh," I said sheepishly, removing my sunglasses, "no, I . . ."

"Ooooh," Frank grimaced. "That's nasty. Did Lainie do that?"

I guess my mouth dropped open because Frank lurched abruptly in a violent laugh, which turned into a cough so long and racking that I was casting about for the emergency button to call a nurse. He waved me down with his free hand as the cough subsided, wheezing out the words, "Don't be embarrassed. She's a tough one. Duz...doesn't let you get away with anything, I bet."

"Nope," I replied, chagrined not about my bruise, but about my problems taking up the attention of a dying man. "How are you feeling?" I said stupidly.

Frank closed his eyes and swallowed hard, grimacing. "I hurt like hell. All over. Have this rash . . . all down my throat. Drugs are lousy in here," he smiled thinly.

"Jesus, Frank," I said sorrowfully before I could stop myself, my knees going weak. I pulled a chair next to the bed and dropped onto it. A few moments passed in awkward silence.

"Heard you're still having some glitches with the software," Frank continued unexpectedly. "Sorry I can't take care of it."

I shook my head dismissively, feeling more useless at every moment. "Forget it, Frank. Really. You must be . . . There must be more important things to think about now."

Frank looked oddly peaceful as he gazed straight up at the ceiling and breathed out with a slight rattle. "To tell the truth, I don't think much now. . . I sleep a lot, and I've been seeing things. Going places." He glanced over at me sheepishly. "I'm not delirious," he insisted.

"Of course not," I responded, glad to affirm him.

"I'm not afraid to die," he continued. "Over that now. Just . . . tired of it taking so long."

I felt awful. "Hey, Frank," I said hurriedly, "I'm sorry I haven't been to see you in a while. A few weeks ago Pierce said you were holding your own. I didn't know you were hospitalized until he called today."

Frank waved me off again. "Don't worry about it. Everything just went to hell all of a sudden . . . like I'm walking down the hall and open the wrong door. Stepped off a cliff . . ."

Frank's eyes glazed and rolled, and I thought he was losing consciousness. But he snapped to, and sharply nodded his head toward Pierce, softly snoring in the corner of the room.

"You have to get him out of here," Frank asserted. "He's pissing off the nurses."

"Okay," I said firmly, relieved that there was something I could do to help.

a novel of sexual initiation

"And Randall?" Frank said hopefully.

"Yeah?"

"You'll have to be his best friend again. At least for a while. He's not accepting this. Still talking like I'm going home . . . Need you to set him straight."

Oh Christ, I thought, but merely said "Okay" again. Then there was a soft knock on the door. A short, round Hispanic nurse entered, saw me and said: "Oh, good. Frank, is this your friend who's going to take Pierce home?"

Frank nodded and chuckled, painfully. The nurse pointed at Pierce and said brusquely, "Please get him out of here. We have no rules left for him to break."

I shook Pierce loose from his nap. Perhaps because he was still half-asleep, he docilely accepted my ushering of him toward the door. I picked up his big bag and slung it over my shoulder. As we exited Pierce called over his shoulder to Frank and the nurse, "We'll be back promptly. Time for a spot of tea."

I couldn't help laughing as we made our way down the drab white hallway to the elevator. "Pierce, I have a news bulletin. This is America! We don't go out for a spot of tea. Besides, it's dinnertime. Let's get a burrito."

Perhaps because Pierce seemed rational over dinner at a taqueria in the Mission, I was not prepared for the scene that followed. Abruptly shifting his focus from our casual conversation and his half-finished quesadilla, Pierce bolted from his seat, announcing that it was time to return to Frank's room. I told him no, the visiting hours were over and I didn't think the nurses wanted to see him for a while. He seated himself again and watched me sullenly as I took a few more bites of my burrito; I felt increasingly like a POW camp commandant. Finally I said, "OK, let's get out of here. I'm taking you home."

Pierce stiffened in his seat and said forcefully, "Frank needs my energy in the room. If I am not there, it will take longer for him to pull out of it this time."

Oh brother, I thought, *here we go.* "Pierce," I said as gently as I could, "Frank asked me to tell you the truth. He's not pulling out this time. He isn't going to make it. He wants you to accept that now and make it easier on everyone."

Pierce jerked visibly, like some internal slip-fault had given way, and his lips trembled with the aftershock. "I can hardly believe Frank would entrust you with such a *news bulletin*," he said sardonically, "when you haven't troubled to keep current with the situation."

That hurt. I wanted to bite back but I had no defense and realized that Pierce's arch tone was complex. He was angry with more than my negligence.

"I'm sorry," I said simply, "I should have called more often."

I was already behind the beat. Pierce had begun rocking back and forth in his chair, tears gushing freely from his eyes, his tentative composure shattered. "I am only twenty-seven," he seethed, looking at me as if I were his mortal enemy, *"and I am going to die."* He rocked forward so hard that he nearly upset the table, causing a clattering that drew the attention of other people in the restaurant, and a nervous shiver went through me. Pierce's dramatic flair often got out of hand over things of no consequence; I had never seen him react publicly to a matter of life and death.

Halfway embarrassed and halfway just plain scared, I barked, "Whoa now, Pierce," like he was a rearing horse, and continued sternly: "Come on, let's go home."

He calmed enough for us to pay the check and get out of there, but inside Liv Ullman Pierce started weeping and wailing like a madman, alternating between grief about Frank and the palpable fear of his own death. I tried to get in some factual questions about whether he was feeling sick, or had been tested, but his answers were unclear and contradictory.

His rising flood of emotion was impossible to check. By the time we parked two blocks from his place in the Castro he was screaming inside the close confines of my car. He didn't stop all the way home. I'm sure people on the street thought he was roaring drunk as I supported him under one shoulder and tried to hurry him along at the same time.

"Wuhh—*ohhh*—ah-ahhhh!!" Pierce bellowed insensibly as I hoisted him up the stairs to his apartment. To my great relief, his

a novel of sexual initiation

neighbor Phillip appeared in the hallway, looking greatly concerned. I realized I couldn't unlock the door. Pierce was out of his mind, writhing around in my clumsy embrace of control, screeching that I couldn't force him to desert Frank. Phillip, thank God, perceived the problem and shouted, "I have a key!" then disappeared back into his place for half a minute. I struggled to hold on to Pierce. Phillip reappeared not only with a key but a bottle of pills as well.

Inside the apartment, I literally tossed Pierce onto the couch while Phillip raced to the kitchen and poured a glass of water. Pierce came at me because I was in the way of the door, but I pushed him back roughly, each of us yelling in turn at the top of our lungs.

"Let me through the bloody door!"

"Oh no you don't!"

As I shoved Pierce backward onto the couch again, I suddenly flashed on slamming Lainie against the wall not twenty-four hours before, and wondered helplessly, *How did my life get so violent all of a sudden?* Phillip was gingerly approaching Pierce with the water and two tiny pink pills in his hand, an armamentarium that would soon surely be flung to the far corner of the room. To my surprise Pierce grabbed the pills from Phillip and knocked them down greedily with the water, like they were candy. Then he lunged at me again!

This time I tackled him at midsection and pinned him to the couch with all my weight, my face in the cushion, my heart racing, my mind amazed at the primitive passion erupting from Pierce. While I held him down at the lap level, Phillip perched himself atop the sofa's back and began petting Pierce's head, saying "Now, now" and "It's all right" and "Let's all take a rest, okay, Pierce?" That sounded like a great idea to me. I was getting wrung out.

In a minute or two Pierce did stop struggling, which was replaced with big sobbing, and then, after ten minutes or so, with soft rhythmic weeping. The pills—"Xanax," Phillip whispered—were apparently taking effect. As if we were the parents of an unruly tyke, I remarked to Phillip, "I think somebody's

MY JOURNEY THROUGH THE PLANT WORLD   206

been at the hospital too long."

Phillip nodded and said, "I haven't seen him for three days. I was over there day before yesterday, but I didn't realize he was staying there. Was he sleeping in the lobby?"

I shrugged my shoulders and we continued to cluck over Pierce as if he couldn't hear us. In a minute or two he shook his head, dried his eyes, and seemed to rejoin our company. Slumping on the couch, his head rolling slightly, he peered at me as if he had recognized me for the first time all day, and said quizzically, "What happened to your eye, old man?"

Once Pierce was asleep and Phillip had departed, I decided I might as well stay the night. I didn't want Pierce bolting back to the hospital in the wee hours, and I was wasted. Not to mention that I could use a break from the home scene as well. I felt a pang of guilt for not having checked in with Lainie yet, but I'd had my hands full for a while there. Who could blame me for relaxing in front of the TV for an hour?

When I finally called home about ten-thirty, Lainie's tone of voice was the worst I could have expected: "Where have you *been?*"

"I'm sorry," I said truthfully, "there was a little emergency with Pierce over here in the city. Frank's in bad shape; we're gonna lose him soon. I know I should have left a message, but I forgot before I left work, and it's been a madhouse over here ever since. And I mean, really a madhouse."

"So you're coming back right now?" Lainie insisted, with the force of a non-negotiable demand.

"No, honey, I'm sorry. I'm completely exhausted. I need to stay here in case Pierce wakes up in the middle of the night."

"But you have to go to the hospital over here!" Lainie cried.

"What?! What do you mean? Why?"

"Your mom called. We've been looking all over for you!" Lainie responded breathlessly. "Your dad had a car accident and he's at Alta Bates. Your mom's there already. You've gotta come pick me up right now!"

WITHIN fifteen minutes I had vaulted onto the elevated freeway leading to the Bay Bridge, high as a kite on an adrenalin surge

a novel of sexual initiation   **207**

boosted by two doughnuts and a cup of rank, pot-bottom coffee grabbed hurriedly at a corner store. I had informed Phillip of my departure, and he elected to sleep on Pierce's couch.

Buzzing over the bridge in Livvy, I kept saying, "What a *day*," marveling at how alive I felt. The abrupt raising of the stakes in three different relationships had made me feel less detached and diffident than usual, and frankly, less depressed. But I didn't quite know what to feel about my father. It's one thing to be chronically pissed off with somebody and secretly wishing he would get his comeuppance, and something else to be confronting that person's actual physical injury. Lainie gave few details on the accident; she'd said Dad had run into a telephone pole at a street corner near campus. That sounded like he was driving drunk, and I couldn't avoid the thought, *Serves him right*, as I careened onto the Ashby Avenue exit into Berkeley at the maximum speed that Livvy's aged suspension could handle. *Not too shabby. After all, she was built as a performance sedan. I hope he's not badly hurt.*

I needn't have worried. Inside a comfy lounge just off the emergency room, I found my father slumped and sleeping against my mother on a couch, Gayle sitting beside them reading a magazine. There was a large bandage on my father's neck, and an arc-shaped bruise traversing one side of his face, leading me to conclude that he'd had a violent meeting with the Porsche's steering wheel. Otherwise he looked okay. *He got off easy again*, I couldn't help but think as I raced up to my mom.

"For goodness sake, Randall," she said sternly, "what happened to your eye? Did you have a wreck too?"

"No, Mom, I . . ." The words stopped coming as I thought of how to explain Lainie's direct hit, because I realized—*oh shit*—that I'd forgotten to pick her up.

"Where's Lainie?" Mom filled in. "Where were you?"

I sat down in a huge plush chair and sighed hugely. "It's a long story, Mom. You remember Frank, Pierce's friend? I had to go to San Francisco General this afternoon because Frank is in really bad shape—he's dying—and Pierce was making a nuisance of himself over there. I forgot to check in with Lainie, and now. . . I forgot to pick her up."

My mother couldn't help herself; the corners of her mouth were picking up in a suppressed grin. "Did Lainie hit you, son?"

I hung my head and blushed; this was terrible. I could not think of a single word to issue in explanation or self-defense.

"My wounded men," Mom sighed, looking over sideways to catch Gayle's eye, who smiled back at her knowingly. "Well, son, at least you're not going to jail."

"Jail?" I exclaimed. "Dad's going to jail?" I'll admit it: something in me felt gleeful.

"Your father ran a red light and hit a young student in a crosswalk before he knocked down a power pole, and plunged half of Southside into darkness," my mother said with a mixture of resignation and sarcasm. "We know the girl's leg is broken. It could have been worse. The police and the doctor say your father was driving drunk. They're talking right now about what's to be done with him."

Indeed, halfway down an adjoining hall I noticed a Berkeley cop and a white-coated doctor talking. "I better call Lainie," I blurted, suddenly feeling in hot water myself. As it turned out, Lainie was relieved when I apologized for skipping over her.

"It's okay. I hate hospitals," she said emphatically. "Is your dad all right?"

"Yeah," I said, "but he might go to jail. He injured somebody."

"Oh wow," she said, and then added meekly, "Will you come home soon?"

I assured her I would make it home as soon as things sorted themselves out. What I didn't know was how long it would take or what it would cost me. The doctor had decided there was no room at the hospital for my dad, but he didn't want him in a cell. Dad was groggy from painkillers and residual liquor, and the doctor said he'd probably suffered a slight concussion. He would need to be watched by someone for a few days; my Mom reluctantly agreed to take him to Albany. The cop was looking at my dad like he was a trophy fish wriggling out of the net. The contemporary sentiment against drunk driving being what it was, the cop was compiling a laundry list of charges, from DUI

a novel of sexual initiation 209

to running a light to reckless endangerment. He said he'd be happier with the medical override of incarceration if somebody posted a bond.

As my mother hoisted my insensibly mumbling father to his feet there was a long, uneasy silence. I honestly didn't think the situation involved me.

"Randall?" my mom sternly inquired.

"What?"

"Of course you will take care of this, won't you, son?"

That's how I ended up leaving the Berkeley police station about one in the morning, after waking Iceberg by phone for legal advice. I stumbled home to wake Lainie in bed and we talked for another hour about all the day's emergencies. Our own difficulty seemed to have receded into the forgotten past. For once, not dealing with our problems seemed excusable.

But our debts to candor would continue to mount. Over the next year, Lainie seemed to start vibrating more than ever. She was always highly tuned and reactive, like Liv whenever Sykes got too rich a mixture going in the carburetor. In our last eighteen months together, Lainie was shaking apart, losing her grip, becoming too unhappy to bounce back from all our crises.

And I didn't know what to do about it. I had my hands full with the business and my dad's post-accident problems and rescuing Pierce in the months following Frank's death. He was drinking and drugging a lot, even getting into fights during the wee hours at various South of Market clubs. I don't know how many times I had to help dry him out or talk him down. Phillip and I, and a couple of other merciful fellows in that neighborhood took to calling ourselves Rescuers of Pierce. We worked out an emergency code that could be left on my answering machine: "We need a quorum. ROP." And off I would go.

But Lainie had no rescuers. She'd always talked to Jeanna, but it so happened that Jeanna and August were in difficult straits during that same time period. Jeanna moved in and out of the apartment several times; we never knew which girlfriend she was staying with. I noticed that Lainie was on the phone long-distance more than ever; not always to Bobby Skinner, but

MY JOURNEY THROUGH THE PLANT WORLD   210

usually to Georgia. I used to kid her about having two jobs: one at the Edible and one fund-raising for the phone company. She didn't laugh as much at my jokes anymore. I guess that one hardly deserved a round of applause.

Even the glue that had always bound us began to weaken. Our lovemaking became more infrequent and angrier. My porn habit intensified, although it had moved out of the old funky theater, which had fallen prey to the video wave. Without really looking for them—the process was more like a bloodhound involuntarily following his nose—I discovered adult bookstores and video arcades, which are still going strong today, although I have since graduated into the ranks of the private mail-order connoisseur.

When I first entered one of those dark, flimsy booths in a downtown Oakland arcade, I remember feeling the same apprehension as when I first entered the porn theater, leavened with the recognition that this was a much weirder situation. Here you fed quarters into a slot by a TV mounted in the wall, and you could flip through eighteen or twenty channels of fuck films, sitting there on a chair with God knows what on it, a tissue box neatly mounted in the side wall at eye level and a little lined trashcan near the feet. Everything one would ever need in a masturbatory paradise, including an oppressive sense of anxiety and shame.

At busy times men haunted the hallways where the booths were lined up, glancing furtively at each other. I was furtive because I didn't want to be recognized, but I figured that some men were there looking for an encounter. About a third of the videos in the round-up were for gay males and a smaller proportion showed S&M. (I watched one of those once for a while, waiting for the black leather-clad folks to get around to screwing. When they never did, I realized that actual sex was not a priority for that crowd. Quite peculiar. I guess it takes all kinds.)

I didn't hang out at those places for long; they made me too nervous. Once somebody knocked on my locked booth door while my penis was out, doggedly pointing toward the TV screen, and I almost jumped out of my skin. Once a guy poked his finger through a hole in the thin wall, and it moved all

a novel of sexual initiation

around like a blind worm. Once outside the booths, a smelly guy with dyed blonde dreadlocks asked me, "Can I have a quarter to jerk off, mon?"

The underworldliness of the arcade induced a dark fantasy in me: that some deranged nut would cut loose there with a semi-automatic. If I were not killed outright, surely I would end up on the front page of the newspaper: **LOCAL BUSINESSMAN ESCAPES HAIL OF GUNFIRE AT PORN ARCADE**.

Is it any wonder I didn't confide in Lainie? I was too busy mainlining the seduction of guilt. At the time, before I had met June, I thought I was a slave to the simple cruelty of hormones. I couldn't help it.

Lainie couldn't help herself, either. She started smoking like a chimney and sleeping erratically. Rest had never been her strong suit; she had always jerked and twitched herself to sleep, as if ready to run at any sign of trouble. When we experienced our first earth tremor together, about a 3.5 late one night early in 1987, I thought she would never calm down.

Then a strange thing happened: Lainie became a sleepweeper. I remember coming home once in the wee hours, after an emergency session of the ROP, finding Lainie huddled on the couch in the living room. The lights were out, the house was still. Lainie was shaking slightly and whimpering. Easing down on the couch beside her, I asked her what was wrong. There was no reply. Gently I touched her arm, and said, "Come on, honey, tell me what's up." She only whimpered some more. This was not her usual way of being obstinate.

Finally, I cautiously placed a hand behind her neck. She leapt up from the couch, shouting, "WHAT?! Who did it, Mama?" and fell over the coffee table in the dark, scraping her shin badly.

Ever after that, I took care not to wake Lainie when her weeping dreams carried her from the bed once every few weeks. She always made the same short transit to the couch in the living room to huddle, mutter insensibly, and shed tears, all without awakening. Over time I learned how to sit beside her and hold her lightly enough so as not to wake her before she drifted back to a quiet, dreamless sleep. Then she could be safely roused.

Or sometimes I would sit with her a long time, until the window facing me was tentatively lit with the smudge of dawn, and I would dry my own tears—feeling both thankful for this rare, delicate communion, and grieved that something like it could find no place in our waking hours.

20

SMART guy that I was, I decided the solution to our problems was buying a house. Iceberg was all for it, seconding my neurotic fantasy that a bigger, more comfortable abode would settle Lainie's nerves and medicate our growing estrangement. He hooked me up with a realtor and I started taking off Saturdays to look at properties.

Lainie came along but she was usually in a daze, wandering with me through empty and still-occupied houses as if they were small museums. I guess she had a hard time seeing herself settled in any of the places. She never really settled into the Virginia Street duplex that I bought, never unpacking six or seven boxes that she used to move from the old apartment. Although the house, where I now sit quietly writing, came with a big back yard, Lainie never gardened here. That should have been a dead giveaway.

When I suggested to Lainie that she might cut back her hours at the Edible in order to play house, she shocked me by quitting her job entirely, inaugurating a chaotic and mysterious lifestyle. One week she might spend organizing and equipping the kitchen; the next week she would seemingly do nothing around the house, telling me later that she went to see lots of matinees or went shopping with Jeanna. And she started hanging out at Brennan's.

She discovered Brennan's. I'd never been there before she left me a message one evening to come pick her up when I got home from work. I suppose she liked it because, as a working-class bar and cafeteria serving heavy meats and exhaustively cooked vegetables, Brennan's has a faintly Southern ambience. Near the end, I got used to driving down there after work whenever

I didn't find Lainie at home.

One evening in late June of '87 I headed to Brennan's in a snit. The sky was still light and the air warm. We'd talked earlier about taking a walk in Tilden Park as soon as I got home. So what if it was a little later than I expected? She could have waited on me. And I knew that she had gone down there on her rickety old bike, which would never quite fit in Liv's trunk for the trip back, meaning I would have to tie it down. That was always a pain.

I entered Brennan's only to discover Lainie holding court at the end of a long table manned by fifteen to twenty softball players, all male. She was pretty drunk, wearing short-shorts and a holey t-shirt. The situation was altogether more than I could tolerate. In short, I was a party pooper. Posting myself like a security guard beside Lainie, refusing to take a seat despite the gregarious invitations of all the guys, I kept saying, "Lainie, we've got to go," as if we had an infant child starving at home. She kept making jokes. Finally I grabbed her roughly by the arm and hoisted her to her feet. A burly guy sitting right beside her also rose, growling at me:

"Hey bud, no need to manhandle her."

Oh, great. I could see the headline: **LOCAL BUSINESSMAN HURT IN BAR BRAWL**. Given that Lainie had once taken me out in the first round, my chances with the softball team didn't look too hot. I relied on artfulness to engineer the kidnapping:

"Look, my girlfriend is diabetic and she shouldn't be drinking. I've got to get her home and give her a shot or she could die. Is that all right with you?"

The big guy raised his hands and said, "Hey, it's cool. Take it easy. We didn't know about her condition."

Outside, with darkness beginning to settle over the parking lot as I continued to hoist Lainie toward the car, her bike rolling under my other hand, she said in a slurred tone, "I thought diabetic was when you can't eat desserts."

"Can't drink either," I said factually. "Could've killed you if you were really diabetic."

"Glad I ain't!" Lainie giggled, and then added, "Oooh, it's so nice and warm tonight."

I should have known what was coming. Lainie often got indiscreetly lustful when she'd been drinking, and the night was sultry. As soon as we were both in the car she was lifting my hand to her thinly covered breast, chewing at my ear, panting dramatically. I kept fending her off, stage-whispering, "Lainie, stop it! People can see us!"

She stopped long enough to gaze out the front windshield, where she could indeed see a few people making their way to the Chinese restaurant on the other side of the lot. Her response: "OK, they can't see *this*." With amazing rapidity she unzipped my shorts, dug me out and started licking and sucking on my rapidly enlarging cock.

Now, I hate to violate a fundamental tenet of the American Male Canon—and thank God this is a private journal, never to see print—but I have to confess that I have never understood the appeal of blow jobs. Well, I take that back partially; they look exciting onscreen, and the *idea* of them is stimulating. But having a mouth around my penis has just never felt very exciting. In my opinion, something designed for the warmly enclosing vaginal glove feels horsey and misplaced in the relative cavern of the mouth, with its hard palate and its tongue and its *teeth*, for God's sake. All in all it's a bizarre undertaking. Who thought of it first, I wonder—Adam or Eve?

Either way, Lainie's drunken mouthing of me that evening wasn't about to produce orgasmic results, especially given my nervousness about being discovered there in Brennan's parking lot with a woman's head in my lap: **LOCAL BUSINESSMAN ARRESTED FOR**... I wanted to lift Lainie's head and say, "Can we stop this and talk about things for a little while?" But that kind of impulse had gone too long unserved in our relationship.

Instead I said, "Here, wait a minute," reclined the seat about halfway, then lifted Lainie just enough to get my hand around myself and start pumping up and down as rapidly as possible. Lainie turned her head and looked up at me glassily, a truly dirty grin on her face. I closed my eyes and kept going, letting the delicious, deeply irresistible tension rise. When I was about to come I remembered something: the seats!

I twisted my head, looking for a rag or tissue, and said in a strangled voice, "I can't come on the upholstery! It's brand new!"

"Okay," Lainie said gamely, closing both of her hands around my own, putting my penis back in her mouth. After a few cooperative strokes, I let loose inside her mouth, again and again. Lainie choked a little, then returned to close quarters and licked me all over. Falling back against the seat, I experienced a disorienting mix of feelings: gratitude, euphoria, alienation, tenderness, a pathetic sadness . . .

I knew from porn that I should have been growling something like, "Yeah, baby, swallow all that hot love cream!" But I said nothing at first, then weakly murmured "Thanks" and "Sorry." One of those sentiments had to be appropriate. Lainie sat up in her seat, wiping her lips with the back of her hand. "Let's go to the pier!" she cried, still chipper and soused.

I zipped up, returned the seat back, started the car, circled the block, and got on the bridge over the freeway leading to the Berkeley Pier. We said nothing on the short trip down there, my mind racing with competing guilts while Lainie fussed with the recalcitrant radio before giving up and humming something flatly. I was heartsick; I knew we were in a bad way.

We walked about half the length of the pier, Lainie weaving slightly as I held her hand. Across the bay San Francisco was taking on its mystical amber glow. At one point Lainie ran to the rail, leaned against it and said, "God, that's always so beautiful. I just love it down here." Then she turned to me and said, quizzically, "Randall?" Before I could answer she lurched up partway over the rail—*my God, is she going to jump?!* I thought frantically—and proceeded to vomit her turkey dinner into the dark bay water. She heaved several times. When she was done, sliding awkwardly back to her feet on the concrete, looking pale and wasted, the only thing I could think to ask was:

"Was it me?"

I guess not. I don't have to take the rap for everything bad that happened. But I remember that incident as the beginning of the end, the opening scene of the last act. The final scene would

a novel of sexual initiation   217

come a few weeks later, on a hot Saturday morning when I had risen early to get the paper and bring it into bed. The windows were open, but to no avail; it was going to be a scorcher. Lainie was still asleep, curled like a puppy beside me. I had just put an arm around her when the floor seemed to ripple from north to south, the dresser across the room jumped, the walls muttered roughly, and the earth said, "BAM!"

"What was *that*?!" Lainie screamed, jumping to her knees and grabbing the footboard.

"Whoa, Nellie," I replied, dropping the paper and jumping to my feet by the side of the bed, holding my hands out to either side like a soccer goalie, my eyes focusing on a framed Goines print swinging gently on the opposite wall. When everything settled I said, "I think it was about a 4.7."

Lainie burst into tears, sitting back on her haunches. "I hate these stupid quakes! They're so scary!"

"It's not a quake," I said didactically, "it's just a tremor."

"I don't care," Lainie wept. "I hate them anyway!" She was deeply upset; I moved back onto the bed to hold her. She cried for a couple more minutes, not unlike the way she cried at night. When she was done, she said "Randall?" in the same quizzical way that had prefaced her vomiting off the Berkeley pier.

"What is it, honey?"

"I wanna go home."

"Home? You are home," I said defensively, "if you would ever finish unpacking."

"I wanna go home to Georgia," she said meekly, like a four-year-old. "I don't belong here anymore."

A cold prickle traversed my scalp. What was it they said back in Georgia? *The crows are coming home to roost?*—anyway, it was something like that, a saying that meant all accounts were suddenly due, the bell was tolling, the piper must be paid. We had let things slide too long without talking; we should have found another therapist; we could have gotten married . . .

I knew it was hopeless. I could think of a lot of things to say that might have delayed the inevitable. But whenever Lainie spoke in this tone of defiant innocence, I knew her mind was made up. I backed away from her and softly said, "All right. If that's what you really want."

Then I went to sit at the kitchen table for a while, staring vacantly out the window, rolling an orange back and forth on the tablecloth. In a few minutes Lainie closed the bedroom door. Soon I could hear her muffled voice on the phone.

When a timid aftershock rolled under the house a half-hour later, it earned no comment—as if there were no longer anyone at home interested in these things, or as if a tree had fallen in the forest without bothering to make a sound.

BUT I AM nothing if not resilient; I can batten down and button up with the best of them. During Lainie's last two weeks in California I was the perfect gentleman, helping her get back home in every way possible, even pressing a check for a couple thousand dollars into her hands at the last minute.

Here's the weird thing. We may never have been better friends than during that process of saying good-bye: gracious, mutually accommodating, considerate and kind. Jeanna, who was in one of her single phases at the time, came over to help Lainie pack up, wandering around the house carrying boxes with a look of pure wonderment on her face. Once she took me aside to whisper, "Why are you breaking up now? I've never seen you two getting along better."

All I could say was, "We got the hang of it a minute too late." Jeanna made a face, the kind she always makes when she's irritated with me. She rode to the airport with us when I saw Lainie off, having shipped all her stuff to her mother the day before. At the gate Jeanna was tearing up, so she hugged Lainie and said, "I love you, cuz. Write me. Now I'm going to the snackbar to have a good cry and leave you two alone, okay?"

Wet-eyed, Lainie nodded vigorously at Jeanna and watched her walk off. Then she said to me weakly, "Well?"

I'd been looking at the floor. I looked up, barely containing the landslide in my chest. "Lainie, I'm sorry about everything, you know, that didn't . . . that wasn't right."

"S'okay," she murmured, dropping her shoulder bag to lean

a novel of sexual initiation   **219**

against me. "I just don't belong here," she said against my shirt. "I have to go home now."

I couldn't help smiling. It seemed that Lainie knew her own soul and I didn't know anybody's. "All right, honey," I said softly, "I guess you're right. You think they'll let you back in the state of Georgia?"

Lainie leaned back and smiled, wiping her eyes. "I'm gonna sneak in. They'll never know."

"Probably not," I said, my voice cracking. "I love you." Inwardly I cringed; had I ever said it before? I must have. Lainie wasn't counting. She hugged me and cried, "Love you too!" then feverishly grabbed her bags, turned and said, "Bye!" and ran off.

I know that I collected Jeanna at the snackbar and drove her home, but I don't remember how. I don't remember a lot of the days that followed Lainie's departure. Some things are forever lost to me, the way a Big Sur rockslide can get lost in the ocean.

Strangely enough, lonesomeness would make me a better person for a little while. When I got refocused on work after Lainie left, I gave everybody a raise, much to Iceberg's consternation. I started being a little nicer to my father, whom I was driving around a lot. There was a lucky man: although the young Japanese woman he had hit suffered a shattered leg and might never walk normally again, her Buddhist parents testified at his sentencing that they believed in forgiveness and rehabilitation, not punishment.

Everyone was so taken aback by this gesture—including the judge (not to mention yours truly!)—that my father avoided incarceration. He lost his license for three years, and was put on five years probation with mandatory enrollment in a recovery program plus five hundred hours of community service, but he still got off. I suspect he didn't stop drinking for a while, but he was severely chastened. I felt sorry for him for a change. We had dinner sometimes over iced tea, and talked more than we ever had. For a while there, we were almost becoming friends.

I also spent more time with my mom, proud to watch her blossoming as a real artist. Not long after Lainie left, Mom had her first solo show at a little gallery in Emeryville. Gayle pulled some connections and got her an advance review in the *San Francisco Chronicle*, although the reviewer didn't quite know what to make of the lushly sexualized still lifes and landscapes that my mother was painting at the time. **East Bay Artist s Erotic Greenhouse**, read the headline. My mother blushed nearly as pink as one of her canvases when Gayle proudly pasted the clipping in the gallery.

Me, I just wandered through the show *hmm-ing* a lot. Once my mother came up to me—nervously avoiding the first group of viewers she didn't know—and asked, "So what do you think of my art, son?"

"Kinda reminds me of my first year in California," I replied inscrutably.

I should never try to get one up on my mom. She gazed at me coolly and said, "Oh, really? Does it remind you of anyone in particular, son?"

How much did she know, and when did she know it? I wondered, but I was afraid to ask. What if she always knew—now what would Anna think of that? If we had sinned, and my mother was a tacit collaborator, what did that make her? A pimp for Satan?

I didn't share this train of thought with my mother, just grinned and lifted my eyebrows. She hit me lightly on the arm like a true chum, and bravely ventured forth to introduce herself to some potential patrons.

I went outside and sat on a wooden bench in the windy sunshine to think about Anna. She still wrote faithfully, and she still wrote about her faith, although she was a little less righteous since she'd had twins and Pastor Kenny had proved to be predictably conservative about gender roles. From Anna's last letter had spilled out several snapshots of the family foursome: dark Anna, still river-haired, and Kenny, blonde as a Nazi, and two little white-haired tykes. *Well, the Indian in them will show up over time,* I mused—then, in deference to my mother, I corrected myself: *Native American, Randall. You've got to keep up.*

By Christmas of 1987, I was both chastened, not unlike my father, and chaste. I had successfully put an end to the weirdness with Etty even before Lainie left, with curiously little resistance

a novel of sexual initiation 221

from the old lady. When I wrote and told her diplomatically that our intimacy was impinging upon our business relationship, she wrote back and said curtly that from now on she would put me up in a Santa Fe hotel when I visited. But she still wanted me there twice a year, and she still talked my ear off! I had given up trying to figure out what was going on with Etty, as had Iceberg.

So I wasn't "getting any" back then. If I'd known that circumstance would remain the same to the current day. . . well, I don't know that I would have done anything different. It's not that I had no romantic initiative, no hopes or dreams. In fact I was prone to dream an impossible dream. Even in my guilty grief over Lainie's leaving, I was acutely aware that Jeanna was technically available. She'd always been warm with me, not one of those hate-all-guys gay women, and maybe, just maybe if I was exceedingly nice . . .

I decided it was worth a try. I was honorable: I waited until three months had passed since Lainie's departure. Jeanna and I had talked several times by phone because Jeanna was worried that Lainie had moved in with Bobby Skinner. I wasn't surprised, although I felt guilty that I'd pushed her back into the arms of a truly violent guy. Lainie hadn't written or called me since moving in with Skinner; I was having to call Jeanna to get any news about her. Using that as a pretense one Saturday about a week before Christmas, I called Jeanna and asked her what the news on Lainie was.

"She's all right, I guess. I haven't heard anything terrible. She actually sounds happier right now than . . . well, you know."

"Yeah," I said. "I know. It's okay. You can say it. Uh, look, Jeanna, I was also calling because . . . I wondered if you'd like to catch a matinee. I should be at work for the Christmas rush, but I really need a break from running all over the place. I thought if you were free, I hadn't seen you in a while, so I thought, maybe we could get together for a movie . . ." Whew! I was sweating on a cold day, and my heart was pounding.

There was a terrifying silence on the other end of the line, for as much as ten eternal seconds, before Jeanna said softly, "Sure, why not? I have to get back home for dinner, though."

"Yeah, of course!" I gushed.

That's how it began: the fruitless courtship of Jeanna. I shouldn't really say *fruitless* because Jeanna has meant so much to me over the years; I mean that I've never gotten her into bed. Back then I thought I had a chance. Especially on my birthday the following spring, when Jeanna loosened up and spent the whole day with me, including a long visit with my mother (who gave me many quizzical looks), plus a jaunt into Sausalito in Liv Ullman, who was proudly sporting a new skylight I'd had cut into her roof at great expense.

I was so on top of the world by the time we sat down at the Sausalito waterfront, looking at the dazzling view of the city, that I impulsively leaned over and kissed Jeanna on the cheek while we were laughing about something. She recoiled dramatically, her face deadening, and said, "Don't do that, Randall."

"What?" I said defensively.

"You know what," Jeanna said cruelly. "We can't start *dating*."

"Dating?" I replied dismissively. "Of course not. That's what you do in high school. For God's sake, Jeanna, I just gave you a little kiss. I like you. I always have. It's not a crime."

"I didn't say it was," she hissed, tamping me down. I hated making Jeanna angry. "Look, Randall, you're a good friend and all that. I've always liked you too, you know that. But I'm still trying to work things out with August, and . . ." Her voice trailed off, then she said, weirdly, " . . . and I'm not completely bisexual."

I couldn't believe my ears. "What the hell does that mean?" I yelped. "I didn't know you were a *little bit* bisexual. Isn't it one of those things you either are or you aren't?"

Jeanna touched me softly on the arm and seemed to retreat a little. "I just mean . . . I've never told you, but I used to sleep with men, and sometimes I . . . Well, I don't want to make you feel bad. I like you, but it's too complicated for me. If we can just be friends like this, that's fine. But anything else is too complicated, all right?"

"All right," I said diplomatically, actually cheered because I sensed there might be an opening for me—to put it crudely—in the not too far-off future. Although I backed off from Jeanna

a novel of sexual initiation 223

after that, disinterestedly dating a few women I can't even remember now, we did get together now and then for "safe" times together, movie matinees and the occasional breakfast.

In fact, we had a very good time once on the Fourth of July. Sometimes I forget because of what followed. Giselle was heavy into her big romance then with Dirk, the German sailor, and she invited me to come with them on Dirk's boat to catch a bay view of the fireworks in the city.

To my surprise, Jeanna accepted my invitation to come along on "Das Boot," as I advertised it. Thence occurred one of the most romantic and peculiar evenings of my life.

Sailing onto the bay proved to be more work than I expected, and by the time we ate a cold dinner while watching the sky show there was fatigue all around. Dirk and Giselle were taking so many kissing breaks that it got embarrassing. I kept wondering how Jeanna felt about it, but I wasn't brave enough to ask her. We talked around it.

After the fireworks were done and darkness had settled in, the wind on the bay mysteriously died and Dirk had to start up the sailboat's little putt-putt motor to propel us back to the Berkeley marina. This took nearly two hours. During that time Jeanna got sleepy; since quarters were cramped she asked if she could lean against me to take a nap. Did I say yes? Do bears wake up hungry?

After half an hour Jeanna jerked awake, but continued to rest against me. Her customary reserve seemed to have been washed away by the waves. I wanted to stroke her hair but restrained myself.

"Randall?" Jeanna asked.

"Yeah?"

There were ten seconds or so of silence. I was starting to get nervous when she continued, in a sad voice:

"Do you ever feel like . . . like you're out of place?"

"What do you mean? Like socially?"

"No," she replied softly. "I mean . . . in this *world*. Do you ever feel like you're in the wrong world?"

It was such a peculiar question that I was stumped for a reply.

As the seconds ticked by on the quiet, windless bay, our two bodies rocking together gently in the boat, I began to feel entranced by Jeanna's inquiry—not unlike the entrancement I felt the first time I met her. I didn't want the conversation to falter so I started trying to think of some clever rejoinder. Then my almost-forgotten inner voice spoke so clearly I thought Jeanna might hear it too:

Be serious. Your time together is precious.

"Well, I guess not," I admitted awkwardly. "What other world would I be in?"

"Oh, I don't know," Jeanna said, sounding embarrassed. "I'm not sure what I'm talking about. But tonight, out here on the water, it's so different than the everyday world, isn't it? As if we crossed over to someplace new without even trying. It's nice, isn't it?"

"Yes," I agreed wholeheartedly. "Very nice."

"Sometimes it just seems that things could be so *different*," Jeanna added.

My heart leapt in my chest. Would we be kissing soon? The voice advised only, *Pay attention.* So I asked, "In what way?"

"I'm not sure," Jeanna admitted. "Easier, maybe? I can imagine living in a world where there's not so much struggle. Or if there was still a lot of struggle, you'd know what it's all *for*. A world where your purpose is clear, I guess. Is that too much to ask?"

I felt troubled; this was a little too philosophical for me. What was she getting at? What did it have to do with us? For the first time in my life, I asked the inner voice a question:

What do I say now?

Speak from your heart.

I felt a distinct flash of fear, but nonetheless tried to visualize my heart actually saying something. Then this came out:

"Maybe you don't have to know what your purpose is, Jeanna. Maybe you do a lot for people just by being who you are. I see you struggling, but still . . . you've always been important to me whatever you do." I paused, breaking out in a cold sweat of truthfulness. "I guess I'm glad you're in *this* world no matter how

a novel of sexual initiation   225

hard it is."

Jeanna sat up so abruptly that I was afraid I'd offended her
somehow. When she turned to me I could see, even in the faint
light of the night, that her eyes were swimming.

"That's really sweet," she whispered. "Thank you for saying
that, Randall."

"Well, sure," I responded lamely.

She leaned against me again. I think she cried softly for a
while; it was hard to tell. Except for quiet good-nights said all
around when we got back to the pier, Jeanna and I hardly spoke
again that night. I dropped her off at one of her girlfriends'
apartments. Rootless as ever, she was still feuding and peacemaking with August in predictable cycles.

Suffused with the warmth of the evening, both climatic and
emotional, I pondered Jeanna's musings on the way home. For
once I was free of anticipation about whether we would ever
become an item. It felt good and I wasn't sure how it had happened. But I did enjoy the fresh memory of her thin frame resting against me on the boat. Entranced with that lingering
imprint, I absent-mindedly walked in my door a few minutes
after midnight. The phone began to ring and my heart leapt up.
It must be Jeanna.

"Hello?" I said happily.

"*Rannnn-dall!*" a voice screamed, veined with terror, its blood-
curdling intensity shocking my ear. I held the phone out a few
inches, and said, "Yeah, this is me. Who is this?"

"Oh, *Jesus!*" It was Lainie, whimpering now, sounding completely wrong, panting into the phone. "Oh God, Randall, I
thought he was gonna kill me!"

I froze. "Who's gonna kill you, Lainie? Bobby? Is he hurting
you?"

"No!" she barked. I heard a metallic clatter, then Lainie
screamed again, this time a long, inarticulate wail.

"Oh, God, Randall," Lainie said when she could speak again.
"Dammit, dammit, *dammit!*"

"Lainie," I said evenly, trying to control my voice, "you've got
to calm down and tell me what's happening. What time is it

MY JOURNEY THROUGH THE PLANT WORLD

there? What's going on?"

There was an indistinct rustling, then Lainie dropped the phone. When she picked it up again, her voice was jumpy but less loud:

"I didn't mean to do it, Randall! But he was drinking all day long and he got so mean. When he left I thought I wouldn't see him 'til morning, but he came back, and when he got out of the truck yelling like he was . . . I knew he was gonna hurt me! I didn't mean to do it, Randall. Really! Oh, Jesus . . ."

"All right, Lainie," I said as reassuringly as possible." I believe you. But you have to tell me what you did, and what's going on right now. Okay? Can you do that?"

"Uh-hunh," Lainie said in her child voice, suddenly obedient. "I shot him."

"Oh, Jesus," I said. "Lainie, is he hurt bad? Where is he?"

"He's right here," Lainie responded, sniffling. "He's . . . kinda all over the place. I got his shotgun when I heard him comin'."

My stomach turned; my heart dropped; my skin crawled. What was I supposed to do, three thousand miles away?

"Lainie," I said tentatively, trying to think fast, "Do you have any neighbors? Anybody close to you?"

"Oh yeah," Lainie said matter-of-factly, "there's the Campbells across the way. I can see their lights."

"Okay now, honey, I want you to . . ." Then I heard a caterwauling sound, barely discernible over the phone at first but growing rapidly in intensity, until I reckoned that the source couldn't be more than a hundred yards away from Lainie.

"Lainie, honey, can you tell me something?"

"Uh-hunh?" she replied waveringly.

"Is that the police coming?"

"Uh-hunh. Sheriff prob'ly."

"Lainie, where is the gun now?"

"Right here. Got it on my lap."

"*Lainie!*" I shouted, abruptly livid with fear. "Put it down on the floor, right now! Put the goddamn gun DOWN!"

21

ON THE plane to Atlanta two weeks after Lainie shot and killed Bobby Skinner, I couldn't keep my eyes open after downing the little tray lunch. I kept slipping into fitful, dream-filled naps. In one dream I was chasing a criminal through some ancient stone ruins like Stonehenge.

I had a partner, an anonymous FBI agent. I knew the criminal was very crafty, so I yelled at my partner to be careful as we split up. My partner disappeared into the filmy mists swirling around the stones. As I crept around one huge, moss-covered pillar, I found myself at the top of a stairway descending deeply into the earth, its destination buried from view.

Then I turned my head and saw my FBI partner, draped lifelessly over the stairway's cold marble handrail. His face was covered by a blank mask, from behind which there issued a trickle of blood. Sticking out of his neck was a gleaming silver needle, which I knew to be exactly seven inches long. Certain that the criminal had fled down the stairway, I grimly contemplated whether chasing him was worth the effort, because I knew—as I said to myself on awakening—*"If caught he will disappear."*

"That's simply wonderful," June had gushed when I told her this dream, about a year after that flight. "It's just perfect, like an engraved invitation to the initiation of your individuation."

Whoa, I thought, *too many "in" words in a row*. All I said to June was, "Individualism?"

"No," she corrected me, "*individuation*. That's the process of claiming your authentic self while shedding the delusive aspects of your ego. For instance: the FBI man who's your partner in the dream? He's your ego. He's a symbol of paternalism and secrecy, two false aspects of your character. Yet he's clearly identified

as not-you: he's both separate and anonymous. The criminal—
that's your shadow, of course—kills him with a seven-inch silver
needle, a pointer toward the journey of integration. Really, dear,
this dream gives me chills, it's so brilliant!"

"Well, thanks," I said hesitantly. "But I still don't get it."

"All right," June said patiently, as if we were reviewing something I should have gotten back in the first grade. "Let's look
more closely. Do you understand the significance of the needle?"

"Nope."

"Silver is the color of the lunar, feminine quality and signi-
fies quickening, the state of impending birth. Seven is the number of reintegration, coming back into the wholeness of things.
Your shadow has collaborated with your feminine energy, your
anima, to indicate that you must choose against the ego in order
to follow your shadow towards integration. The Stonehenge
ruins in your dream indicate that you are near the portal of the
collective unconscious, a realm of psychic energy that both
underlies and transcends your individual psychology. Indeed, by
the end of the dream you are at the top of the stairs leading into
your own depths. But the dream also shows that you are indecisive about the next phase of the process: pursuing your shadow."

"Of course," I piped up, trying to sound like I was keeping
pace with June's dizzying analysis, "because I know that he'll
disappear if I catch him."

"That's right!" June beamed. "If caught, the shadow will disappear *into you*. Your shadow, Randall, is something that seems
dark and evil, yet is really made up of positive, powerful qualities—in your case, I'm presuming, a profound tenderness and
open-heartedness. These are the kind of qualities that have been
driven from your everyday personality. Mind you, that's not just
your personal problem—it's also the problem of Western patriarchal culture as a whole."

I blinked, stuck on the words *profound tenderness*. A wise-guy
part of me wanted to say, *Like crying over dead puppies?* but I realized I'd only be giving June ammunition. For once I held my
tongue.

"Anyway," June resumed, "those tender and powerful energies

a novel of sexual initiation

want back into consciousness, to find expression in your everyday life. But your ego is so afraid of them that it masks them as bad and shadowy. To get back your most positive, transcendent qualities you have to courageously confront your negative shadow qualities. The shadow would then disappear into you—not all at once, of course, but gradually, step by step. Do you see? The steps are right in front of you, at the end of the dream!"

I felt like I'd been injected with some kind of mental speed; my poor brain was racing with unfamiliar firings of untried neural connections. Thank God June has always insisted on my keeping a tape recording of our sessions. Otherwise I wouldn't have remembered one-tenth of what she said at the time. Copying it into this journal, I get a little more of it than I used to.

Of course I understood nothing when I had the dream. At the time I jerked awake, filled with foreboding, and let my eyes drift groggily up toward the TV angled down at me from the ceiling of the jet. One of those Eddie Murphy actioners was playing itself out silently. Just as I looked up a bad guy was blowing away another bad guy with a sawed-off shotgun, which made me flinch in my seat. Then there were bad guys and cops and Eddie Murphy shooting guns all over the place. From my seatmate's headphones I began to overhear, very faintly, the sound effects: BLAM BLAM BLAM! Ka-POW! *Ka-CHUUNG!*

I had reason to be sensitized to gunplay at the moment and I stared at all of it, aghast. When Eddie Murphy pulled out an enormous handgun and started blasting away at a Rich Bad Guy inside a luxurious estate, shattering mirrors and china cases, I suddenly saw the gun in a way I had never seen a gun before: as an erect penis.

That was probably how guns got invented, it occurred to me: as a subconscious attempt to correct the inconsistencies and inefficiencies of the male sex organ. After all, a gun is always erect and can be fired at will; it's never impotent. Instead of a messy hot load, it fires hot *lead*, straight to the target. And it kills right away, whereas what the penis delivers takes years to kill. Since whatever is born must die, the seed of life is also the seed of death. But the gun's seed saves a lot of time; it can kill right away. What power, what gleaming efficiency, compared to the humble, unreliable penis, that must spawn a baby in order to eventually produce a corpse!

I suppose this irrational line of thought evidenced my morbid state of mind at the time. But it did help me understand the National Rifle Association. They weren't really defending the Second Amendment to the Constitution; they were defending something far more intimate—a deeply emotional attachment, as it were. For if guns were outlawed, only outlaws could have hard-ons! No wonder this issue was passionately fought by gun lovers. This was *personal*.

By the time the plane landed, I was more or less in my right mind again, though keyed-up for a number of reasons: I hadn't been home since leaving at age seventeen, I was to be met by my sister who had always resented me, and I had to find a decent lawyer, pronto, for my ex-girlfriend, who happened to be a murderer. No, wait: that didn't sound right. What had the newspaper called her? In between naps on the plane, I had been staring at the *Atlanta Constitution* story Carolyn had sent me: **ABUSED KILLER LAY IN WAIT FOR VICTIM.**

Lainie, an abused killer? That I could imagine. But "lay in wait"? That brought a rueful smile. The only time I could remember Lainie "lying in wait" was one evening during our last two years together, when she had taken the initiative to do something about our sputtering sexual relationship by investing in a sexy teddy set from Victoria's Secret. Erotically semi-clad, she lay in wait for me in the candlelit bedroom one evening.

Except that by the time I actually got home, after a long dinner and a drink or two with Iceberg, she had blown out all the candles, made some popcorn and turned on the TV. That's how I had found her, with a big wooden bowl on her belly and bedcovers obscuring her seductive attire. It was just as well. The scene she had planned would have made me nervous, echoing all the porn I had seen. I would have laughed at the wrong times.

There wasn't much to laugh about now. With only an overworked public defender at her side, Lainie would be convicted by the press of the charge brought swiftly against her—Murder

a novel of sexual initiation 231

One—well before a jury got around to it. The story Lainie's court-appointed attorney had told me squared with Lainie's wild call that fateful night:

By July 4th the bloom was well off Lainie and Bobby's reunion honeymoon. He had reverted to his habitual violent ways, precipitating frequent fights that had brought the sheriff to their door twice already that spring and summer. On the day of the shooting, Lainie was afraid to go to bed because Bobby's all-day drinking binge was sure to result in bruising punishment whenever he returned home. When he showed up, Lainie met him at the door with shotgun in hand, and told him to go sleep it off at one of his buddies'. He slammed her against the wall, she thwacked him with the gun butt, and when he lunged at her again she unloaded at very close range.

Oh, Christ. I couldn't get away from the feeling that all this was my fault. After all, if I'd been better to Lainie, married her or something, she wouldn't have ended up back in Georgia embroiled in a lowlife tragedy. I had told Iceberg that I wanted to find the very best legal representation available, and he answered:

"Sounds like money down a rathole to me."

"What?!" I replied, shocked.

"Well, she blew the guy away, didn't she?" That's when I remembered that Iceberg and Lainie never had gotten along, eyeing each other testily at their very first meeting and ever after that. When he saw my determination, Iceberg agreed to shake loose some ready money from some of the investments he had made for me.

"Don't go overboard," he warned me when I was getting myself together for the airport. "Let's leave F. Lee Bailey out of this, okay? You're not a rich man."

My unexpected ally in the attorney search was my own sister Carolyn, who had taken up Lainie's cause with unexpected vigor. I had called her as soon as Lainie had abruptly hung up the phone that night, praying that she would drop the gun (she did), before some trigger-happy Barney Fife could storm the premises and send her to the same fate as Bobby Skinner.

Carolyn, who had a reasonably happy and stable family life by that time—Cody had actually grown up, to everyone's surprise, and become a successful salesman of GM's hip new auto line, the Saturn—started working on Lainie's case day and night, peppering me with phone calls prior to my flight home. So after greeting Carolyn, tow-headed Frank and two-year-old Grace, my undeniably cute niece, at the airport gate, I was not too surprised to learn that my sister was already a step ahead of me.

"I found a great lawyer for Lainie!" Carolyn exclaimed, so excited that she stepped on one of little Frank's lines about his junior football league. "Somebody who really, really cares. Are you ever gonna be surprised!"

"Surprised?" I replied as we threaded our way through the airport throngs, while I mussed Frank's hair as a consolation for the adults changing the subject. "I'm not surprised that you found somebody already. You've really been working on this, and I appreciate it."

"No," Carolyn smiled conspiratorially, "I mean surprised by who the lawyer is."

"Is it somebody I've heard of? I can't afford F. Lee Bailey, sis."

"No," she giggled, "It's somebody you know. Wanna guess?"

I was stumped. I knew no lawyers in Atlanta, unless it was some guy I'd gone to high school with. "No, just tell me," I sighed as we passed through a turnstile into the baggage claim area.

"JoEllen Sanders," Carolyn replied. "Known to you as JoEllen Jones."

I had seen my suitcase and bag approaching on the carousel, but I let them drift on by. My scalp was prickling. "What?!" I exclaimed. "JoEllen from high school? But I thought she lived in Florida . . ."

"Used to," Carolyn explained, seeming proud of herself. "She got divorced and came back up here. I don't know how she did it with a little girl to raise on her own, but she put herself through law school and just took a position with a big firm downtown. She does corporate law, but when she heard about Lainie she called the public defender. Her firm's gonna help her out. She seems really smart, Randall. I don't see how we could do any

a novel of sexual initiation   233

better. Aren't you excited?"

I sat down on the ledge of the baggage carousel; I had forgotten why we were there. I had an impulse to burst forth in tears, but it passed. Instead I looked up at Carolyn, my eyes only going a little wet, and said: "Yeah, sis. That's great. They don't come any smarter than JoEllen Jones."

I WAS doubly glad I'd planned to stay in a downtown hotel. It wasn't just that I hadn't looked forward to bunking with little Frank. Now there was an even better reason to be on my own in comfortable accommodations. The setting could very well prove useful for a tryst, a most unexpected romantic reunion.

The possibility of consummating my long-deferred passion for JoEllen Jones grew so prominent in my mind that Cody and Carolyn must have thought me terribly absent-minded during dinner with the family. Cody, who simply could not grasp my love affair with a twenty-year-old Volvo, was working hard on a sales pitch for a new Saturn—"I could have it shipped to you by the time you get back to California!"—and I kept shaking my head politely, mumbling brush-offs. I completely missed a couple of things that Carolyn said. Instead of getting pissed with me like she did when we were teens, she asked with genuine concern, "Are you all right, Randall? All this must be hard on you."

"I'm okay, just tired from the flight." I repeated this excuse several times before begging off from a TV evening with everybody. By 8:30 I had hopped into my rental car to drive back downtown. My mind was racing.

I couldn't believe the unexpected twists and turns of my life, how so much misdirection, poorly chosen forks in the road, and tacky melodrama had magically led me to this incredible resolution: JoEllen Jones! It made a crazy kind of sense, after all. JoEllen wasn't just an old flame, but the truest and deepest love of my life, inadvertently truncated before our full potential could be realized. Not to mention: before we ever got to bed.

Of course I'd kind of forgotten about her in recent years, but fate had seen to it that we should be reunited at this dramatic moment. It was so perfect! After a madly passionate week in

Atlanta, drenched nightly with sexual passion while we spent the days together assembling a bulletproof defense for Lainie, JoEllen would visit me in California and eventually move out there . . . with her daughter. My enthusiastic plan got a little fuzzy at that point. I couldn't see how JoEllen's child fit in; I was hardly ready to be a stepfather. Maybe I would warm up to it. *We'll see,* I thought, *but first things first.*

Yet the very first thing—seeing JoEllen again for the first time in ten years—didn't happen the way I envisioned. I thought we would rendezvous in a downtown park, perhaps, spending a minimum of time on small talk before embracing passionately on a bench, then retiring to my hotel room when that got out of hand. Instead, in the morning I had a message at the hotel desk to meet JoEllen at her law firm—McRae, Baker, McClelland, Schene—at ten a.m. Upon entering I was ushered into a conference room where a young male stenographer sat. We chatted about the weather East and West for ten minutes or so before an elderly gentleman, a middle-aged gentleman, and JoEllen Jones, or Sanders, entered the room.

I was paralyzed. I could hardly leap up and embrace her, given the circumstances. I was also transfixed by her appearance; with her swept-up hair, high heels, and conservative Ann Taylor look, she was not quite the ripe young thing I remembered from high school! Also, she was a little zaftig, her natural fullness of figure having graduated into an undeniable plumpness over the years. She was a mother, after all. Upon seeing me for the first time, she hopped a little on one foot, waved the fingers of one hand like she used to every morning at school, then gave me a dazzling smile and a wink. The message seemed to be: *Later, honey!* That was good enough for me.

For the duration of a forty-five minute meeting with one of the firm's senior partners and JoEllen's immediate supervisor, she was strictly business. The old man—McRae, I believe—issued his misgivings about JoEllen partnering on a big case in public view outside her field of expertise. Her immediate boss kept coming to her rescue, reassuring the old man by getting the discussion around to money—specifically the amount of the

a novel of sexual initiation   235

retainer that I could lay out in order to get Lainie's defense into high gear as soon as possible. They had thought at first that this would be a pro bono defense.

Immediately I proclaimed (partly to impress JoEllen) that I would provide "whatever it takes." When they started laying out hard figures, I almost choked aloud. Iceberg was going to kill me. Unless the trial proceeded quickly and cleanly and concluded in Lainie's favor, the whole process, including possible appeals, would easily outstrip my personal resources. I was feeling progressively clammy as the discussion went on, deferring more and more of the lawyers' inquiries to Iceberg.

Still, by the end of the meeting we had established an initial plan of attack. JoEllen was impressively articulate and businesslike; it was as if we'd never met before. But when the old man, JoEllen's boss, and the stenographer had filed out of the room, JoEllen carefully shut the door, turned to me, and squealed:

"Ooooh, Mister Kendricks! Can you *believe* it?" Then she rushed into my arms, her soft but tailored substantiality filling up my embrace. She hugged me tightly then leaned back and said, in a chiding tone, "Boy, have we ever been out of touch!"

"Yeah," I laughed, "I didn't know you had . . ."

JoEllen interrupted me with a peculiar look in her wonderful eyes, a look somehow both stern and merry. "Randall, you were *living* with Lainie?"

I grinned, oddly embarrassed. "Yeah, six years, I guess."

JoEllen's embrace loosened a little. "It's so weird, isn't it? I mean, that things turned out that way. But she always had a crush on you."

"She did?" I said wonderingly. "In high school I thought Lainie couldn't stand me."

"Well, that's also true," JoJEllen laughed, deep and throaty. "It happens that way sometimes. I've even done it myself." She blinked and looked at the floor as if she were remembering something intensely personal.

I didn't like the drift of the conversation. "Hey, JoEllen, are you free for lunch?"

"Oh God, Randall, no, I'm not. I'm sorry, I'm just so busy.

Maybe tomorrow, after I get back from meeting with Lainie."

My heart fell. "How about dinner tonight?" I proposed gamely, trying to salvage something of my anticipations.

JoEllen backed off from me, frowning, and turned to open her briefcase and extract a thick calendar book. "I'd love to, Randall, but I don't have a sitter tonight. Let me see. Hmm . . ."

"Hey, come on," I pleaded, "we haven't talked in ten years and I'm only going to be here for a week. Can't you make it work somehow?"

JoEllen flashed me an irritated look, then smiled, conciliatory. "Okay, I'll make the sitter an offer she can't refuse. And by the time I make it right with Sandy—that's my daughter—she'll have me where she wants me for the rest of my life." She shook her head helplessly and added, "Meet you at the hotel about seven-thirty?"

"Great," I said, feeling triumphant.

"This'll be fun!" JoEllen beamed, as if we had decided to go to the zoo.

I WANTED to see Lainie that afternoon but the county jail authorities were being imperious about her incarceration. Lainie was regarded by local law enforcement as that most dangerous of creatures—a violent woman—and she was considered a flight risk due to her California connections. Thus the sheriff had gotten a local judge to refuse her bail, one of the things that JoEllen wanted to fight immediately.

Once it became clear that I would not be allowed to see Lainie until two days later, I took off in my rented car and did a nostalgic tour of the old stomping grounds: around town, out past the high school, then to one of my favorite cemeteries where you can find the graves of slaves with worn, unintelligible headstones huddled in the back, near the woods. I sat in the shade there for a while, escaping the oppression of a Georgia summer afternoon, and marveled about how foreign and familiar home felt to me now. And I contemplated, in increasingly gray tones, the peculiar set of circumstances that had finally brought me there.

a novel of sexual initiation

When I headed downtown my spirits rose as I contemplated a happier matter: what JoEllen might wear to our romantic dinner. I knew she wouldn't be as daring as back in high school, when she used to expose her pubic hair for my titillation. I was visualizing a low-cut evening gown that would tastefully advertise her ample bosom.

So I suffered a considerable disappointment when JoEllen showed up in the hotel lobby, twenty minutes late, wearing exactly what she had on in the conference room that morning: Ann Taylor, wrinkled.

"God, I'm so sorry about the time," she said sincerely, "I had to go home and deal with the sitter, and then drive all the way back in. I didn't even have time to change, and I'm really wiped out. Hope you don't mind if I don't last too long?"

I nodded as I took her arm and lightly kissed her cheek, but what she had said sounded awful. We decided to take dinner in the hotel restaurant because it was the easiest thing to do. We had no more than started in on a little wine before JoEllen started in on me.

"I missed you a lot for a while, Randall. You hardly ever answered my letters after you left."

Ouch. "Yeah," I admitted awkwardly, "I'm sorry. I guess I left everything behind me when I got to California. Things were so different when I got there."

"Hmm," JoEllen said neutrally, obviously unconvinced, then took another tack: "Lainie said she used to live with two gay women out there? And one of them is some kind of a witch?" Her eyes widened in the candlelight.

"Yes," I reported, "one of them is Lainie's cousin Jeanna. The witch is her girlfriend, more or less—August. Tough old bird."

"Goodness gracious," JoEllen replied disapprovingly. "You Californians are so weird! I'll have to keep this stuff from coming out if we get to trial. If those good old boys at the DA's office get wind of Lainie hanging out with lesbians and witches . . . well, it just can't come out. We'll have to keep you under wraps, too."

"What does that mean?" I shot back, offended.

JoEllen retreated. "I mean we want to limit the disclosure to

Lainie's life here in Georgia. The problem is that you could be subpoenaed by the prosecution, since she made that call to you right after the shooting. I don't like it. I'll have to ask Craig about how to handle this." She pulled a notepad and pencil from her pocketbook on the floor, and set to scribbling with a forceful hand, making the table shake and the candle waver.

"JoEllen," I said firmly, feeling increasingly irritated as she wrote her notes, "can we talk about something else for a minute?"

She stopped scribbling, gazing at me quizzically as our salads arrived. She started right in on hers but I sat there with fork in hand and asked thoughtfully, "JoEllen, what did you think when Carolyn told you I was coming home?"

JoEllen raised her eyes ceilingward like she was trying to recall some arcane legal point. Through a busy mouth she said, "Well, I guess that it would be nice to see you after all these years, and I was happy to have some help for Lainie. And . . ." she paused, stabbing at a cherry tomato like it was a fugitive, "that it was all kind of *strange*, you know."

"That's it?" I replied, disappointed.

"Yes."

"Hmm." I started in on my salad, my excitement about the evening dropping like a stone. We both ate in an increasingly uncomfortable silence until JoEllen stopped abruptly, laid down her fork, and put her hands in her lap.

"Randall." JoEllen's tone was motherly.

"Yes?"

"Do you mean that you were expecting . . ." She scanned the elegant, nearly empty room, leaning forward to whisper: "Did you think we were going to *sleep together?*"

That really stung. "No!" I blurted defensively, "I mean, not just that. The first thing I thought when Carolyn told me you were Lainie's lawyer was that, you know, we were pretty big sweethearts, and we never really got the chance to . . ."

"Randall."

"Yeah?"

JoEllen pushed her salad plate away, averting her eyes from mine. "You left me *twice*."

a novel of sexual initiation 239

I was stunned. "But I was just a kid, both times! It was beyond my control."

"So now that we're adults and you're in control, you're ready to consummate our high school romance." JoEllen's tone was steely, like a cross-examination. "Let's say we did. Have you thought about how Lainie might feel?"

"No," I said truthfully, startled that this connection had not occurred to me. But on first glance, I couldn't see a problem. After all, Lainie had left *me* for an old boyfriend!

"And let's say we don't worry about that, we just fall in love again. Then what would happen?"

I leaped at the unexpected opening. "Then you could come visit me in California . . ."

"Not in the near future," JoEllen interrupted coldly, "not with me taking on this trial on top of trying to establish myself in the firm. And I would never move to California; my life is here. I promised Sandy I would never move her again. She's happy here in school."

I stared dumbly at JoEllen as our entrees arrived; the sight of the main course clearly pleased her. Her tone softened as she dug in: "Of course, if you wanted to move back here and take a chance on *courting* me in a proper way . . ."

My shock must have been apparent, for JoEllen smiled merrily and moved in for the kill. "You know, that's still the way we do things back here. We don't jump into bed on the first date like y'all do in California."

I flashed on my first, accidental "date" with Lainie. Finding nothing there to use in my defense, I tried to imagine pulling up roots and moving back to Atlanta. That lasted about three seconds. So I had nothing to say. The broiled trout on my plate looked entirely unappetizing, its cooked eye trapping me with a vague accusation from beyond the pale.

"Randall." Now JoEllen's tone was kinder.

"Yeah?"

"I don't mean to be hard. I'm actually flattered, really I am, that you were thinking of me romantically after all this time. Romance is just not a big concern in my life right now. I'm still sorting myself out from my divorce."

"Uh-huh," I replied neutrally, flaking some fish away from its spine. Ten or fifteen seconds passed as I disinterestedly dissected my dinner, not looking at my companion.

"Well," JoEllen said gamely, "would you like to hear about it?"

"About what?"

"My *life*," she replied pointedly.

"Sure," I responded, jerking to attention, "of course."

A DAY and a half after that bracing course correction, I finally got to see Lainie in the county jail. Having imagined we would be forced to talk over phones through a glass partition, like in the movies, I was surprised that we met in an open room where several female prisoners were meeting with friends or relatives. We were allowed to hug each other before we sat down across from each other at a plain table. But there were two armed guards in the room. In a yellow jumpsuit with a number over her left breast, Lainie looked unexpectedly cute, like some kind of girl paratrooper. She felt really good to me when we hugged; I had forgotten how she always seemed to fit me somehow, at least physically. She had lost weight and looked a little pale, yet seemed in good spirits considering the circumstances. Then I remembered the circumstances: where we were, and how each of us got there—and my heart began to tear open.

Yet Lainie smiled brightly at me from across the table, her jaws working busily on some gum, and said for openers:

"I quit smoking!"

"Really?" I laughed awkwardly. "That's good, I guess."

"They don't hardly let you get cigarettes in here anyway," she said in a low tone, as if that revelation could get her into trouble. "So I figured, it's now or never, huh?"

"Yeah," I said inconclusively, suddenly nervous about our surroundings. "Look, Lainie, we don't have a lot of time, so I want to say some things that are pretty important."

"Okay," she replied calmly, then smacked her gum.

"First, I'm going to be working with JoEllen on your defense, so you don't have to worry about the money or anything. I think

a novel of sexual initiation 241

she'll do a pretty good job. You know she's trying to get the charge reduced to manslaughter before it gets to trial, right?"

"Uh-hunh." Lainie was looking at me as if I had spoken Latin.

"We'll see how that goes. The other thing is . . . well, I want you to know that I feel partly responsible for all this."

"You do?" Lainie exclaimed, obviously surprised. "Why?"

"Because, you know. . . of the hard time we had and everything. Seems to me now that if I'd worked a little bit harder on our relationship, we could still be together and none of this would have happened."

Lainie had begun slowly and dramatically shaking her head before I finished confessing. "No," she said firmly, "I wasn't gonna stay in California no matter what. And you know what else, Randall?"

"What?"

"When we were together was the best time of my life. I just couldn't keep a hold on it. I was gonna come back here and fuck up sooner or later." Lainie's confident pose had broken down; now I saw how troubled she was. But what she said about us truly surprised me.

"Lainie," I responded intently, and then trailed off, at a complete loss for words.

"I don't wanna be locked up forever," Lainie said, her voice cracking a little, "but part of me sorta feels like I deserve it right now. Because I came back here and got myself right in the middle of an old mess. You know I didn't mean to . . . to kill Bobby, and I still can't hardly believe it happened. It's like somebody else did it. It's like it was gonna happen anyways and now I have to pay for it, 'cuz that's just the way it is."

"Oh, Lainie," I said, abruptly feeling weak all over, wanting to defeat her logic but not knowing how.

"You and JoEllen are so smart," Lainie whispered as she leaned toward me, eyeing one of the guards, "I'm not really too scared. Really!"

I believed her. But that meant I had to believe in myself. A few days later on the plane back home, that was hard to do. After the emotional roller-coaster of the trip, I felt like a fool, a heel, a dolt—about as smart as the dumb, wandering crawdads I used to catch in the creek not far from home when I was a kid. The dashing of my crazy dream about JoEllen had affected me deeply, so much that I'd avoided her for the rest of the trip, spending more time with C & C and the kids, which seemed to make them happy.

I did have two more meetings with JoEllen, one of them a brief strategy session at her office and the last one a lunch before I flew home. She was very sweet all through that final meeting, perhaps sensing that I was not feeling good about myself. She kept reaching across the table to touch my hand. As we were about to part, she reached into her enormous handbag and pro-duced a plastic bag full of buttons, from which she withdrew one that said in plain white lettering on a dark blue background:

FREE
LAINIE

I laughed out loud despite my blue mood as JoEllen said, "Aren't they nifty? The DA and the press have been so hard on Lainie, I decided to counter-attack. We're going public with this as a symbolic case about spousal abuse. Although I wish Lainie had bothered to get married for once in her life. It would make for an easier case around here."

I must have winced because JoEllen changed the subject. "Oh, by the way, the Atlanta Women's Center is going to hold a music benefit next week for Lainie, and Carolyn and I are going to cook up some other stuff. So you don't have to worry about all of this being on your shoulders. I know you're not a wealthy man, although it seems like you've been doing all right with your stores and everything. And for such a young man!"

JoEllen's eyes were dancing in her round, full-moon face, and I suddenly recognized her as the JoEllen of the old days, a young woman changing the world. "Well, what about you? You're really going for it, aren't you?" I said in frank admiration. "You're not worried about taking on the DA or anything."

JoEllen smiled warmly at me as she pinned the button to the

a novel of sexual initiation

lapel of my coat and then patted it. "Those good ol' boys," she drawled softly, "will never know what hit 'em." Then she kissed me full on the lips, said, "Write me for a change, okay?" and that was that.

By the time I got to the airport I had pulled the button off, embarrassed. On the flight I spent a long time staring at it before deciding resolutely to wear it after all, every day until Lainie's trial was done. Because I really did want Lainie to be free: free from jail, free from her hard life, free from more pain and suffering. So far as I can remember, this was the first time that I ever committed to repairing some of the consequences of my indecisive drift through life.

22

JEANNA met me at the airport. She was full of questions about Lainie. Before I'd left she had made tantalizing noises about coming with me, but she had fallen ill several weeks before I left, with mysterious, recurring abdominal pains and attacks of fatigue, like a flu that wouldn't go away. When she picked me up she didn't look well, but maintained that she was feeling better.

Over the next year, Jeanna and I would hardly talk unless it was about Lainie. There was quite a lot to talk about: JoEllen and Carolyn succeeded in making the case a regional cause célèbre, a kind of public referendum on abuse among Dixie intimates. Lainie had outrageously violated the traditional code which said Southern women were supposed to take it and keep their mouths shut, protecting the reputation of their homes and families. Taking out your spouse was frowned upon, to say the least. Thus, Lainie's claim of self-defense initially had little appeal to the traditional mindset.

However, the stirring-up of urban feminists caused a panic among the prosecutors, who were afraid of compromising their masculinity either by losing the case they had prematurely staked out or accepting a plea bargain. As a result the case was delayed from reaching a jury for a full year. Six months into that time JoEllen somehow got Lainie sprung from jail, creating a whole new round of controversy. Not long after that JoEllen sent me a newspaper profile of herself, citing her as one of Atlanta's "upcoming legal stars" as well as one of the city's most eligible single women. Jeanna read the profile while sitting with me at the Edible one Saturday, her eyes widening all the way through. When she was finished, she said wonderingly, "This was your girlfriend in high school? Very impressive!"

I beamed and took the honors, keenly aware that all my romantic peaks seemed well behind me. For soon after returning from Georgia, I had embarked on my Disastrous Dating Period. Determined not to fall prey to fantasies á la JoEllen, I had backed off from trying to convert Jeanna and started searching deliberately for a normal girlfriend. I asked Giselle if she had any available chums, which netted me a ludicrous evening with a San Francisco punkette—me holding my ears in a dingy South of Market bar on the fringe of the mosh pit, absorbing body blows from disaffected youths ten years my junior. Then I answered a personal in a weekly paper, leading to an uncomfortable afternoon in a cafe with a "young at heart" divorcée fifteen years my senior. There were other encounters, but I don't want to bore myself here.

Then there was Ava, a tall, striking, well-heeled blonde who picked me up in my own store in San Rafael. She was looking for a gift for her nephew. We had a long run, three-and-a-half dates altogether, each one dominated by increasingly heated discussions of sexual politics. We argued so much about what *would be* acceptable or not acceptable in a committed relationship that the fourth date was on the rocks after two drinks. I was pissed because I had left work early for Ava's sake, then waited twenty minutes for her at a bayside Sausalito restaurant. Perhaps because I was drinking on an empty stomach, things were getting a little voluble when, to our mutual surprise, the Loma Prieta earthquake struck, all 7.1 of it.

Ava started screaming bloody murder, which I would have done if she hadn't beaten me to it. The earth had no sooner settled down than she rushed home to see if her goddamn parakeets were alive. (If their cages had fallen and popped open, Ava's cat might have had unexpected delicacies for a post-quake repast.) I rushed back to the San Rafael store. Both my business and my house got through on the lucky side. Remembering how a much milder quake had signaled the end of my relationship with Lainie, I took the Loma Prieta as an omen about Ava. We never talked face-to-face again.

Thus the Disastrous Dating Period only extended my Siege of Celibacy. I compensated by converting one entire wall in the house to a massive home entertainment center, complete with

a novel of sexual initiation 247

giant-screen TV, global sound system, and top-of-the-line VCR. I began building my collection of porn tapes, safely mail-ordered and anonymously received in brown-paper envelopes. My sexual surrogates, eventually numbering in the hundreds on scores of tapes, were only two-dimensional. But I could control them completely, even halt their passion at precisely the moment of orgasm. I would stare at the open-mouthed screams or arcing ejaculations, in utter stillness, for minutes at a time, usually deep after midnight when I was unable to sleep following a disastrous date or punishing hours at work. At least and at last, masturbating would put me to sleep.

After seven or eight months of this, the challenge of converting Jeanna to heterosexuality looked not too daunting after all—alas, my seesaw heart!—and I began calling her more frequently. On my thirtieth birthday in 1990, she took pity on me and came out to an evening movie, despite an episode of her so-called "chronic fatigue." When I boldly suggested that she could come back to the house and rest there til morning—with completely honorable intentions on my part—she eyed me wearily and said, just like JoEllen might have done:

"Randall."

"Yeah?"

"Did I tell you I'm moving back in with August?"

I felt a flash of anger. "No, you didn't. Again?"

"Yes, again," Jeanna said firmly. "I haven't been doing very well and she wants to take care of me. It's not romantic this time. I just need a stable place to get over this . . . whatever it is."

"Great," I said coolly. "What makes you think it will work this time?"

"Randall," Jeanna repeated firmly, "I don't want to argue about this. You're not my boyfriend."

"You can say that again."

"But I know you're pretty lonely. Pierce says you're not acting right."

"Pierce?" I replied, shocked. When had she talked to Pierce? Since he had fallen ill himself a few months before, he had moved back home with his mother in the Oakland hills. After helping him move, I hadn't seen much of him, even though he called regularly. I guess I didn't want to think about where he was headed. "When did you talk to Pierce?" I added accusingly.

"He called me about a week ago," Jeanna replied defensively. "He said you seemed angry all the time and wouldn't talk to him. That doesn't seem like you. Ever since you came back from Georgia, you've seemed really negative. I know you've not been enjoying your. . . dates."

"So?" I said meanly, getting really steamed.

"So I want to know if you'll talk to somebody. A therapist. I think she's really good."

"Oh, shit," I seethed. "Here we go again. I thought Shanti Valentine moved to Oregon."

"She did," Jeanna protested. "She got married to a stockbroker after the Ranch broke up, and moved to Portland. This is an older woman, a Jungian who actually met Jung! Her name is June Jacobs. I have a feeling you'll really hit it off with her."

This was humiliating. I halfway wanted to slap Jeanna on the mouth, and halfway wanted to accept her recommendation. After all, excepting Shanti Valentine, Jeanna's intuitions were more often on the mark than off. Then I heard the inner voice for the first time in months, stern and uncompromising:

Accept this gift!

"Okay. I'll think about it," I muttered, having the odd feeling of answering two people.

"Good," Jeanna said, grinning conspiratorially, then handed me a business card. "Don't think about it too long. Your first appointment is my birthday present for you."

That's why I think I can be forgiven my insolent attitude at the outset of my first meeting with June. I'd been shoved into therapy for the second time by the woman who had been holding out on me for years, a woman whose own emotional life was hardly normal.

So I was determined not to waste time on this therapeutic adventure. I decided before the appointment to volunteer my insecurities up front, immediately dumping all the stuff that a therapist might expect to spend months digging out of my psyche. Based on my previous experience, I figured I could blow this particular busybody out of the water on the first go-round. Then maybe Jeanna would stop trying to get me fixed. Who did she think she was, anyway?

After polite introductions and thirty minutes of factual chit-chat about my life circumstances, I informed June Jacobs, Ph.D., that I was not a therapy neophyte, and had read up considerably on her profession, including the Jungian angle. (This was true. I had read part of *Man and His Symbols,* and saw a movie about Jung at the UC Theater, too.)

"I know, for instance," I ventured, "that therapists spend most of their time trying to get their clients to focus on their real problems instead of all the false problems and excuses that they put up as straw men. But as Jung himself said, one's real problems can never be fully solved. How did he put it?" Here I paused thoughtfully, as if working hard to recall something when I had actully rehearsed this quote the night before . . .

"Oh, yes . . . 'The meaning and purpose of a problem seems to lie not in its solution but in our working at it incessantly.' Have I got that right?" I asked pointedly.

"I believe so," June said, smiling impartially.

"Doctor Jacobs, I don't mean to steal your thunder, but the fact is that I already know the big, central problem of my life. I can honestly say that I've been working at it incessantly for some time now."

June nodded encouragingly.

"Well, okay," I said, suddenly feeling hesitant. "Here it is. I'm in love with Jeanna." My face flushed but I took this as a sign I was really being truthful. Things were going according to plan. This was brilliant!

"Yes?" June answered neutrally.

"And you know she's gay."

"Yes, I do."

"Well, there it is. I'm in love, and have been ever since I met her, with a woman I can never have. That's the big problem in my life, and I'll just have to keep working at it. It's no mystery. It's simply my challenge, my cross to bear. I don't blame anybody for it, and it hardly demands further analysis. That's just the way it is." I peered at June confidently, thinking silently, *Case closed. I'm outta here.*

As June leaned forward to make a few notes in her clothbound record, I really thought I had aced her. Furthermore, I thought I had told the whole truth and nothing but. That's why I was all the more surprised when she leaned back, smiled pleasantly and asked:

"Given all that, Randall, what do you think your *real* problem may be?"

I stared dumbly at June, my mind a complete blank. I had run out of script and she had asked an utterly unexpected $64,000 Question. I smiled wryly at first and wiped my forehead, then chuckled involuntarily. That turned into an uncontrollable giggle that soon broke into several rough, ragged barks of bitter laughter. With tears rising to my eyes, I finally responded:

"Well, Doctor, you've got me there. I don't have the slightest idea what my real problem is. I don't have a *fucking clue.*" The last few words rushed out of me with such an unexpected, vile wrath that I shocked myself, glancing quickly at June to see if she disapproved of my language. All she said was:

"Please call me June. See what excellent progress we're making? We've gotten one of your straw women out of the way already. You really did come prepared, Randall, and I think there's a lot we can learn together. Shall we set a time to continue next week?"

THAT'S HOW it got started, the last few years of reflection under June's probing guidance—not to mention how *this* got started, this ridiculous opus that sits on the corner of my desk, mocking me with that same old question: *Do you have a fucking clue to your real problem yet?* Even June's optimism seems to be flagging lately. I think she expected this journal to work some kind of miracle. But as I come close to wrapping up my sexual history I seem only to be going further down the tubes.

At least I used to make money in the midst of all my problems. Now I don't even do that very well; Giselle and my other

a novel of sexual initiation 251

managers are always calling, wondering where I am. I write here at home, or ruminate moodily at one cafe or another, sounding like any other Berkeley nut-case muttering to himself. Or I sit for hours under my secret bay tree deep in the Tilden Park woods, like some melancholy, numbskull Buddha without a fucking clue.

It's ironic, considering how the first year with June raised a bright hope of redemption—or at least redirection—of my hapless life. Maybe I was just seduced by some genuinely scintillating conversations.

In the early days it seemed that I learned as much about June as myself. A physicist in her first career, she was involved in various projects working with the "peaceful atom." By the mid-1950s June had concluded that there was no truly benign nuclear research in her field and abandoned it. After several years of what she called "tumultuous self-examination," she ended up at the Jung Institute in Zurich, where she had a few dramatic encounters with the Old Man himself in his waning years.

"He didn't particularly like gay women," June once recounted, "because he was personally conservative, and he was resentful of any woman who didn't immediately respond to his charms. Actually, I wasn't quite as resistant as I convinced him I was."

June moved back to Berkeley in time for the Free Speech Movement, the People's Park brouhaha, and all that fun stuff— seeking at first, she said, for "some reliable catalyst common to both personal and political revolution."

"But I've been humbled over the years," she admitted quietly, "by the gap that still exists between my worldly, political self, who looks upon the world and says 'Things are not as they should be,' and my ancient, knowing self who says, 'Nothing is as it seems to be.' So I am hesitant to act at times. As I know from my first career, you can be convinced of the worthiness of your intentions and chosen direction in life, only to find that you have been hornswoggled by your predecessors—that all your efforts have been unknowingly bent to the service of deadly intentions. The challenge of my later life has been not to hornswoggle myself, I suppose."

That self-revealing speech has certainly stuck with me. Not because I fear the same situation in my own life—"the inadvertent service of deadly intentions"—but because I fear that I have served no serious intentions whatsoever, deadly or lively, throughout the course of my life. Instead I have reacted only to whatever events fell upon me, trying to get by without taking any serious risks, thus ending up with a pointless, trivial life—a life devoid of winning or losing, outright failure or undeniable success, irreparable tragedy or saving grace.

I can prove my point by taking almost anybody's life for comparison. Lainie, for instance: now there's a compelling life story, worthy of retelling by Oprah for an audience of millions. Not long after I began to see June, Lainie's legal adventure finally began to accelerate. The Atlanta DA's office decided to go to trial with their original charge of first-degree murder despite the public furor of sexual politics that JoEllen and my very own sister had worked up. To make a long, exciting story short, those fellows really took it on the chin. With the expertise of her firm behind her, JoEllen proved to be a stunning courtroom performer who outmaneuvered her opponents on every count, including the courageous decision to put Lainie on the stand in her own defense.

Lainie, who could never really lie, apparently got up there and just told the truth in her innocent and sometimes profane way, eventually convincing both the jury and general the public that she was almost as much a victim of the hard life as Bobby Skinner. At any rate, who got killed had more to do with who controlled the gun than any kind of premeditation. That Lainie got hold of it first came to be seen as canny, not vicious. I suppose those common folks on the jury, both black and white, could identify with Lainie too easily to condemn her. They voted for acquittal free and clear.

I got all this second-hand, by newspaper and frequent phone contact with Carolyn and JoEllen. In one of her brilliant moves, JoEllen blocked the prosecution's attempt to make me testify by pouncing on some procedural error the good ol' boys had made. Thus she succeeded in limiting the disclosure of my relationship

a novel of sexual initiation 253

to Lainie. She didn't even want me there for the trial, afraid the opposing attorneys would somehow manage to open the "can of California worms," as she so eloquently put it to me. Thus, my role in Lainie's dramatic adventure was reduced to several mentions, in court and in the press, of "the post-shooting call to a friend in California." Perhaps my not being present actually helped Lainie for a change.

In the end, not too much of my money was needed either, JoEllen and Carolyn having raised substantial donations through a nationwide network of women's organizations. After the trial JoEllen took Lainie under her wing and wisely got her out of town, helping her move up to Charlotte to live with an elderly aunt. Lainie also enrolled in a community college and got a part-time job as a receptionist. Because of her notoriety—those buttons were everywhere!—Lainie legally changed her first name. To "Lana."

Compared to a story like that, what have I got to show? Not much. Take another case for comparison: the Berquists. I came into the Berkeley store one day to find Iceberg sitting there with an expectant grin on his face. I thought he was going to say he'd found a seventh store site, in which case I was going to tell him no way, I was done with expansion. Instead he said:

"Big news on the Berquist front."

"Oh yeah?" I said. "Don't tell me Etty wants me in Santa Fe again. I can't listen to one more of her transcendental lectures."

"Nope," said Iceberg with great satisfaction. "Etty's off both our backs. For good."

"What do you mean?" I replied, puzzled.

"I mean this," he said, proffering a letter but talking so feverishly I couldn't pay attention to it. "She's backing out, surrendering her interest, asking only that we contribute $15,000 to some charitable organization for Indian kids. No explanation, no nothing. I've checked it out with her lawyer and it looks to be for real. The letter says only that Diversions no longer figures in her portfolio. Of course, she never explained how it figured in the first place! She just wanted her old spotted hand in. Now she wants out, and it's okay with me. That is one weird old biddy."

"Jesus, this *is* odd," I said softly, staring uncomprehendingly at the letter.

"But wait," Iceberg bubbled, beside himself with excitement. There's *more*." Now he held up an envelope engraved with an official imprint I had seen only once before: The Independent State of Papua New Guinea. No sooner had the words registered in my brain before Iceberg said, "Old Chuckie's disappeared."

"Disappeared?" I said wryly. "You mean he made off with some government assets? Or kidnapped some chieftain's nubile daughter and spirited her off to a strip club in Sydney?"

"Nope," Iceberg said proudly, as if he had personally had a hand in the news of the day. "I mean *disappeared*. As in, from the face of the earth!"

Or, take Pierce as yet another contrast to my dull and useless life. Pierce has had a dramatic life, full of meaning and hair-raising adventure. Just a little while ago he asked to borrow my car for a few days while his mom's was in the shop. He'd been feeling a little better, he said, since he cut down his dosage of AZT, which I didn't think was such a hot idea. His mother wanted him to try some traditional African herbs and he was going to have to drive to Sacramento to get them. Feeling bad that I hadn't been talking to him much, I said sure, I didn't need the car. I liked to walk in the hot, windy weather of Indian summer.

Pierce made the trip okay. When he got back he called and said he felt too tired to return the car, so could it wait until tomorrow. That was October 19, 1991. A little fire started that day behind the Claremont Hotel in the Oakland hills and was put out, but got blown alive again the next day. Everybody knows what happened next: the firestorm consumed everything in its path. Pierce and his mom got out of her house in the nick of time, Pierce gunning Livvy down the hill for their lives. They were forced to stop in front of a wall of flames, abandoning the car and running back part of the way they had come. Miraculously they found a ditch in the semi-wild hillside that they managed to slip, slide, and fall their way down to safety, galloping singed but unhurt into the arms of some astonished firemen.

Liv Ullmann was not so lucky. Engulfed by Mother Nature's

a novel of sexual initiation 255

fiery embrace, she exploded and burned to an ashen hulk that I paid to have hauled away two weeks later. Her burial fee, as it were, was the last expensive demand the aging Swedish movie star would ever make of me.

IV

23

3/11/92

NOW WHAT? For several weeks I've been grappling with the realization that I've come to the end of my sexual history. In fact, I've been padding it near the end, bringing life in general up to the present. Because my sexual history, insofar as it involves real, three-dimensional people, ended a long time ago, with Lainie. The Siege of Celibacy continues, unless I count various partial gropings and awkward kisses from the Disastrous Dating Period. I've abandoned the hunt now, eschewing sexual intimacy in favor of the lonely thrall of pornography, and work, and this dubious record of self-absorption.

All in all, real sex is just too fucking dangerous. And that's not just me. It's all over the news.

At least I'm not without friends. A silver lining to the Oakland hills fire was that Pierce ended up living in my apartment downstairs, the one I had always meant to rent out but never got around to sprucing up until Pierce was suddenly homeless. I don't charge him anything.

His mother moved to Sacramento so the care of Pierce has largely fallen to me. That's getting easier, thank God. Despite some heated arguments about his abandoning conventional medical treatment for his AIDS condition, he seems resolute about his chosen path and—what can I say? After all, he is getting better, at least as far as apparent symptoms go. And he seems calmer than I've ever seen him. When he first got ill, I think he faced the music about his risky lifestyle.

Of course, this evolution has not come without an accompanying wardrobe shift and, as always, Pierce cuts a distinctive figure in his chosen style. I can only describe it as a blend of African chic and Western yogi. He's often going about in one of several handsome, colorful dashikis, a tribal pill-box hat if he's feeling chipper, and loose, flowing drawstring pants with either sandals or Nikes, depending on the weather. He's gotten into yoga in such a big way that I'm a little worried about him. He's not only taking three classes a week, but also holding down a part-time job in the offices of *Yoga Journal*, a weird magazine published here in town.

It's irrelevant to his financial training but he insists that the job is more meaningful to him than anything he's ever done. "I'm getting out the healing word," he playfully boasts in his best (which is not very good) imitation of a televangelist. He keeps trying to get me to read stuff in the magazine, but please—it's too bizarre. Everybody in the advertisements looks like God.

But how should I know from weird, when I'm helping Pierce with his rituals? Three months ago he first asked me to come on a hike with him up in the hills, in order to help him with a healing ritual that his mother had taught him, something out of their tribal heritage. I was more than a little anxious when he stopped before a large, commanding cedar tree atop a hillock, about a half-mile into the woods from Grizzly Peak Boulevard, and started taking things out of his backpack. I didn't know what was going to be asked of me.

It turned out that it wasn't much. After asking me to walk with him, silently, three times clockwise around the tree, he then directed me to stand off to the side while he slowly circled the trunk once more, dropping ash from his hands until he had ringed the tree with it. Then he picked up a stick, and holding it out to me, asked me to take hold of its other end and come into the ring with him.

I hesitated. "Are you sure this is right, Pierce? Should I really come in there?"

"Why not?" he asked, curious.

"Well, because, you know. . . I'm not African."

Pierce chortled and said, "Neither am I, bwana."

"Yes, but your mom is," I responded, deadly serious. "And she taught you this. What if I don't belong?"

"You belong if you're invited in to help."

a novel of sexual initiation   261

That seemed all right, so I took hold of the branch and went in. Nothing much happened after that, either. We both kneeled at the base of the tree, while Pierce prayed in some unknown language. Then he buried an old earring of his in the dirt, and poured water from a wooden bowl over the burial. He had carefully carried the water in the open bowl all the way from his house, explaining before we got up there that it was "sky water" that had fallen directly into the bowl.

When Pierce rose, he asked me to help him gather a bunch of rocks, which half-filled both our backpacks and made the way back considerably more of a chore than getting there had been. Then Pierce built a ceremonial ring in the backyard, in which he's always burning things. Once he invited me to join him in that ritual as well. At dawn one morning I was supposed to bring a piece of paper that represented something I no longer needed to hold onto, "a memory you are prepared to liberate," as Pierce put it. I brought the title to Liv Ullmann; Pierce brought an old picture of him and Frank in Yosemite.

"Pierce," I said, alarmed, "that's not your only picture left of Frank, is it?"

"No," he replied softly, "it's a snapshot of one particular time that I have mourned a lot, and need to let go of. What about you?"

I showed Pierce the title.

"Hey, man," he blurted, "I feel awful about the car, you know."

I waved both hands in protest. "Nonsense. Livvy went out nobly, saving your lives. I need to let go of her now so I can let my brother-in-law ship me something spiffy and modern, something that leaps forward when you touch the gas pedal. You know, one of those *male* cars."

Pierce smiled broadly at me and put one long arm around my shoulders. "You're a funny chap, Peanut Man." We both burned our offerings and Pierce said the benediction. I went straight into the house thereafter, called Cody, and made his day. He made me a pretty good deal on a turquoise sports sedan. It's sitting out there on the driveway, gleaming unashamedly, at this moment. But its gender is ambiguous.

I wish Pierce had an effective ritual for Jeanna. She's been sick on and off for a while now. The worst part of it is that she's firmly in the clutches of August again. The upshot is that I don't see Jeanna very much. When she's not feeling well she doesn't leave home, and when she's feeling better she puts in her hours at the bookstore. I know she's sick, but her life seems so aimless now. She's getting on toward forty and doesn't seem interested in much besides her poetry. Where is that going to get her?

The last time I saw her, about a month ago, we met at Au Coquelet, a cafe downtown where I've been hanging out so much that Giselle calls it my office. Jeanna told me she had a poem she wanted me to keep for her. This is what she gave me:

Lullaby
I am not a body. I am the rain,
falling all over your house
and in the deep fold of the distant hills.
I cover the leaf, the roof, the field grasses
and the shiny street. A billowing wind
carries me through the swirling branches
and drives me against your window.
I strike and coalesce, fall and spill
into the soil and the swallowing gutter,
taking a wild ride to the sea.
Later the sun may draw me up,
but the clouds will lose me when
they let down their burden in water
again. I am not a body. You can
sleep to the sound of my falling.

Stupid me, I thought a poem she wanted to give me might be *about* me, so I couldn't make much sense of it at first. Plus, we've been in the middle of a drought for a few years so I didn't know why Jeanna was thinking about the rain. When Jeanna gave me the poem, I shrugged my shoulders and said, "That's nice. Why do you want me to keep it? Aren't you keeping a copy?"

"No," she said, shaking her head fearfully, making her dark hair, longer than ever, swirl around. "It scares me. I don't know

a novel of sexual initiation   263

what it means."

Surprised at her reaction, I looked at the poem more closely and tried to dig out a reassuring meaning. "Well, you've been sick a lot," I said helpfully, "and that probably makes you feel like you'd rather not be in your body. And it is like a lullaby. It's very calming."

"You mean you might like it?" Jeanna said sensitively.

Boy, am I dense! The last thing I said should have been the first: "Yeah, of course! It's wonderful! I always like your poems, you know that." Jeanna, to whom I've always looked to lift my mood, looked genuinely happy for a change.

3/15/92

SO I thought I was done with this thing. I put it away in a box after the last entry, but now something peculiar has happened that's got me thinking again. Last night I went to a slide show at a local Sierra Club chapter, an impassioned presentation about the clearcutting and burning of tropical forests worldwide, put on by a group called Forests Forever.

I seldom make time for this kind of thing, but I was invited by a customer who's become a new pal lately. His name is Wayne Dennis. He showed up in the store a few months ago with his six-year-old son Greg, nervously casting about for "something fun," as he vaguely put it, for him and the boy to do together. Wayne was so awkward with the kid I would have thought he met him no more than five minutes earlier, and that impression turned out to be not far from accurate. Wayne had inherited Greg by getting married less than a year ago, "at the grand old age of forty," as he put it.

Prior to that, he'd put in fifteen years as a forest ranger in the Sierra, sitting alone in a tower for six months of the year watching for fires, and the other six months in an office a couple thousand feet lower in elevation. Finally deciding that he was "missing out on life at sea level," as he confided to me in a long in-store chat, he had retired from the Forest Service, moved to the Bay area to take a more politically activist job with Forests Forever, and promptly fell in love with a single, divorced mother. "Sometimes I'm scared to death by all this," he had whispered.

The puer comes down to earth, I remember thinking, but I said nothing.

Anyway, Wayne invited me to his slide show of the burning, scarred, and wasted rainforests. I felt disturbed when he referred to the "vicious, piece-by-piece destruction of the literal lungs of the earth." The next picture I saw—of a raw, naked swath of exposed earth next to verdant forest—made me think of something else entirely, and I couldn't get the highly disturbing association out of my mind.

Whispering my apologies to Wayne's wife Deborah, I hurried out of the building and urgently drove home to slap into the VCR one of the most recent porn tapes I had received, one of the most up-to-date. It confirmed my peculiar association: every woman in the tape had her pubic hair shaved off, or shaved down to a neat little strip or thatch. This is a trend I've been observing in porn for five or six years now, this sexual clearcutting of women. It has disturbed me almost as much as the growing prevalence of surgically enlarged, balloon-tight breasts. Not enough to make me stop watching, but . . .

Here I sit, mightily disturbed by the connection I have seen between the clearcutting of rainforests and vaginal forests, and I don't know what to do about it. I can't help but think that this is the kind of thing June could intepret brilliantly, but I've never confessed my dark habit to her. It would be too scary. I can imagine she might finally lose her intellectual objectivity, and dismiss me with a scathing lecture about porn and violence. I couldn't take that.

Recently Wayne laughingly invited me to change careers and go to work for Forests Forever, "because we sure could use a marketing genius," as he put it. "Don't think we could match your income by a long shot, though." So why am I sitting here having a vague fantasy of working for nothing, writing impassioned direct-mail letters for Forests Forever? Is it guilt? Do I feel some weird complicity in the ravaging of the earth's natural resources

a novel of sexual initiation 265

because I have supported the industry that's clearcutting feminine vegetation?

Jesus, I'm getting nutsy. I am becoming one sick fuck.

3/30/92

NOW *I'VE* written a poem. Here it goes:

List for a Bad Mood
a mudflow, stopping
an iron bar sinking
the gray stone buried
a fossil cracked by a hammer
a thought never told
a bone without a body
a wheel, a planet, a dropping bell
small animals watching the moon
rain gathering in a sliver of the sky
children with nothing to say, walking
a river with nowhere to go
the simple principle of fog
an old building, burned, waiting
nothing given, nothing gained
a white wall, stucco
leaves from the stream
action or inaction
sorrow

Oh, well. No Pulitzers here. I was working on this garbage
yesterday in the Berkeley store office when Giselle materialized
at my shoulder and said, "Whatcha doin'?"

I almost jumped out of my skin. It was tough to cover; I lied
poorly. I hate to lie to Giselle, my most loyal manager, happily
married woman that she is nowadays. Isn't it odd how you can
never tell who will stick with you through thick and thin?

Back to the bad mood. June has taught me to confront these

things. It's the parent trap this time. On the one hand, there's my mom: "If it's not one thing, it's your mother," as the bumper-sticker says. It's not that she's causing a big problem; I guess I'm a little sad for her. I helped her move to a new, cramped apartment yesterday, since Gayle left for the East Coast and they gave up their nice house in Albany.

Through the whole thing my mom kept saying that the split was "completely amicable" and Gayle really needed to pursue her studies at Columbia, and blah-blah and so on. I got fed up with Mom's sterling self-control. I've been more sensitive to it ever since June said to me that my historic hostility toward my father was peculiar to her "since your most troublesome emotional habits seem to have been borrowed from your mother."

I mean, sometimes June irks the hell out of me! She stirs up things that have been no problem in my life and offers me precious little salve for the obvious wounds.

Then there's what happened two nights ago. Dad's new girlfriend Lacey, a ballsy little Texan whom he met at AA, called and invited me to hear Dad's little speech to his recovery group on the occasion of his achieving one full year of sobriety. Since he left the University and took that job at Cal State in Hayward, he's seemed a little more real, less driven to fulfill conventional expectations. But the idea of being around a bunch of addicts bugged me, and I tried to beg off. Lacey would have none of that.

The meeting started with a big circular hand-holding—never one of my favorite rituals—and after a couple of other people spoke, Dad got up, and said, "Well, everybody, here I am—one year old!" (General laughter, applause, hoots of caring support.) "It feels odd at my age to be starting over at anything, yet recently I've had to start over at almost everything, it seems: my career, my love life" (warm, wet-eyed look at Lacey), "my relationship to my family" (warm look at me, for God's sake), "and, most of all, my idea about what's really important in life." (A revival-style "Amen!" from a beefy black guy in the circle.) "Some of you know that when I first got into trouble, driving drunk and seriously injuring a young girl" (Dad choking up), "I was forgiven by her family. That confused me. I didn't know what to make of it."

a novel of sexual initiation **267**

("Nawssir," seconded the black man, completely uninhibited.)

"But somehow that's what got me here today. If I hadn't been forgiven, I think I would have defended myself, you know, talked my way out of the mess I was in. Then I'd still be out there, weaving all over the road tonight." (Dramatic pause.) "I wouldn't have met you people, and gotten born here, a year ago tonight." (Now, Dad weeping softly.) "Well, that's it, I guess, if that makes any sense. Thanks, everybody." (Standing ovation. I got up slowly.)

After hugging my father and handing him over to a clutch of his recovery chums, Lacey threaded her way over to me and said, "Well, what did you think? Isn't he something?"

I like Lacey, I really do. Only a few years Dad's junior, and definitely not one of his usual pretty young things—considering her acne-scarred face and bleached hair with dark roots—she's smart and canny, and she's obviously been around the block a half-dozen times. I didn't want to make her mad, and I didn't even want to trash my father one more time. I don't know what came over me. Something old and worn-out; something bitter and dying.

"I don't know," I sighed, "as long as I've been old enough to see Dad as just another person, it seems like he's been playing one role or another. Now it's the humble role. I guess I like it better than some of his earlier ones."

Lacey gave me a glinty-eyed look, then grabbed my shirt sleeve and pulled me over to the corner of the room, out of the earshot of the others. "Listen to me, young man. Your father has his share of problems being real, just like you and me and everybody else. But we talk to each other late at night when he's falling apart, and I know he's trying harder than he's ever tried in his life. Maybe that's something you could learn from him, if you ever get one foot out of your own bullshit. If you don't go over there, right now, and give him a hug and tell him you give a good goddamn about him, then I will personally kick your ass from here to Abilene. Is that clear?"

"Yes, m'am," I blurted. "Yes, m'am!"

24

4/13/92

EVERYBODY'S worried about taxes; I couldn't care less. I asked Iceberg to file an extension for me; I have far more compelling things on my mind. Things seem different; things seem a little more possible. I don't know what may happen next.

I did it; I told June the secret a couple days ago. I didn't go into the session meaning to confess, yet things seemed somehow set up for it. I was her last appointment for the day, at 3:30 in the afternoon, and she wanted to meet on the patio out back of her house, a Julia Morgan original that's always seemed too big for June's solitary lifestyle. On the patio, an exquisite Japanese tea tray stands in for her desk. The circumstances were relaxed, while I was not. I started off telling June about the long talk with my father the day after the AA meeting, about all his changes and my own sense of stagnation.

Soon it was as if I were a volcano brimming with tension, and then it came out. It started with a slip of the tongue about the VCR. It came out in a frightful torrent: how it had started in the porn theater years ago, how I'd kept it a secret from Lainie, Jeanna, everybody, how I'd built the library of tapes at home, how I had to rush to build a secret storage cabinet before Pierce moved in downstairs, so he would never know, and finally—almost two hours later, with neither of us having commented on the time gone by—how I knew it was all so petty that it probably wasn't worth talking about.

I noticed that my shirt was soaked at the armpits and that I stank. "It's not like I've been going to prostitutes or anything like that," I said. "I'm practically a Puritan. I mean, I've never even been to a strip club, or one of those live sex shows."

"Why not?" June asked objectively.

I'd thought about this before so I had an answer. "I'm too chickenshit. That would be too real. I've reduced all of my sexual life to two dimensions. I guess you could call me an image man. It's all I can handle."

June leaned back in her wicker chair in the fading light of the late afternoon, and said, "Well, it could have been much worse."

"What could have been worse?" I asked, mystified.

"Your secret. I've known there had to be something drawing off your vital energy for some time now, some hidden compulsion, but I couldn't figure it out exactly. You keep your secrets well, Randall. But you do have a trapdoor personality, just as I thought."

"I do?"

"Yes. Your fear drives you to control everything and limit your vulnerability, with the result that your passion for life is increasingly withdrawn from the uncontrollable real world. Sooner or later it has to dive into a shadowy underworld, where you erroneously believe you can have greater control. Of course, any such obsession ends up controlling you."

"You're certainly right about that," I sighed. "But now, I'm really going to end it. I know it's not healthy, so I'll stop it."

"How many times have you already attempted this already?" June inquired knowingly.

"Hundreds," I said, steeling myself to sound unusually determined. "Now that I've told somebody, you especially, I couldn't live with myself if I . . ."

June had begun shaking her head vigorously. She leaned forward over her tea table and placed both hands on it, a sure sign that she was about to launch a major address. I felt drained and wavery, completely open, ready to let her rip.

"Listen," June continued urgently, "it's brave of you to tell me all this, Randall, and there's a psychological value to confession itself. But if you're looking for me to either pardon or condemn you, I'm only going to disappoint you. Because it's not what you've been watching that's the problem—it's what you're not seeing."

a novel of sexual initiation   271

"What I'm not seeing?" I asked dazedly.

"I have no love for this porn stuff, Randall, and I can sometimes sympathize with the puritanical urge to stamp it out. Stamping out seems so efficient and total, were it actually possible. That's why it appeals to fundamentalists, be they religious or feminist. But porn is only one symptom of our cultural psychosis, which has to do in part with our attempt to master nature and separate ourselves from it. Nature is full of shadow, you know, all those frightening things that whistle and rustle in the night, not to mention quakes, fires, and floods. By believing we can control and eventually forget nature—ostensibly to make our lives pain-free and luxurious, and to put death out of our minds—we drive all the shadow energy into our own psyches. Then it rises up and looms over us in various forms, but most obviously our sexuality, the part of ourselves that we do still recognize as nature. And the shadow *will not be long repressed.*" June thumped the fragile tea table, making it jump along with me, but she drove on.

"When you tell the shadow that you're going to stamp it out, Randall, well, it couldn't be happier. You've made its day, as the saying goes, because the shadow draws as much energy from our opposing it as it does from our giving into it. That's why your pornography habit has been unbeatable, Randall. It's not your hormones. It's not your lonesomeness or sexual frustration. No, it's the collective, cultural shadow with its teeth in you, like a rabid dog. Fight it, and the tear in your flesh worsens. Give in, and it will eventually consume you."

"So what do I do," I mewed, "if I don't fight *or* give in?"

"Learn to respect and negotiate with the shadow. That's a big part of individuation, remember? Of course you've been struggling already, but your struggle could be more conscious. The more you keep the struggle conscious, the more you learn what the shadow wants. It doesn't want to destroy you, drive you to violence, or enfold you in blackness, even though it seems to threaten these things. Actually, it wants back in, to be a part of you again. Do you remember how we've talked about your shadow energy concealing a profound tenderness?"

I nodded mutely.

"All right, then. Your sexual shadow represents not just your earthy energies, but also the energy of tenderness trying to find a place to root within your psyche. Tenderness is a quality of your spiritual nature, Randall—it comes from above, not below. What's difficult about being human is that we have both an earth nature and a spiritual nature. Where they meet and mix is called the soul. We're the only species trying to live with these two natures at once. It's a profound and dangerous enterprise, and most people back away from full engagement with the soul's struggle. Spiritual types tend to deny their earth nature. Most everyone else forgets their spiritual nature. In fact, Western culture has grown increasingly anti-spiritual, trying to find its salvation in rational materialism. But when you disown spiritual yearnings, you end up neurotic and unhappy no matter how well-fed, secure, or wealthy you may be. The soul is starved without spiritual yearning and some degree of spiritual discipline. That soul starvation is the story of our culture, Randall. It's your story, too."

"It is?" I said weakly.

"Yes," June confirmed. "Now, whatever is driven into the shadow will make ugly but compelling faces to get your attention. Pornography is just one of the vulgar faces resulting from our culture's rejection of nature and the disowning of tenderness. That face has certainly gotten *your* attention. But remember that the shadow's face is a lie, a mask of the real thing. That's why you can look and look at porn, always hoping for that wonderful thing you think you'll find there, and always be disappointed. To see what you really want you have to look *through* the mask. As you learn to do that the mask itself will gradually become less appealing. On the other side of the shadow's mask is your own soul, and that's the real reward."

I nodded vigorously as if I'd understood everything June said, when in fact I would have failed a pop quiz. Hoping not to sound too dumb, I tentatively asked, "So what do I do now?"

June leaned back and laughed softly, then regarded me with warm eyes. "Ever the pragmatist," she said. "That's good. Do

a novel of sexual initiation   273

you remember the first time you came here, Randall, when you quoted Jung to me?"

"Yes," I replied with great embarrassment. "That was really arrogant. I'm sorry."

"Never mind that. Do you remember what old Father Jung said about the real problems of our lives?"

"Something about not being able to solve the big problems, but that you find their meaning by working at them all the time?"

"That's right," June said with obvious satisfaction. "That's what I mean. Keep in mind that your struggle is not just your struggle, Randall. The struggle to see through your shadow and put your two natures together is part of humanity's reaching toward soulfulness. It's not a simple moral decision; there are no foolproof strategies. It's something we don't know how to do except through struggling. The best you can do is try to stay conscious of your struggle, Randall."

"Stay conscious," I repeated numbly. "How do I do that? I mean, I feel conscious here with you, but in day to day life I never know what to do. Things catch up to me and I fall back into my habits. How do I stay aware?"

"You can always ask for help, Randall. Ask to be shown what to do."

"Ask to be shown? By who? Who's gonna show me?"

"In your particular case?" June mused, looking sneaky. "I don't know. I guess you'll have to ask around. Listen carefully for voices wiser than your own."

I knew what June was up to. As long as I've known her she's had the annoying tendency to lead me up to some kind of precipice, patiently assuring me that there will be a stairway down the cliff, or a parachute neatly prepared for me on the ledge, or a hang glider waiting. When I'm actually teetering on the edge, unable to avoid the fall, it becomes obvious that I have to make the leap unassisted and somehow learn to fly on the way down.

But this time I've figured it out. Who else could I ask for guidance but Jeanna? We have a deep connection, after all, even if it has never been physically intimate. That desire I am finally ready to surrender, in order to be a truer friend. I don't know what to expect of a deeper, more serious friendship with Jeanna; I don't even know how to proceed. But I'm willing to face the inevitable awkwardness and certify my intentions to both of us. Who knows? Maybe asking Jeanna for this guidance, and offering her my stronger, truer support, will help her make sense of her life, even help her get well. Maybe she has secrets to confess, too, secrets that I cannot even imagine. Maybe she needs someone to hear her out who has no selfish agenda.

I accept that giving up my agenda about Jeanna is where I must begin. I have to be fearless for a change. I have to go over there—even though I hate it when August answers the door—and ask Jeanna's forgiveness for my flirting with her and badgering her over the years. Then I will offer the strongest, tenderest friendship I have ever managed. No—*more* than I have ever managed. Then I'll really, really try to listen. I have the feeling that, once I have begun this, I won't need this journal anymore.

4/17

But Jeanna is dead

25

4/20/92

THE MOON looks like a recessed ceiling light, a wan white circle punched in the night sky. By concentrating on it I can get myself away from the frayed, panicky edges of my mind, onto steadier territory. This is better; this is an improvement. When I got up here just after sunset, I was still wild, a feral child rabid with loneliness and terror, a brute whirlwind of hatred. I fell upon my bay tree, the one I have been visiting ever since I got jealous of Pierce and his ritual tree, and I began scraping at its bark with my bare hands, screaming like an idiot for the tree to "let me in."

I don't have the faintest idea where I got that inanity from. I remember the feeling of being excluded from something, of having my chance for a fair and bearable life cruelly stolen away. All I could think was that Jeanna was dead and I was not; she didn't have to feel anything, and I had to feel *everything*.

I guess I wanted to be absorbed into the thick, fibrous silence of the wood. Wouldn't June love that? I really wanted to be one with nature. But I was excluded; there was no admittance allowed. I scraped and clawed until my hands were burning. Now, in the glare of my flashlight on this journal, I see that I am leaving a bloody smear all down this page. How melodramatic!

Finding my journal and flashlight in my backpack, along with a candy bar and a half-filled water bottle, was a big surprise. I must have been planning this little camp-out, but I'm sure a lie detector would confirm that I can't vouch for anything I thought, said, or did over the past few days. I remember only the "high spots." The first and the worst:

Brimming with good, therapy-induced intentions and afraid I'd lose my nerve over the phone, I drove to Jeanna and August's

MY JOURNEY THROUGH THE PLANT WORLD 280

place the morning after writing up my long talk with June. I had to park a full block from the apartment because of a strange preponderance of automobiles in the neighborhood. When I came close my enthusiasm chilled a little. There were four or five women standing out in the courtyard.

I could see that the door to the apartment was open, as if there were some kind of party going on. At ten in the morning? I stopped dead in my tracks, halfway convinced that I should talk to Jeanna at some other time, rather than interrupting a meeting of August's coven. But then I decided, no, I'd chicken out if I turned back. I should at least go in, apologize for the interruption, and ask Jeanna when we might be able to get together later. That seemed sensible and respectful.

I was almost at the door, having nodded in a friendly way to the women talking outside, when I nearly collided with August on her way out. Her eyes were red and her face puffy. She looked at me as if she had seen a ghost, and murmured, "I was about to call you."

"Really?" I said, mystified. "I guess I heard you on the psychic network. Is Jeanna here? I don't want to interrupt your meeting or anything. I have to ask her one quick thing."

August looked at me like she'd rather be anywhere else in the world at that moment. It was a look both strangely tender and hopeless. "Randall, Jeanna died last night."

I wished August had said something I could misinterpret, or something not clearly heard; something that would bear repeating, and in the repeating, could be reversed. But she was perfectly clear. I stood there feeling my feet become strangely heavy and my head sickeningly light; I was so rapidly adrift!

"How could Jeanna die?" I asked wonderingly, as if I were a child stunned to learn that it was raining on parade day, or that Santa was a drunk. Then a hard fact with which to fight back came to me, and I let August have it in a firm, certain voice: "People don't die from chronic fatigue."

August rubbed one eye with the back of her chubby hand, like a toddler. "It wasn't chronic fatigue. It was her heart. She had a heart condition."

a novel of sexual initiation   281

"She had a *heart condition?*" I shrieked, startling myself and the women nearby. "Since when did she have a heart condition?!"

"Since always," August said matter-of-factly. "When she got so ill this year, we knew it might be the beginning . . . that this might happen. She was born with an inoperable defect. It got worse over the years."

A massive anger was coalescing inside me, red-hot and out-of-control, like all the rods pulled on a nuclear reactor at once. "Why have I never known this?" I demanded of August.

She backed away from me a step, a rare reaction for her. "Well, Jeanna never talked about it much. I guess she told you what she wanted to. Maybe she told you what she thought you could handle."

"Oh, *fuck that,* August," I seethed, beginning to lose my grip. "Fuck that shit. This isn't right."

August backed away even further; one of her friends came up to hold her. Everyone was looking at me strangely, as if they were all afraid. One of the women caught August's eye and tilted her head toward the open door. August shook her head in response and addressed me again.

"Randall, I know this is a terrible shock, and a terrible way for you to find out. But we have to accept that it was Jeanna's time. She was an old soul."

"What?" I said incredulously.

"She was an old soul. We talked about it a lot, about her feeling that she didn't have much to do in this life. I think it was because she had done most of her work in other lifetimes. She may have been here to help a few of us in one way or another, and when her work was done, it was time for her to go. That's the way I'm looking at it, if it's any help."

I shook my head vigorously, and halfway turned around as if to go, but I wasn't sure I could take a step without falling down. This was too much, this metaphysical bullshit, and I wasn't going to let August get away with it. I wanted to demolish her intellectually, but instead I thrust myself at her fat little face and screamed, "I said, fuck that shit, August! You can't make this all right—it's all wrong! I don't wanna hear any more of your good-witch crap, dammit. Why don't you . . . why don't you just go fuck yourself? Isn't that what all you dykes do—fuck yourselves? Just go do that, okay?!"

The other women were now circling and enclosing August, ushering her toward the apartment door, perhaps because I had started doing some kind of mad, raving dance in place, something for which I was not responsible. Before they disappeared behind the door, however, August called out, "Please call me, Randall! Jeanna left instructions!"

I didn't remember that until a little while ago, and it's just as well. If it had registered then I might have tried to storm the apartment door. Instead I took off running, and I've been running ever since, until a little while ago when I collapsed against this tree, looked up, and noticed the moon.

Perhaps there is a God because I don't know how I could have driven the car up here alone without plunging off the hillside or crashing into someone. I don't even remember what I did yesterday, the second day of living with the ghastly news. Did I go to work or was I at home? I honestly don't know. I do know that I drove up here today soon after noon, and I ran, in a vast, stumbling grief for a while, then napped atop a picnic table, drawing the curious looks of casual hikers who may have mistaken me for someone homeless. They could not have possibly understood that I was more alone and abandoned than that.

I haven't told anyone; not June or Pierce or my mom or dad or Giselle or Iceberg or even Lainie; let them find out on their own. Leave it to death's little grapevine. This is still my private news; this is the crushing insult intended just for me, exquisitely timed to shatter all my petty, silly hopes for becoming a Better Person. What complete bullshit that was! What crap.

At least I'm sleepy now, and I have a candy bar. There's a brilliant, two-step plan for the future. I could put some high-octane sugar in my belly—have I eaten anything recently?—and go to sleep under this goddamn tree. If I stay with it all night, perhaps it will see that I am really faithful after all, and it will take me in. The park ranger will find all my stuff here, my light and the candy wrapper and my journal, but I will have disappeared.

a novel of sexual initiation

I will be living inside the bark, where I will feel nothing but the water rushing ceaselessly upward all day, drawn by the warmth of the sun. Maybe I won't eat ever again. Who needs food when you've got photosynthesis? It's a plan; it could work; I'm completely serious.

Please, please take me in! I don't want to find myself still in this body in the morning, huddled, stiff, and broken on the cold fucking ground, feeling even sillier for having written all this crap, then having to live for another impossible day in this goddamned vacant world, without Jeanna.

26

4/26/92

MY LEG hurts like hell, and I can hardly move it, but at least it's not broken. Apparently I just sprained my knee badly when I fell and then lay in the snow for a couple hours, up there in the mountains. That makes it sound so ordinary, like I just fell down, passed out, and came to—which, on the face of it, is all that happened. But there was the Dream. Compared to the few "big" ones I've had in the past, this one is off the charts, too big for measurement. June will go crazy. I bet she'll want to write me up for some Jungian journal. I can't wait to tell her.

First I've got to get down as much of it as I can remember. I have some notes I scribbled while lying in the back of the station wagon on the trip back yesterday, but some of them are indecipherable and my memories are fading. Pierce has fixed me up on the couch with some tea and scones and my laptop. I hope he hasn't given me too much painkiller. For a guy who's gone organic in his diet and lifestyle, Pierce still has quite a stash of fun chemicals.

Let's see . . . when I woke up in the park, the morning after I last wrote, I was exhausted and depressed, but stable. I drove home and washed up, and played back my messages. By then everyone seemed to have heard the news, and was wondering where I was. I made some calls, including to Lainie—I mean Lana—who said she had wanted to come for the funeral, but August had told her there wasn't time. I had two messages from August, too, both ordering me to call her immediately. So I called, and August sounded more than a little irritated.

"Where have you been?" she asked brusquely. "We're all leaving tomorrow morning for the Sierras and you're supposed to come along."

"I am?" I said, confused. "Who's we? Is Jeanna's funeral in the mountains?"

"No," replied August, "we're holding a ritual of passage. We're driving up in several cars, and you're supposed to come. Jeanna insisted on it, when we talked this over a few months ago."

"Oh Lord, August," I sighed, "what kind of a ritual? Can't you give it a rest for once and do things the normal way?"

"The way we're doing things is the way Jeanna wanted it," August declared defensively, "and she wanted you to come. That's the last time I'm telling you. Come to the apartment by six a.m. if you're going to join us."

"All right, all right," I surrendered. "I'll drive, if anybody wants to ride with me."

"No, you can't drive," August commanded. "We have enough cars, and we all have to stick together to maintain the proper focus. What we have to do is very difficult, and we don't have much time. There will be one person in each car to help each group get prepared. I'll be riding in the same car with you, since you probably haven't done anything like this before."

"I've done rituals before with Pierce," I said defensively, realizing how contradictory I must sound.

"Well, maybe that will help," August allowed. "But you'll have to be serious and not make fun, okay? Jeanna promised me you would help out for her sake if I ever had to ask."

"All right," I said softly. "Of course." I realized this might be my last opportunity to serve Jeanna's wishes instead of my own.

"Oh, and Randall?"

"Yeah?"

"Don't eat anything between now and then. And no caffeine or alcohol. Bring a sleeping bag; we'll be staying overnight."

"OK," I replied, abruptly feeling my first pang of hunger in several days. I realized that I had probably not eaten in forty-eight hours, and wished that I still had that candy bar from the night before; I didn't know if I'd eaten or lost it.

By the next morning when I drove to August's, I was so famished I was feeling weak and dizzy, but I'd kept my promise.

a novel of sexual initiation 287

It looked like there were about twenty people standing around, with a few of them, including August, bustling about frenetically, piling flowers and bundles of herbs and sleeping bags in the trunks of four cars. As none of the cars were very large, this meant that it would be pretty close quarters wherever I was riding. Although I was feeling better, I was hardly sociable.

Most of the trip to the Sierras was taken up with listening to August give us a pep talk for the ritual, including teaching us all a song in some unknown language, a song which she said would be the "vehicle for Jeanna's passage to the next world." The words sounded something like *"Ha-wa, ha-way, ha-wa my consommé,"* but we could just as well have been singing "Open sesame, Safeway" for all I knew. I listened and sang along with everybody like we were all on the way to camp.

We headed up the highway toward Yosemite, but turned off on a road unfamiliar to me, and kept climbing into ever more remote territory until we passed the snowline. When all four cars pulled up in front of a large wood-hewn cabin, almost the size of a lodge, it was somewhere around ten or eleven in the morning. A station wagon with windows obscured from the inside was parked in front of the building.

For perhaps an hour and a half, I disconsolately wandered the building and the grounds, weak from hunger and disoriented, while almost everyone else busied themselves with preparations. A few people were meditating, one group was practicing the song, several people were stretching out on the floor, others were decorating the large central room of the house with tree branches and flowers while removing every last stick of furniture. There were some peculiar cooking smells issuing from the high-ceilinged kitchen. Every time I would hang out near there August would walk by and give me a stern look.

Finally, just before noon, I slumped down against a wall in the main room, next to a fireplace which was working up some radiance. I noticed for the first time that the impressive sliding doors to the next room, probably a dining room, were not only closed but also barred with a large **X** made of two split halves of logs, each one about ten feet long. I was trying to figure out the

MY JOURNEY THROUGH THE PLANT WORLD   288

point of this when the African couple entered.

She was tall and regal, and reminded me a little of August's painting of Nzinga, the warrior queen of Angola. He was shorter and rotund, and he carried a long drum slung around his neck, which he started slapping almost the moment he got in the door. He would not stop for six hours, and that's just as long as I was around. How he did it I'll never know. The two of them were dressed in full ceremonial garb; Pierce would have loved to meet their tailor. *Where does August find these people?* I remember thinking.

Everything swung into action right after that. The curtains were drawn everywhere, making the room semi-dark in the middle of the day. The tall African woman began dancing slow, sensuous circles around the main room while August and three other women, also dressed ceremoniously in long flowing pants and embroidered caftans, walked stiffly through the gathered assembly, offering everybody some kind of warm, grainy mush from wooden bowls.

I was so ravenous I was sure I could devour two bowls by myself, but when August came up to me she silently indicated that I was to take only one handful. And that turned out to be enough. The stuff tasted like some kind of foul, sour buckwheat, and the chaser, offered next, was a tiny cup of bitter, rooty tea. I don't know whether it was a protein rush or something August put in the food or tea, but I was soon as high as a kite, yet piercingly focused on the goings-on.

My most difficult moment came in the first hour of the ritual, after August spoke the only English words I would hear for hours. While Nzinga, as I had decided to call her, continued to wreathe her way around the room to the hypnotic roll of her partner's drum, August announced that each of us was invited to express our deepest feeling for Jeanna in the center of the room, without words. Everyone else was to begin singing the song we had been taught earlier, and to keep singing and dancing like Nzinga around whoever was in the center.

All this made me exceedingly anxious. I hung back from the crowd for over an hour while people moved, one by one, into the

a novel of sexual initiation 289

center and danced, or laughed, or wept aloud, sometimes ending up screaming and writhing on the floor. The crowd was mostly female but there were two or three guys I had never seen before. One had produced a drum and joined the African drummer. Another had put on the head and pelt of a real wolf over himself, which I thought was very New Age. Yet I found his balletic leaping about in the center of the singing, increasingly energetic group strangely hypnotic. As the afternoon progressed I would find my snap judgments constantly being challenged in this way.

I had almost decided I was safe, and that the group would move on to some other activity without noticing that I hadn't participated, when I felt an urgent shove at my back—it had to be August!—and I found myself in the center of the group. Feeling silly and out of place, I was about to beg off when I got the strongest feeling that that would be a serious mistake. The inner voice suddenly reminded me:

This is not about you.

And so, despite my embarrassment standing there, I tried to think about Jeanna. All I could see was her black hair swirling around as she laughed and turned her head quickly, so I started turning that way, trying to swirl somehow, which reminded me of a picture I had once seen of whirling dervishes. I decided to be one of them, imagining myself with one of those funny vertical hats. I started spinning madly and laughing at the image, then thought of Jeanna whirling with me, dancing in my arms like we had never done. I felt a flash of anger, then deep and pained regret.

I flung myself into spinning with complete abandon until I started to lose my balance and stumble, crashing crazily into one person and another. People always gently pushed me back to the center until I tripped over my own feet, meeting the wooden floor roughly with my two hands out in front of me just in time to keep from knocking my head. With my head reeling and my ears filled with the unbearable noise of singing all around me and what seemed to be the pounding of a hundred drums, I began to scream.

I'd have never thought this possible before, losing control in a group like that. Now I didn't care what anyone thought. I vaguely remember being carried from the center of the room by two or three people, and laid on a big pillow, where I must have kicked and yelled with grief and anger, coming completely unglued, for most of another hour, while somebody firmly kept me in place. Somebody else put cooling water on my forehead. Somebody else sang the song, ever so softly, right into my ear.

And when I was done, all the grief having flooded from the broken dam in my heart, I slept for a while, perhaps an hour. When I awoke the room was a little darker, the sun probably having passed below the high ridge outside, and the atmosphere in the house was wilder than before.

While I'd been out of it, another phase of the ritual had been inaugurated. Almost everyone was sitting against the walls while five or six people, all dressed in some kind of animal skins, were having at it in the center of the room, grappling with each other, battling and throwing each other about, yelping and howling and barking. I sat up and rubbed my eyes and watched in amazement, distinctly aware of the altered atmosphere in the room, and how avidly I was taken into something that, had I heard it described to me while I was in my right mind, I would have mercilessly denigrated.

But I was so captivated that when the wolf-man crashed against the wall and breathlessly handed his sweaty skin to me, I took it without question, rushing into the center of the room with a feral roar, knocking down someone. Then three people piled into me, and I hit the floor laughing, forgetting myself, got up singing that damn song, then decided to follow Nzinga around the room a while, dancing, gesticulating, aware that my mask freed me from the usual limits and incessant demands of my personality. The former me seemed to have been exiled to some distant room.

I don't remember everything that happened; I do remember the growing intensity of it all. I must have been singing and dancing for another hour when the fun suddenly evolved into deep, deep weirdness. Without warning August burst into the room at the height of one whirling, bouncing, full-group dance,

a novel of sexual initiation   291

wearing nothing but mud, a brown and ochre paste covering her
from her feet to her head. Even her hair was matted with it. She
was groaning and roaring and spinning around while bent over
at the waist, her eyes closed tight and her hands grasping forward for something invisible. She was obviously out of her mind.
I kept blinking, hoping I was hallucinating.

All of a sudden somebody in the corner of the room thrust a
cedar branch into the fire and raised it above her head, creating
a *whoomp* sound and a lot of crackling and smoke, and I began
to get seriously afraid. They were going to burn the house down!
August unexpectedly made a charge at the barred door at one
end of the room, and soon she was being helped by two other
people, a male and a female, to take down the split logs and pull
back the sliding doors.

On the other side of that door, laid out on a low table and
ringed with flowers and candles, was a body. Like everyone I
crept forward to take a look, the volume in the room suddenly
decreasing down to the level of the drums, only a few people
remembering to sing half-heartedly. When I got close enough to
the room to see that the body was Jeanna, dressed in a simple
white robe, I recoiled and plastered myself against the wall, just
outside the entrance to the room. My rational mind slammed
back into gear with a vengeance. This was sick; this was too
weird; this had to be illegal!

I was ready to bolt, and I looked around in a panic to see who
might run with me, just as Nzinga began to sing "*ha-wa. . .*" in
her bold and piercing soprano, more passionately than ever.
Everyone but me joined in, clasping their arms around each
other and swaying back and forth around the bier. August had
said nothing about this part of the ritual in her pep talk. I was
split in half by two fears: the fear of staying to see what would
follow and the fear of possibly disrupting everything. The result
was that I kept peeking around the entrance to the room where
the corpse was, keeping my eye on the goings-on without getting
involved. I resumed singing in a soft, guarded voice.

Soon August assumed a position behind Jeanna's head and
slipped her hands underneath the body's shoulders. She wailed

something unintelligible and began lifting the body. *Oh shit*, I thought, a chill going all through me. Other people were now helping to lift the body off the bier and soon it was standing erect, supported only by a few hands. How was this possible?

And then I heard it: a high, unearthly whine, a weeping call unlike anything I had heard all day, and the sound seemed to be coming from Jeanna. And she was walking! Or was she? Assisted by August and another woman, she seemed to be moving forward of her own volition, one slow step after another. Now I had to be hallucinating; this couldn't be real! My breathing became labored and panicky, and I was ready to run when Jeanna and her entourage came within a few feet of me. Her head turned gravely toward me and I saw that Jeanna's eyes were half-open. She was regarding me with a peculiar, heavy-lidded look and an ancient, far-away smile. Then she had passed me, headed with the group toward the rear of the house.

That did it. If they were going out the back door, I was going out the front. I was going as far as I could, as rapidly as possible, away from the eternal drumbeat and the song, which seemed to have erased every thought in my mind, leaving only the impulses of fright and a desperate alienation.

I heard someone call my name as I flung open the heavy wooden door and ran past all the cars into the mercifully quiet twilight, a light snow on the ground giving the woods a bluish, supernatural glow. At breakneck speed I ran over the near ridge and then down the steep incline on its other side, paying no heed to direction or my insufficient clothing. I had shed my pullover sweater hours before, during the sweaty dancing. For the moment, the bracing, high-altitude cold was of no concern.

I was escaping from the lunacy I had witnessed, the lunacy that was a complete affront to everything I thought possible, much less wise or decent. Before I knew what was happening, I had lost control of my own momentum. My shoes were slipping on the brown leaves and the white snow. I realized that I was hurtling out-of-control toward a small stream about twenty feet down the hillside, a gurgling brook decorated here and there with tissues of ice along its banks—a harmless, lovely scene if I

a novel of sexual initiation

were not about to collide with it at high speed.

As I lost my balance and went down on my side I tried to heave myself toward the trunk of a tree by the creek. I partially succeeded, with the result that one knee slammed against the tree as I pinwheeled on the ground toward the water, and then—too late to do anything about it—I saw a large gray stone looming in my blurred, ground-level vision. I felt an instantaneous, searing pain and saw a flash of purple light.

27

THE DOG was barking furiously at me from the center of the stream—a fat little terrier with no better sense than to be standing in the middle of a freezing mountain creek in the dead of night. He was such a scruffy animal that I wasn't afraid of his hysterical barking, much less his bite. But he had an urgency about him, hopping this way and that, every few moments running downstream only to turn around, hop up on his hind legs, and yap ever more ferociously.

He wanted me to follow him. Cold and stiff from the awkward position I had landed in, with one arm trailing in the ice-cold stream for God knows how long, I roused myself with some difficulty and brushed myself off, feeling my head for a bloody wound but finding none. The dog ran madly upstream toward me again, making such a fuss that he was splashing me with more freezing spray.

"All right, Lassie," I said irritatedly, "hold your horses." As soon as I stood up he was dashing away again, this time without turning around. If I hadn't started after him, galloping down the middle of the stream, he would have soon been out of sight. He was fast for such a short-legged bugger!

As the creek descended gently into an ever deeper canopy of trees, I began losing moonlight and feared that soon I would be able to see nothing at all. Indeed, it wasn't long before the stream plunged into a pitch-black tunnel. I stopped short before going in, tilting my head to hear how far ahead of me the terrier had gotten. His bark was very faint and I heard no splashing at all.

Trying to figure out what was going on, I remembered one of Etty's lectures about the "shamanic journey into the under-world" and about how one would always be greeted at the outset by a "power animal" who represented one's guardian nature spirit, functioning as a guide to all the visions to come.

My power animal is a chubby little terrier? I thought. *How humiliating.* Was this a trip worth taking? I took one more cautious step forward. It proved not to be cautious enough because my foot went out from under me on solid ice, then I landed hard on my rump. In a second I was body-sledding down a slick, black conduit into nowhere, the ice eventually dropping away from underneath me so that I was in a vertical freefall. I cursed myself for following the scruffy dog, since this was clearly the end of me.

Yet only an eyeblink later the sun was seductively warm and the calm, lazy river drifted through a meadow as if it had no place else to go. The dog and I were on a log raft. The ratty little beast was panting heavily after our laborious excursion, but I was enjoying myself, stretched out languidly in the generous sunlight. Every once in a while the dog would stick a paw in the water, like an oar, to guide us this way or that. I didn't see why he bothered.

Once the dog reached so far over the edge of the raft that he almost fell in, scrambling back to safety at the last moment. When I sat up to chide him I saw, to my great disgust, that he was smoking a cigar.

"Stupid dog," I said disapprovingly, "no wonder you can't catch your breath."

Then the raft bumped gently against the bank of the river and snagged there. The dog bounded off and up into the long, luxurious green grass. "So we've arrived," I sighed indifferently, and hopped off the raft onto solid ground. Atop the bank, the meadow scene spread out before me looked strangely familiar. Off to one side a beautiful dark horse grazed behind a fence, looking up once to acknowledge my arrival. Right in front of me was a cheap, bare card table with two wooden chairs. I sat down on one of them. The terrier jumped onto the chair on my left, put his paws up on the table with the ridiculous cigar hanging from his teeth, and turned into Chuck Berquist.

"Hullo there, Randall," he chirped, "what can I do you for?"

"What?" I said, stunned.

a novel of sexual initiation 297

Chuck plucked the cigar from his teeth, exhaled blue smoke and smiled like a chimp. "Excuse me," he said merrily, "I meant to say: How can I help?"

"Help?" I said, looking nervously around but finding nothing but acres of achingly lovely, green waving meadow in view. "Help with what?"

"Oh, whatever," Chuck said casually, leaning back in his chair to put both feet up on the table. "Questions. Possibilities. Points of view."

"Chuck," I said wonderingly, "where are we?"

"Oh, we're here now," he said factually. "Not to worry."

"Ah," I said, uncertain of how to pursue the question further. Then I felt a knife in my heart: "Chuck, Jeanna died!"

"Yeah," he said wryly, taking his feet down from the table and leaning toward me, "it's a pisser. It happens. Or seems to."

"Seems to?"

"Yeah. That's the problem with the plant world. Shit happens, and it seems like you can't do anything about it. Whereas *here*," he paused dramatically, waving his stinky stogie in my face, "you can change anything you want, but other things happen too fast to keep up with."

I leaned back in my seat, the cigar smoke making me nauseous. "Chuck, would you mind getting rid of that damn thing?"

Chuck put the thing between his teeth again and growled, "Don't bug me. S'not real, after all." Then he smiled eerily, his eyes glinting green in the sunlight in a way they shouldn't.

"Chuck!" I yelped, my heart racing. "Am I having a dream?!"

The cigar abruptly disappeared like something vaporized on *Star Trek*, and Chuck laughed heartily. "Hey-o," he crooned, perfectly appropriating Iceberg's voice and style, "there you go!"

"All right!" I shrieked excitedly, falling backward out of my chair into a perfect martial-arts roll, something I had never practiced but could now do at will. Then I ran a few steps and leapt into the air, marveling at how the sky had turned three shades bluer, how the grass was so green its color had become a new dimension, how I could smell every scent of the meadow like a bloodhound. And I could do this from fifty feet in the air, because now I was flying, my arms out to the side just like Superman!

So this was what Etty had called a "lucid dream." The warm wind whistled by my ears. I cut a few rolls, dips, and loop-the-loops with the greatest of ease, buzzing Chuck a few times, who was laughing and jumping up and down in the meadow's deep waves like a small, ecstatic child.

"See me?" I cried out to Chuck. "Do you see that I can fly?!"

"Yessir," Chuck yelled from the ground. "So what are you going to do now? Goin' to Disneyland?"

I swooped down from mid-air and stationed myself as close to Chuck as I could get, so I could whisper into his ear. "Do you mean I can do anything I want? No limits, no rules?"

"Sure," he confirmed.

"The hell with Disneyland," I muttered darkly. "I wanna fuck my brains out."

"Hey, go for it," Chuck replied cheerily. "I'm the last guy to get in your way."

SO I took off again, not having a plan so much as a heady imperative of lust, and as I soared beyond the meadow's borders I soon spotted a town. I thought I would zoom into some lovely lady's bedroom, giving her a big surprise on a sultry afternoon, but abruptly found myself in the old porn theater I used to visit, simultaneously sitting in the audience and involved in the activity onscreen.

There was an orgy scene going on in a dark, watery grotto, with a gaggle of ten or twelve people clumped in groups of two, three, and four, everybody fucking or sucking and crying out "Oh, oh, oh!" and "Yeah, baby!" and "Give it to me now!" Everywhere I looked I saw women's rumps and tits proffered invitingly to me. There was a regular sexual smorgasbord going on, all you could fuck forever, and I couldn't wait to get docked with somebody, then pull out when I was bored with her, and go screw somebody else, and feel all the soft flesh I possibly could with my hands.

I was in a literal panic of desire; I couldn't believe the good

a novel of sexual initiation

fortune that had materialized out of thin air. The only problem was that I was sitting in the audience at the same time, my erection out in the dark air, and it felt more real there than in the grotto. By concentrating intensely for a few moments I managed to pull my awareness fully into the movie world, and got ready for action. This was great!

"Randall!" my mother called. When I looked out I saw her sitting where I had been in the theater seats, holding up a list of "Things to Do Thursday for Mom," a list that unrolled like toilet paper over the rows of seats in front of her.

"Dammit," I whined. That list could take me the rest of my life to complete! When would I ever have any fun? Fortunately, at that moment Giselle appeared before me, greedily clasping my thighs. With copious tears running down her cheeks she cried out, "Let me show you what a really good blow-job is!"

Well now—I wasn't about to turn that down. So I said "Sure, baby," like it was in the script, and thrust myself toward her. *Oh yes,* I thought, thrilling to the first few flicks of her tongue, *everything I've been missing.*

I looked down toward Giselle, thinking gratefully that here was a woman who really knew how to give head—especially considering that she didn't have one to give it with! Not at all, nada! Just a little rounded bump between her shoulders where her neck should begin. Recoiling, I looked all around the grotto and saw that everyone was like that: headless bodies pumping and humping away on each other, the only sound now being the slapping of wet groins together and the sploshing of water. Sickened, I stepped out of the water and hastened to a wall mirror, where I could somehow see, to my deep horror, that I was headless too!

"Aaaiiuuugggh!" I screamed, losing my footing on the wet, slimy tile of the grotto, tumbling over backwards and landing squarely in Chuck's lap at the card table, back in the lovely green meadow. Embarrassed but relieved to have escaped the underworld scene, I softly said "'Scuse me," easing myself over into my chair.

"Bad trip?" Chuck inquired casually.

I ran my hand through my hair and said, "Chuck, you would

not believe . . ."

He interrupted me with a knowing grin, flicking a few ashes from his cigar (back again!) onto the table. "Yeah," he mused, "that's the trouble with the fantasy realms. They'll turn on ya. If you're not careful, you can get stuck between worlds that way."

Something clicked. "Chuck," I said suspiciously, "how did *you* get here?"

His cocky demeanor wilting, Chuck dropped both hands beneath the table and slumped his shoulders like a little kid. "I got lost," he whimpered.

"But wait," I said, confused. "If this is *my* dream, then how did you . . ."

"My dream, your dream, the American dream . . . what's the diff?" Chuck mused. "I'm just trying to redeem myself, provide a little service, do my stint as a tour guide. Then maybe I can get back on track. Who knows?" Chuck looked skyward and sighed wistfully.

"They said you disappeared," I reported.

"From the plant world?" Chuck replied. "Well, let's say I'm on hiatus. Just like you, Randall, *my good man*." The last three words came out in Pierce's voice, so I did a double-take. But it was still Chuck sitting there. The way things seemed to be morphing brought a new query to mind.

"What about time, Chuck?"

"What about it?"

"Can I mess with it here? You know, like, rewind and record over some things?"

Chuck held his two palms up in the air and protested, "Hey, I said I'm the tour guide, not the projectionist."

The hell with him. I lifted out of my chair and flew backwards, spinning heels over head to back up time. I knew that would work, even if I didn't know how I knew. Momentarily I landed with astonishing accuracy in Anna's apartment on New Year's Eve, the second time we slept together.

I remembered getting a little rough with her and I'd always wanted to apologize. I called to her from the bed, where I could smell the herbs from the good breakfast she was making.

a novel of sexual initiation   301

"Anna?"

"Yes, baby?"

"I'm sorry."

"That's nice," she said without affect, and then added, "Could you ask the kids what they want for breakfast?"

"What?" I replied wonderingly, and then looked down to see that Anna's two blond little tykes were on either side of me in the bed, pointing and laughing gaily.

"Who's this, Mommy?" cried one of the kids. "Is he Satan?" laughed the other.

I was about to protest my innocence when I heard a metallic click, and looked up to see Anna's Christian husband advancing on me with a shotgun, muttering, "You Godless pervert." By the time the twin barrels were right in front of my eyes, Lainie was holding the gun, and asking, "But why can't we go, Randall? Why *can't* we go on vacation?"

"Lainie, I swear," JoEllen said disapprovingly as she entered the room and pushed the shotgun away, narrowly saving me from bloody oblivion. "You Californians are all so crazy! Randall, please get rid of that hard-on and get dressed. I'm going to need a full deposition on your Disastrous Dating Period." Then JoEllen opened the door to a courtroom. In there was my father, sitting and smiling flirtatiously in the judge's chair, surrounded by all the women I'd never gotten to second base with.

"All right," I said disconsolately as I flipped back into my seat at the card table, "so that doesn't work, either."

Chuck's eyes were merry and his moustache was curling with his smile. "The past isn't what you think it is," he said gently. "It wasn't even what you thought it was when it was happening. Nowadays, of course, it's *only* what you think it is. And mere thoughts, as I'm sure you know, are notoriously unreliable."

This sounded suspiciously circular to me, but I decided to let it go. My mind was drifting erratically; for no good reason I remembered August telling me that Jeanna was an old soul who'd been through many lifetimes. So I said, "There's something else about the past that I'm curious about, Chuck."

"Shoot."

"Is reincarnation for real? I mean, have I known some of the people I know, before?"

Chuck recoiled like a used-car salesman who's been asked for the papers on a lemon in the lot. Eyeing me warily, he replied, "Depends on how you look at it."

"How do you mean?"

"Depends on whether it's *useful* to look at things that way."

"Okay, let's assume it might be useful to look at it that way. Have I lived before, and known some of the people I know now, in other lives?"

"S'possible. If you want to look at it that way."

"Jesus, Chuck. Can you just tell me who was who in other times?"

"Try me."

"My mom."

"Recently? Your brother. Before that, you were marauders in fourteenth century Spain. Looting, pillaging, that kind of thing."

"And Dad?"

"Oooh. You've got a problem with him. Murdered you not too long ago." (Well, that I could believe.)

"OK, June?"

"Nobody. New entry. You never knew her before."

"Really?" That was kind of surprising. "Pierce?"

"Nzinga. You were her favorite slave until she gave you away, trying to score points with somebody."

"Really?" I laughed. "Well, whaddyaknow. How about JoEllen?"

"Ah, that's sweet. Your wife, big family in the last century. Tragic death, though. You're carrying a lot of sadness for her."

"And Lainie?"

"Surely you know this one, Randall. Recently your mother."

I took a big breath and paused, partly because I had a lot of information to digest, and partly because I wanted to ask the next question coolly, without betraying anything in my tone of voice.

"How about Etty?"

"Ah yes," Chuck mused, leaning back in his chair and cross-

a novel of sexual initiation 303

ing his hands over his potbelly. "Etty's a gatekeeper, a watcher of the portals between worlds. You wouldn't be here without her."

"A gatekeeper?" I replied wonderingly. "Is that why she gave me all the lectures?"

"Yes," Chuck said knowingly, "not to mention the . . . "

I blanched. Obviously he knew everything. "I never understood that," I confessed, "especially since she didn't seem to . . ."

"She needed only your acceptance," Chuck interrupted, "your reverence of her unseen function."

"But I didn't know what I was doing!" I protested. "I don't think she did either. I think she just liked young men. I'm sure there were others."

"Several, yes. But I didn't say *anybody* knew what they were doing," Chuck said sternly. "Most everyone in the plant world is unconscious of their true purpose until they begin to accept guidance."

The last phrase intrigued me, but I had one more pressing question. "Who was Jeanna, Chuck?"

"Ah, Jeanna. The poet, the old soul. She was your loving sister more than once. But all in all, nobody special . . ."

I was incensed. "How can you say a thing like that, Chuck? She was . . . wonderful. There was nobody like her, ever."

"I didn't say Jeanna was nobody special to *you*," Chuck corrected me. "I said, *nobody's special*."

CHUCK AND I talked a while longer, but I don't recall everything. I do remember asking him why he had lied so much and all he would say was "Sometimes the truth must come in the form of a lie." I didn't entirely buy that either, but let it go. After a while I began to get antsy. I felt somehow that time was running out and something was incomplete. There was some important question I had not yet asked.

"Chuck?"

"Yup?"

"Flying around and learning the secrets of time is fun, but . . . isn't something else supposed to happen?"

"Don't know," Chuck replied, leaning forward to blow noisy

bubbles in the Alice-in-Wonderland hookah that had replaced his cigar a little while before. "What do you think?"

I pressed both my hands against my skull, as if the pressure might make something pop out. "I can't tell," I mumbled, "it seems as if there's something I should ask . . ."

"Yes?" Chuck said expectantly.

"Something I should ask *to be shown*," I sang triumphantly, having thought of June in the nick of time.

"Beautiful!" exclaimed Chuck, and threw one arm out in the direction of the dark horse a couple hundred yards away from us. The horse snorted, pranced in a circle and then took a running leap over the split-log fence enclosing it, heading for us in a full gallop. I rose and leapt atop the charging animal as it thundered by, completing the whole motion with the practiced grace of a Native American warrior of old.

I hung onto the horse's mane for dear life as we sped through the meadow into a rapidly shifting panoply of natural territories and wild topographies. We galloped over snowy mountains, across endless tundras, through vast painted deserts, over the Arctic icepack, into the Australian outback, and deep into South American rainforests. It was an epic journey of great learning compressed into minutes; my body sweated, chilled, thinned, toughened, and strengthened as the passing climes demanded. Finally, the horse slowed as I realized that we had arrived in the rolling hills of the East Bay, above Berkeley. I patted my great steed affectionately as I slid off his back, rubbed my sore bottom, and looked around.

It was one of those pristine spring days with a few puffy clouds in the sky, a day so clear I could see the Farallon Islands out in the ocean to the west. About thirty feet in front of me to the east, partially obscuring a dramatic view of Mt. Diablo, was a simply perfect tree in a glory of recently unfolded leaves. It seemed to have been torched with a luminous green fire. The tree was perhaps sixty feet tall, with a whitish bark covering great, strong branches lifted prayerfully toward the sun. Its thinner, higher branches waved softly in a tranquil breeze. Standing there, watching the tree living and growing in its proper spot,

a novel of sexual initiation   305

gave me a feeling of complete serenity.

From behind me, however, a roiling thunderstorm materialized out of nowhere and raced overhead with incredible speed,
sending a shower of lightning daggers into the ground and thoroughly soaking me with one strong deluge of rain, like an auto-
matic car wash. Sputtering and laughing, shaking off the water,
I saw that running underneath the raincloud, matching its pace
perfectly, was Jeanna, wearing the simple white gown of the ritual, wetly matted against her slender body. She seemed to have
passed by without seeing me.

"Jeanna!" I cried, taking off after her. I had no sooner broken
into a full run than Jeanna ran headlong into the tree—and I
mean *into the tree,* vanishing into the bark when she should have
collided with it. *If she can, I can too,* I thought aggressively, but
what I saw as I came within ten feet of the tree made me slow my
pace. Forming on the surface of the tree was a vertical, pulpy
gash, somewhat like the images in my mother's recent artwork,
and definitely vulva-like.

"Whoa, Nellie!" I cried as I came upon the sexual entry to the
tree, stopping short to consider the ramifications of what I was
about to undertake. Could the situation be any more obvious? I
reached my hand toward the fissure, and slowly plunged it in; it
felt pretty much like what I had expected, only bigger, of course—
prodigiously so. Standing there with one hand up to the elbow
plunged into the tree's . . . whatever, I laughed and said aloud,
"Sorry this is so *Freudian,* June," then stepped all the way in.

Inside, I felt enveloped by something like Jello, but with
more character: something veined and pulsing, warm and rhythmic, soft and yet relentlessly powerful. To say enveloped is actually an understatement. I was literally absorbed and unified
with the tree's inner tissue, which was flesh, blood, and fibrous
wood all at once.

And then, with a great shock, I realized that my body had
become the tree's body. I could feel a fantastic network of roots
plunged into the dark soil; I could feel those roots' tiniest fila-
ments taking water from the soil, a devilishly tickling feeling. At
the same time I could feel my lofty branches soaring toward the

MY JOURNEY THROUGH THE PLANT WORLD   **306**

sky, all the way to the most tentative, budding tips of new leaves. I have never felt more alive; I have never felt larger; and I have never made so much sense to myself before. I could have stayed that way forever, but then a voice spoke to me—a voice inside my head like my own, but distinctly feminine and not unfamiliar.

How can I help you?

Where am I?

You have entered the plant world.

But Chuck said the world I came from is the plant world.

There you have only journeyed on the surface, alone and apart in your delusions. Now you are inside the plant world, joined to your nature.

Who are you?

I am your real lover, your truth.

Why haven't I ever heard from you before?

You have, but seldom listened. I have also spoken in dreams and accidents of fate, in coincidences, and in the ceaseless return of love even as you have turned away from it.

I wanted to protest at this point—she was being a little harsh—but she had so much authority that I trembled to object.

Well, I've done the best I could with what I had.

Everyone does. But the dream grows less painful as you begin to hear.

Which dream? This one?

All dreams. The world is dreams upon dreams, in which there can be found worlds upon worlds.

So what am I to do?

Regain the dream of your nature, which is closer to wakefulness than the dream of bitter separation that you have fallen into.

And how do I do that?

Tenderness. For tenderness is the strength most needed in your world now.

Tenderness. That's what June says. That sounds so simple.

So simple that you have mastered it?

Well, no.

So simple that you have even begun?

a novel of sexual initiation   307

All right, you've got me there. How do I begin?

Forgive, to begin removing your curse of anger upon the world. Be grateful, in order to restore your will. Surrender to your true purpose, so that you may steward your time well. And then act wisely at every moment of decision.

Hold it. How do I just be wise? Isn't that a little vague?

Listen for me whenever you are unsure.

How do I find you, except in here?

This is one dream. As you are now within me, I am always within you in your daily waking dream.

Where?

On the other side of fear. Confront your fears, and my voice will be clear.

And that's it?

That's it.

Amazing.

Then something really amazing happened: for a split second the sky above cracked and emitted a blinding silver streak of light, a light so intense I had to turn from it, but a light so compelling that I wanted to see it again and follow it immediately to its source.

What was THAT? I wondered.

The tree quaked. **That was reality.**

Reality?

What is beyond this dream, your waking dream, all dreams. Awakening. Where you are eventually headed.

Let's go now.

You are unprepared.

The hell you say. It's my dream. I can go if I want.

As you wish.

And so, with a great upward intent I shot forth from the tree, its roots, trunk, and branches dropping away like a landing pad beneath me. I went flying about the sky, seeking that great silver flash. At first I thought it had disappeared for good, but then I saw it out of the corner of my eye, rippling here and there at random like cloud lightning. Tracking it down was like trying to trap mercury, but with a little dodging and weaving I was finally in

MY JOURNEY THROUGH THE PLANT WORLD

the right place at the right time when the sky cracked open again, and I fell into it.

The funny thing is that I was falling up and down at the same time. It's hard to describe, and even harder to describe being inside the light, which was no longer silver, but more like an ivory liquid, almost a dish soap. *This isn't so special*, I remember thinking. That was before I noticed what was happening to my body. Apparently the liquid light was some kind of solvent, because my hands and feet and limbs were dropping away from me, getting smaller and smaller as they floated away in the vague off-whiteness all around me.

Dismemberment, I vaguely remembered Etty saying, but I was rapidly losing the capacity for memory and rational thought. I was becoming nothing but a blind pulse, a single recurring beat in the middle of nowhere. Then I became aware of the Big Pulse, something far below—or above?—where the light was getting more silvery and intense, like the first time I had seen it crack the sky.

Ah, reality. . . I let myself drop and I let myself rise, and my little pulse was getting ever closer to the big one: LUB-DUP, LUB-DUP, LUB-*DUP*. Then I understood: I was going to be annihilated. I would be absorbed into the big pulse of reality, which would accept me totally into a vast sea of love, unity, and unchanging constancy. It would be like an eternal orgasm, a perpetual paroxysm of acceptance. That would be the end of me, and the beginning of everything real—but *I* wouldn't matter anymore.

I'd still like to matter a little bit, I thought, quite innocently. Right when I could have merged with the big pulse, I bounced off it instead and there was a giant sucking sound down south. In a flick I was back where I'd started, warm and ensconced in the tree again.

You were right. I'm not ready for reality. I'll hang out with you instead.

No. You must go. Your time here is almost up.

A dizzying panic of abandonment flashed through me, and I screamed, *No! How can that be? I like it here!*

Of course. You have crossed the barrier between yourself and

a novel of sexual initiation   309

*your nature, but you are only visiting. You have much work
ahead to secure your conscious passage.*

I'm not going anywhere! I declared desperately. To prove my
point I started grasping at the soft tissue enveloping me, but to
no avail. Everything was totally slippery; there was nothing to
hold onto.

Why can't I stay with you? I wailed. *Why can't I stay and be
your lover?*

The strong feminine voice within my head began to recede,
like I'd pushed the FADE button on the remote control of my CD
player. The last words I heard as I felt myself slipping and sliding from the tree's vaginal embrace were:

You cannot hold me. I am not a body. I am free.

"WHERE WERE YOU?" Chuck bellowed as I plopped unceremo-
niously onto the top of the card table, snapping it in half, which
dumped me even more ignominiously upon the earth.

"Well, you see, I had a shot at reality . . ."

But Chuck was having none of it, vociferously insisting,
"We've got *to go*! We've got to get *out* of here!" He grabbed me
roughly by the arm and dragged me down to the riverside, where
the raft we'd arrived on had been replaced by a sleek, racy power-
boat. "Thank God it's easy to manifest what you need around
here," he said irritably, "or we'd never make it." Practically sling-
ing me to the floor of the boat like a sack of potatoes, Chuck
jumped to the front and started the engine with a fearsome roar,
fishtailing the boat in a wide half-circle before heading straight
upstream.

I was so depressed about my expulsion from the warm womb
of the tree that I didn't pay any attention to Chuck's shouting at
first. When I did, I couldn't hear what he was saying over the
surges of the boat's motor.

"D'you (*rooaarr*) member (*rooaarr*) axe?" he seemed to be
screaming, turning his head back and forth from me to the water
ahead, the low fringe of hair on his head flying horizontally in
the rushing wind.

"What?" I shouted back.

He repeated his shout, but I didn't catch any of it this time. Crawling forward on the floor of the boat, which was bucking every time it leaped over the water's surface, I eventually managed to get myself up to the control panel where I might be able to hear what Chuck was saying. By then it was too late. The boat ran aground violently in the middle of a small mountain stream in the dark of the night.

Chuck grabbed me again and flung me out of the boat, then took off running ahead of me, turning his head to holler, "Do you remember what to ask?"

This time I heard him clearly. It was hard to think as I ran forward in the moonlit darkness, trying to avoid falling or getting slapped in the face by tree branches. "What to ask about what?" I yelled back.

"Do you remember *what to ask*?!" he bellowed again with even greater urgency. I racked my brain for the correct answer, wishing Chuck would slow down for a second. Searching backward in my mind over my most recent adventures, seeking a clue, I finally hit upon something: what both Chuck and the inner voice had first asked me.

"How about . . . uh . . . *How can I help?*?" I yelped.

"Bingo!" Chuck nodded even as he raced ahead, turning just enough to flash me a finger-circle sign. "Don't worry! We're almost there now."

Almost where? I wanted to ask, but I suddenly remembered a recent, useful piece of advice. "Hey, Chuck," I yelled forward, "thanks! You've been a great guide. The best I've ever had under these circumstances!"

"You're welcome!" Chuck replied, then took a great leap over a fallen tree trunk in his path. As he hit the high point of his arc, he changed back into animal form. But not into a fat little terrier this time: now he was a sleek, loping coyote with an auburn coat, and his new physique gave him even greater speed. Feeling near the end of my reserves, I too leaped forward over the tree trunk with a final burst of energy. In the dim moonlight just ahead, I saw a body slumped by the streamside, one arm trailing in the cold water, with a bloody head turned to the side next to a

a novel of sexual initiation 311

large stone. It was me!

Too late, I realized that my forward momentum was going to carry me right into that unconscious body; I couldn't stop. I started trying to run backward, getting an image of myself as a cartoon character with my legs churning in a reverse circle, but it was all to no avail. Chuck, that goddamn little trickster, had pulled his last fast one on me—getting me going so fast toward the world I'd come from that I was going to crash right through the invisible barrier, despite my passionate desire to stay on the other side. I wanted to stay in the marvelous territory where I could fly, traverse great distances, and perhaps once again merge with the wise womanly tree, the tree that Jeanna had apparently joined forever.

It was not to be. Losing my balance and catapulting head first toward the body slumped by the stream, my mind went into a blur and I heard a great *ka-chunk,* like two gears engaging roughly, tooth against metal tooth. Then I groaned, wondering how I'd gotten my head into a sink full of running water. But there was no sink; I was hearing the mountain stream I'd fallen toward, the one that my chilled-numb arm was resting in.

"Oh, Jesus," I moaned, pushing myself up into a sitting position, feeling a nasty, searing flash of pain shoot from my right knee to my groin. "Oh, shit." My body was so heavy now, and painful! And I was freezing cold. I'd been passed out in the woods for God knows how long, and I wasn't sure I knew the way back to safety.

"Randall!" came a man's voice from a hundred feet above. "Randall Kenn-dricks!" A flashlight beam wavered crazily from the ridgetop.

"Down here!" I yelped. "Down by the creek! I hurt my leg!"

HALF AN hour later, I was back in the cabin by a warm fire, greedily knocking back a hot chocolate and some cheese crackers. My leg was in a makeshift sling because the wolfskin-guy thought I had broken it and we didn't want to take any chances. I'd been cleaned up a little, but I could feel matted blood in my hair and my clothes were muddy and torn. August came out of the bathroom, her hair wet against her skull, wearing a neat pair of jeans and a flannel shirt. She squatted down beside me, a kind but amused grin on her face.

"Where did you go, Randall? We missed you on the last part of the passage."

"I got scared," I said truthfully.

"That's okay," she replied softly. "Jeanna's gone on now, and everything's fine." Then she flinched slightly as I reached up and tenderly rubbed one of her earlobes.

"Still got a little mud behind the ears," I explained.

"Thanks," August chuckled, then gingerly placed her fingers on my bloody spot, whistling like a cowboy. "Wow, Randall. Looks like you got yourself kicked from here to Houston and back."

"Yeah," I grimaced, noting the encroachment of a headache at the back of my skull. "Somewhere in Texas, anyway."

28

5/13/92

ONE BY ONE, I've been decommissioning my porn tapes. It's sort of a ritual that came to me a few days after my big dream. Beginning with the most recent tape and working backwards chronologically, I'm watching a few minutes of each one with a new focus: I'm trying to see through the mechanistic sexual action to perceive what else might be going on. Because of my otherworld experience, I've been paying special attention to the people's heads, scanning their often blank facial expressions to guess at what they might have been thinking when the video was being shot.

After the first few attempts I laughed out loud when I realized what they were thinking about: *Work!* After all, they're just doing a job, like I do everyday. They're in the same old world I am. That's when it hit me, for the first time really, that there is no porn world where all that untrammeled, repetitive sex goes on perpetually. Somehow I had long believed that such a world could exist and felt a childish anger that it did not. In my lonely youth, when I was unconsciously looking for something I'd lost—my tenderness, maybe?—I found a tawdry but compelling substitute: a false world of self-absorbed lust.

For years I have mistaken the fantasy world of porn for the lost ecstatic world of my own nature, the plant world I briefly joined inside the tree. I've been stuck between worlds, as Chuck put it, right here on earth: distanced from my own nature, distanced from intimacy, distanced from any real purpose. Pornography is just one of the allies I have enlisted over the years in my conspiracy of distance. Having been inside the tree in the otherworld, I know how the world I'm seeking feels. But I have to get into that world consciously somehow, climbing assiduously over the jagged rocks of my self-created obstacle course, trying to close the distances . . .

That's why I'm decommissioning the tapes. I study each one and then erase it, all the while hearing the voice within me saying: *Forgive*. If I turn away from this stuff with bitterness I will only come back; that's always been my cycle of compulsion. With time and a lot of deep breaths I am trying to release my curse of anger upon sex, shake hands with my shadow, and reclaim the nature I have lost from within myself. Step by step, I am undoing the countless miles I have traveled deep into a lonely wrath.

But I have learned that nothing changes on its own; everything is connected. The voice within also directs me: *Be grateful*. So I have to write letters of thanks: to my father and mother, for everything they gave me, and tried to give. To Lana, for always seeing through me, and for being so much fun; to JoEllen, for being just plain magnificent; to Etty and August for opening the door to unseen worlds. And to Anna, of course, for initiation.

Then I hear: *Surrender to your true purpose*. I don't know what my true purpose may be, but at least I've recognized what it isn't. I need only look at the fancy neon sign in all my storefronts to see one of my big problems: DIVERSIONS. But since it's the only way I have ever made money and killed most of my time, I don't know what else I am qualified to do.

I discussed my options with June the other day, on our second meeting after the ritual. The first meeting was taken up with debriefing my dream; June kept a tape of that one! This time, I mentioned my tentative interest in working for Forests Forever—imagine me, a late-blooming environmentalist! June was soon mounting her bully pulpit, her eyes flashing with excitement.

"Your dreamworld journey is pointing the way, Randall, toward the purpose you've been unable to recognize before. I believe the meaning of your life lies in serving the feminine, an incredibly important function in this age when the patriarchy is disintegrating so violently. You've never heard this call for what it is; that's why you've felt that women were always leading you on or threatening you somehow. But really they were trying to call you out, to catalyze your potential to serve.

"That's why I'm all for this rainforest thing. I think it's calling out your archetypal energy. You have the potential to serve Mother Earth in a conscious yet sensually charged way. That's so rare, and so needed right now. Everything feminine needs you, Randall. *So serve her.* Serve Her!"

By this point June was leaning forward in her chair and shaking her rosy spectacles in my direction. Given what I'd been through recently, her odd little speech was making some sense. But I wasn't about to let on.

"I don't know, June. I don't seem like a good candidate for serving the feminine. I haven't really been close to any women for a while because they scare me to death. Or no, I guess it's the nature of sex itself that scares me, and women are how I know sex. How can I serve something that terrifies me?"

June sat back and beamed, looking supremely satisfied. "How can you *not*, Randall? It's how you get to touch the face of God."

That's what I love about the Jungians: their grandiloquence.

6/12/92

I'VE DONE IT. A week after that last entry, I called Iceberg into my office and told him I wanted out. I had to repeat myself five or six times, because he kept thinking that I wanted a little more time to myself, or a little less pressure, or a little more variety: anything besides wanting out completely.

I asked him to help me figure out how to keep a little income rolling in for the next couple years, but otherwise, I wanted to turn the enterprise over to Giselle and all the other managers, and let Diversions become one of those employee-owned corporations. That sounded cool to me (and to the employees, as it turned out), and crazy to Iceberg. He came around eventually, once assured that his retainer wouldn't change. Thereupon followed lots of meetings and confabulations and general hysteria,

MY JOURNEY THROUGH THE PLANT WORLD   316

during which I had to cancel two appointments with June.

In fact, I've felt less need to see her since the ritual. My life seems to be reorganizing itself at breakneck speed. I've had several talks with Wayne Dennis, who seems ecstatic that I am prepared to join Forests Forever. I don't know what I have to offer, but I suppose I can keep asking "How can I help?" It appears they can use all the help they can find these days. I'm taking some time to read up on the worldwide rainforest situation, and the news is bad, like it so often is in this world. But I feel strangely chipper, ready to sally forth, ready to give anything a try.

After all, you never know what will happen next. A case in point: my last appointment with June a few days ago. When I got to her house, I was fairly bursting with the news about my change of purpose and blurted it out right away. June seemed oddly distracted, saying only that the decision felt right to her and she wished me "the best," a peculiarly formal thing for her to say. Here I was doing what she had encouraged, but all of a sudden she seemed not to care. Then:

"Randall, I have the oddest feelings right now, and I don't really know where to begin." June sighed hugely, her hands trembling slightly atop her chair. "First things first, I guess. I'm afraid we have to curtail our professional relationship."

"Really?" I said, more curious than shocked. I'd been prepared to propose the same.

"Yes," June said, then blushed beet-red. "Look, two weeks ago I was at an art therapy conference, and I met Kay. Your mother, I mean. She's doing wonderful work, you know."

I laughed out loud. "You met Mom? What a hoot! You mean we can't talk anymore because you've met my mother? Hell, we could make it a family therapy thing, couldn't we? I'm ready for anything now."

"Well, you may not be ready for *this*, Randall." June pursed her lips and seemed to make a great effort to compose herself. Her voice slipped anyhow as she spoke again. "You see, Kay is moving in here with me. We decided that I should tell you."

My brain suddenly felt like a taffy machine, with elastic bands of sweet protoplasm churning, folding, and recombining

a novel of sexual initiation 317

into each other.

But I couldn't figure this one out on the spot. I turned my head and looked out the window for a moment, suppressing a gut-busting guffaw, before I returned my gaze to my therapist and said, therapeutically, "Isn't this a little *impetuous*, June? Have you talked to anyone else about this? Like a professional?"

June's lower lip trembled in response, then she whispered, "I'm so happy." I realized for the first time ever that June, my wise, omniscient mentor for the last three years, was a lonely person. Was I supposed to have understood that earlier? Or had she just done her job well? I decided that it hardly mattered. Then I realized that I actually liked the prospect of dropping by June's, on Sunday afternoons perhaps, just to hang out with her and her . . .

We hugged on my way out. I leaned down conspiratorially and whispered, "So should I call you *Aunt* June now?"

WHAT WAS there to do after *that* but take a walk into the woods? Feeling lighthearted, amused at life's strange turns and unexpected recombinations, I trekked up the Berkeley hills to my secret bay tree, which I had not visited since the nightmarish evening after learning of Jeanna's death. I was almost afraid to see it again, but instead I was surprised by a distinct shift in my perception. Although it was a windless day, my tree seemed to be moving in place, almost trembling with life, and illumined from within by a vital light.

I looked around to see if the whole scene was lit up this way, but it was only my tree that had changed. *It's come alive*, I thought, but that made no sense because it had always been alive. Yet something had surely happened to it, some new infusion of energy. I walked up to touch the bark, and out of nowhere a strong breeze came up, making the highest branches of the tree swirl about. I looked up, hands on bark, and in my mind's eye I saw Jeanna's long dark hair swirling, just as I'd remembered it before I started dancing in the ritual.

Then, glad that I was alone in the woods with no one watching, I leaned fully against the broad trunk and became a tree hugger. In a flash I was transported to that soft night on the Fourth of July when Jeanna had leant against me in the sailboat and I'd felt closer to her than ever before. Somehow this was the same feeling—and then I knew with utter certainty that Jeanna was *here*, and Jeanna would always be here, within the tree and somehow also within me, ready to give me strength and guidance and unfailing wisdom at every step of my way. I would have other lovers and friends, more journeys and adventures, times of exceptional joy and deep despair, but I would never be quite so alone as I used to be. For somehow my heart had found access to a well of profound tenderness. I turned about, leaned my back against the tree, and slowly sank to the ground whispering *thank you, thank you, thank you* to someone; it didn't matter who. I laughed softly with tears streaming from my eyes for perhaps half a minute. When I was calm I silently called, *Jeanna?*—and she answered *Yes* right away. And then we began to talk.

About the Author

D. Patrick Miller is a widely published novelist, journalist, and poet, with books previously released by Viking, Henry Holt, Hay House, Celestial Arts/Tenspeed Press, and his own imprint of Fearless Books (*www.fearlessbooks.com*). He is the author of *Love After Life*, his first novel; *A Little Book of Forgiveness; The Book of Practical Faith;* and *Understanding A Course in Miracles*. He has published over 100 articles in the "journalism of consciousness" in print magazines and online, and also provides editing and literary consultations for other authors, literary agents, and publishers. He is a member of the Authors Guild and the American Society of Journalists and Authors. Miller is a native of Charlotte, NC and has lived in Berkeley, CA since 1977.

Author's Note

Although I did not know it when I wrote this novel, Forests Forever was (and is) a real educational and activist organization focused on the preservation of California's diverse woodland ecosystems. See their website at *www.forestsforever.org*.

−D. Patrick Miller

LaVergne, TN USA
12 November 2010
204685LV00010B/33/P